MW00683152

SPIDER LINES

SPIDER LINES

TERRY TRAFTON

Columbus, Ohio

This book is a work of fiction. The names, characters and events in this book are the products of the author's imagination or are used fictitiously. Any similarity to real persons living or dead is coincidental and not intended by the author.

A Fox Lane Book

LCCN: 2018947117
ISBN: 9781619848443

First Printing August 2018

Printed on Acid Free Paper

Printed in the United States of America

terrytrafton@hotmail.com

For my mother and father

Acknowledgements

THROUGHOUT THE WRITING of this book, it was always apparent how significantly the contributions of others mattered. I am grateful to those at Gatekeeper Press whose suggestions and patience were invaluable, Tony Chellini, Rob Price, who worked closely with me during every aspect of this project, and my editor, Wendy Thornton who corrected the mistakes I missed. Always polite, always positive, and always willing to provide constructive feedback, the publishing team at Gatekeeper Press was excellent.

Thanks to the visionary thinkers unwilling to bend to those who refer to their ideas as too impractical, too radical, too far from mainstream academic thinking. These are the bold independent thinkers unafraid of ridicule. They are the critical and creative thinkers who will not stay silent.

Special thanks to Dr. Virginia Grabill, Michael Foltynewicz, and Paul Berlanga for their exceptional friendships. There are those whose names I have forgotten, the silent ones that influenced to a large extent both the dialogue and characters in this book. Although research was necessary in the writing of this story, in the end, it remains a work of fiction. The author is responsible for any inaccuracies, omissions, or other egregious errors.

Finally, I express my gratitude to my own family, especially to my wife Joyce whose constant encouragement motivated me to write, even on those days when the sentences came together awkwardly and when paragraphs were not so easily conceived. Her interest in my work was not without criticisms, which, after consideration, I realized were perceptive suggestions intended to make the writing stronger.

Author's Note

THE POWERS OF ley lines are not to be underestimated or disregarded. Unusual and unexplained phenomena occurring at places where there are high concentrations of earth's energies have been documented and continue to be regarded as highly credible accounts of things unexplained. Life is not always neat and orderly. It is often messy, chaotic, enigmatic and even unsettlingly creepy. We observe the beauty and symmetry of lines in a spiderweb without ever realizing the mysteries that exist in all those empty spaces. This is where imagination lives—in that realm of unknown possibilities, a place where coincidence makes the impossible achievable. There are no walls, no parameters or restrictions, but plenty of open space in which to experience, not only illusion, but also truth. Like the spiritual energies of ley lines, the pathways of spider lines will take each of us on a journey to those blank spaces in our own lives, and it is there that we will realize the profound magic and fascination of the human psyche.

T.T.

Chapter 1

AS A ROSE-COLORED moon began to fade pale and small, an extraordinary event was taking hold of this bizarre and remarkably uncommon night. Without warning, sharp slashing claws lacerated the sky, ripping and shredding the very fabric of space and time. Lightning flashed. Thunder was so loud and intimidating that words spoken among the crew were too indistinct to be fully comprehended. In this freakish eerie chaos, a gaping mouth belched fire, before its flaming lips snapped shut with tremendous force. The beast was alive—its gluttony rapacious as it devoured the starry night. An enormous rupture—bulged increasingly wider, until reddish-black walls resembling molten rock appeared. The craft was being compressed, squeezed on all sides, sucked into a violently-churning vortex. As it was hurtled deeper into space, a heavy metallic fog clung tenaciously to its exterior skin.

The sky, an explosion of vivid surrealistic colors, was becoming increasingly hostile. A thrashing bludgeoning force so devastating and maniacal, it had the power to extinguish starlight and obliterate entire constellations. As a whirlpool of unbridled energy spun insanely into a funnel of concentric circles spinning counterclockwise, stars wobbled loosely on their cosmic axis. It would not be long before the sky became a debris field of untethered floaters, a wasteland of macabre images contorted grotesquely into an impossibly real nightmare.

Smoke! A rancid burning sensation filled their nostrils. White billowing smoke, increasingly intense, made it difficult to see the navigation screens clearly. Extreme vibrations in the controls, discernable malfunctions and failures in the instrument panels, as spikey red lines convulsed into heavy black circles across each screen. Other monitors showed a series of thin configurations resembling cobwebs. As seconds passed, as the spidery lines scrambled erratically into meaningless data, resignation took hold of each crew member—its grip severe, unrelenting. There was no attempt to conceal what each was thinking.

Panic! The craft could not survive much longer. They prepared for the inevitable. There would be no change of course. For them, home would soon be nothing more than a swarm of cruel and mysterious shadows. But when the images swirling around them began to melt into a stony-gray haze, the craft steadied momentarily. An uneasy calm set in long enough for them to distinguish pinwheels of green light, which resembled deformed eyes slowly converging into one enormous unblinking eye.

If it was the eye of God, in its gaze was fierceness, and no hint of absolution. Unable to escape the gaze of the horrible and foreboding eye, each knew what had happened was a catastrophic breach of the space–time continuum, an aberrant twist of fate that waited to apprehend their identities. Impossible as it was, the three travelers had been transported to another time and place. They had entered a hole in the sky, a deep black hole filled with new and exotic starlight.

With the beast finally gorged and glutted, and a tumultuous sky caving in behind them, they brushed smoke from their visors, in a desperate attempt to see what was ahead of them. As frightening as their thoughts were, the possibility that they might survive the crash brought a momentary sense of hope. Descent was coming too fast. Still, the open space beside the water might be large enough to make a controlled landing.

Then, without warning, a church steeple—a monolith that stretched high into a crisp moonlit sky. There was a devastating sound from deep below. The church steeple! The craft had collided with the church steeple. Then, as the craft struck the ground, strange vivid images of things to come.

A large mysterious house built near a church.

A stone foundation under which a sinister black shape was interred.

A stone bridge across a blue stream.

The portrait of a young woman without eyes.

The sky was noticeably off—stars blinking in the wrong places, constellations broken and scattered across an alien sky. The years were wrong. They had moved backward in time, and as they stood beneath a sky on fire with flaming stars, each searching among these stars for their place in the firmament, they realized again the impossibility of going home.

Chapter 2

IT WAS A 30-minute drive on a sunny fall day to the law offices of Whitman, Whitman, and Burke in downtown Evansville, Indiana. Heading west on Riverside Drive, past the Casino Tropicana, or Aztar, as it was still referred to by many longtime customers and supporters of riverboat gambling, Ben recalled the time when he hit a large jackpot on one of the quarter slots. Ben Manning was a man who took chances and on that rainy July afternoon, with no specific place to go, he felt lucky. As he was leaving the casino, he dropped one last quarter into another slot. That's when, much to his amazement, the lights started spinning. Later that same day, he deposited his winnings into a savings account at First Trust and Savings.

The Whitman, Whitman, and Burke offices were on the top floor of the Mason Building. From there the scenic view of the Big Bend in the Ohio River was stunning in the morning sunlight, and from this height the Kentucky landscape, with its long bean fields and cornfields, looked deceptively near. On the sandbar, just off the Kentucky shoreline, boats were anchored and people waded and splashed in the shallow water.

As he entered the office, "Mr. Manning?" asked a young woman politely, coming out from behind her desk to shake his hand.

"Ben Manning," he replied.

"Jenna Newland. Rikki is expecting you."

Her handshake was firm, and when she spoke, her smile was warm and genuine. "So, we're going to be neighbors."

"Really?"

"My father owns the property south of Atwood House beyond the woods."

Before he could reply, Rikki Whitman appeared in the doorway of the conference room. "Ben, won't you please come in? Max is waiting, so let's get the paperwork completed and get you back outside into that glorious sunshine."

Rikki was in her late 30s, expensively dressed, and with an air of urgency, she led him into the conference room where realtor Max Palmer was seated. The scent of perfume was heavy, or was it cologne? At length, he decided it was perfume.

"Afternoon," Max said, looking up from the papers in front of him.

"How are you, Max?"

"Right as rain, as they say."

Rikki gestured him toward a chair next to Max, then went around to the other side of the huge rosewood conference table. The perfume seemed to hang in a cloud around him, and for a moment he thought the heavy smell would trigger his asthma. As seconds passed, the sweet smell slowly dissipated.

"Well, gentlemen," she began, "as you know this is more of a formality than anything else. Ben, all the paperwork is in front of you. I'll go over it and you can sign as we go through it. I'm sure you'll find everything as we previously discussed." Then following a slight pause, she added, "I'm happy to answer any questions at any time." She poured a glass of water, took a sip, and then ran the polished fingernails of one hand through her dark hair.

There were no questions. After the papers were signed and notarized by the perky secretary, copies were appropriately distributed and Max handed Ben three keys on a plastic key fob, saying, "It's all yours, Ben. Good luck with it."

"I certainly hope I've made the right decision on this one," smiled Ben.

"As you know, the house has been unoccupied for several years, so it's going to need some work," Max stated.

With two feet of polished rosewood between them, Rikki and Jenna sat across the conference table from the two men. Ben looked from one to the other before speaking again. "It's the location I like . . . private, but still close to town."

Before he left the office, Jenna handed him a business card, which read, Klassy Kleen, and said, "I do weekend work."

"What do you mean?" he asked before reading what was printed on the card.

"Housework. It's good supplementary income. My mobile number is on the card, so if you need help with that big house, please give me a call."

"I will. Thank you, Jenna. I'm sure there is much to be done, so I'll definitely be in touch."

He went back outside into the sunny day, thinking Jenna would work out fine. To say that he'd not had second thoughts about buying Atwood House would be an understatement. But as he had told them at the closing, he liked the location with its lofty view of the Ohio River, and five acres of wooded property offered plenty of privacy. It would be nice to leave behind the cramped quarters of the apartment in which he had lived and worked the past 12 years.

At 35, Ben was just beginning to experience some significant success as a landscape artist. Commissions were strong, and he had several profitable exhibitions behind him. Beyond that income was the $200,000 his uncle Keith had left him. There would be renovation money available, and if the paintings continued to sell, he'd be fine financially.

The door creaked, and creaked . . . and creaked a bit more, until it was open wide enough for him to enter a large foyer with a dusty pastoral scene hanging above a mahogany table. Slowly, as his eyes adjusted to the dim light, he saw white sheets draped across furniture in what he knew had been used as a parlor. When he had seen the house that first time in late August, he was very much intimidated by its size. It was considerably more house than he needed, and the high ceilings gave the rooms an even more spacious impression.

The faded velvet curtains covering the tall parlor windows, and the even taller library windows, were heavy and kept out sunlight. The velvet was worn in several places. When they were new, these curtains would certainly have given the rooms an expensive ambience. They would have to go, though.

Electricity and water had been restored over a week ago. He'd contact Indiana Bell next week. Cable was an easy installation, so he could arrange for that next week as well. Getting the house back together would take time, but with some hired help, he hoped to have most of the work done by Christmas. Although he could do minor carpentry work, the more extensive renovations, like ceiling and roof repairs, and plumbing, would have to be done by professionals.

It was too soon to think about decorating the entire house. Ben had decided to keep some of the upstairs rooms closed until he knew what to do with them. Previous owners had left behind several pieces of furniture, which were included as part of the closing transaction. Max had told him that most of the furniture had been there since William Gilbert Atwood owned the house. Despite the extraordinary walnut library table, an early 20th century parlor set, mahogany bookcases, a mahogany bedroom set, a couple of couches, and miscellaneous tables and chairs, the house still looked miserably empty.

In the car, Ben had a bag of groceries, an easel, acrylic paints, and three blank canvases. It would be a working night and a chance to convey some further impressions of Atwood House. Although he'd been through the house several times, it was the library he liked most. One architectural feature that stood out was the ornate built-in bookcases with their heavy beveled glass doors and flashy brass pulls. Several boxes were stacked in one corner of the room, and after opening the first three, he decided these were books that had been left behind. He'd find time to sort through them later in the week.

For a few minutes, Ben's first night in Atwood House seemed about to begin, until he realized he hadn't brought an inhaler. Though his asthma was completely controlled and hadn't bothered him during the last few years, he always felt more at ease when he had an inhaler. There was a drugstore no more than 15 minutes away. He'd get the prescription refilled, pick up some other things he needed, then return to spend his first night in Atwood House. When he returned an hour later, there was a car in the large circular drive and a young woman standing on the stone porch steps. It was Jenna Newland and she was holding something in one hand.

Coming down the steps rather hurriedly when she saw him , she yelled out a shaky, "Hello."

"Jenna," he answered.

"Rikki asked me to drop this off. She forgot to give it to you this afternoon."

"What is it?" he asked, taking an unclasped folder and briefly glancing inside at what looked to be photocopies of newspaper articles.

"She didn't say . . . just said she thought you would find these interesting."

"Thank you."

"When I knocked on the door, it opened, but no one was there. Then I saw your car approaching."

He could tell by her expression that she was slightly shaken, and before speaking again, he glanced at the front door which was open slightly. "I can assure you there's no one in the house."

"I heard footsteps," Jenna said deliberately. Before he could say another word, she was waving to him as she got into her car.

"Thanks again," he called, watching the car drive away into the trees that buffered Atwood House from the highway.

Three steep dormers and three tall brick chimneys cut sharply into the purple sky. Evening shadows had already climbed high up on the front facade, muting the ornamental angular cuts of the cornices and corbels, and giving the impression that the dentils along the edge of the roof were dominos stacked in a long horizontal line. The last rays of sunlight lingered in the upstairs windows, while the bay windows on the main floor were flat, dull, and appeared more like those seen in black-and-white photographs of old houses. Suspicious eyes, the dormers stared down at him as he approached the house. Just for a moment, a dark shape was silhouetted in one window. When he looked again, there was only a gleam of pink sunlight.

Ben closed the door behind him and heard the lock snap shut. He didn't think more about what Jenna had said until later. After setting the folder on the mantel beside the Klassy Kleen business card, he went into the kitchen to make coffee. Footsteps in an empty house . . . that just wasn't possible.

Chapter 3

IT WAS CHILLY in the house and heat off the burner felt good. Unsure about the tap water, he used bottled water for coffee. Recalling what Jenna had said, he shrugged his shoulders, dismissing footsteps as nothing more than her imagination. Even though the house did have a kind of eeriness about it, there was no reason at all to believe occupants from another time still walked the wooden floors.

Opening the folder that Jenna had given him, he was surprised to find several copies of newspaper articles dating as far back as 1905, and each had direct references to the Atwood property. There was no indication at all who had compiled these articles, or where Rikki had gotten them. Who would have taken so much time to locate them, and why? There were even pictures of the house taken several years after its construction in 1903. One picture showed a young woman standing on the back patio, looking at the lens of the camera. The photo appeared in a 1904 newspaper, *The Boonville Enquirer*, and though the resolution was grainy, the woman seemed to be standing in a beam of sunlight. and Ben thought her expression evocative, provocatively poignant.

The focus on the house was most likely the photographer's primary interest, but it was the slender shape that dominated the picture. Dressed in black and holding a lacy parasol, her face partially concealed by a sort of blusher veil, she wore a feathery hat tilted to one side. The eyes, however, were clearly visible through the gauzy veil, and they looked intently at Ben Manning—so it seemed to him. The entire countenance of the woman struck him as familiar; but that was a thought quickly dismissed with the realization that she belonged to a past century.

William Atwood Dies in Motorcar Accident. Beneath this 1910 headline in the same newspaper were the details of a rather bazaar story of Atwood's accident on a late summer night when he lost control of his car on State Road 66. There was an older passenger, James Alexander, with Atwood when the automobile went over the cliff into the Ohio River. Little information was given about Alexander, other than that he had worked for Atwood and was from Ferdinand, Indiana, visiting relatives in Newburgh at the time of the accident. There were mortuary photographs of both Atwood and Alexander that Ben considered offensive by contemporary journalistic standards—despite his doubt that propriety in journalistic standards prevailed at all.

Until his untimely demise at age 42, William Gilbert Atwood had been president of the First National Bank of Newburgh, one of only a few local banks to survive the Great Depression. For several years after the Depression, the house remained occupied by Atwood's young wife, Anna, until 1955, when a young military officer returning from the Korean War, bought the estate with the intention of turning it into a hotel. Before renovations began, two of three investors got cold feet and plans for the hotel fell through, leaving the house vacant for several more years. It wasn't until the 1960s that a young physician, David Young and his family purchased Atwood House and renovated much of it. The house stayed in the Young family until it was sold to an eccentric businessman who intended to make it into a gambling casino. But the businessman eventually abandoned the idea when he was unable to secure the necessary zoning permits. At some point in this legacy of owners, the realty company had obtained the property and once again Atwood House remained vacant until Ben bought it.

Unexpectedly, one story caught his eye. Apparently, there had been documented accounts of strange occurrences in Atwood

House that began shortly after the Young family had purchased the property. The family frequently reported hearing footsteps, floorboards creaking, and doors opening and closing, especially late at night after they had gone to bed. The stately house soon took on the reputation of being haunted. No one really took it seriously, until one evening in June when ten-year-old Amanda Young was playing on the stone bridge near the house. She told her mother that a shadowy figure resembling a young woman in an old dress had passed her without saying a word.

Several years later, a story in the *Evansville Courier* reported alleged sightings of apparitions in the foyer and parlor. Members of the Young family had frequently "observed ghosts" and were afraid their children might be harmed. One account of a young woman in a long black dress was so vividly recounted that it read like the description of a visiting relative. Ben considered these accounts imagination, resulting from living too long in a large house surrounded by dark woods. He put the folder on the desk and went to bed.

Early Saturday morning, he cut and stacked nearly a cord of firewood. With cool evenings increasingly prevalent, he was already looking forward to the warmth of an evening fireplace. Anxious to engage Jenna's cleaning services, he took the business card off the mantel, dialed one of the phone numbers printed there and waited for her to answer.

"Klassy Kleen," declared a cheery voice.

"Jenna?"

"This is Lacey. I'll get Jenna for you."

Twenty seconds passed before Jenna answered the phone. "Hello."

"Ben Manning."

"Hi, Ben. How's that great big house?"

"Dirty . . . could you possibly work me into your schedule . . . soon?"

"Lacey and I can begin today if you like."

"Terrific."

"See you in an hour—if that works for you."

"Works fine. Thanks, Jenna. The front door's unlocked."

About an hour later when Jenna arrived, dressed in jeans, a

sweatshirt, a red apron, and a ball cap, with her blonde hair funneled into a ponytail through the opening at the back, she had another younger girl with her. Both women had big smiles and as they walked toward the front porch, Ben gave a slight wave.

"Glad you called," Jenna said. "We had nothing at all scheduled for today. This is Lacey Laurens."

Lacey was a couple years younger than Jenna but didn't have the same perky demeanor. She was just kind of there. Quiet, pretty in an old-fashioned sort of way, she nodded and forced a smile before returning to the SUV to get supplies. Her dark hair caught the morning sunlight as she walked away from them.

"How do you want to lay this job out?" he asked.

"Well, it's certainly more than we can do in a day. Why don't we start with the rooms on the main floor," she suggested, "unless you want to do the house from the top down."

"The upstairs rooms can wait," said Ben.

"Any carpets that need cleaned?"

"Just a lot of dirty wooden floors, and the few pieces of furniture can be pushed aside easily enough."

"It really is a beautiful house," admitted Jenna. "I've been by it several times, but this is the first time I've been inside." Then after a slight pause, she asked, "Are you going to put down carpet?"

"I have oriental rugs for all the rooms, except the great room. Don't know what I'll do there yet. Floor's good, so will probably leave it like it is."

Standing in the doorway to the library, Jenna did a cursory survey of the large room. "What are you going to do, if you'll excuse me for asking, with those awful drapes?"

"Replace them," he smiled. "They really are awful, aren't they?"

"Well they've definitely seen better times."

Lacey brought in everything they'd need to clean the main floor and seemed anxious to begin. "My God, this is a huge house," she declared.

Ben shrugged as he spoke. "I suppose I could always rent some of it out, but not until I've had a chance to enjoy it," he joked.

"Let's get to it, Lace," Jenna suggested, giving Manning the impression that the two women were quite comfortable together.

"I can help if you want," he told them.

Jenna looked at him a moment before saying, "No, you'd just be in the way. If we need you, we'll call."

"Then, I'll be cutting firewood."

The morning passed uneventfully. Ben cut, split and stacked firewood. Jenna swept, mopped and waxed the hardwood floors in the parlor, library, and great room, while Lacey cleaned the three bathrooms on the main floor. As Jenna was finishing up in the library, something shiny caught her attention. On the floor near the fireplace was an ornate brooch, silver, octagonal, and embedded with what looked to be small diamonds. After looking at it for a minute or so, she dropped the brooch into her apron pocket and went on with her work.

It was nearly five o'clock, and the sun was a sheet of orange draped over the branches of distant trees. When Ben came in, Jenna and Lacey were in the foyer. Both women stared at the stairway, which stopped at a large landing before splitting into two separate stairways leading to the upper rooms.

Lacey's expression struck Ben oddly. She pointed to something on the landing. Eyes narrowed, face blanched, her hand shook as she pointed. Her body was noticeably tense, rigid, as though her feet were fastened to the floorboards. She was clearly frightened by something . . . but what?

"There's someone there," she declared anxiously. Her eyes rolled back in her head and she grabbed Jenna's arm and shook it slightly. "This house is not what it seems."

"Psychic," announced Jenna. "She sees things."

"You're not serious," replied Ben.

"Look at her," Jenna told him. "Does that look normal?"

"What?" answered Manning, obviously confused by Lacey's actions.

"She looks scared out of her skin."

He looked at the staircase and landing. "There's nothing there."

"There!" Lacey shouted, her shaky hand and arm gesturing emphatically, wildly. "There!" she repeated, eyes still focused on the landing.

Again, he looked to where she was pointing, and again saw only stairs and the landing soaked in soft pink light that was coming in through the opening in the curtains. Eyes wide, complexion still paling, Lacey continued to point, while Jenna and Ben regarded each other curiously.

"Do you see anything?" he asked Jenna.

But before she could answer, Lacey whispered loud enough for both to hear, "There's a woman in a long dress standing with both arms stretched out in front of her, as though she's waiting to hold someone."

"Oh, my Lord," blurted Jenna. "It's her. It's Anna Atwood."

Manning looked from one to the other for an explanation. "What's going on here?"

Lacey began coughing as her head rotated in slow circles. Ben expected her to go into convulsions at any moment. He glanced at Jenna who was now laughing uncontrollably.

"Very convincing," Jenna complimented.

Lacey dropped her arms, and she, too, began to laugh, "Do you really think so?" she giggled.

"We really had you going, didn't we?" said Jenna. "She's auditioning for a part in a community theater production. Tryouts are next week. We thought this might be a good opportunity for her."

"I'm sorry if I startled you," Lacey confessed apologetically.

Ben was looking at the landing. He took a couple steps closer to the stairs. "My God, there really is someone there."

At first, both women seemed surprised, and looked at him suspiciously. Not smiling as he looked at them from the bottom of the stairs, he wanted them to know he was serious.

In the silence that followed, they heard a perceptible creaking . . . and the sound of footsteps coming closer to where they were standing. Although the heavy velvet curtains were parted slightly, the trailing tints of the evening sun were nothing more than purple stains on the oak staircase. In the center of a strange white light that was becoming increasingly intense, was a distinct image, and that image was coming down the stairs toward them.

More footsteps on the stairs. Then, before any of them could say another word, the walls began to shake. A door slammed shut somewhere deep inside the house. There was a tremendous gasp as though the house was exhaling. Whatever was happening was more than the spin of light and shadows . . . but was it more than progressive imagination? When the figure was only steps away from them, it suddenly became more indistinct, a vacillating shape about to vanish.

"I don't believe it!" exclaimed Jenna who was visibly shaken. "I saw it, but don't believe it."

"There was something . . . someone there," began Lacey . . . "on the stairs."

Ben shook his head. "There has to be a logical explanation."

"Good luck with that . . . but if you figure it out, tell me," Jenna said. "I just watched a person vanish into thin air, and there wasn't anything logical about it."

A peculiar calmness settled in the house, as each attempted to gather their thoughts about what had just happened. Lacey was the most distressed, but even she had regained composure before speaking again. "I feel like we're being watched. Call it intuition if you want. But there is someone or something in this house watching us."

Late that same night, after Jenna and Lacey had left and the fire had burned low, he went outside to get more logs. That's when he saw her. She was a distinct shape emerging out of the night and stopping near the stone bridge. For a moment, he thought it was Jenna Newland. Walking across the damp grass toward her, he suddenly hesitated, reluctant to take another step. There was something strange in the way the figure moved. With a full moon spreading its fire across the lawn, he pulled up his collar to keep out the cool night air. His shadow stretched in front of him as he came nearer the stone bridge.

Not more than 20 feet away, Ben tried to distinguish the face, which was partially concealed behind a black lace veil. She wore no coat, only a sweater with several buttons that resembled pieces of icy starlight. The hem of her dress touched the grass as she stood completely still, regarding him carefully. The wind stopped blowing in the trees. A rush of cold damp air sent a shiver through him, and the rattling inside him could have been his bones clattering. Suddenly, an eerie silence took hold of the night, and the only sound was his heart banging against his chest.

"Please, I must find it." It was a fragile voice that reminded him of his mother's crystal. Was she asking for his help—pleading for his help?

Before he could speak, she turned away from him, and after a few steps, vanished. It was as if she had entered a hole in the night, a deep cavernous hole that swallowed her while he watched. The cold damp air warmed. Frogs croaked. Crickets chirped. Stars blazed against a black sky. Moonlight burned silver on the grass, and still, he stood motionless, watching, hoping she would return.

After the fire had been replenished, he took up a sketch pad and began drawing the comely shape standing on the stairway, her arms stretched out in front of her. He left the face entirely without features. This was a preliminary drawing for the painting he would begin later that same night. He had recently stretched a new canvas, which was on the easel in the study. His earlier intention to paint a landscape had now changed. It would be a portrait of a mysterious woman who had appeared on the stairs and who had only minutes ago stood in the moonlight—a shadowy enigmatic shape that had spoken to him.

Chapter 4

Dr. Adrian White was napping on the couch when the doorbell rang. Professor emeritus, internationally respected authority on the Einstein Rosen Bridge, White looked much younger than his 70 years. Unshaven, with his dark hair uncombed, he stood erect in the doorway, his light gray eyes looking curiously at Ben Manning.

Once the two men were seated comfortably in White's study, and with small talk out of the way, Ben felt his body relax. Adrian White, however, seemed a little apprehensive as he listened to Manning describe the mysterious figure he had seen appear and disappear, first on the stairway, and later, on the lawn—just a few nights ago.

"I don't mean to be rude, Mr. Manning, but what you told me on the phone seems to me a pretty ordinary occurrence and not the mystery you seem to think it is. After all, people do come and go."

"But they don't just vanish into thin air."

"You're not a scientist are you?"

"I'm an artist, mostly landscapes."

"We really are at opposite ends here. I deal with facts, while you deal primarily with imagination."

Dismissing White's rather caustic remark, Ben asked seriously enough to keep the man's attention, "Is time travel possible?"

"Can I get you something to drink?"

"I'm fine thank you."

"You asked me that same question last night on the phone."

"Is it possible, at least theoretically?"

"Yes." Taking his glasses off, White ran thin pale fingers through his hair, stopping once to rub the gray sideburns, and then the corner of his right eye with a bent index finger. "Let's back up a bit. When this happened, had you been drinking?"

"Nothing at all."

"The figure, this woman, dressed in early 20th century clothing, suddenly appeared one afternoon on your staircase?"

Ben nodded. "I didn't imagine this. There were two others who saw what I saw, and each of us saw her clearly."

"And it was the same woman that night on the lawn?"

"I think so. She was dressed in the same black dress and had a veil across her face."

"Did she come out of the woods?"

"I'm not sure. When I saw her, she was crossing the stone bridge, coming toward me. I thought it was a neighbor out for a walk."

"Did she speak to you?"

"She said she was searching for something . . . then she was gone."

"Tell me about this bridge."

"It was built over Archers Creek at about the same time as Atwood House. It's ornate and has carved granite posts and panels. There are several acres of trees on one side and a few acres of open land on the other side."

"You believe in ghosts?"

"Never thought much about ghosts, but I do know what I saw, Dr. White. If you'll excuse me for saying, people just don't come and go this way."

"That's not entirely true. There are numerous accounts of people disappearing suddenly, without any plausible explanation. But it's my opinion we're talking about another phenomenon that could have something to do with what you suggested."

"Time?"

Nodding, Dr. White's stony eyes bulged a deeper shade of gray as he continued, "Einstein's Rosen Bridge."

Ben smiled. "I'm in over my head already."

"When Einstein introduced his Theory of Relativity in 1916, it became the template for gravitation research. Twenty years later when Nathan Rosen collaborated with Einstein, they published a paper, in which they included with the theory of general relativity, a curved space concept that connects two different regions of space." White took a piece of paper off the desk before speaking again. "A straight line might not be the shortest distance between two points. If I fold this piece of paper like so, the distance between two points is shorter, resulting in what might be referred to as a wormhole."

"But didn't Einstein say nothing could move faster than light?"

"Yes, Einsteinian causality it's called. But here it gets much too complex to discuss."

"Can you put this idea in language I can understand?"

"It's a shortcut from one part of the universe to another."

"Sort of like a black hole, then?"

"Similar in some classic respects," White replied. "A black hole results when a large star explodes—a supernova. The remaining mass collapses to a point of infinite density . . . or singularity. The intense gravitational field traps any emitted protons. Since no light escapes, the result is what John Archibald Wheeler referred to in 1968 as a black hole."

"So, they actually exist?"

"What I'm about to tell you is absolutely true. It has nothing at all to do with imagination or inspiration. It actually happened one summer morning a few years ago when I was driving from Bloomington to Evansville on Interstate 69 . . . a two hour drive I've made many times."

"Yes, I know the route well."

"I remember it was a particularly cold day for late June. About an hour or so before noon on a long stretch of highway between Washington and Princeton, referred to locally as Peddlers Run, I saw coming out of the southwest a bank of gray clouds or fog. At first, I thought rain was coming in across the corn and bean fields. Suddenly, I was totally immersed in this strange fog and had to turn on my headlights to see the road. Even with the lights on, the highway was nowhere in sight. It had just dropped out from under the car. Lightning snapped all around me, but there was no rain . . . not a drop of rain. There were no headlights, no other cars, just this long dark tunnel of electrified clouds, or a sort of swirling magnetic fog which seemed to attach itself to my car."

Before speaking again, he lifted his eyes to regard Manning seriously for several seconds. "I no longer heard the car engine and had the unusual sensation of floating, almost like the car was being pulled—funneled into a bright light at the end of the tunnel. When the fog dissipated, I was driving west on Interstate 40 toward Nashville, Tennessee. The sun was shining and there wasn't a cloud in the sky. And here's the strange part. When I looked at my watch, 22 minutes had passed, and I was 200 miles southeast of Evansville, Indiana."

"That's incredible," returned Ben.

"It's absolutely impossible, and yet it happened."

"I've read accounts of people who have experienced missing time."

"This is where it gets interesting. I was in Tennessee the day before I left Bloomington."

"You're telling me you went back in time?"

Dr. White rubbed one thumb across the back of the other as he spoke. "Yes, 18 hours in fact."

"That's astonishing. Are you sure?"

"Absolutely positive."

"This is the Einstein Rosen Bridge theory . . . the actuality of it?"

"Yes, to some extent, but although what happened to me might sound like science fiction, there are mathematical foundations that can explain at least some of it. I experienced a quantum jump in time . . . a time–warp."

"This is way more than I expected," Ben remarked. He was slightly suspicious to hear White recount such an astonishing event so openly.

"There are hot spots, areas of intense energy where anomalous events consistently occur."

"Like the Bermuda Triangle?"

"It's certainly one of those places with an expansive profile. But there are numerous other known places across the globe. Some are only now gaining provenance."

"Already mapped and researched, I suppose."

"Not so easily done as you might expect. Since we're not using crucibles and Petri dishes, empirical data are thin."

After a pause, Ben asked, "So it's possible that not all these sites have been located?"

"That is very much the point. There could be hundreds, even thousands of these portals and most remain undiscovered."

"I'm sure the government would want to control these sites."

"Without a doubt, but do you grasp the importance of what I'm telling you?"

"I'm not sure. It's definitely extraordinary," admitted Manning.

"The important thing is that it happened. Time was somehow bent or squeezed."

"How is such a phenomenon possible?"

"To some extent, I think it was coincidence. When I entered the portal, I was in the right place at the right time, or wrong time, depending on your perspective."

"These portals just appear out of thin air?"

"Don't know. Research shows that location of portals requires mathematical calculations—foundations, if you will."

Ben walked across the room and stared into the sunny afternoon, giving Adrian White the impression that he was trying to comprehend at least some of what must seem a preposterous account. "You're positive this really did happen to you?"

"Absolutely, just as sure as I'm standing here now."

"This figure I saw, this woman, she came through one of these portals . . . out of the past?"

"Possibly."

"That would explain it, wouldn't it?"

"This is not something easily understood. It involves energy fields, grids, parallel realities, and much, much more."

"But you've given me a possible explanation, and that's what I needed."

Standing beside Manning, hands in his jeans pockets, Dr. White's expression conveyed serious interest in what Ben had told him. "We might be onto something here."

"What do you mean?"

"I'd like to spend a couple days in Newburgh."

Ben nodded. "Great, but I can't promise she'll appear again."

"A friend of mine is a leading authority on psychic phenomena. I'd like to bring her along."

"When?"

"The end of the week, if that's okay. I'll call you."

"That's fine with me."

"In the meantime, if anything unusual occurs, please call me." After jotting two phone numbers on a desktop notepad, he tore off the sheet and handed it to Ben. "My home and mobile numbers. Call me anytime."

Ben thanked the man and left, anxious to get back to Atwood House. Whether he would ever really understand this business of quantum leaps, he couldn't say. One thing was sure, and that was that Adrian White had believed him, and that was certainly important in Manning's mind.

Remembering Lacey's performance at Atwood House, he quickly realized how gullible he was. Maybe White was also having a go at him—but he didn't think so. Though the man's strange narrative seemed highly suspect, even implausible, White seemed genuine.

Chapter 5

BEN WAS ADDING paint to a long black vintage dress when the phone rang. "Hello."

"It's Jenna. Lacey's out of town for a couple of days, but if you want, I can finish the big room tomorrow."

"You sure you want to come back after what happened?"

"This girl has got to make a living."

"I'm sure you realize what a huge task it is putting this house back together and how very much your help is needed and appreciated."

"See you around nine in the morning."

The painting was unlike any he had done. Portrait painting was not what Ben preferred, but this was more than that. Since he saw the woman, she had been in his head, drumming against his skull, as though trying to escape confinement. Or, was it the face he had painted, the face behind the veil that was enduring confinement? It was a face that continued to haunt him. Had he painted the wrong face and made the veil a barrier? Why had he so often hesitated when painting her face? Regarding the portrait with a more critical eye, he began to doubt the integrity of the portrait. But then, he hadn't seen her face clearly, and what stared back at him now was only paint on canvas. It was a portrait that could not be finished, not until *her* face appeared behind the veil.

Footsteps in the foyer. The room brightened. Was it her?

He had lost track of time, and when he looked at the mantel clock, was surprised to hear it striking ten. Floorboards creaked, causing Ben to draw back, maybe afraid of what he might see. From somewhere, light spilled into the library, covering first the walls then the floor, revealing clearly the intricate designs of the large oriental rug that he had laid down only the day before. Still he hesitated. Glancing at the painting covered in white light, he could not believe the remarkable thing he was seeing.

Emerging on the canvas was another face, slowly appearing behind the black lace veil. Unpainted, but right before his eyes, the face gradually took shape. Two eyes, the color of midnight, vacuous eyes without light became clearly visible. Where a mouth should be, a hole in the canvas was sucking him inside, and he had the suffocating sensation of being devoured by a mouth he had not painted but only imagined.

The veil was being lifted by long delicate fingers. But the arms that held those long fingers were melting into pools of vanilla wax on an expensive oriental rug. Was the veil gone all together? And where had the light in her eyes come from so suddenly? Darkness had set in hours ago.

The lips in the painting went thin as a whisper and he knew they were about to speak. "If you are to find the truth, you must look at what you cannot see. The veil I wear is a mourning veil. It must be lifted by your fingers—and only by your fingers. It is then that you will see what I cannot hide."

"You ask me to see what is not possible," Ben admonished softly.

"I ask you to imagine the impossible, sir."

"If removing the veil will permit me to see you clearly, then that is an action easily done."

"Did you find it?" asked the mouth in the painting. "It was a gift, a wedding gift," and as she spoke, her voice grew faint and trailed away, leaving behind a perceptible echo.

Each word seemed to paint itself on the air. He heard a shudder coming from deep inside the house, a clatter, or banging, and it was getting louder.

It stopped suddenly. The house went ghostly silent. Then, from the darkness, a hand thrust out toward him—a white hand with a black ring on the index finger. The slender hand was only inches away from his arm. He backed away abruptly, bumping the library table behind him. The index finger with its shiny ring pushed into the wet paint on the canvas.

A second later, the hand vanished. Hurriedly, he switched on the overhead lights and immediately the deeper shadows faded. Pulling himself together, he glanced around the room. No one. So, he had imagined it all. Imagination might account for some of the strange occurrences, but something unexplainable was happening at Atwood House.

Strange things happened in darkness, especially in such an old house with so much history. A little nervousness in such a big house was to be expected. Another thought persisted, though, and this was what had motivated him to contact Dr. White. He looked forward to White's visit later in the week. If anyone could explain these curious events, Dr. Adrian White seemed, at this point, the most credible source of information.

After closer examination of the smudged paint on the canvas, he saw the unmistakable impression of a fingerprint. Ben was sure he had not imagined the hand. The evidence was in the swirls of black paint, where there was a definite imprint of an index finger.

Jenna arrived at precisely nine o'clock the next morning. She looked stunning in the bright sunlight. A tan scarf was wrapped around her head, and trailing down her back, her hair was tied off with black ribbons. Dressed in blue jeans, tennis shoes and a plaid woolen shirt, she looked very different from that first day when they had met in Rikki Whitman's office.

"How's your morning, Jenna?"

"I'm still trying to figure out what happened, who we saw on the stairs."

"That might take more time."

"By the way, with all the confusion, I forgot to give you this." She opened her palm and handed him a brooch, the one she'd found earlier in the week.

"It's beautiful. You say you found it?"

"In the library. It was in a crack at the base of the fireplace."

He turned it over in the palm of his hand. "It looks old, really old—Victorian maybe. I'm going to town later this morning, so maybe I can get Bob Bergman to look at it."

"Okay, then. I have lots to do, so better get at it. Strange place to find a piece of jewelry though," she said as she walked deeper into the interior of Atwood House.

At a few minutes before noon, Ben opened the door to Bergman and Son Jewelers. He was carrying the brooch in a small box. A thin man in his late 60s saw him come in and gave a slight wave. Bob Bergman was dressed in a dark blue suit. His dark eyes were set far back in his head. The neatly manicured beard gave him a distinguished kind of old-school appearance.

"Morning," Bergman greeted him warmly.

"It's been too long, Bob. How are you?" replied Manning, reaching out to shake the man's hand.

"Business could always be better, but got my health and that's what counts." He smiled broadly at Manning before speaking again. "I got some nice engagement rings, Ben."

"Thanks," Ben laughed, "but marriage just isn't in the cards right now."

"You're not getting any younger as they say."

"I'm kind of set in my ways, Bob."

Ben put the box on the glass counter top and removed the brooch from a thin wrapping of tissue paper. In the fluorescent light, the piece took on an expensive shine. It caught Bergman's attention immediately.

"So, this is what you called about," said Bergman, picking up the brooch and turning it over in his fingers. "It's beautiful . . . haven't seen one of these in some time."

"Then it's not costume jewelry or paste?"

Bergman had an eye loupe on the end of a nylon cord, which he used to magnify the brooch. "No, it's certainly not paste. It's a late 19th century bullseye agate mourning locket, or brooch pin. Provenance of the agate is probably German. The rope edging is 24 karat gold.

The five embedded diamonds are two-carat." He paused a moment before adding, "Flawless, no inclusions of any kind, and the color does have some very minor tint. The cut of these stones is European." He lowered the loupe until it dangled again at the end of the cord. "This is most interesting."

"What's that?"

"These gems set between each diamond are blue cap tourmaline. I've seen that only a couple times. Such an arrangement is rare."

"What's the purpose?"

"Tourmaline is thought to have healing properties and has long been used as an energizer to align the power of the crystal with higher forms of human consciousness . . . a talisman. If you look carefully you can see that the points of the tourmaline are higher in every instance than the diamonds."

"Any particular reason for that?"

"None that I can think of . . . it could be a deliberate setting, but I don't know why. There is also some wear to the tips, as though they have been rubbed or pressed against something . . . very peculiar."

"I've read Internet accounts of people using various gems to enhance spiritual powers, even sexual prowess."

Bob nodded, "Let's look at the back." Again, using the loupe to magnify the brooch, he said at length, "Sterling case and clasp." He looked at Ben and smiled that warm ingratiating smile. "It's an extraordinary piece."

"Excellent."

"You said you found it in the Atwood House?"

"Jenna Newland found it when she was cleaning the library. Said it was in a crease around the fireplace casement."

"Julia and I use Klassy Kleen frequently. Jenna is certainly a lovely young lady, Ben."

"She is, and extremely dependable and efficient. I'll recommend her every chance I get."

"That's interesting," said Bergman, looking again at the back of the brooch. "I don't know how I missed that."

"What?"

"There's a maker's mark, barely visible, but let me see if I can make it out." Again, he used the loupe to examine the mark. "It's a Martin Mayer stamp—German." He looked at Manning. "I do know Mayer was in Chicago to exhibit at the World's Columbian Exposition in 1893. If it could be traced to the Exposition, it would certainly have tremendous provenance," he concluded, holding the brooch in the natural light of a large window behind him.

"You said it was also a locket."

"It can be worn either as a brooch or as a locket. These two small eyes are chain fasteners."

"I guess the biggest question now is its value."

"If you want to sell it, I'd be willing to pay 30,000 dollars." He regarded Ben who was silent. "I've got customers with deep pockets, and they'd pay huge for a piece of this quality."

"Are you serious?"

"I am."

"Wow, I don't know what to say, Bob."

"The patina suggests it's been in the same spot for several years, probably since the Atwood family lived in the house."

"I certainly appreciate the offer. Let me think about it."

"If it's the price that bothers you, I can assure you it's a fair offer."

"No, it's not that. I just need to think about it before making any commitment to sell it. I'm sure you understand."

"Whatever you say, Ben. The offer stands if you change your mind."

Ben thanked him again and went back out into the morning sun, which was not as bright as it had been when he went into the jewelry store. Maybe he had refused Bergman's offer too quickly. Why should he hang onto a piece of jewelry this valuable? He couldn't help but feel something was compelling him to keep the brooch. Though $30,000 was certainly a considerable sum of money, Bergman had said the offer would stand, and for now, that was good enough for Manning.

Chapter 6

ADRIAN WHITE CALLED late that afternoon to say he and Dr. Liz Raymond would arrive Friday morning before noon and were planning to stay in Newburgh the entire weekend. "That will give us time for a consistent investigation."

"No need to get a hotel. There's plenty of room here," he told White.

"That's a generous offer, Ben. It would keep us involved in a sustained way, and there'll be no need to hurry between places. Dr. Raymond and I have discussed at some length what you told me, and we have a few ideas we're anxious to try. Maybe we can explain what's happening."

In the library, the painting remained unfinished. Standing in front of the canvas, he looked carefully at the veil over the woman's face and was sure he saw the faint trace of a face behind it—again, one he hadn't painted. Yet, it was there, and the longer he looked, the more distinguishable were the features. Strangely, when he held it up in the weak sunlight coming in through one of the tall library windows, only the veil was visible. The face was more evident in dimmer light.

It was much later in the day, in the gray flat tones of evening, when he saw clearly two black eyes staring intensely from behind the transparent veil. As he looked, they became even more intense. The eyes were fixed firmly on his, and the longer he looked at them the more conscious he was of a tightness in his chest. His breathing was irregular and had an audible raspy edge to it. It was as if the eyes were pulling him into the painting, holding him with unexplainable force against which he had no defense. He had the odd impulse to speak.

"Is it you?" he asked, immediately thinking how ridiculous the question sounded, especially when no other person was present. "Who are you?"

The index finger with the ring moved. He saw it move. He hadn't painted the finger in a pronounced position, but there it was, raised slightly and making features of the ring easier to see. Examining the ring more closely, he thought the center stone identical to the black agate in the brooch, and there were other indisputable similarities.

A loud knocking on the front door startled him and turned him away from the painting. He was not expecting anyone, and when he opened the door, he was surprised to see the jeweler, Bob Bergman, standing in the last rays of a purple sunset that pinched the horizon above the Ohio River.

"I wanted you to see what I found after you left this morning," said Bergman.

Closing the door behind them, Ben showed Bob into the library. "Please excuse the mess."

"What mess?" Bob laughed. "Houses are not museums or furniture stores. They're made to live in, and what you call a mess, I call homey." He put a picture on the library table. "I thought I had seen the brooch before, and here's a picture of it."

Ben examined the photo. "They sure look the same."

"It was sold by Martin Mayer at the Columbian Exposition to John Allen Dale at an undisclosed price. Seems it was an anniversary gift for his wife Esme. If it is in fact the same brooch, as I think it is, the piece has a rather odd narrative attached to it."

"In what way?"

"Esme Eleanor Dale was a devout Spiritualist rumored to have undeniable psychic powers, which she frequently displayed during séances in their Long Island home. Her husband made his fortune largely from investments in the railroad and was a man of some prominence among the New York elites, some of whom were frequently in attendance at Esme's séances. There are accounts from some in attendance, including John Allen Dale, of the brooch having strange properties."

"Properties?" asked Ben curiously. "What sort of properties?"

"That's the really strange part. The agate was said to cast strange beams of light at certain times of the day and night. Esme was convinced that it enabled her to connect with 'the other side' as she called it."

"That's a real stretch, Bob."

"I don't know. Agate does have properties that allow it to show brighter in sunlight, but this was apparently more than that. There are accounts of jewelry being made specifically for mediums by lapidary specialists who realized the interactive properties of gems, especially the pronounced attributes of crystals."

"Then Esme's intention was to own something more than just a piece of expensive jewelry."

"It looks that way. I'm sure there is more to the piece than what I've told you. It most likely changed hands when Esme passed a few years later. There was a reference to a John Allen Dale collection sold at Sotheby's in a 1905 auction in London. The brooch could certainly have changed owners there."

"I want you to see something," Ben said, turning Bergman's attention to the painting. "Look at this."

After looking at the ring, Bergman agreed that it was similar in many respects to the brooch. "It's not uncommon to see matched sets. There could have been a bracelet, or even a matching necklace."

"Seems like overkill, all that bling at once."

Bergman smiled. "Although the Victorians liked expensive bling, I doubt if all the pieces were worn at the same time. One thing is sure. We have what I feel is irrefutable provenance, and if you do decide to sell the brooch, this kind of provenance will undoubtedly increase the overall value."

"Could there have been more than one of these?"

"It's possible. I've seen other similar pieces. This kind of jewelry is often made for very affluent people who want something no one else has."

"Can I get you something to drink, Bob?"

"No thanks. I was on my way home and wanted you to know what I discovered. Besides, I wanted to see what you're doing with this historic place."

"Well, Jenna and Lacey have done the cleaning. Several pieces of furniture were left behind, so I put them where I thought they were placed originally."

"Might be some *mabui* in that furniture," Bergman smiled.

"*Mabui*?"

"It's an Asian idea. Inanimate things can take on part of a former owner's soul, or something like that. The furniture has a kind of immortal soul, which might require exorcism, or a separation ritual called *mabui-wakashi*."

"Really," Ben answered.

"A friend of my wife mentioned it once when they were antiquing. It did seem to keep her curious though. She seemed to lose her interest in furniture that other people had owned. Julia can be that way—as superstitious as anyone I know. I don't think I'd take it too seriously, Ben. Just makes for good conversation when I see antique furniture."

"I suppose the house has its own *mabui*. Several people have lived here at one time or another, and to some extent, I'm living in their lifetimes," said Ben with enough seriousness to turn the conversation away from trapped souls.

"It's the first time I've been inside," admitted Bob. "Quite a place."

"Thanks for the information," Ben said as Bergman prepared to leave.

"By the way," he began, "is that a portrait of Anna Atwood you're painting?"

"Just an idea I had."

"What about the ring? Do you have it?"

"No, just coincidence," Manning answered.

"It's one peculiar coincidence," Bob replied, opening the door into the early night.

Chapter 7

DRS. ADRIAN WHITE and Liz Raymond arrived at a few minutes before ten Friday morning. Ben was raking dead leaves into a pile when the black SUV rolled to a stop in the driveway. Waving, he walked across the lawn to meet them. "Nice to see you again, Ben," Adrian said. "This is Dr. Liz Raymond, a professor of parapsychology at Indiana University."

The two shook hands, while White went back to the SUV to get two satchels. The woman was in her 40s and slightly overweight. Her red hair was a stylish cut and hung to her shoulders. Dressed in jeans and a light jacket, she appeared anxious to get started. "What a fabulous location," she announced after several seconds of surveying both the house and landscape.

"Glad you could come, Dr. Raymond."

"When Adrian told me about your experience, I decided it was too good a chance to pass up."

"I don't know what's going on here, but strange things continue to happen."

She looked at the house before speaking again. Staring at one of the upstairs windows, she asked, "You live alone?"

"Yes."

"Who's that in the window?"

Manning looked and saw Jenna looking out at them. "Oh, that's Jenna Newland. She's been helping with the cleaning. Actually, she's been *doing* the cleaning."

Just then, Adrian joined them. “We have some equipment we’d like to unload, Ben . . . just wondering where you want to put it until we decide where to set it up.” Adrian looked at the house as he spoke. “I can just imagine what this place was like a hundred years ago.”

“Why don’t we put it inside the foyer for now?”

After the equipment had been offloaded, Ben introduced Jenna, who was coming down the stairs as they entered the house. She had finished for the morning and was on her way to another job. “I’ll finish later if that’s okay,” she said in a breezy voice, which caught Liz Raymond’s attention.

“That’s fine, Jenna,” Ben replied.

“Pretty girl,” Liz commented after Jenna left. “Seems to have a lot of energy.”

“She’s working her way through graduate school.”

“And smart, too.” Liz smiled.

“Did she see the figure?” asked Adrian.

“She did,” Ben answered.

“Maybe we’ll have a chance to speak with her when she returns,” suggested Liz.

“Yes,” Ben nodded. “Although she was a bit shaken by what happened, I’m sure she’s put most of that behind her.”

When they went into the library, Liz stood in the center of the room, looking first at the fireplace. Putting her hand on the mantel, she focused on the small box that contained the brooch. Cocking her head to one side as though listening for something, she turned away from the fireplace abruptly and looked back at Adrian.

“What is it, Liz?”

“What a sweet smell,” she said, looking around the room as she spoke. “Flowers, the wonderfully fresh scent of flowers.”

There was an undeniable aroma in the air, sweet like the fragrance of cut flowers in a vase, though there were no flowers anywhere in the room, only a tall empty vase in the center of a round mahogany table near the doorway. Before either Ben or Adrian could speak, Liz made somewhat casually what both men considered a rather startling declaration. “We’re not alone in this house.”

Expecting to see someone else, Ben looked around the room. Maybe Jenna forgot something and had come back for it. Except for the three of them, the room was empty.

Then it was the painting that held her attention. "Who's that?" she asked, coming closer to get a better look at the unfinished portrait.

"It's her, the woman I saw on the stairway, and then again on the lawn near the stone bridge."

"What's this smudge?"

"A fingerprint. It happened a few nights ago."

Dr. Raymond regarded the ring with some curiosity. "It's her fingerprint."

"How can you know that?" Ben asked a bit startled at her quick and emphatic revelation.

"She has been in this room many times. She's looking for something."

Ben immediately thought about the brooch. At first, he hesitated to reveal the circumstances of the other night, but at length, disclosed what had happened. "I saw a hand and arm come out from behind the easel. The finger with the ring pushed into the paint. Seconds later, the hand and arm disappeared."

"Did you see the woman?" Dr. White questioned.

"No, only the hand and arm."

"It was the woman in this painting," Liz surmised. She was talking to Ben but continued to look around the room and not at him.

"Yes," said Ben. "I can't explain what happened, but it happened. There was a presence. It's not something I imagined."

"And the face behind the veil, did you imagine it?"

"No. It just appeared on the canvas."

"It seems she's trying to tell you something," smiled Liz.

Manning nodded. "Hope you can explain what's going on, Dr. Raymond. I don't like to admit it, but I'm becoming a bit uneasy with what's happening here."

"We'll figure it out, Ben."

To check for possible changes in electromagnetic fields, Raymond removed from her jacket an *electromagnetic field meter*, or EMF, a device shaped like a television remote control. Very slowly, she continued to survey the room with it, pausing at times to observe the readings on the screen. Both Ben and Dr. White watched as she moved the device methodically from one area to the next. On first impression, Raymond might come across as a woman short on personality, but one very long on determination.

"What's she doing?" Ben asked.

"Looking for energy disturbances," said White. "The paranormal disrupts energy levels."

Just then, Liz turned to White. "I think this would be a good place to set up an infrared camera."

Undeniably, this energetic woman had a primary agenda that had everything to do with the paranormal. She was all business. Ben felt sure that if there was another presence in Atwood House, Dr. Liz Raymond would find it.

He showed them two other rooms located at the back of the house on the main floor. Liz said little about these rooms, only that the readings on the EMF showed nothing to get excited about. Later, near the main stairway, she hesitated, telling them EMF readings were indicating a disturbance, a possible paranormal presence.

"Do you feel it?" she asked them.

"No, nothing unusual," returned White.

"Me either," Ben agreed.

"Cold, it's extremely cold here."

White sensed his obligation to keep Manning informed, especially when explanation depended on the EMF Liz was using. He came up beside her, looked for a moment at the reading, and then turned to Ben who waited anxiously for him to reveal what was happening.

As Liz moved through the room, White said, "The EMF can determine instantaneous changes in ambient temperatures, which could suggest a paranormal presence."

Liz asked, "Is there another staircase to the upper rooms?"

"Yes, a small one behind the library."

"What's that room?" Liz asked.

"The great room."

"May we see it?" she requested politely.

He led them down the hallway, before stopping in front of two large ornate walnut doors. The doors open, standing in front of them was a young woman—and she was holding something in her hand.

"My God!" whispered Adrian.

Dr. Liz said nothing but stood with her eyes fixed on the figure directly in front of them. Her face relaxed, she smiled slightly. It was almost as if she expected to find someone there—so Ben thought.

"Lacey," Ben said at length. "I didn't know you were here."

"Hello," returned Lacey cheerfully, "didn't mean to startle you. I came in the back way a few minutes ago."

"I'd like you to meet Drs. Liz Raymond and Adrian White. They're here to do research," Ben informed her.

Lacey did a little curtsey before saying, "I'm sorry if I frightened you."

"Not at all," returned Liz affably. "Mr. Manning said you had a paranormal experience in this house."

"I certainly would not call what happened normal in any way."

"Well, if you don't mind, maybe we could talk about it later."

"I don't mind," Lacey smiled. "In fact, I think it's all kind of exciting." With that, she nodded and walked away toward rooms at the back of the house.

"The upstairs rooms are not entirely furnished," Ben informed them as they walked down the wide upstairs hallway. He was somewhat apologetic when he said, "Some remain exactly the way they've been for years. However, we have a couple of bedrooms prepared for you, which I hope you'll find satisfactory."

"It must be an enormous job maintaining a place this size," said Adrian. "Thank you again, Ben for inviting us to stay in such a beautiful house."

"Adrian's right, it is a marvelous place, and I'm excited to see if there are other—uninvited guests," smiled Liz.

"These two rooms are ready for you." He opened the door to the first, and across the hall, the door to the second room was already open. Though both rooms were sparsely furnished, new curtains had been hung, and, overall, these would be comfortable quarters for the two guests. Ben was glad to have the company.

"This is excellent," said Liz.

"Each room has its own bathroom."

After thanking him again, Adrian suggested they get settled before continuing with "their work," as he called it.

About an hour later, they met in the library and spent a few minutes discussing preliminary strategies. Liz had definite ideas about how to lay it all out, and both Adrian and Ben were agreeable to the logistics she proposed. Maybe there was something to this paranormal aptitude as Ben had referred to Dr. Raymond's expertise.

"Let's put cameras at the bottom of both stairways," Liz said decidedly. "The primary corridor seems to be there," and she nodded to the main stairway. It took nearly an hour to set up four infrareds in places that Dr. Raymond referred to as "hot zones."

The large landing at the top of the main staircase was backed by a stunning set of stained glass windows. Beautiful flower patterns in intricate lines and swirls, and cranes and butterflies were all caught in the morning light that washed across the molasses-colored wainscoting. Noticeably absent in these patterns was the religious iconography of early church stained glass. A walnut bench, which was an architectural feature below the three windows, was cushioned in burgundy velvet. This was one of Manning's favorite places in the entire house. Late afternoons often found him sitting there with a book, reading in the warm streams of sunlight that lingered in the stained glass for nearly three hours.

"It is truly stunning," began Liz, as she regarded the stained glass closely. "I can imagine the excitement of living so many years ago in such a magnificent house. Can't you just see the matron of the house pausing momentarily, before descending this huge stairway, and probably wearing a dress like the one you painted into your portrait, Ben? And the parties, people waiting anxiously for Mrs. Atwood to make her grand entrance. What exciting times this house must have seen."

Though she was speaking to both at the same time, there was a hint of nostalgia in her voice, which Ben thought exciting. It struck him a bit odd that her personification of Atwood House was so casually made, as if she honestly believed the house to be a living breathing thing.

Chapter 8

A FEW MINUTES BEFORE five o'clock, Jenna Newland entered the house through the front door. She was carrying wallpaper samplers, and when she saw two cameras set on tripods, she placed the books on a foyer table and went into the library to find Ben, who looked happy to see her. "Hi," she said warmly.

Liz, standing by the monitors, said, "Nice to see you again, Jenna."

"Sorry I had to rush away this morning." Jenna shook hands first with Liz then with Dr. White. "When Ben said you were coming, I asked him if I could be a small part of this investigation."

"Ms. Newland," White nodded courteously. "It might be premature to call this an investigation—more like curiosity at this point."

Liz put one arm on Jenna's shoulder and said, "We're happy to get all the help we can. There is definitely something, maybe I should say *peculiar,* about Atwood House, and it's our intention to discover as much as possible about that incident on the stairway."

"What I saw was certainly strange—not easily forgotten."

"Must have been somewhat unsettling," Liz remarked with an air of compassion.

"It was certainly that, wasn't it, Ben?"

"It was all that and then some." He laughed slightly, not wanting to attach too much seriousness to an event that might still have an explanation outside the paranormal realm.

Computer monitors were set in a row on the library table. If there was movement in any of the designated areas, it would show on at least one of the monitors. Jenna, who was showing renewed curiosity in the current activities, detailed her account from the previous week when she was one of three witnesses who had seen the mysterious figure on the stairs. Ben and Dr. White observed the monitors while Liz listened to Jenna.

Minutes later, Jenna pulled Ben aside. “This is fascinating, kind of like the big event in town. Do you mind if I hang around to see what happens?”

“Seriously?”

“Why not? It’s not every day something like this happens in Newburgh, Indiana.”

“Like what?”

“The ghost on the stairs.”

“Come on, Jenna. Don’t you think that’s a bit much?”

“Not at all. You saw it, too.”

“I saw something. It could have been *pareidolia* for all I know.”

“What?”

“Seeing something that really isn’t there, like seeing a face on Mars when the image is nothing more than shadows and light, or seeing Abraham Lincoln’s face in a cloud formation.”

“Yeah, I saw that face, the one on Mars. It’s spectacular,” she said.

He regarded her inquisitively. “You’re playing me, aren’t you?”

Laughing, she asked again, “So, can I stay for the ghost hunt?”

“Stay as long as you want,” he smiled. “I’m actually glad you’re here.”

A red light flashed, indicating one camera was activated. Liz watched the monitor intently. Although the camera in the foyer was focused on the landing, the entire staircase was visible.

“What is it?” asked Ben.

Without answering, Liz grabbed a *forward-looking infrared radiometer* called a FLIR, a thermal imaging camera, off the table and hurried out of the library toward the foyer.

Adrian shook his head. “I’m not sure, but I think something activated one of the cameras.”

"We've got a hit, a heat signature," Dr. Raymond announced when the others arrived in the foyer.

"It could be residual heat," suggested White.

Dr. Raymond slowly lowered the FLIR to her side. "The sunset, the windows face west."

"Yes," Ben said.

"Shadows," she went on, "probably the wind blowing the branches of a nearby tree. The equipment is extremely sensitive and these false signatures have to be logged."

"How do you determine which signatures are authentic?" Ben began, "those that are . . . paranormal?"

It was Adrian who said, "The computer records a determination, especially regarding the FLIR, but it's often based on tangential evidence and observation analysis."

Liz Raymond shook her head as though something wasn't adding up, and for her, loose ends were too frequently dead ends. She panned the FLIR from one side of the landing to the other, and then began moving it slowly down the staircase, stopping abruptly just a few steps below the landing. "That's peculiar. The FLIR shows movement on the stairs. Someone's coming this way."

Ben, taking a few steps closer to the stairs, deciding closer would quickly support the FLIR image, looked at the stairway but saw nothing out of the ordinary. His arm extended, he brushed and wiped the air as though he expected to touch what he could not see.

Suddenly there was a piercing scream. Jenna brushed one hand over the back of the other, and stepped hurriedly to the side, nearly knocking Adrian into the foyer table. "Something touched me. I swear to God, something cold and damp brushed against me."

Adrian, who was startled by Jenna's disconcerting outburst, moved back and looked at Jenna, who had gone pale. "She obviously felt something. Look at her."

Ben guided her to a wooden chair beside the table and eased her down gently. "Take it easy, Jenna. This thing can get freaky if you let it."

“I don’t think she imagined it.” Liz seemed confident that Jenna had certainly experienced something unusual. “Something was there, moving deliberately down the stairs.” She looked again at the FLIR. “Whatever it was is gone.” Her grip on the plastic handle of the FLIR loosened.

Hours passed with nothing out of the ordinary taking place. The autumn sky darkened quickly. Long claps of thunder announced the severity of an approaching storm. Already, the first drops of rain could be heard against the windows. As lightning flashed across a black sky, they sat in the library discussing how the night would lay out.

While Adrian and Dr. Raymond considered whether to reposition one of the cameras, Ben lit the fireplace. Almost immediately the chill that had settled on the night, and especially in the room, relented. Though Jenna had pulled herself together, she had subsequent reservations about continuing her vigilance too much longer into the night.

“How do you feel?” asked Ben after placing another log on the fire.

“Have you ever been touched by a ghost?”

Shaking his head slowly, he replied in a voice barely audible, “Never.”

“Well it’s not a thing you want to experience.”

Her fragile state of mind kept Ben from saying that what she had considered paranormal might have been nothing more than a draft blowing in from the hallway or from one of the adjoining rooms. Instead, he asked if he could get her something to drink. “As soon as the storm breaks, I’m going to make a run for it,” she announced.

But the storm didn’t break. Its intensity raged late into the night. The curtains had not been drawn and as Ben went over to close them, spikes of lightning created surrealistic patterns in the windows. Glancing outside during one large flash of lightning, Ben caught sight of a figure standing near the stone bridge. Not wanting to alarm Jenna, who was asleep on the sofa, he kept quiet about what he’d seen and returned to his chair beside the fireplace. He thought his own imagination was responsible for the mysterious mirage in the rain.

The night wore on without anything unusual occurring. That all changed at three o'clock, as rain continued to drum and splash the windows. It was Liz who first saw the movement on the camera positioned at the end of the hallway near the great room doors. Clearly discernible was a momentary shadow. But it was the opening and closing of the doors that gave the incident significance and veracity.

"Look at this," she called to Adrian, who left his chair beside the fireplace to join her. "I'd call that a serious hit."

Ben came over to look at the replay on the monitor and shook his head in disbelief as Dr. Raymond replayed the EMF clip a second time. "Someone's in the great room?"

"Yes," proclaimed Liz.

That the door to the great room had opened and closed was undeniable. It was not something imagined. It had happened. The proof was right there in front of them. Dr. White watched the monitor as Liz and Ben opened the two large doors.

As Liz panned the room with the FLIR, Ben aimed the EMF at the center of the room. "Oh, sweet Lord," she shouted suddenly. "Do you see this, Adrian?"

But it was Manning who replied, "Remarkable, this just can't be possible, and yet there they are, several shadows moving around the room right in front of us."

Rain beat against the library windows so fiercely that it was difficult to hear Jenna who was just waking from her nap on the couch. Stretching long and lanky, she walked over to White. Eyes narrowed and shaking her head, as though trying to shake off two hours of sleep, she asked, "What's happening?"

"We've found something," Adrian admitted.

"Ghosts?"

"Look," Adrian pointed to the monitor.

"Wow, all kinds of things are happening in there."

In the great room, Ben came over to where Liz was standing so he could see the images in the FLIR viewfinder. For some strange reason, he recalled an Edgar Allan Poe story, *Masque of the Red Death*. He had read it in grammar school, and apparently it had made a more indelible impression on him than he realized.

Liz handed the FLIR to Ben and took from her pocket an *electronic voice phenomenon*, or EVP, which she held in the palm of one hand. Shaking her head and looking excitedly at Ben, she acknowledged a strong reading.

Wherever he aimed the FLIR in the great room, he saw movement—a lot of movement. The back wall was a backdrop against which shadows twirled and whirled. Lowering the camera, and then slowly surveying the entire room, Ben admitted that he saw "nothing, no movements, nothing at all." Except for them, the room remained empty. It was only when he used the FLIR that images appeared.

"This is absolute textbook," Liz shouted.

In the center of the room, contorted shapes jerked and twisted whimsically, while others moved in more coordinated repetitious cadences. Liz had moved into the center of the room and her shape was distinguishable in the FLIR viewfinder. Standing in pure amazement, Ben tried hard to conceptualize what he was seeing, but he could not. The room was alive. Yet, he and Dr. Raymond were the only ones there.

Finally, and most importantly, was the deliberate way the shadows gathered in one corner of the great room before disappearing. They vanished in a strange procession of silhouettes, moving easily through the wall, leaving behind a huge empty room, shining in the brilliant light of two ornate chandeliers.

Later, with light from the fireplace casting thick heavy shadows across the library, and rain continuing to beat on the house intensely, they downloaded data into one of the computers. Four apprehensive figures crowded around the library table anxious to see the monitor. The rhythmical movements of the shadows were frequently repetitious and coordinated.

Music, and its presence astonished each of them momentarily.

"Dancing," said Jenna, "the ghosts are dancing."

"It sure looks that way," agreed Ben.

"This stretches the limits of imagination," White confessed slowly.

"It's no longer imagination," Liz informed them.

"What's the explanation?" Ben wanted to know. "What are we seeing?"

It was Jenna who attempted to clarify what each had seen that night in the great room of Atwood House. "Ghosts."

Chapter 9

JENNA LEFT LATER that morning with the intention of returning with Lacey around noon, telling Ben that despite the "ghosts" she was determined to finish cleaning the upstairs rooms. In the meantime, both Liz and Adrian were busy analyzing computations, so Ben had a chance to look again at the articles Rikki Whitmore had sent him. As he leafed through them, he became more curious about what Liz and Adrian were discussing—even when he knew that what they were considering was extremely complex.

"Look at these." Adrian pushed his calculations across the table for her consideration.

"You realize what this means?" he heard Liz ask Dr. White. "If you're correct, we're on the verge of one of the biggest scientific discoveries of the millennium."

Adrian nodded his agreement. "The idea of a separate reality coexisting with the one we know—what an opportunity."

"A multiverse," Liz added. "We actually caught a glimpse of a past event. We'll need to test these data further to eliminate any possible kinks or inaccuracies." She looked at White as she spoke. "But I think we've got something extraordinary."

White responded, "We have preliminary evidence that magnetic portals open and close at various places in this house. Invisible, unstable, elusive as they are, these portals do exist. However, there are no markers, no known data, which indicate in what respects these magnetic fields are similar and what their commonalities are."

"Incredulous as it may seem, something astonishing happened here last night. Technology has enabled us to glimpse a startling phenomenon, which would not have been possible otherwise," confessed Liz Raymond.

"We got lucky," Ben suggested.

"Yes—but more than that," continued Raymond, "we have data that confirm paranormal activity occurring simultaneously in time and space, but not without some incongruence, leaving us with a mystery not so easily solved."

"To put it allegorically," began White, "we have seen the other side of the looking glass and been over the rainbow. More to the point, we have witnessed an event that happened at Atwood House possibly more than a century ago."

Ben, wanting to remain in the conversation, stated skeptically, "I know what we saw . . . what the technology recorded. Maybe there is an explanation that doesn't involve the paranormal."

"No," Adrian persisted, "the heat signatures corroborate the hypothesis of a gateway or portal. We observed several figures that appeared to be—" and he hesitated momentarily before suggesting, "dancing, and then disappearing at one end of the great room."

"If you're right, how do we find this portal?" Ben asked.

"We begin where it happened—in the great room." Dr. White was emphatic about what had occurred and his recommended course of action also sounded direct and discerning. "There are several accounts of magnetic fields with divergent locations, and most recently, both the Air Force and NASA have contributed heavily to the literature."

With a look of confusion, Ben asked, "Maybe the bigger question is what happens if we actually discover one of these portals or gateways? It would be a gateway to where?"

Dr. White answered quickly. "Documenting the actual existence of a portal might be enough. That itself would be incredibly significant."

But it was Liz Raymond who gave the answer Manning expected but was not at all sure he wanted to hear. Still, he listened as she articulated the words slowly, precisely, and thinking with each word she spoke how serious she was.

"As incomprehensible as it sounds, we go through," she said in a nonchalant tone that was evident to both Ben and Adrian.

"That's way too risky for me. I like where I'm living—if you know what I mean," Ben said flatly.

"Relax, Ben, we're a long way from anything that serious," acknowledged Liz with a slight smile. "Let's analyze again those EMF data," she suggested. "Maybe we've missed something that will help narrow the search."

"Since there are no signposts to guide us," began White, "it's time to think outside the box, which means determining alternatives that might possibly alter known laws of physics." Then after a short pause he added, "Based on NASA-funded research, we begin with x-points, but we go beyond those. Let's correlate magnetic field data with EVP strengths."

This was all getting much too technical for Manning, who excused himself and went outside. Just as he left the house, he saw the Klassy Kleen SUV roll to a stop. He'd been anxious to see his favorite cleaners again, if for no other reason than to have the other upstairs rooms cleaned. He was sure Jenna would be glad to finish the work and move on to another job.

She smiled when she saw him. "Any more ghosts?"

"It was a Strauss waltz," he told her.

"What?"

"The music we heard last night in the great room."

"Oh, you're talking about the dance, or waltz of the zombies."

Lacey came in during the middle of the conversation. "What's this talk about zombies?"

Before either Ben or Jenna could answer, Dr. Raymond came out of the house with a camera. "Where was it you saw the figure?" she asked.

Pointing, Ben answered, "Over there by the stone bridge. She was standing just a few feet away."

"I'd like to put a trail camera near that spot, attach it to one of those nearby cedar trees," and as she spoke, she pointed at a specific tree near the bridge. "Maybe we'll pick up something there."

Jenna and Lacey went into the house to continue cleaning a couple of upstairs rooms. Ben helped Liz secure the camera and watched as she adjusted it. The ground was wet, still spongy in places from last night's heavy rain. Near the bridge were several puddles that in the morning sun glistened like chunks of broken glass.

After the camera was set, Liz seemed preoccupied with something. She was on her knees and looked intently at the ground in front of her.

"What is it?" Ben asked.

"There's something down there."

"It's probably a septic tank."

"No, it's something else, something that doesn't belong there."

"I don't know," he said, shaking his head. "Could be anything. I got a metal detector in the shed."

"Do you mind getting it?"

"Not at all."

She continued to walk around the area close to the bridge. Sticking out of the ground and glinting in the sunlight was a piece of what appeared to be metal. But when she touched it, there was a sudden rumbling far off on the horizon, causing her to draw back quickly.

Minutes later, Ben moved the metal detector across the lawn a few feet from where Dr. Raymond was kneeling. Rain had washed away some of the topsoil and when he looked closer, he noticed a slight depression. Nearer the bridge was another sunken area. Since moving in, he hadn't paid much attention to the lawn or landscaping. Rikki Whitmore had told him that a man named Tyler had kept up the grass and shrubs during the time Atwood House was the property of the realty company.

"Did you find something?" Ben asked.

Liz looked up. "I'm not sure. Bring it over here a minute."

As soon as he moved the metal detector across the piece that protruded no more than an inch or two out of the soil, it began beeping strongly. Liz had found a broken branch and began digging into the soft earth, trying to uncover more of whatever it was shining so brightly in the sunlight.

"It's more than six feet down." He showed her the depth reading on the metal detector. "And it's not metal."

Liz tossed the stick into the bushes. "Would it be okay with you if we get a GPR unit in here?"

"What's that?" asked Manning.

"*Ground penetrating radar.* It's extremely sensitive equipment, and it will give us a good idea what's down there."

"Sure, if you think it's important."

"We won't know until we do more expansive scans of the area."

They went inside to look for Adrian to tell him they had found something of interest in the yard. Holding a dust mop, Adrian was standing in the center of the great room, his head laid back, and staring either at the ceiling or at the decorative cornice around the upper windows. He penciled information into a notebook, and after returning the small notebook to his pocket, he began thrusting the mop out in front of him, jabbing it at the back wall, then lunging with it higher up near the ceiling cornice. Though deliberate and methodical, his actions seemed ridiculous to Ben who was looking at Liz for her reaction.

Suddenly, he turned to them with a revelation that was not necessarily unexpected. "We saw the shadows disappear at the back of this room."

"They had to go somewhere," Liz agreed.

It sounded like he was letting them in on his thoughts. For a moment, Ben felt he might be in the way and thought about leaving. White, however, regarded him curiously as though he had something to say, but didn't know how to say it without sounding impulsive.

At length, Adrian asked, "What's in there?" he pointed to a door on the other side of the room.

"Another room, empty as far as I know. Probably a sitting room at some time or another, or possibly a storeroom." Ben went over and opened the door. The air was hot and stale, and with only light shining in from the great room, it was hard to see the interior clearly. But there was enough light for him to see the dark figure standing motionless in a thin stream of light. "There's somebody in there!" he yelled, as he pulled the door shut. "It's her."

Chapter 10

ONCE THEY LOCATED the light switch and entered the room, which was larger than Ben expected, they found a storeroom with a few pieces of antique furniture pushed up against two walls. A couple of oil paintings were partially covered with a soiled cloth, dusty books in stacks on a table, and a carpet was rolled against one wall. Some early 20th century men's clothing on a hanger caught Ben's attention. Under an ornate chair was a pair of vintage men's shoes. In one corner was an aluminum ladder. What they had earlier thought was the figure of a woman turned out to be a dress form draped in a Victorian gown.

"That's strange," Ben declared.

What resembled a doorway, possibly one opening into an adjoining room, was bricked shut, and it had not been done recently. For a moment, Ben thought it might originally have been a fireplace, but quickly dismissed this idea, largely because he knew none of the chimneys corresponded to this area of the house.

They thought nothing more about it. White seemed anxious to return to the great room and asked Ben to bring the ladder so he could continue his observation, or search, closer to the ceiling. With too many loose ends for Dr. White, it was beginning to look like resolutions would take more time. Though he was not as tenacious as he had seemed earlier, Adrian's continued determination and resolve remained evident to Ben who regretted that this investigation was pulling him away from his painting.

Increasingly excited, Liz realized the importance of what she referred to as a "signature investigation with paranormal overtones and influences." She continued to study those data already compiled, trying hard to find something they had missed—something that would explain what had happened, while also searching for indications that there were considerably more paranormal events to come.

"I think we're looking in the wrong place. We need to turn the room the other way—spin it," Adrian suggested. "Maybe it's like the image on the retina of the eye, an image in reverse."

Ben, who was holding the ladder while White continued to poke higher up near the tops of the windows, considered these random attempts to locate a portal, ridiculous. In appearance, the event had taken on aspects of theater, an air of absurdity. Adrian White was hoping for the miracle that would reveal a gateway. He was a believer and wanted faith to be a tenant of the scientific method. Maybe it was faith that kept him poking another 30 minutes into the many nooks and crannies in the great room at Atwood House.

Jenna and Lacey had finished cleaning and packed their supplies into the SUV. Jenna asked Ben for an update on the investigation, which he embellished, hoping to keep her interested. Having Jenna around was a pleasant experience that he looked forward to, and each time she showed an inclination to stay, he was glad. Lacey, who was busy with school, said she would try and find time to stop by and help in any way possible.

Around three o'clock that Saturday afternoon, a red pickup truck with *Jennings Surveying* stenciled in black letters on both doors pulled up in front of Atwood House. Herb Jennings and his 25-year old son, Matt, had been called in by Liz, who said she had used their services before and considered them dedicated professionals. Matt had told her that one summer night when he and some friends were swimming at Fischer's Lake, they had seen "quite clearly" a V-shaped UFO land in a pasture less than a mile from the lake. Indiana MUFON was called, and several other witnesses came forward to confirm the sighting. Even though the military had cordoned off the area, investigating authorities referred to the event as nothing more than a meteor strike.

Both Liz and Adrian were there to greet them and help them offload GPR equipment. The area by the bridge had been flagged and everyone was anxious to discover what lay beneath the surface. Ben stood near Matt on the stone bridge, observing Herb as he pulled the GPR unit over one quadrant at a time. Matt also watched for anomalies that might appear on the monitors of two computers set adjacent to each other on a folding table.

"Using two computers, we can actually merge data into a three-dimensional image," Matt told Ben.

"How far down can you go with this equipment?"

"That depends on the frequency of the antenna and the subsurface geology to a large extent. We can go deeper in dry sandy soils and in a subsurface like granite or limestone. Lower frequencies have more depth capability than higher frequencies. After 40 feet, signals weaken and become considerably less reliable," Matt explained. "The equipment is cutting edge impact echo, infrared capable, and uses electromagnetic radiation radar pulses to actually image the subsurface."

"Sounds complicated," Ben offered.

Matt smiled. "It's like a lot of other things in life—takes time and training to understand how to use it."

"A three-dimensional image should provide a fair indication of what's down there?" continued Ben.

"The integrity of the signal is usually reliable, but when radar signal attenuation occurs, reliability diminishes." He saw the confusion on Ben's face. "Readings indicate signatures. You see these horizontal lines, and the uniformity of the signal?" Again, he glanced at Ben, who nodded. "This ground is uncompromised—no intrusion. A subsurface disturbance will register as an anomaly."

Five minutes passed. Ten minutes passed. When Herb ran the GPR closer to the protrusion that Liz had found, the readings began to change.

"Hot zone," yelled Herb.

After mapping the rest of the area near the bridge, they gathered around the monitors to sort through these data. Several vertical lines spiked as Matt tried to control the resolution and keep the transmission from fluctuating. Then, a three-dimensional image slowly emerged on one of the computer screens.

"What is it?" Ben asked excitedly.

"Septic tank," Herb said assuredly.

It was Matt who offered another opinion. "Awfully far down for a septic." He pointed to the freeze frame on the screen as he spoke. "Look at the edges. They don't look like manufactured or prefabricated sections—too jagged. Could be an obsolete septic system maybe." After looking closer at the image, he added, "Whatever it is appears to be in several pieces, possibly something deliberately destroyed."

Herb studied the scans carefully before admitting, "Could be broken foundation." He turned to Ben. "Was there a structure here, an old pump house, a concrete foundation for a storage shed maybe?"

"I don't know. I suppose it's possible, but I don't know of anything."

Matt made another suggestion. "They might be left over pieces of stonework from the bridge." Again, he pointed to the image on the screen. "These striations indicate a natural formation, granite or possibly limestone. If the pieces are concrete, we'd see less uniformity."

The son was schooling the father, Ben decided. More scans, more speculation about what was buried more than six feet in the ground. White looked closely at the piece now protruding nearly a foot out of the soil, the same piece Liz had attempted to dig out with the end of a broken branch. Still convinced that it was a piece from one of the andesite panels, probably discarded during the construction of the bridge, Ben ran his fingers over the smooth surface. One corner of the rectangular piece glistened white with sunlight.

"It's definitely a larger structure that has been deliberately buried," White concluded.

"Something really alien," Liz suggested boldly, "and it has been down there several years, probably since the house was built. I get an impression of catastrophe."

Whether anyone else heard what Liz said was uncertain. Or if they heard it, maybe they dismissed it as incidental talk. Ben heard it clearly enough and was already trying to comprehend the implications of something catastrophic happening so close to Atwood House. The first thing that came to mind was an explosion—but an explosion of what?

"It's a signature we've seen before, on construction site surveys, where there were old church foundations or cemeteries," Herb proclaimed. "But the mapping shows no indication of graves, so a cemetery can be ruled out."

"I'm sure there's historical information available. Maybe a local historian can identify a particular structure that used to be here." Ben was trying hard to find a solution that would delay excavation of the site.

"There's not enough down there to suggest a really large structure," Matt confessed, "not a large stone structure anyway."

It was Adrian who noticed what the rest of them had missed. That section which had been recently exposed showed no indication of being in the ground—no soil line, no noticeable patina. White continued to study the anomaly as Manning watched.

"Any ideas?" asked Ben.

"Maybe it's nothing more than an aberration, a fault line, or even scratches from a mower blade," Adrian replied, "and yet there seems to be a pattern, an impression intentionally incised into the surface."

Ben watched intently as White continued to examine the indentations. "Is it stone?"

"This does not feel like stone," White confessed.

"Maybe this will help," said Jenna, handing Adrian a bottle of drinking water.

He splashed water across the surface and almost immediately two shapes were visible. Both looked to be a triangle, one inverted on top of the other and resembling an hourglass. Although the top triangle was larger, they converged at their apexes. Exactly at the point where it disappeared into the ground was the beginning of what looked to be a series of lines. White attempted to wiggle the piece, perhaps thinking he could extract it, but it was too deeply embedded in the earth and not moving at all.

Liz pushed the idea of digging, saying, "Matt might be right. What's down there might be discarded or unused pieces from construction of the bridge. But I'm convinced it's more than that, and I'm sure there are several other pieces to be found." She glanced across the field in the direction of the large woods to the northeast. "There are several perceptible undulations in the ground on an otherwise flat terrain, and they head off toward those trees. The soil has been pushed up somehow, not deliberately, but possibly because of whatever it was that happened here."

Herb spoke directly to Adrian White and then to Ben. "We can get a backhoe in here, or Bobcat, something less invasive than heavier equipment that would tear up the lawn."

Drs. White and Raymond looked at Ben. Even Jenna regarded him anxiously, after glancing again at the scans, which were still freeze-framed on the monitors.

"If you think what's down there is significant, then let's dig," Ben suggested.

Before a decision could be made, Liz called Adrian back to the monitors. "I want you to see this." Her tone was serious, as though whatever it was she had discovered had taken on new meaning.

With each of them looking at the monitor, which was in the shade enough to keep the image from washing out, Liz pointed to a shadowy part of the object just below the surface. "Look closely and you can see what seem to be marks in a sort of deliberate pattern."

They did, and it was Jenna who said, "Symbols."

"Possible iconography," stated Dr. Raymond.

White tapped the piece gently with a coin that he had taken from his pocket, and immediately the metal, or whatever it was, reverberated like the soft echoes down an empty hallway. "Resonance," he declared. "Whatever it is has distinct resonance."

"Does that have some importance?" Ben asked curiously.

"Well, we know it's not rock formation," stated Adrian White authoritatively.

Kneeling beside White, Liz rubbed an index finger along the surface, and twice attempted to push in her fingernail. Looking at Adrian who was now sitting on the ground, she said, "Plastic maybe."

"I don't know. I never knew plastic to reverberate like that," admitted White.

Matt kneeled beside Liz and ran his own fingers over the smooth surface. "It might be a combination of materials," he suggested.

"You have a hammer in the truck?" Adrian asked Matt.

Matt nodded, and seconds later he returned with a hammer, which he immediately handed to White. "Here you go, Dr. White."

"Let's just see what we've got here," Adrian replied evenly.

The small group gathered in a circle around the protrusion and watched Adrian strike the object softly. There was no reverberation, just a strange sound that reminded them of sonar pings. White gripped the hammer tighter and struck another blow. This time, there was no sound at all. Instead, the object took on a deep green color. "Now that is weird," admitted White.

"It's moving," Jenna shouted. "Look."

"Vibrations," said Adrian. Placing his hand flat on the surface, he looked from one to the next. "This thing has a heartbeat."

Chapter 11

THE DIG, AS it was referred to, was scheduled for the following Wednesday. Professor Raymond returned to Bloomington to resolve University protocol that would free her up for a few days. Jenna Newland resumed her work at the law offices of Whitman, Whitman and Burke. Ben used the time to paint, attempting to complete the portrait of the woman he had started days ago. With the lifting of the veil came imagination, but not the truth he had expected. The impossible tore at his conscience, kept him awake at night, left him thinking and searching long after midnight for a face conceived, not from imagination, but one painted with authenticity and veracity.

Adrian White was in Newburgh to interview Larry Collins, a self-professed historian who, ten years ago, had published his extensive and comprehensive knowledge of the small town of Newburgh, Indiana. Paperback copies could be found in many of the local tourist attractions and antique malls across Southern Indiana. They met at a local Denny's Restaurant on the western edge of Newburgh and sat facing each other in one corner of the restaurant. A pot of hot coffee in a white ceramic container was between them on the table.

Collins was a tall well-built man who looked much younger than his 58 years. His black hair was combed straight back, leaving a noticeable receding hairline. Hazel eyes regarded Adrian inquisitively. "You say you're going to dig the yard at Atwood House?"

"Only an area southwest of the bridge," White began. "An anomalous GPR signature has us curious about what's there. Might not be anything significant, but we want a closer look."

Collins leaned forward in his chair, his square jaw rigidly set, and his lips drawn tight. Eyes narrowed, head inclined to one side, his words were a declaration that White had certainly not expected. "You might be digging in the wrong place."

"Well that's certainly possible," Adrian replied., waiting for Collins to explain.

"Several years ago, the Air Force had an unprecedented interest in property northeast of Atwood House. I remember my father talking about it several times. Not much got past my father. Anyway, the cover story had something to do with the discovery of a meteorite on the east side of the bridge. The area was roped off for several weeks. During that time, they dug the hell out of several square feet of land. They obviously expected to find something out there. But the meteorite cover became transparent after only a few days, when a sergeant from Grissom Air Force Base had a little too much to drink one night in town."

"Probably nothing more than bar talk," suggested White.

"According to accounts of those who were there that night, the man mentioned repeatedly the words 'magnetic vortex.' Of course, no one knew what he was talking about, until a reporter from the *Indianapolis Star* picked up the story and tried to authenticate it through military channels."

"What happened?"

"Times were different in those days. The military was a hell of a lot less diplomatic than today. There was unwavering commitment to both military dictate and mission. The Air Force passed the incident off as nothing but rumor. When the reporter tried to locate the mouthy sergeant, the Air Force had no record of the man at all."

He poured hot coffee into Adrian's cup and then into his own. It was clear that the story had little effect on White who was staring out the window in the direction of the Ohio River. "It must have been a big event for such a small town."

Collins nodded. "My father said the town had a campy atmosphere for several weeks, and even after the Air Force had packed out and returned to Grissom, people, many of them strangers, continued to visit the site. Pine trees had been planted where they dug, and there were only a few indications that the ground had been disturbed at all." He took a couple sips of coffee before leveling a serious look at Adrian White. "What are you digging up out there?"

"I honestly don't know."

"Atwood House has an exciting history, especially if you're into this paranormal stuff."

"We're investigating phenomena that have scientific explanations," White said stiffly.

"It's a small town, hard to keep a secret for long."

"No secrets, just methodical fieldwork."

"There's always been talk of ghosts, apparitions that bump along through the night," admitted Collins. "My father talked often about strange occurrences at Atwood House."

"I'll stick to facts and leave ghost hunting to the paranormal people," replied White.

"People like Dr. Raymond?" suggested Collins.

"That's right." White appeared surprised at the mention of Dr. Raymond and realized Collins knew much more about their research at Atwood House than he had disclosed.

"Be that as it may," he smiled. "I'll give you the name of a woman who has, as crazy as it might sound, firsthand experience with Atwood House. She worked for many years as a housekeeper for the Young family. Still lives in Newburgh not far from Atwood House. If anyone can speak to strange phenomena, it's Millie Stewart."

White took a small notebook from his jacket pocket and wrote the woman's name on a blank page. "I'll contact her."

"Address and phone number are in the Newburgh directory." Then after a pause, Collins added, "On a more scientific note, Professor Jeffery Trafford, I think he's still teaching at the University of Evansville, has spent months mapping what he refers to as ley lines—based on something Plato wrote about."

"The *dodecahedron,* the fifth Platonic solid that Plato used to describe the cosmos?"

"Yeah, that sounds right. Don't have any idea what it is, but it sounds right."

"It's extremely complicated. Essentially it deals with global geometry, and the possibility that the universe is not just flat and infinite, but instead finite, and in the shape of a polygon with twelve flat faces." Instantly, Dr. White realized this was getting way too technical and drew back.

"I see . . . well, not really. Trafford wrote of magnetic energies, which increase proportionately in areas where ley lines intersect."

"I'm familiar with Dr. Trafford's work," admitted White. "In fact, these lines have been mapped before by researchers. It's widely known by the scientific community that around the world we find this convergence of powerful magnetic lines, especially at sacred sites in England and France."

"Trafford said there is a crossing of these lines on Atwood House property," revealed Collins.

"That might explain the Air Force presence to some extent."

Collins nodded, "Yes, it certainly could." Then he added, "Let me just say this before you leave, Dr. White." Again, he leveled a serious look at Adrian. "It was my father who first told me about the sightings."

"Sightings?"

"Isn't that the reason you're there, to investigate the sightings?"

"There have been strange occurrences at Atwood House. I don't deny that."

"I'm assuming you have seen the apparition on the stairway?"

"Yes," White admitted.

"And the activity in the great room, the dancing, and heard the music?"

"Yes, all of that. You seem very informed, Mr. Collins."

"Let's just say that Millie Stewart has often mentioned the strange events that have happened in Atwood House."

"You mentioned your father?" prompted Adrian.

"He spoke of a room on the first floor of the house. Told my mother and me that once a man had entered that room and never came out. He just disappeared into thin air, so it seemed."

Recalling the room off the great room, the one with a bricked doorway, White wanted Collins to continue. With his arms folded on the table, Adrian drew a deep breath, exhaled it, and waited anxiously for what he thought he might already know.

"In fact, my father was the man who closed the gateway."

"Gateway?" asked Adrian cautiously.

Collins nodded. "Said the room gave off peculiar odors. That didn't seem unusual, since many different odors would linger in a musty old house like that one, so I didn't think much about it. But according to him, these were not the kinds of odors frequently associated with old houses."

"I don't understand," Adrian admitted. "Are you suggesting that these odors were coming in from outside the house?"

"That's what he thought at first. The scent of flowers was heavy. So was the smell of rain. Other smells seemed to be more prevalent in this one particular room where he was working."

"What kind of smells?"

"Thermal, thick in the nostrils, and sustained in the air for minutes at a time, not the smell of burning wood, but something much more intense—like an engine overheating, or wires shorting out. Mechanical is the word my dad used."

"That's all very interesting, but smells not entirely uncommon in a house. There might have been a short in the electricity, or it could have been radiator heat."

"It was summer, and the house was not occupied during the time he did the work. There was one smell my father knew well." Again, he leaned across the table closer to Adrian. "The smell of jasmine."

"Jasmine?" repeated White.

"Yes."

"I don't understand."

"There's no jasmine growing anywhere on the property."

Still unclear why this was so seemingly important, White looked at the man with narrowed eyes and repeated, "Jasmine?"

"That's right, Dr. White, its sweet floral aroma is powerful and has a kind of narcotic effect."

"I'm sorry but I wouldn't know the smell of jasmine, not even in a room filled with its aroma."

"My mother and father planted several jasmine shrubs around our house. Most are still there. The smell is pungent. I remember it well. But to find it filling interiors of an empty house is a bit strange, don't you think?"

"What if your father had the smell of jasmine on his clothes when he worked at Atwood House? Wouldn't that explain it?"

"That's precisely what he thought. But the smell seemed to be especially strong in the great room. He was convinced that it was a processed aroma—the kind of fragrance used in the production of high-grade perfumes, particularly popular with women during the late 19th century."

"I see where you're going with this, but it's just too implausible. You're telling me your father suspected inclusion—some sort of outside interference?"

"If I say what I really thought happened, you would call me crazy."

"We all take risks of one kind or another, Mr. Collins. Besides, I'm not making judgments so much as trying to get an understanding of what is going on at Atwood House."

"Entities from another time are coming and going through another open gateway. They are using Atwood House the way it was used since the house was constructed." He looked at White, expecting the man to shake his head and walk away. But that didn't happen.

"That is a huge statement."

"Not to be denied, Dr. White. Just as sure as the sun rises in the morning sky, people continue to come and go, seemingly at will, and they're not neighbors from across the way—if you get my meaning."

"We're excavating near the bridge. Do you know of anything at all that might have been near there, a collapsed building or an old foundation perhaps?"

"When the Air Force excavated a large plot of ground on the east side of the bridge near the woods, they certainly uncovered something, and according to my father who probably saw much more than he expected or even wanted to see, it was not a meteorite, which was the initial story floated in the local papers." During a short pause, maybe to emphasize the gravity of his next statement, Larry Collins fixed his eyes on White's and lowered his voice to a whisper. "There is still something in the ground somewhere on the Atwood property, something that shouldn't be there, and no matter how deep the Air Force dug in 1947, there remains some speculation among some of the old-timers in town, that the military left something behind, something they never intended to find. Maybe that's what you've located."

Chapter 12

WEDNESDAY MORNING EARLY, a little too early for Ben, who was just coming downstairs, the Bobcat arrived on a construction trailer. Herb and Matt Jennings were talking to Adrian White on the grass near where the dig was to take place. Liz Raymond had called to say she was on her way and "only minutes away." Jenna, taking an early lunch and possibly an afternoon off, was just now driving the last mile or so to Atwood House.

A specific area had been designated, and as the group assembled under a large yard canopy, they watched Herb sink the steel teeth of the backhoe into the soil. The first two feet were not so much clay, as expected, but a large layer of sand, which seemed to extend all the way to the creek. Digging was easier than anticipated and in less than 30 minutes there was a sizable hole more than six feet deep. After shutting down the Bobcat, both Herb and Matt eased down into the hole on an aluminum extension ladder. Matt ran a handheld GPS over the ground and got a series of strong beeps, which indicated a solid hit.

Climbing up the ladder, he shouted at those standing around the hole. "It's time to bring in the hand tools. We're just inches away from whatever's down there."

Since White had done several digs in his early career, he volunteered to supervise the excavation from this point forward. After Matt had shoveled off a foot of dirt, White climbed down into the hole, and using a hand trowel, dug away an inch or more of soil. Something white came into view. He carefully brushed away loose dirt to get a better look at what they had uncovered. Yet, there was not enough of the piece exposed to make an identification, so the digging, slowly, carefully, continued.

An hour later, the first piece unearthed lay on the grass, glistening with sunlight. Liz examined peculiar markings with a magnifying glass and began making copious notes on a pad of yellow legal paper. She also made several scans of the symbols to be studied later. Precise and crisp like laser incisions, seven symbols, which Liz continued to refer to as iconography, were clearly discernible and arranged in a horizontal row about five inches apart. Each symbol was six inches tall and different sizes in width, with the middle symbol two inches wide, and the others about half that width. Dirt embedded deep inside the cuts and creases had to be dug out and brushed away. Pouring water across the block of symbols helped revive them, and slowly the ancient dirt disappeared.

Neither Liz nor Adrian had any idea what the symbols or icons meant. They looked alien, and that was the presumption each had. Although they assumed the icons had specific meanings, conjecture at this point was not possible. The first symbol created the most interest. White was convinced it represented a symbol in an equation he had seen, but he couldn't be sure where that was, or when.

Even more curious than the row of seven icons was an octagonal depression seven inches below the center symbol, and three inches deep. It was evident that something was missing. This space was designed to hold something . . . but what? At least, that was Liz Raymond's assumption.

As the day wore on, several more pieces were uncovered. The smaller ones were arranged on tables that had been set up under the canopy. The larger pieces, some nearly six feet in length, were placed on the grass near the canopy.

Jenna was running her finger across the smooth surface of a smaller piece when she noticed something strange. "It feels warm," she said.

Ben had also noticed that pieces he touched were not exactly hot but had become increasingly warm. "They seem to absorb sunlight."

Dr. White, who suspected there might be low levels of radiation, passed a Geiger counter over the artifacts. "Nothing to worry about," he informed them. "Readings are extremely low. No danger at all. We get more radiation from X-rays, even from the sun."

Jenna finally asked the questions that they all wanted answered. "What is it? What have we dug up? Is it dangerous?"

Liz shook her head slowly. "I don't know," she admitted.

"I have some ideas," White told them, "but that's all they are, nothing stronger than suspicions."

Herb and Matt had resurveyed the site with GPR and got no additional anomalous signatures. "Clean," they both said at the same time.

Herb came over to where Ben and Adrian were standing. "Should we fill the hole?" he asked.

"You're sure we've got all the pieces?" asked White.

"There's nothing left down there," Herb replied. "We even scanned a wider perimeter and found nothing unusual."

White looked at Ben who nodded. "Fill it."

Again, the Bobcat roared to life, and in less than 20 minutes the hole was filled. The 21 pieces they had uncovered continued to be the focus of that afternoon. White was inclined to consider the substance a composite of mineral and metal, but Liz was not so quick to accept this assessment.

The longest piece measured six feet, and the shortest, that piece with the seven symbols, was about two feet long and 12 inches in width. The edges of each piece, originally thought to show deliberate breaks, were now being referred to as stress or compression fractures. Liz Raymond, however, held on to the thought that there had been some deliberate attempt to alter the integrity of the pieces, that they had been intentionally compromised, though, at this time, it remained a notion unsupported by anything more than conjecture.

Ben rubbed his hand across the iconography. Suddenly, he pulled it away abruptly, shouting, "This thing is pulsing—vibrating!"

The more pieces they fit together, the stronger the vibration, which not one of them could comprehend. Dr. White suggested the pieces had become a kind of conduit for electric charges, possibly a long obsolete trunk line housing for cables buried in the ground. Because of the mysterious iconography, and the fact that there were no cables present, this idea was quickly dismissed as not a very plausible presumption.

For the time being, they went on with their efforts to fit the remaining pieces together. Seven pieces, and none more than ten inches in depth, were already assembled on the lawn. Adrian, kneeling beside Liz, passed the Geiger counter across the surface of each piece, and told her the readings were still consistently low.

Finally, all 21 pieces had been connected into a two-dimensional shape that lay on the grass. What they had put together in less than three hours, none of them could identify. One thing was sure, except for a few rough edges, each piece fit together perfectly—like the interlocking pieces of a jigsaw puzzle.

"I don't think this was meant to be a two-dimensional structure," White concluded, looking at what resembled a tower with three spindly legs that converged into a triangular enclosure. Measuring over 12 feet as it stretched flat on the grass, it resembled in some respects a surveyor's transom.

"I don't think we can stand it up, if that's what you're thinking," Liz replied.

"It's not going to stand on its own," Herb agreed, "but supports might hold it up."

With several scans of the pieces already downloaded, Matt ran a Microsoft Windows image manipulator called GIMP on his laptop. This platform allowed him to produce and edit several possible images, and eventually he rendered a structure that resembled a three-dimensional triangle. "What about this?" he called out from the shade of the canopy. "We could use the three long pieces as the verticals," he proposed, as the group gathered around the monitor. "Some of these shorter pieces could be used as capstones, others to provide horizontal support."

An hour later, after nailing together a wooden support structure to the same measurements as the pieces, they stood back and looked at it with interest. Seeing the three-dimensional image made of lumber gave each a feeling that they were getting closer to learning what the image might have looked like originally. What if they did figure out the shape? It did not come with a set of instructions. It wasn't one of those do-it-yourself kits accompanied by directions. It was something dug out of the ground and that was just about all it was. Even with the three-dimensional framework in front of them, no one seemed any closer to solving what had become a conundrum of sorts.

"It's a tower. Maybe it transmits a signal," said Manning at length.

"Needs batteries," laughed Jenna, regarding Ben with a huge smile.

"What?" asked White seriously enough to attract their attention.

"Batteries," repeated Ben. "She said the thing needs batteries."

White looked at Dr. Raymond with the same serious expression. "She might be onto something."

"I was only joking," Jenna told them.

Dismissing Jenna's remark, White said, "What if we put a deliberate electrical charge on this thing?"

Matt rubbed his fingers through two days of whiskers. "Are you serious?"

"I don't know," answered Adrian. "It's like nothing I've ever seen. At some point it had a purpose, and that purpose might be one we can't even begin to imagine, so we begin with possibilities."

"If it is a communication tower, something must activate it," Ben surmised.

It was Matt who offered another possibility. "Maybe it's nothing more than yard art—a kind of abstract architectural structure. We've seen some weird stuff come out of the ground. Some people got peculiar ideas about decorating lawns."

"Perhaps," smiled Liz. "But I have a hunch there's something more to it than yard art."

None of them was confident about the purpose of what had been constructed from the 21 pieces, unless it was Dr. White, who continued to suggest that they hook an electrical charge to at least one of the three vertical pieces. They'd apply a voltage charge, then stand back and wait for something to happen. After backing the truck closer, Matt taped generator cables to opposing sides of the largest pillar. Gradually increasing the voltage to 4500 watts of power that surged through the anomaly . . . nothing.

Shaking his head, he shut down the generator and removed the terminals from the structure. "That's all we got," he told them. "Maybe it needs higher voltage, or a sustained charge."

"It was just a hunch," admitted White. Then after a pause, he added, "There has to be some way to wake this thing up."

"Maybe it's been dead too long and isn't going to wake up." Ben's remark was intended to break the solemnity that had taken hold of the dig. It was just something to say—words to fill the spaces between too much serious dialogue.

Before anyone could answer, "I hear something," Jenna whispered. "Listen carefully, and you can hear a kind of buzzing or snapping sound."

"That's just residual power off the generator poles," Matt assured her.

"Oh, well, how would I know that?" she laughed.

"You probably wouldn't," returned Matt with a smile.

Soon, everyone was laughing slightly—except Liz, who stood on the bridge looking down into a winding stream of clear water that trailed off into woods in both directions. With her head bent over the railing, she seemed intent on something in the water. Whatever it was, held her attention for almost a minute, until Adrian came up beside her. The others watched them from a few yards away.

"What is it, Liz?" White asked. "Is there something there?"

"A face," she replied slowly. "There on the surface of the water," and she pointed to the stream ten feet below.

"Your reflection?" he asked cautiously.

"No, it's not my face."

No matter how hard he tried, Dr. White could not find a face reflected in the water, not even his own. Instead, white puffy clouds and the low branches of a large oak tree spread out across the surface in a mosaic of fall colors. Liz insisted there had indeed been a face looking back at her, a face from "another time," as she later told them. "I'm not a person inclined to invent or exaggerate. It was there as clearly as my own face was *not* there."

Dark clouds gathered low on the horizon and the temperature dropped several degrees once the late afternoon sun had set. Matt and his father had packed it in about six o'clock, telling the others they would be out of town for a few days and wishing them all the best with the investigation. Liz went back to Bloomington, and Adrian White spent much of his time working on a new book. Ben decided it was time to reconsider what White had referred to as "strategies." There had been many documented observations. Time was needed for analyses and syntheses of field notes. And maybe they all needed time away from the paranormal.

Chapter 13

MANNING WAS SITTING in front of a small fire, reading, when the phone rang.

Jenna said, "I'm on my way with a bottle of wine."

"Great, another Friday night, and all I'm doing is sitting alone in this big empty house waiting for some company."

"You probably have more company than you realize," laughed Jenna. "I'll be there in a few."

"Are you walking?"

"There's a beautiful moon, or haven't you noticed?"

"I'll wait for you at the bridge."

"You better get started. I'm almost there."

The moon had risen high above the horizon and washing across the lawn was a soft silver brightness that gave at least form, if not substance, to surrounding trees and shrubbery. Lower in the northern sky, where a long heavy bank of black clouds had formed, sharp flashes of lightning advertised a storm, soon to be above Atwood House.

For Manning, there was something comforting about the sound of rain. It was particularly enchanting when it struck the windows in the library and splashed into puddles on the grass. Thunder, though it could certainly be unsettling, carried the message of any rainstorm, and that message always spoke of power—the incarnate power of nature. It was lightning he didn't like. It had always frightened him tremendously. He remembered a story his father had told him when he was ten, about a man sleeping near a window during a raging storm. Only seconds after the man got up for a glass of water, a bolt of lightning struck the bed in which he had been asleep. Every Sunday after that day, the man could be found in church praying to a merciful God.

The thing they had dug out of the ground cast a heavy shadow, stretched wider and taller by moonlight. He glanced at it, curious about what they had uncovered—wondering if it had any significance at all. Its glossy surface glistened, as if each piece had recently been polished. The closer he came to it, the more ominous it became. Propped up by a wooden frame, the thing had a kind of malevolent appearance. For a moment, it seemed to move, as though it had legs, twisting and turning as it grew out of the ground like something alive.

"Ben." Jenna's voice was muffled and sounded strangely far away. He saw her shadow on the bridge, a long thin shade, unmoving against the sky, almost as if it was a piece of the night waiting for moonlight to breathe life into it. Again, she called his name, and again he stood transfixed to the spot not more than 20 yards away from her. Something moved closer to him. Then, before he realized it was happening, the entire night with all its darkness began to close around him, causing him to breathe deeply as though he expected to be suffocated by a night that grew blacker and stranger with each second that passed.

"Ben," Jenna called again.

Suddenly, a thin veil of mist fell across the grass. Jenna was little more than a shape against the far sky, a silhouette with blurred edges. Claps of thunder shook the ground. A blast of cold air sent shivers through him. He felt extreme shaking as though the ground beneath him was about to open. Lifting one foot, then the other, he was conscious of the ragged sounds of stiff awkward breathing as he tried to walk. Ben Manning was afraid and did not know why. The threatening dark kept closing in, until Jenna's voice was eclipsed by a spikey wind that blew the mist nearer to where he stood.

"What's wrong with you, Ben? I'm here, on the bridge. Can't you see me?"

Her voice was incredibly faint, the words increasingly indistinct—

ephemeral whispers pushing anxiously through the night, only to die in the grass at his feet. Manning stood immovable, his eyes focusing on the thing in front of him, his brain trying to comprehend it. He felt an offending numbness take hold of him, even felt this bitter apprehending cold in his shoes and socks, which were soaking wet. The same dampness seemed to be creeping up his legs and when he looked down at his feet, he didn't see them. Had they sunk into the ground? Was he sinking into the earth? How could such a thing be happening right there in his own front yard?

"Look at me, Ben. Turn your head away. Turn away from the cold. The stars are in the sky above you—starlight encloses you. Lift your collar to keep away the cold."

But there was a force that kept him from moving. His eyes closed. He attempted to move his head. His entire body was rigid—stiff as statues he had seen in museums and city parks. And as he sank deeper into the ground, mist filled in the spaces of the night, until the only thing he saw was the strange image in front of him. From far away, a voice called faintly, "Look at me, Ben. See the moonlight shining on the water."

With the ground continuing to shake, and his heart about to beat right out of his chest, he was conscious of movement. A dark slender shape appeared near him in the mist. He'd heard stories of people disappearing, never to be heard from again, and now it was happening to him. Still visible in the sky was a pale moon. He could still distinguish its white edges, but the closer he looked, the more doubtful he was that it was the moon at all. And where had all the stars gone? The entire night had transformed into an alien landscape.

"Moonlight is all around me, Ben," whispered a familiar voice he knew was Jenna's. "Though a storm is on the horizon, the clouds are far away and the moon is brighter than I've ever seen it, so large above the trees, such a pristine moon, climbing higher in the sky. The coming rain has only dampened the air. Can you see the moonlight, Ben? It's in my eyes, and my hair is on fire with moonlight. Please look at me, Ben."

Taking another deep breath, he tried to pull himself together, attempted to understand the unfamiliar sky. At length, the ground back under his feet, and the mist beginning to dissipate, he managed to turn his head to see Jenna running toward him. She was moving much too slowly and seemed suspended in the air. With her arms stretched in front of her, and her fiery hair fanned out on the sharp wind, she took on an ethereal presence that startled him even more. Everything began to spin wildly—until someone grabbed his arm.

Beside him, a long thin silhouette rising out of the shadows caused him to draw back. Then he saw her, her mouth wide open, her lips moving slowly. Where were the words? He knew she was talking but heard only crickets and cicadas roaring in his ears. He felt her fingers gripping his arm, pulling him toward her. They were digging into his jacket, pinching his skin.

"Jenna!" he yelled, surprised how far away his voice sounded.

She tugged on his arm, pulling him nearer; but another equally strong force, this one invisible, pulled harder from the other side, both trying to take control of his body. Then before he realized what was happening, more nothingness, as the ground disappeared once again. He felt the distinct sensation of ascending. His body weightless, the perception of floating off into space was more euphoric than unpleasant. Except for the persistent tugging on his left arm, his body was entirely without feeling. The conscious numbness in his legs and hands, a tingling throughout his entire body, were disturbingly intense as he hovered motionless, buoyant, severely afraid under a sky filled with strange constellations. But the grip on his arm was deliberately strong. Whatever it was, a determined force, a chain that anchored him to something substantial, it was the security that kept him from floating into another time.

Squinting in the intense light, he tried to see what he suspected were fingers digging into his arm. Just for the slightest of moments, he saw a small blue sparkle near his elbow. The smell of flowers filled his nostrils. Something wet and cold struck his face and hands. Rain. The blue sparkle dimmed. The smell of flowers faded. He no longer had the sensation of floating. Even the mist had disappeared into the woods, leaving behind a black sky with no moon present, and Jenna, who continued to grip his arm fiercely.

"Snap out of it, Ben!" she yelled, her breathing labored, hair disheveled.

"What happened just now?" He felt the grip on his arm relax. Still a little shaken, he looked at Jenna who stared past him with wide eyes. "What is it?"

She pointed to a dark figure standing on the bridge. "There."

In the faint glow of a yard light near the bridge, a figure in black stood unmoving in the light rain, which had just started to fall. Lightning snapped across the sky. The storm had come in much quicker than either Ben or Jenna had expected. Only minutes before, they had been standing in moonlight. Taking her hand, Ben pulled Jenna toward the safety of Atwood House.

When they were seated in the library in front of a flaming fire, it was Jenna who spoke first. "I'm glad that's over." Her voice was flat as though what she was saying had no meaning at all to her. It was just a thought that needed to be disclosed. If there was another thought that it really wasn't over, that thought was not expressed.

They sat next to each other, watching the fire. His arms were folded. Jenna's hands were in her lap, and at times, she rubbed them together, possibly rubbing heat from the fireplace into her skin. The heavy furniture in the room left shadows on the rug. Rain beat noisily against the house as minutes passed in silence. It was possible that each was trying to decide what had happened out by the bridge. What was clear to both was the realization that they had seen a familiar figure standing in the rain.

Shaking his head, Ben managed to explain to Jenna that when his uncanny, inexplicable disassociation had happened, he was looking at the thing they had dug out of the ground. "I saw you standing on the bridge, but something powerful took hold of me. And the light was so bright, a huge explosion of white, vibrating in concentric circles that weakened before finally disappearing—compelled me to close my eyes."

Jenna put her hand on his shoulder. "It's getting spooky, and way out of my comfort zone."

He shrugged, gave a slight laugh and asked, "What can I get you to drink?"

"Oh, no, I left the wine on the bridge railing." Watching him get up and start toward the doorway, she asked seriously, "Surely you're not going back out there?"

"I'm not even considering it," he laughed. "You couldn't get me back out there tonight." He added, "There's plenty of wine in the kitchen."

Jenna was a few years younger than Ben and both her youth and good looks made her extremely appealing, especially desirable on a rainy night such as this. Whatever it was that had happened to them had brought them closer together and it was a relationship both seemed anxious to move forward.

With rain still pelting the house, the long arms of a nearby oak tree swept against the windows with each new gust of wind. These intermittent gritty sounds were fingernails, scratching, scraping urgently—the anxious fingers of the demon night trying to get inside the house. In the windows, the sky blanched white with lightning. Claps of thunder in long deep crescendos were jagged ruptures in the cold autumn rain.

Though the storm continued to be intense, both tried to relax in the comfortable surrounds of the library. Manning had poured two glasses of red wine and set the bottle on a table near the desk. Jenna, her hair pulled into a loose upsweep, looked at rows of old books. "So many books," she mused.

"Most were in the house when I bought it."

She walked across the room and stood for a minute looking at a shelf of books directly behind the desk. "Have you seen these titles?" she asked as Ben stoked the fire.

"I don't remember paying much attention to any of the books. They're just there, taking up space."

"It seems someone had a keen interest in the paranormal." She leafed slowly through the pages of a book as she spoke. "I guess I shouldn't be too surprised, especially when signs of the paranormal are all over this house."

Manning walked over to Jenna and looked for a few seconds at some of the titles. "One thing's sure, those left on the shelf have been there for a while."

She blew dust off the book she was holding. "They certainly have."

Jenna's presence in the house was increasingly appreciated by Ben, who found her a charming companion. In the beginning, their relationship had been casual without any expectation of something more. If any experience had brought them closer emotionally, it was what happened an hour earlier near the bridge. There was agreement that each was involved with something strange, something surrealistic; but neither fully comprehended the extent of their involvement, or how deeply they would become embedded in the supernatural. Atwood House had a hold on them—and so they waited for the inevitable to happen.

It happened later that same night. Power failure. Except for light from the fireplace, Atwood House was entirely in the dark.

Chapter 14

Dr. Adrian White spoke with Professor Jeff Trafford on the phone. Their conversation was frequently disrupted by the stormy night. White repeated the same thing several times before he was finally convinced that Trafford understood most of what he was telling him.

"Yes, I recognize some of the symbols," Trafford said, "though it took time to remember where I saw them."

"You know what they are then?"

"Three, maybe four of them," Trafford answered with a clear note of authority.

"I don't mind telling you that our research came up empty."

"It was coincidence that I recalled them at all."

"I see," returned White. "Well, we're definitely anxious to know what they mean."

"I hesitate to bring this up at all, especially when it has already received so much notoriety."

Dr. White nodded, as if Trafford could see him, "Regardless, we need a place to start . . . something tangible so we can push ahead with what we've discovered at Atwood House."

"Roswell," said Trafford sharply, the word sounding alien to both men.

"Roswell?"

"Yes, you heard me correctly—Roswell."

"I don't understand. How could any of this connect to Roswell? I thought all that had been settled years ago."

"That depends on your perspective," declared Trafford flatly.

"About the only perspective I have is what the military has published," Dr. White said.

"Jesse Marcel—that's where I remember seeing these symbols," Trafford went on, with the intention of getting to the point quickly, "the famous Roswell I-beam hieroglyphics."

"You're saying this thing we dug out of the ground in Newburgh, Indiana has some relevance to Roswell, New Mexico—1947 Roswell?"

"I don't know. What I do know is that those same symbols, at least some of them, can be seen transcribed in shades of lavender on what Marcel referred to as a piece of debris that his father showed him in 1947, telling him it was from a crashed UFO."

"Wasn't all that attributed to the crash of a top-secret weather balloon?" Adrian asked. "There have been a dozen television documentaries and numerous books, even an Air Force investigation that concluded Roswell had nothing at all to do with a crashed UFO. It's the others, MUFON and other UFO organizations that still perpetuate that myth."

"Yes, like many others who know the narrative, I remain skeptical. Call it weird improbable coincidence if you want, but the symbols you found in Newburgh match at least some of those described by Jesse Marcel," persisted Trafford.

There was a pause before White spoke again. "Coincidence or not, there has to be an explanation."

"Quantum physics," declared Professor Trafford. "The symbols are very similar to the various forms of electron clouds found in hydrogen atoms—and could be modifications or variations."

White admitted, "You're losing me here."

"I'm saying that we're dealing with very sophisticated quantum mechanics, and," after a pause, Trafford added, "they show up on something you dug out of a patch of ground in Newburgh, Indiana. How did they get there and why? And is there any connection at all to what Marcel said he found in Roswell?"

"Well, it's certainly something to think about," agreed Adrian White.

"I've done some checking into the adjacent property around Atwood House, and if you're not too busy tomorrow afternoon, say around three o'clock, I have some things here at my office that I'd like to show you."

At a few minutes after three the following afternoon, Adrian White sat with his legs crossed, staring across three feet of glossy walnut at 65-year-old Jeffery Trafford. On the desk in front of him was a thick folder, which had not yet been opened. Adrian continued to watch and wait, while Trafford tapped his fingers on top of the folder.

"A few years ago, maybe seven or eight," he began, "Larry Collins brought these papers to me. He said they were declassified documents of a military presence on Newland property, that property that adjoins the southeast part of Atwood House property which begins at the woods beyond the creek."

"Yes, Collins mentioned that when we met last week. He said the Air Force had gone away with something on a flatbed truck. Apparently, everyone involved remained very quiet about it."

"My field of study is ley lines, you know, the apparent alignment of specific land forms significant to the ancients."

White nodded, a slightly skeptical look on his face. "I'm familiar with the term, but my comprehension of ley lines is limited."

"Like some others out there, I've devoted my entire professional career to locating and plotting them." He tapped the folder again with an index finger before continuing. "And what I have here will verify how extensively property adjacent to Atwood House has been investigated by the Air Force . . . and reasons why."

Adrian nodded his understanding. "I'm sure you can imagine how anxious I am to learn what you have."

"Let me begin by pointing out the authenticity of the papers. Though they are revealing in many ways, they do not offer a complete narrative of everything the Air Force discovered. But there is enough to indicate that something of significant importance took place on that particular property."

"These ley lines you mention, what are they exactly? I've heard them discussed briefly but would certainly like some clarification on their significance."

"Alfred Watkins first mentioned ley lines in a book titled, *Early British Trackways*, published in 1922, I think. His primary focus was on alignments of manmade structures, and to some more recent extent, he combined the study to include mystical arrangements of land forms."

"I'm somewhat familiar with literature describing how Britain has numerous archaeological sites, mounds, Neolithic structures, graves, and sacred places. Some researchers, for whatever reason, have shown how many of these sites can be connected to one another in straight lines. I assume there must be some valid significance in that research."

"Yes, Dr. White, and because of the high densities recorded at these various sites, the studies were heavily criticized as little more than wishful thinking. What many of Watkins' contemporaries failed to consider was that he did not claim these lines had any kind of supernatural powers. They were at best ancient pathways used for trade or religious and other cultural practices. The supernatural ideas all came later when researchers like John Michell connected Watkins' ley line theories with Chinese mystical concepts of *Feng shui*. And then there were others who made subsequent assertions that ley lines produced a kind of powerful spiritual energy."

"So, these ley lines have taken on entirely different meanings from what Watkins intended?" suggested White.

"Definitely," remarked Trafford emphatically. "In fact, there are increasing numbers of researchers who proclaim these ley lines to be maps of hot spots, magnetic vortexes, where earth energies are extreme." He continued after a slight pause, during which he passed his fingers through sparse white hair before opening the folder. "One of the more controversial conclusions is that ley lines cover the entire planet and that several of these sacred sites have a high concentration of UFO activity."

"You're talking about this ancient astronaut business now?"

"To some extent, yes, but there's something more, something that until recently has not been too seriously considered." Thirty seconds later a map was unfolded on the desk in front of White as Trafford came around to where Adrian was sitting. "Here's what I wanted you to see."

The map, old, and folded several times, had declassification notices stamped at various locations. Heavily creased, slightly soiled, and brown from aging, the map showed all seven continents distinctly. Most noticeable were numerous straight lines overlaying the entire surface. Some lines were deep blue and others red or black and were clearly not as old as the map. It was obvious to White that they had been added recently, probably by Dr. Trafford. Indicated were parallels of latitude, meridians of longitude, along with the names of many major cities.

Guessing at the significance of the many lines, Adrian suggested, "These indicate ley lines?" He glanced at Trafford, who nodded.

"The red lines indicate places of frequent UFO activity, places like Sedona, Arizona, Dulce, New Mexico, and here in the Hudson Valley of New York State."

"Yes, I see."

Trafford cleared his throat before speaking again. And laying a somewhat shaky index finger on the map, he said excitedly, "Look at these two red lines, one of only three places on the entire map with two heavy red lines."

"Okay," Adrian replied, waiting for an explanation that was slow to come.

"Do you notice anything a bit unique about the pathway of these two lines?" He traced the path of the lines with his finger as he spoke.

Standing up, then stooping to get a better view of the map, White ran his hand alongside the two red lines, stopping near the bottom of the map. "They pass through the Midwest."

"Not just the Midwest, Adrian. These lines pass directly through Indiana . . . Newburgh, Indiana. They bisect an area near the 37th latitude. That's Atwood House property." He pointed to a spot where two red lines were circled.

Adrian lowered himself into the chair slowly, staring hard at the map and then looking up at Jeff Trafford who was smiling. "Are you absolutely sure about this?"

Jeff nodded. "I've had it checked and double-checked." Then after tapping the location on the map with his middle finger, he added, "Do you understand what I'm showing you?"

"I'm not sure."

"Something important happened out there, something the government tried to conceal."

"I don't know," returned Adrian hesitantly. "It just seems much too improbable."

"Not when you consider how invested the government was in locating what was buried either on Atwood House property or on adjoining properties."

White sat shaking his head. Finally, he thanked Professor Trafford for the information. As he got up to leave, Jeff took a picture out of the folder and laid it down in front of Adrian.

"What's that?"

"One afternoon about 20 years ago, Larry Collins snapped this picture from the woods northeast of Atwood House. He said the Air Force had at least some interest in whatever was there."

"Looks like part of a wall, one heavily damaged," stated White.

"Or, and I know this sounds more ridiculous than controversial—a portal," said Professor Trafford evenly, one the Air Force overlooked or disregarded for one reason or another.

"What if it's nothing more than what remained of an old wall or building?"

"That's possible," answered Trafford, "but why so much interest in that specific area?" Pausing momentarily, he added, "Whatever it is, there's a good chance it's still there."

"I've been out there with Ben Manning and we've seen nothing at all on that part of the property."

"According to Collins, there used to be a structure somewhere northeast of the house."

"There's a section of brush out there, probably nothing to get excited about. I suppose the stones could still be in the weeds," decided Adrian.

"Maybe—I'm only passing along information that might have some relevance," concluded Trafford.

Chapter 15

ONE NIGHT, AFTER several rainy days, Manning went outside for some fresh air. It was a stinging cold night. Millions of silver stars looked like specks of white paint on a black canvas. A crescent moon was a sharp incision—precisely cut into the eastern sky, and on the Ohio River, the sparkle of star fire reflected off the calm surface of the water. Rain clouds, earlier crowded on the low horizon, were moving west and taking with them the threat of more rain.

Although the night had become daytime muted to shadows, its sounds were distinctly different. The soft sound of water splashing against rocks, the incessant croaking of bullfrogs near the stream that flowed beneath the stone bridge, the scraping chatter of the crickets, the distant hoots and screeches of an owl, all were distinguishable sounds in the night. Most noticeably missing were the cheery sounds of songbirds that had settled for the night deep in the foliage of the oak and chestnut trees, the high-pitched bark of the squirrels, and the traffic noise on the French Island Trail highway.

With his head laid back to regard the stars, Ben Manning realized once again that he was not a man who would ever comprehend those profound mysteries above his head. He was convinced that the possibility of other intelligences in the billions of galaxies had to be enormous. The Drake Equation had been revisited often in recent years, lending further assurance that the people of Earth were not alone in the cosmos.

When he was young, his mother had told him at bedtime that fairies did their play at night. Often hiding among the flowers and shrubs, they waited for the deep hours of night when the grass was damp with dew. This was the time when they washed the dust from their clothes. "You have to wish to see fairies. If you believe, the chance of seeing them some moonlit night is always possible," she had said more than once. As a boy, he'd looked for them many nights, and on one magical night he was sure he'd glimpsed a white dress in a glimmer of moonlight, as one of the fairies scurried across the yard into his mother's flower garden.

Standing on the large patio at the back of Atwood House, Manning looked across the lawn toward the woods. He heard movement, clumsy at first, then gradually stealthier and more carefully measured, as though whatever it was had realized it was being observed. Deer often grazed long into the night near the edge of the woods. Often during late evenings, he had watched as they made their way along the perimeter of trees, always careful to stay concealed as much as possible in the heavier shadows. Deer moved their heads to regard their surroundings, and, if threatened, always disappeared into the deeper woods where their movements were no longer noticeable. The movements that had caught his attention were the movements of something walking awkwardly, breaking branches, a thing unfamiliar with the woods at night, and it stayed fastened to the long shadows, making it impossible to recognize with certainty who or what it was. But, Ben Manning was convinced it was not deer that were making the noise.

A flash of light. Then another. He caught the silhouette of what he was sure was a person. It was the realtor Max Palmer who had told him that Andy Shanklin owned most of the woods farther north and that his sons Ray and Kevin liked to hunt and were often in the woods at night coon hunting. Manning had seen the men once or twice in late evening, walking in and out of the trees with two dogs. He thought little about it at the time. Even though more than three acres of the woods was Atwood House property, it had long been a hunting site, and Manning had done nothing to stop the hunters, even when they encroached on his property. He knew people fished the pond that was farther back on Shanklin property. Strangers usually came as they pleased, using an old dirt access road that ran along the edge of the woods, a road that Ben felt sure crossed property lines.

But it was the light shining along the ground, a light that never went high into the trees, that held his attention. Someone was searching for a pathway in or out of the woods and seemed to have difficulty keeping the light steady. At times, the long beam cast a large circle on the lawn, a crisp white circle that did not move for seconds at a time. When it did move, it was to a place not more than ten feet away from where he had last seen it. This movement happened four or five more times before the light turned back into the woods and finally disappeared. Someone was searching for something on the ground, but what? More importantly, who was in the woods?

Before going inside, he walked around to the front of the house, the wet ground soft with each footstep. Looking out across the lawn to the tower, as it was now being called, he remembered the unusual event that had occurred there. The bridge glinted blue-white in the dull moonlight, its shape nearly indistinct against the tall trees behind it. How much longer they would leave the strange anomaly standing, he couldn't say, probably until Drs. White and Raymond had done enough with it to understand what it was or wasn't, and that could certainly take significantly more time. If it hadn't been for the strange thing that happened to him that night with Jenna just a few yards away, it might just as well be a piece of abstract yard art. Even though it had done little more than exist, Ben sensed something evil about it, and would be glad when the strange thing was gone.

The fire felt good. He was tired and stretched out in his favorite recliner to watch the hypnotic flames as they sparked high up in the fireplace. Despite the odd occurrences, Ben was beginning to feel comfortable living in Atwood House. Even alone, he felt the house to be a special place far enough away from the busy streets of the city, and to some extent, insulated from the politically correct dictates that society had become. Here was refuge, and Ben Manning felt sure the house, in its own way, was happy to have someone living in it again.

He couldn't say how he knew that—just that it was something he felt deeply.

It was a quiet house, no dripping faucets, no squeaks or groans. Even the occasional sound of a whiney floorboard was all but silenced beneath the heavy oriental rugs, which covered the floors of many rooms. Music brought Atwood House to life, and those silences that were often disconcerting vanished in the concertos of Mozart and Vivaldi.

It was not just the music that brought inspiration, but maybe even more, the overall atmosphere of Atwood House. Each room had been lived in by people whose lives were in some ways connected now to Ben's own life. There had been parties inside these walls. People had spoken of other times that Manning could only read about. Those times had been lived out in each of these rooms. If anything, it was the high ceilings that he loved most. That kind of space was rare in most contemporary houses.

The unfinished painting was still on the easel and covered with an old bed sheet. As the fire crackled, Ben removed the cloth and regarded the portrait with new interest. What if he put in Jenna's face? No, that wouldn't work he decided. This face was from a time and place that did not belong to Jenna Newland.

A few minutes passed before he noticed it. After a closer look, and even in the firelight, he saw it clearly, and knew at once he had not painted it there. But there it was, an exact image of the brooch Jenna had found by the fireplace. Then again, maybe he had painted it and had just forgotten he did it. That had to be the case.

No, he remembered leaving the blouse loose at the neck until he could decide how to finish it. A brooch or necklace had been considerations, but he was sure he had left the blouse open. Jenna! Only recently, she had suggested how right the brooch would look. No, Jenna could paint a wall, but this was done carefully, with artistic skill. Jenna didn't paint it.

Immediately, he was conscious of someone else in the room. He felt his body tighten as he turned around to face her. "Anna?" he whispered.

"Yes," replied an airy voice from the shadows at the back of the room.

"This cannot be happening."

"There are things you do not understand," said the woman gently.

"This is sure one of them."

"There is no reason to be afraid, Ben Manning."

"You know my name?"

"I have heard it spoken in this house."

There was a soft rustle as she moved closer to him. Trying to separate her from the shadows, his heart pounding, he thought he could no longer keep his phony composure and might collapse at any moment. "Who are you?"

"You have just spoken my name."

"But how? I mean how can you be standing here talking to me like someone who just came in off the lawn?"

"It is too soon for that," she told him. "Do you have the brooch?" she asked.

"It was you who painted it there?"

"Yes."

"Why?"

"I wanted you to see where it belongs."

"Then it *is* your portrait I'm painting?"

"It is," she replied. "It is a portrait of what I was in this house."

Ben wanted to step nearer for a better look at the woman, but hesitated. She was taller than he expected, or was she hovering in the air? At present, he could not be sure of anything, except that he was talking to a young woman he could not see clearly—and she was talking back.

"Do you have the brooch?" she asked again.

"Yes."

"It was a gift from my husband before he died."

"This is too preposterous to believe. If you are who you say, then I'm talking with someone who lived more than a century ago. That's not possible."

A long white hand came out of the shadows toward him. He

instantly saw the ring that matched the brooch closely. Her hand was just a few feet from him, and for a moment he thought about reaching out to take it in his own. Was she offering it to him, or did she want him to see the ring?

Behind her was a very faint glow, almost imperceptible at first, but unmistakably there. Slowly the hand and arm receded, but not before he saw a green flash from the ring. A slender shadow, blacker than night, was cut sharply against a burst of white light so intense it caused him to look away. It only lasted a few seconds, and when he looked again, the light and the woman were gone.

Chapter 16

"I'M TELLING YOU, Jenna," began Ben with Jenna standing next to him, "she was really here. Her hand reached out to me. As crazy as it seems, I talked to her."

Shaking her head slightly, Jenna looked closely at him before speaking. "I don't know what to say. You're sure you weren't dreaming? You've been noticeably obsessed with the woman in the painting."

"It all happened just the way I told you. She spoke to me. I heard every word clearly. It was an experience as real as you talking to me now."

"Where's the brooch?" Jenna asked.

"Bergman has it in his safe. I asked him to keep it for me until I decide if I want to sell it."

"Get it back. Give it to her. Maybe then this craziness will end."

"We're talking about 30,000 dollars."

"Wow, that is a lot of money."

"What if this entire thing is a clever scam, a setup?" After a pause he asked, "How well do you know Lacey?"

"Ben, you don't expect me to believe . . . "

"It could be an elaborate setup is all I'm suggesting."

"Why? Who would go to all the trouble of spooking this house, and all the rest of it? It would be an impossible thing to pull off, and you know it."

"I don't know. I just think what's going on here has a rational explanation and has nothing to do with the paranormal."

"I saw her Ben—remember? And I don't care what you say, there *is* something freaky about this house. It's much more than it seems—more than just an old house." After pausing, she asked, "You said she just disappeared?"

"There was something behind her, a flash of light across the wall. It all happened so fast."

Jenna took his hand in hers as she spoke, "It might take time, Ben, but with Liz and Adrian helping, we will get to the bottom of all this."

"I have to admit that it's stressing me out a bit. I'm not even sure I can go back to the painting. I don't know if I want to finish it."

"You can always sell the house," she smiled.

He shook his head. "I can't do that—too much like running before I know why I'm running."

"This apparition has substance. I don't know where she's from, but she'll come again, you know," said Jenna seriously.

Nodding, "I know. It all happens quickly, though. There's no warning. She's just there, and then gone."

"If you don't mind, why don't I hang around tonight?"

"I don't mind at all. It'll be good to have someone else in the house," and he gave a slight laugh that made him feel a bit more relaxed. "I'll make some coffee," he said. "Only take a minute or two."

The overhead lights were on in the library. The foyer was lit brightly. The light on the stairway was bright enough to soften shadows. He had left more lights on in the house than usual these past few nights, trying to convince himself bad things came out of shadows, but hesitated to appear in rooms that were brightly illuminated. He'd been sleeping on the couch in the library and had not been in any of the upstairs rooms in several days. Although size was a consideration when purchasing Atwood House, Manning had recently considered a smaller place in town—a studio space where he could display his paintings in a gallery setting. Infrequent as those thoughts were, he did not deny them so much as momentarily dismiss them.

When he returned with a pot of fresh coffee, Jenna was standing with her back to him—in the same place where he had seen Anna. For a moment, the thought that it was not Jenna startled him. When she heard him place the tray on the desk a few feet away, she motioned him to look at something. Kneeling, Jenna brushed her fingers over a section of rug directly in front of her.

"What?" he asked curiously, kneeling beside her.

"The rug is damp. Feel it."

Looking up at the ceiling, he answered nonchalantly, "Probably nothing more than a leak."

"This is where she stood?" she asked.

"I think so."

"She came out of the rain."

He looked at Jenna for an explanation. "What?"

"She must have been wet and stood here dripping on the rug."

"I don't think she was wet at all."

"There was a storm," Jenna persisted.

"I don't think she was ever in the rain."

"You're telling me she lives in the house with you?"

"Come on, Jenna, you're making too much out of this."

"Maybe so," she said, walking over to sit in a chair beside the fireplace. "But if that's the case, maybe we better search the house."

Ben handed Jenna a mug of coffee. "If I told you what I think, you'd call me a lot more than crazy."

"Try me . . . maybe I already know some of what you're thinking," admitted Jenna.

Putting himself in the empty chair beside her, he said, "It's something not so easily discussed. Practical doesn't seem to work here . . . especially when you consider all that's happened. The more I try to rationalize what I've seen, the more I realize there's no workable explanation, no convincing reason for any of it."

"There is if you believe in ghosts," she replied sharply.

"Don't you think that's pushing it too far?"

Jenna looked thoughtful. Then she said, "Not anymore. If what you told me really happened, and I have absolutely no doubt that something unusual is going on in this house, then rational explanations aren't in the cards, that is if you really want to understand this—this phenomenon."

"It's constantly on my mind, Jenna. I just can't shake it."

"Shaking away a ghost isn't that easily done," she said candidly.

He looked at her for a few seconds before speaking again. "You're really serious."

"I'm not the only one who feels that way, Ben. I've heard the rumors about Atwood House. And what about those others who have reported seeing things out of the ordinary?"

He tried to play this down by saying, "But things out of the ordinary aren't necessarily ghosts."

"If you're saying you think someone is fabricating what's going on here, it's one tremendous piece of work. And why would anyone go to so much trouble?"

"I'm not sure, Jenna."

"Atwood House is haunted and has been for over a century," she insisted.

Before the conversation could continue, footsteps came from the foyer, as though someone was walking toward the library. They were distinct enough for both to hear clearly. Jenna and Ben looked at each other before she asked, "Expecting anybody?"

"No one," he answered. "I keep the house locked at night."

Slightly shaken, Jenna got up and stared at the main entrance to the library, as though she fully expected someone to enter at any second. "Did you lock the door after you let me in, Ben?"

"I think so but can't remember for sure."

Jenna gasped . . . a long uneasy sigh, then told him rather assuredly, "Well you definitely got a visitor."

With enough visible light in the doorway, they would see anyone entering the room. They waited, and the footsteps grew louder. At just about the time they expected to see someone, a bolt of green light cut sharply across the oriental rug. There for only a few seconds, it was harsh enough to cause both to cover their eyes.

Then came the huge silence of a large house. Both knew someone was now in the room with them. The large overhead light in the library dimmed, leaving the room in shadows. In the large doorway that opened into the room was a woman, and behind her was a long fissure of green light.

"It's her," Ben said softly. "She's back."

"I wasn't serious about the ghosts, Ben," Jenna said nervously, clutching his arm with enough strength to get his attention. "I didn't know what else to say."

The apparition before them was a striking silhouette, tall, shapely, and stunning in a pink dress. She was wearing a large hat tilted to one side. In one hand, she held an umbrella. Her other arm was above her waist, and she carried something Ben could not distinguish. Backlit in green light, the shape seemed more like a statue, a comely figure chiseled from polished marble—until it moved.

"Say something, Ben. Talk to her," urged Jenna.

"What do you want me to say? I don't even know if she's really there."

"Oh, she's there all right."

"How are you?" Ben asked politely. "Nice to see you again."

'"How are you? Nice to see you again"' Jenna repeated. "That's the best you got?"

"Come on, Jenna. What do you say to a ghost?"

More footsteps. The woman was moving deeper into the room, closer to where they stood. Their feet were stuck to the floor. No matter how much they wanted to move, they could not. The statue was coming closer, and they too had turned to stone.

"My time is short." The voice, though plainly audible, was little more than a whisper.

Somewhat to his surprise, the woman was not floating two feet above the floor. Her gait was deliberate and with purpose. She passed so close to them that her dress brushed against him. An ornate Victorian table was pushed back a little into one corner of the room. Ben had considered moving it to another room but had forgotten to do it.

"Can you smell them?" asked Jenna.

"What?"

"Flowers, she's carrying flowers."

They heard the glass vase placed on the table. The sweet smell of cut flowers filled the room. But it was what the woman did next that held their attention. Placing her parasol on the table, she bent lower to arrange the flowers in the vase, standing over them several seconds before turning to leave.

"There were always flowers in the house," she said. The green slice of light from the foyer shot once more into the room, and in little more time than it took to blink, the woman was gone again.

For several seconds, Jenna and Ben stared at the empty spot. Momentarily distraught, neither knew what to say. Thoughts of what just happened surged through them with such emotional charge that both were once again on the verge of denial.

His body had tensed so much that it was entirely stiff. He heard Jenna's breathing, uneven, rapid, and was afraid she was going to pass out. "Snap out of it, Jenna. It's over. She's gone."

"I don't believe it," she managed to say. "It's too incredible to comprehend. I saw it happen. As sure as I'm standing here, I know it did happen."

He helped her over to the couch and dropped down beside her. She sat rubbing her hands together as she stared into the fireplace. Above them, the overhead light burned bright. Even the deepest corners of the room had shaken loose their usual shadows—in the air, a sweet seductive aroma. The room had taken on fruity scents, possibly of pomegranate, persimmon, or jasmine—pungent, intoxicating scents.

"Perfume," remarked Jenna abjectly.

Chapter 17

EARLY ONE MORNING, the sun still low on a pink horizon, Dr. Liz Raymond drove south on Highway 231 from Bloomington toward Saint Meinrad. She looked forward to spending a few hours with an old acquaintance before driving to Evansville for the weekend. Sixty-year-old Carl Hewitt had spent his entire life working at the Archabbey that stood like a medieval fortress at the top of one of the highest hills in Spencer County. She had recently read a news story in the *Bloomington Herald Times* about an excavation near the Abbey and was sure Hewitt would have all the pertinent details.

When she found him, he was dressed in bib overhauls, drinking coffee in an empty cafeteria. Even seated, his size was undeniable, and in any room filled with people, Carl Hewitt would be considered a big man—at least in stature. His unshaven face and disheveled hair gave him the appearance of a man who was not used to being stared at. In his gray eyes, the reality of living in a cold indifferent world had softened to resignation. The world was what it was, and his place in it was little more than coincidence.

"Dr. Raymond," he smiled warmly when he saw her come into the cafeteria. "My goodness, what brings you to the Abbey?" Standing to greet her, he added, "It's been such a long time."

"Nice to see you again, Carl. It's been much too long."

"Life's like that, isn't it?"

"Seems that way, some days more than others," replied Liz.

"The wife was talking about you only last night. Said you'd be interested in this thing they dug up out on the ball field."

"How's your Jenny getting along these days?"

"Much better than anyone expected. Still has a few bad days, but the treatments seem to be working."

"You be sure to give her my regards and best wishes when you see her."

"You can bet I will," he answered. "How about a cup of coffee? Just made it?"

"Thanks, but I've had plenty this morning." Sitting across from him, she regarded Carl thoughtfully before speaking again. "About this thing that's in the news, what is it?"

"Don't know what all the fuss is about. Looks like nothing more than a big rock to me. But the way people are talking, it must be something important."

"You say it's on the ball field?" asked Liz.

"Well, under it, really. They found it when they were installing new drain tiles. They thought it was an outcrop of limestone. The roof of a cave someone said. This area is full of caves. Used to run those caves every chance I had when I was younger." Pausing to refill his cup, he said, "Sure I can't get you some coffee?"

"Thanks, I'm fine."

"Never in my life did I think I'd see a rock create such a sensation. People been coming from all over the place to see it. Even the government's been here and had a look." He sipped his coffee slowly before adding, "Air Force had the entire field blocked off for nearly a week and wouldn't let anybody near the thing. Don't know what they expected to find—maybe a meteor. They finally packed up their people and equipment and went away. Strange thing though . . . "

"What's that?"

"The more they dug, the bigger it got. Still haven't uncovered it all."

"I'd like to see it if that's possible," Liz said.

"It's just sitting down there big as life—and just about as strange."

The walk down to the ball field took nearly 15 minutes. A few pickup trucks were parked in a lot near the Abbey, and in the distance, an excavator lurked like some prehistoric animal. Even from 50 yards away, the rock, as it was most often referred to by those who had seen it, eclipsed a building used to store maintenance equipment. The closer they got, the more imposing it became.

"There are times when I think it's actually growing in size," admitted Carl. "They've probably exposed more of it is all. Still, it looks real strange, like it just doesn't belong there."

"It certainly does look out of place," Liz agreed.

"Looks like it just rolled down the hill and right there is where it stopped."

Five feet above them, the rock tapered only slightly, and once out of the ground, it might certainly be symmetrical. Carl was right. It was huge and looked severely alien. A couple of people nearby were taking pictures of it. One man rubbed his hands at various places on the smooth surface, but for what reason, Liz couldn't imagine.

"Two geologists from up north, Chicago maybe, said it was prehistoric. They didn't think it was indigenous to this area," Carl proclaimed rather officiously. "How do you figure that?"

"What do you mean, Carl?"

"If it's not from here, how did it get here? Who put it here?"

"That's curious all right," agreed Liz.

"It's more than that, Dr. Raymond. It's another of those cosmic mysteries handed down to us by God."

"You might be right, Carl," she smiled.

The man who had been rubbing his hands across the surface of the rock stopped long enough to take several photographs, after which he took a small notebook from a canvas bag and jotted down some notes or calculations. Still curious, Liz came over and waited patiently for the chance to speak with him.

Before she could speak, he looked up at her and said so bluntly that it took her completely off guard. "I knew it."

"Excuse me?"

The man, in his late 30s or early 40s, looked rough around the edges, unkempt, and the closer she got to him, the stronger the smell.

His clothes were muddy and soiled, and although clean-shaven, he looked grungy, as though whatever it was that preoccupied him had precedence over anything else, even hygiene. Oddly, it seemed to Liz, the shoes he was wearing were wingtips, and highly polished, and seemed a contradiction to his otherwise disheveled appearance

"Put your hand here," he directed authoritatively. With Liz's hand pressed against the rock, "Can you feel it?" he asked.

"Feel what?"

"The heartbeat," he replied.

Liz jerked her hand away. "It's stone for God's sake."

He smiled at her before saying, "It has a pulse. Not like you or me, but it has a distinct pulse."

She looked at him, only this time with displeasure instead of curiosity. "I'm sure it does," she lied.

"An electronic pulse."

Something about the man held her attention, though she could not say what it was about him that kept her from walking away. "I don't understand."

"X-ray eyes that see the trinity of light," he laughed before hurrying away in the direction of the woods at the east end of the ball field.

"Don't take him seriously," Carl told her.

"You know him?"

"Not exactly. People in these parts call him Walking Einstein."

"You can't be serious."

"Nobody really knows who he is, but everybody knows him. If that makes any sense."

"I'm not sure," answered Liz slowly.

Twenty minutes later Liz was driving the remaining 30 miles to Evansville, where she would meet Adrian White and Ben Manning at Atwood House. She continued to think about what Walking Einstein had said and wondered if he really *did* know something. Or was he just one of those kooky characters found in any small town? The term "X-ray eyes" kept turning over in her head. Did it have any real meaning? The image of that man wearing high gloss wingtip shoes was what she recalled longest.

When she drove up, Adrian, Ben, and Jenna stood in a circle around the tower that still stood like a piece of abstract yard art near the stone bridge. She parked the car and hurried to meet them, waving to each as she crossed the lawn. "It all looks the same," she said, stopping between Ben and Adrian after giving Jenna a slight hug and smile.

White spoke for the other two. "A few things have happened since you were last here . . . nothing earthshaking."

"Well I'm anxious to hear about them."

"Welcome back," said Manning cheerfully. "Room's all ready for you, and Jenna has prepared a meal for this evening, so I hope you're hungry."

"Sounds terrific," Liz smiled.

"Hello again, Dr. Raymond," said Jenna who was obviously glad to see her.

"Jenna, call me Liz, please."

Jenna's smile was warm and ingratiating, "Nice to see you again, Liz."

"I heard about the incident." Liz went over to where Jenna stood and took her hand. "It must have been extraordinary."

"Yes, it was every bit of that and then some. Even though I saw it happen, I'm sure I can't explain any of it." She glanced at Manning before speaking again. "There were moments when Ben thought it was spectacle."

"Spectacle?" asked Liz inquisitively.

"Theater—the kind that involves Lacey Laurens," Ben answered.

Ready with an explanation, Jenna looked at Liz and said, "I think I've managed to convince him that what happened was not something I arranged with Lacey to frighten him."

"Oh, I see, your friend—the young girl who works with you."

"Yes," answered Jenna. "She's always anxious to develop a convincing character." She continued to look at Liz before speaking again—this time more seriously than any of them expected. "It's not every day a woman steps out of another century to put a vase of flowers on a table, is it?" Jenna's smile was forced slightly. She realized

Liz Raymond would eventually ask again about the encounter with Anna Atwood. But Jenna was already looking ahead to Anna's next visit, which she knew was inevitable.

Liz put her arm around Jenna's waist. "We're going to figure this thing out, honey. I promise you that. We'll get to the bottom of what's happening at Atwood House."

Still smiling stiffly, Jenna responded, "I hope you're right."

Chapter 18

JUST AFTER DARK on the ball field at Saint Meinrad Archabbey of the Benedictine Order, with a slice of moon low in the sky behind him, Walking Einstein pulled the long collars of his jacket tight at the neck, and taking a rag from his pocket, bent down to wipe dirt from his brown wingtips. Even with a nippy wind blowing out of the north, he was anxious to resume his study of the rock in front of him. Methodically, like a physician about to perform routine surgery, he laid the things needed on the ground.

Setting the bag to one side, he began walking around the rock, poking the sharp end of a metal pole into the sand until he struck something solid. At each of these spots, he placed a chunk of quartz about the size of a softball. Regarding the rock carefully, he aimed the beam of his flashlight at one specific section, a circular depression about two feet from the top. Picking up from the ground a larger stone, the size of a ripe Posey County melon, he worked it as deeply as possible into the cavity, which was no more than four or five inches deep. Next, he took up a small trowel and whiskbroom, scraped, then brushed surface dirt off six locations near the rock—those same places he had earlier marked with pieces of quartz. Looking back at the enormous rock, he folded his arms, drew in a long breath of cool air, and waited . . . and waited.

Autumn nights in Southern Indiana were spectacular. He watched the erratic movements of fireflies across the Abbey lawns and adjacent soybean fields, as the snappy night woke to the music of bullfrogs bellowing in the Lake of Galilee near the Abbey cemetery. Still, he stood motionless, waiting, expecting something to happen. Minutes passed. Still he remained in front of the stone that he had earlier embedded in the large rock.

With the moon higher in the sky, its soft light sinking into creases and crevices in the stones, a small white light sparked to life in all six smaller stones, as though someone had lit birthday candles. The longer he waited, the brighter each became. But it was the larger stone that caught fire—a greenish-white fire. He watched the light gather into a column of more protracted illumination that shot several feet into the sky. The display lasted no longer than a minute.

Walking Einstein gathered the few stones into the canvas bag and headed in the direction of the small town of Saint Meinrad. The bag slung over one shoulder, he leaned noticeably, as he tried to manage the weight more easily. Above him, a streak of purple light shot out into space. He stopped for several seconds to regard it, until it disappeared among the stars.

It was nearing ten o'clock at Atwood House. Dr. White was talking with Liz in the doorway to the library. With the late evening meal finished more than an hour before, and the kitchen cleaned, Jenna prepared to leave, saying she had a busy morning the next day and wanted to turn in earlier than usual. Ben walked her out to the car and kissed her lightly on the cheek, then asked if she could spend Saturday afternoon with him.

"Doing what?" she asked coyly.

Speaking about Liz and Adrian, "I'm not sure what their intentions are for tomorrow. I do know that I'd feel considerably more at ease if you were around."

"I'll be here as soon as I can," she assured him.

Ben watched her car drive down the long driveway, taillights glowing like the red eyes of a large primeval reptile. Except for a mild breeze rustling leaves in the large oak and chestnut trees that were everywhere around the property, the night was unusually quiet. Above Atwood House, the starry roof of the sky seemed higher than ever—all those primordial mysteries of the universe immutably silent in that coldness that was space.

The sound of an engine starting, in the direction of Shanklin's pond, caught Ben's immediate attention. Walking around to the back of the house, he saw headlights in the woods, probably on the trail road that led back to the pond. It sounded more like a truck than a car engine. Pickup trucks and SUVs had pretty much taken over the roads, and in a small rural setting like Newburgh, there were few exceptions.

Whatever it was moved steadily deeper into the woods, until only a trace of the lights remained visible. Then almost as quickly as it had come, it was gone. Not thinking too much about it, he went back inside the house to find Dr. White, who was searching through a folder of paperwork that he had removed from his briefcase. Liz studied the vase on the Victorian table as if she were attempting to determine its provenance and authenticity.

"Have you looked closely at this, Ben?" she asked when he entered the room.

"Not really. Is there something significant about it?"

"A couple things maybe," she admitted.

"It's Limoges porcelain."

"Sounds expensive," he told her.

"I've seen similar vases in antique stores. It's French. I remember a friend telling me how much she loved a Limoges vase that she and her husband had bought while traveling one summer in France. She always referred to it as the most beautiful and most expensive piece of porcelain they owned, and when people saw it on her dining room table, they were absolutely taken by its beauty."

"The colors are vibrant. It looks brand new."

"It's certainly the kind of vase you'd expect to find in a house built in the early 1900s, particularly among the furnishings of a family as wealthy as the Atwood's."

The bouquet of mixed flowers was stunning. They were not the colors of summer, but the darker shades of fall, and their aroma was pungent and pleasantly musky. Looking as if they belonged right where they had been placed, the vase and flowers breathed life into the large room. The vase more than ten inches tall, was decorated in an array of hand-painted flowers and infused with bursts of pink and yellow.

"You say she came into the room, set the flowers and vase on this table and left them as they are now?" Liz asked.

"That's right. Her dress brushed against me as she passed. Once again, it all happened so fast," he added. "Maybe the strangest part was how effortlessly she moved. Her single purpose was to put that vase of flowers on that specific table, as though she had done it several other times."

"A routine," suggested Dr. Raymond, "done so frequently during her lifetime that it was an entirely ordinary action."

"You see, Liz, and if you'll forgive me for saying so, that's precisely what bothers me most," Ben said.

"Her lifetime?"

"Exactly," Ben replied. "How can her lifetime be in my lifetime?"

Liz, stepped back away from the table and with Ben watching, concentrated, not on the vase, but on the flower arrangement. Tilting her head to one side, then the other, she bent lower to observe those smaller flowers near the rim of the vase. She was searching for the subtle messages revealed in the flowers. "It's all here in front of us," she nodded.

Catching her attention, Ben asked, "You're saying she uses flowers to convey messages?"

"Emotions. Simple meanings in the choice of flowers and colors—we do the same thing today. Most women in the early 20th century felt they had to bite their tongues when it came to topics like love, sex, intimate feelings. Propriety was everything to them. Subtlety usually prevailed."

"I never thought anything about it, just assumed cut flowers made a room smell pretty."

"I'm sure that is often the case." She regarded him carefully before speaking again. "It was a very good friend who taught me about flowers and their perceived meanings. For example, take the yellow primrose, the strongest color in the arrangement. It's often used to convey young love. See how they seem to rise out of the darker shades of the hawthorn?"

"And that means something special?"

"Hope, and maybe the innocence of youthful love. When tied together with the long clutch of honeysuckle in the foreground, it means sweetness and bonding love. I'm sure there's much more meaning here than I see."

"I don't think I'll every look at flowers the same way again."

Dr. Raymond gave a slight laugh, adding, "This could certainly be the bouquet of a young bride wishing for good fortune and lasting love." She turned away from the flowers rather abruptly and regarded Manning. "If she brought these into the room, her fingerprints should be on the vase."

"No, I distinctly remember she was wearing lacey white gloves. She held a parasol in one hand. I saw the gloves clearly when she passed me."

"But if at any time the vase had been handled without gloves, there would be prints."

Before the conversation could continue, Adrian White remarked from a few feet away, "You've mentioned this slip, this bulge or wrinkle of green light, which often accompanies her appearance and disappearance."

"That's right. Sometimes brighter than at other times, but always present, and coming from behind her."

Adrian looked from Manning to Liz who were both anxious for an explanation. "I have an idea," he admitted. "Strange as it sounds, it might actually have legs."

"I'm certainly open to any ideas you might have," Manning replied encouragingly.

"I think we have a time slip, a hole in the fabric of time. Only momentary, but existing long enough so that another universe can be breached."

"Another universe?" questioned Ben, with a distinct air of doubt, "a doorway to another time?"

"Or portal," answered White. "The research is out there. Cutting edge as it is, it offers at least one possibility."

It was Liz Raymond who attempted to put a provocative, somewhat edgy spin on what Dr. White said. "If Anna has found a gateway or portal, then what's to keep us from using it?"

"I like the time I'm living in now," admitted Ben. "Even if I had a guarantee that we could come and go into another time, I'm convinced that I would never take that chance."

White nodded. "The risks would be great. There would be no guarantees."

"Then we stick with observations for now," declared Liz.

"Yes," continued White, "we begin with what we already know. Reanalyze our field notes to date, and then document every detail of Ben's encounters."

"Don't forget that Jenna was here, too. She saw what I saw," Ben reminded.

"Yes, of course," agreed Liz. "We already know the hot zones. We reset cameras near the stairway and one here in the library."

"And maybe another in the great room," suggested Ben.

For the next hour, the three of them arranged cameras at locations that had been previously active. With computer laptops placed on the long walnut table in the library, they were ready to settle in for the night. To say that surveillance was tedious business would be an understatement.

Until four in the morning they sat, waiting for something to happen. The huge silence of Atwood House filled every room and hallway. The anomalous activity they anticipated never occurred.

Away from Atwood House, in Saint Meinrad, Indiana, Walking Einstein was sitting on a park bench drinking coffee from a thermos when the black SUV rolled to a stop on the street in front of him. Two men in suits helped him to his feet, and in less than a minute, the SUV and Walking Einstein had disappeared into the night.

Chapter 19

"HOW WAS IT last night?" Jenna asked. "Anything happen?"

"Nothing." Ben reached out for her hand. "Thanks for coming."

"You're welcome," she smiled.

In the kitchen at Atwood House, Liz and Adrian looked at the map given to Adrian by Professor Trafford, a map denoting numerous ley lines crisscrossing the planet. It was spread out on a round table that Ben used in a breakfast nook. White traced the lines that passed through Newburgh with the fingers of his right hand.

"Hi, Jenna," Liz said, when she saw Ben and Jenna enter the kitchen. "Hope you can spend some time with us today."

"Ben said you had a quiet night."

"Absolutely nothing to get excited about last night, but there's always tonight," Liz returned hopefully.

Jenna made her way to the kitchen table and glanced down at the map, "It's a regular spider web, and look at all those spider lines. They're all over the place."

"Ley lines," corrected Adrian.

"And what are ley lines exactly?" Jenna asked with enough curiosity to get an immediate response from Adrian White.

"Simply stated, they are lines that pass through sacred or significant points on the earth's surface. According to Professor Trafford, they are high energy resolutions. You see *these* lines, Jenna?"

"The two heavy ones passing through Indiana?" she asked.

"They pass directly through Newburgh," White acknowledged, a hint of authority evident to the rest of them.

"That's interesting," Jenna said. "They must indicate places of some significance then."

"Exactly," White agreed. "Although documenting a planetary grid system might still be considered pseudoscience, we know that Plato recognized energy grids and their patterns. But maybe it's the New Agers who have continued to push the authenticity of energy grids, by widening the boundaries to suggest ley lines resonate energies that provide battery and navigation power for UFOs."

"If I understand you correctly," began Ben, "these circles identify places of unusually high concentrations of energy . . . "

"Vortexes," interrupted Adrian. "They're called vortexes."

"These vortexes are points of navigation?"

"That is fundamentally correct, Ben," White assured.

Many lines bisected small red circles. The two heavy lines that passed through Newburgh had a small grouping of these circles northeast of the Ohio River. Near this grouping was an intersection where several lines crossed through one large red circle.

White took from his briefcase another aerial map with similarities to the map on the kitchen table. "This map gives us a more detailed topography of Newburgh and the surrounding area. You can see how the lines pass through specific places from the Ohio River all the way to the Great Lakes."

Ben looked closely at the map, reading the names of towns on the two parallel lines which passed through Newburgh. "Wouldn't it be interesting to know what these circles identify, especially those around Newburgh?"

Jenna surprised them all by saying, "That might be possible. We might be able to do an image overlay, using Google Earth. Better yet, geocoding would enable us to get a specific address of a geographic location. If that doesn't work, we'll try reverse geocoding."

"You can actually do all that?" asked Manning.

"Welcome to the 21st century, Mr. Manning," Jenna laughed. "I should have something in a few minutes." She was taking a laptop from her backpack as she spoke. "I'll send this to the printer in the library, and we should soon have some definitive data."

"You're absolutely amazing," he replied.

"Maybe more technologically informed than you is all," she smiled.

Later, Ben and Liz left Atwood House through a backdoor, leaving Adrian and Jenna to run the software that would show the geographical locations they needed to continue their "reconnaissance work," as it was now being called. A sunny cool afternoon, a high blue sky filled with white clouds, this was another beautiful autumn day in Indiana.

"Jenna's quite a young lady," Liz began as they walked among several apple trees that skirted the lawn near the woods that marked the northeast end of Atwood House property.

"She's been a huge help in many ways."

"You had another interesting experience the other night."

He nodded, "The kind of experience that hits you pretty hard, keeps you awake at night thinking."

"I guess Jenna was shaken by it to the point of denial?"

"Maybe at first, but she doesn't really talk much about it. She realizes it happened and leaves it at that."

"And what about you, Ben?" Her tone was caring and not at all deprecating.

"Ambivalence has set in, and what happened—just happened."

"Acceptance, even of something we can't explain, but know with assurance actually happened, takes courage," she admitted.

"What occurred a few nights before out by the bridge, that still haunts me. I'm not sure if it happened at all, and yet I know something very unusual happened out there."

"Maybe it'll help if we talk about it."

"I was suddenly caught in dense fog so heavy that everything around began to change. At first, I thought I was hallucinating. Jenna was there. I heard her calling me. It was deeply disorienting and unnerving."

"You said it was near the bridge?"

"Yes, near that damn thing."

"We may actually have an account of what happened on the trail camera."

"I forgot about that."

"When we can't explain something rationally, within the framework of our everyday orientations, we often have a tendency to set it aside, realizing a different perspective is needed. Maybe that perspective has been photographed."

"A paranormal perspective," replied Ben dispassionately.

"You're an artist, Ben. Imagination is a fundamental requirement . . . and without it, everything stays black-and-white. There are no spaces, no cracks, no chance to breathe life into a two-dimensional painting. Your brain has to see that third dimension."

"That third dimension does not have to be paranormal."

"No, but it *can* be paranormal. Aren't there inferences in your paintings? Don't you allow for interpretations uniquely different from anything you have considered or intended, or are those parameters too rigidly fixed?"

"Parameters are the enemy of creativity."

"Exactly."

In the arboretum of apple trees was a circular concrete bench, behind which a trellis of red and yellow roses was sharply accentuated against the deep blue sky. The two of them sat there, Ben watching the grass grow as Dr. Liz stared into the woods more than a hundred yards away. Near the apple trees, sharp morning shadows looked imprinted on the grass. It was a day of spectacular sensations, and both knew the only way to save these impressions was with a camera.

"This is such a stunningly beautiful place," Liz confided, clicking off a couple pictures with her mobile phone. "In so many ways it reminds me of a place on the Upper Peninsula."

"Your family still lives in Michigan?"

"No family, Ben. I grew up in a home for orphaned girls."

"I'm sorry."

"No, not at all. It was a great place to be a kid. We all saw ourselves as free spirits born to roam, as we would so often say." She had a far-off look in her eyes as she added, "That was such a long, long time ago." She looked apologetically at Ben. "Sorry, it's strange how a place can take you back so many years and get you there so quickly."

"If you don't mind me asking, how did you acquire this . . . this ability?"

"It happened one summer in Bloomington, several years ago, just after I moved there. I was painting the kitchen and fell off the ladder. My head struck the counter. Days after that fall, I seemed to have a heightened sense of intuition."

"I assumed that it was a predisposition acquired at birth."

"And it can certainly be that, but it wasn't like that with me. The trauma caused a rewiring in my brain."

"Really?"

"I'm sure this sounds preposterous, but I assure you it is real."

Ben looked at Liz closely before asking, "Is it something you can turn on–and–off?"

"It's extremely complex. I'm not so sure I understand it." She smiled warmly. "Usually, it just happens."

Another few minutes passed before they walked back to the house. Jenna, who had only recently returned from town, motioned for them to look at what she had just placed on the table. Dr. White was already looking at an enlarged copy of a map with specific locations that Jenna referred to as placemarks, most of them indicated by a specific icon.

"She did it," said White enthusiastically. "We now have something to work with, and you'll be amazed at what we have in front of us." When he had their full attention, he smiled broadly before speaking again. "If these ley lines have the significance I think they do, then we are truly on the brink of a major discovery."

Chapter 20

MILLIE STEWART WAS a small wrinkled woman hooked to a portable oxygen bottle. A mound of gray hair was held in place by two matching celluloid combs. Most of her recent days were spent sitting in front of a large flat screen television in a 1920's two-story clapboard house on Pine Street, which had been in the Stewart family since it was built. Despite the twinkle in her blue eyes, the woman looked tired to the two visitors sitting a few feet away on a faux leather couch. The room, messy, and cluttered with newspapers and books, was dimly lit and had an odor of spoiled food.

Swallowing hard, Ben wished they had not come, wished also that Dr. White, who had arranged this meeting, had not been called away on family business. But in White's absence, Ben and Jenna were the ones obliged to keep the appointment. He glanced at Jenna, as if to tell her he wanted this to be a quick conversation. She smiled and nodded as though she knew his thoughts.

"It's very kind of you to meet with us," Jenna said sincerely.

Millie's smile was slight, and with her head inclined to one side, the woman nodded almost imperceptibly. "You're welcome. I wish Mr. Collins could be here. He's such a nice man. I don't get many visitors these days. Everybody's too busy anymore. My daughter's a physician, and her work is important, so she only comes sometimes on weekends. I like riding the Presbyterian bus, and once or twice a month two of the church ladies will visit."

Mr. William Stewart, gone for three years, was resting comfortably behind a small headstone in Rose Hill Cemetery near a large oak tree. On the walls were numerous family photographs, each a testament to Millie Stewart's 78 years. The small space heater near her feet warmed the room and gave it a kind of cheery atmosphere.

"Mrs. Stewart, this is my friend, Ben Manning. He's the new owner of Atwood House."

"It's certainly a beautiful house," she smiled, "and yet, I have so many disturbing memories, the kind that stay much too long in your head."

In front of them was a woman who knew about Atwood House, and who had just confessed that at least some of her many experiences there had been distressing. She seemed anxious to speak, but in a cautious way, as if she wanted to reveal the strangeness that was Atwood House.

"It was such a long time ago," she continued, "and those years have been so long in the past that I have trouble remembering clearly. I have so much difficulty talking with strangers."

Anxious to leave, Ben nudged Jenna, who just shook her head without looking at him. She was not going to give up so easily. Diplomacy would have to prevail if they were going to get anything pertinent from Millie Stewart. He admired Jenna's tenacity. Always with tact in mind, she was usually willing to keep pushing, and these moments with Millie Stewart were no exception.

"Atwood House must have been a happy place, especially during a time when life was so much simpler than it is today. I can just imagine parties on the lawn and dances in the great room, and all the guests dressed in fine clothes."

Millie looked long at Jenna, before replying. "I was about your age when I began working for the Young's. I remember how excited I was to be employed in such a fine home. Though I was one of the service staff, Mrs. Young always made each of us feel as if we were family, especially on holidays." She adjusted herself in the chair, which was worn heavily on both arms. "How very much I enjoyed Christmas there. No expense was spared in decorating the house. The decorations were so elaborate that people came from miles to view them, especially the outside light displays. Even when it snowed, the Young's insisted on putting up a large tent on the front lawn to serve people from town hot cider, tea, and steaming coffee. There were pastries and fruits of all kinds."

"I'm sure it was quite spectacular," said Jenna warmly.

"Yes, but as wonderful as those times were, there were always the shadows." Her memories caused her to drift a bit and even the soft expression on her face hardened noticeably when she mentioned the shadows. Yet, she gave them the impression that she was reliving experiences that she had not discussed with anyone in years.

"Shadows?" repeated Ben.

"They came and went without intruding."

"Did you ever speak to them?" Jenna wanted to know.

"They spoke to us sometimes."

"To you personally?" inquired Ben.

"Only once, when I was dusting books in the library," she answered calmly. "Anna Atwood was suddenly in the room with me. She was a very beautiful lady, but deeply saddened and troubled by the passing of her husband. It was her habit to leave a bouquet of flowers on a small table. Such delightful flowers. There was one other time when I came into the library from the foyer and she was standing beside the fireplace with her back to me. I don't think she knew I was there." Millie leaned forward in the chair before asking, "Have you seen her?"

"Yes," Manning replied.

"And does she still bring flowers?"

Jenna nodded.

"And there were others who came to Atwood House?" Ben inquired gently.

"Yes, but not from around here. They used gateways in the house and on the lawns. It seemed they were living their lives in the same space as we were living ours, but they were from another place . . . another time. They were always kind, especially Miss. Anna. Her pain must have been a great burden. I never tried to understand how any of this was possible—just accepted it and did my job."

Somewhat stunned at Millie Stewart's rather nonchalant reference to gateways, Ben and Jenna looked at one another noticeably surprised. Neither had expected such casual comments about phenomena still considered by most in the scientific community to be little more than science fiction. It was clear to both that Millie had decided years ago that these strangers she saw at Atwood House were not coming to the house in cars from town. They appeared suddenly at various locations, and disappeared suddenly, as though they were passing easily from one time into another.

"You mentioned gateways," Ben began cautiously, "in the house, on the lawns. Do you remember where precisely?"

Millie nodded. "In the foyer and near the bridge," she answered. "I think there was another in the storeroom near the great room. It all sounds so strange to me now, like it never happened at all."

Manning saw something crawling up his jeans—a roach. Jenna also saw it. Much to his surprise, she brushed it away with the back of her hand. Both knew it was time to leave Millie Stewart's house.

Back at Atwood House, Ben dialed the phone number to the Newburgh Presbyterian Church and spoke with an associate pastor. "I think Millie Stewart is a member of your congregation."

"Yes, for many years," returned Assistant Pastor, Gary Evans, "and she never misses Sunday morning service."

"This is Ben Manning. I own the old Atwood House."

"Yes, one of Newburgh's great historical houses. How can I help you?"

"A friend and I visited with Mrs. Stewart earlier today, and I'm sorry to say that living conditions in the house are disgusting. She mentioned that a couple of ladies from the church visit her occasionally, so I'm wondering if any of this has been brought to your attention?"

"No, I've heard nothing at all about this."

"Is there a chance that you could visit Mrs. Stewart, maybe get some volunteers to put the house right, if you know what I'm saying?"

"Yes, and you have my personal assurance that it will be taken care of with discretion."

"I'd be happy to help out, if you need me."

"Thanks, Mr. Manning for bringing this to my attention. We have a conscientious church congregation always willing to lend a hand."

"A friend," said Jenna abruptly, once Ben hung up the phone. "I thought I was a little more than that."

Laughing slightly, Ben replied, "You know what I mean, Jenna."

"That was a nice thing you did, Ben."

"Yeah, I feel better about it."

"We could clean it ourselves, you know."

"Let the church do it. Maybe it will set a precedent of sorts."

She kissed him lightly on the cheek. "Okay."

Later, sitting on the front porch, they watched the afternoon transform into a stunning sunset. Under the orange glow across the southwestern horizon, the Ohio River looked smaller and less foreboding. Peaceful, serene in its journey, it seemed in no hurry to find the big Mississippi. On one of the sandbars near the Kentucky side, a couple boaters gathered their gear, and soon disappeared around the bend on their way toward Evansville.

"She's a nice lady," Jenna said, her eyes on the sunset.

"It's a sad thing to see a person feel so used up. Maybe she really was glad for the chance to talk again about Atwood House."

"I was surprised to hear her speak about things so casually," Jenna admitted. "It was like she was seeing her experiences there, especially those at Christmas, happening all over again."

"Maybe reminiscing is that way. I can't imagine living alone like that. It can't be easy for her."

"Then why don't we visit occasionally?" Jenna suggested.

He put his arm around her, "Nice thought."

Chapter 21

WALKING EINSTEIN SAT alone in a small room painted putrid yellow. The only furnishings were four wooden chairs, two on each side of a large table that had nothing on it. An observation window made it clear people were watching him even now. He was sure it was an interrogation room and decided he was only moments from being interrogated. About what, he didn't know.

His canvas bag had been confiscated. While waiting patiently for someone to come into the room, he snapped a dirty handkerchief across the tops of his wingtips. He didn't have to wait long before a short man wearing an impeccably-tailored suit walked in and sat down at the table across from him. Attempting to size each other up, the two men looked at one another for several seconds.

At length, the short man in the expensive suit began, "You can call me Smith."

"That's fine, and you can call me Jones," replied Walking Einstein.

"We know who you are, Dr. Charlie Chase."

"Well, Smith, why don't you tell me why I'm here, why you zapped me off the street? And I'd like to have my bag returned."

"In good time, Dr. Chase," answered Smith courteously. "You can understand why we would be concerned about a man walking the streets with a bag of rocks."

"Can we please cut to the chase?" he smiled.

Smith opened a folder and began reading. "'Dr. Charles Chase, 35, unemployed, and referred to most often as Walking Einstein.' Very flattering name for an itinerant such as yourself, don't you think?"

"I'm definitely humbled by it."

"Let me continue please. Let's see, 'PhD in physics, University of Chicago,' where you taught seven years before being released. Never tenured and frequently at odds with not only your administrative superiors, but also most of your department colleagues, and even students. To put it frankly, Charlie, most of them thought you were stark raving nuts."

"Bunch of sheep really. It was a bad relationship right from the start. What else you got on me?"

"'*The Truth About Interdimensional Travel*, published by The Free Press' four years ago, but peer reviews were not altogether favorable."

"Academics, most of them need specific instructions on how to blow their noses. The few that have courage enough to propose anything outside the constraints of mainstream thinking are looked down on, and often referred to as educated idiots, sensationalists whose research is ridiculously short of empirical data is usually how they put it."

"That might well be true," Smith offered generously. "We know all about glass towers and prima donnas of every description and temperament."

"Oh, one point of contention in this fascinating biography you've got there. I resigned before they had the satisfaction of dismissing me."

"We think your research is cutting edge," said Smith abruptly.

"Listen, I'm not too thrilled about being picked up the way I was." After pausing to glance at what he was sure was two-way glass, he added, "Who is this we you're mentioning? NSA, OSI, CSI, FBI, NASA? Help me here. I'm running out of letters. Give me another vowel and a couple of new consonants."

"We're none of those, and yet all of those," acknowledged Smith.

"So, you're deep, and there aren't enough letters to define your organization. And probably no congressional oversight either. How am I doing?"

"Let's face it, Charlie. You need a job and we're offering one."

"I'm listening."

"You've been to the Abbey every day for the last month, and most recently you've made frequent visits late at night. Your fascination with that hunk of rock out there has us curious." He cleared his throat and leveled a look at Chase that was direct yet inquisitive. "We saw the beam of light."

"I knew you guys were doing more than laying drainage tiles." He bent over to wipe his wingtips with the fingers of his left hand. "I suppose you found the quartz veins?"

"Yes."

"There's your answer—quartz."

"We already know about the conductive properties of quartz. But there are pieces missing, and we think you know what those pieces are and how they fit together."

"I've spent years studying what mainstream science considers—let's see what's the term they use—fallacious lunacy . . . or words close to those. While they were anxious to publish the same old crap in various scientific journals, I was enduring endless rejections and criticisms for hypotheses that rattled the righteous foundations of academia."

"That's a reputation people like you have to accept."

"People like me are as devoted to facts as any of these smug bastards in ivory towers. Any theory away from their narrow-minded thinking borders on scientific blasphemy. There's not one willing to take a shot in the dark, because they're too damned wrapped up in protecting their tenures. Imaginative thinking just doesn't cut it, too many risks, so they play it safe. The few forward-thinking, innovative, unpretentious researchers still out there endure constant ridicule by these complacent, egotistical, and suffocating academic elites."

"You've been branded an overzealous radical among your contemporaries," Smith said.

"You brought me here to tell me that? Come on, Smith, or whoever the hell you are. My boat's still floating, and I got both oars in the water, if you follow the analogy."

"Relax, Doctor. We didn't bring you here to dress you down. I'm sure you've had enough of that already."

There was a knock at the door. When Smith opened it, a tall man, probably pushing 50, dressed in Air Force blues, filled the space. Chase knew he was an officer but couldn't tell the man's rank. Whatever words exchanged between the two men in the doorway were inaudible to Chase, who was beginning to get increasingly uneasy with being detained.

"We're working on a project, Dr. Chase," Smith announced after the officer had gone and after Smith returned to the table, "one requiring your expertise."

"There aren't already enough overpaid academics in your think tanks, Mr. Smith?"

"We need a freethinker, an individual not confined to main-stream scientific research, an individual unaffected by prevailing theories." He leveled a weighty look at Walking Einstein, who was sitting with his arms folded on the table. "Are you interested, Dr. Chase?"

"I'm interested, but not much more than that. What I know, you must also know."

"You sell yourself short, Chase," declared Smith sharply. "But if you want to continue with this persecution complex, that's your cross to bear—not the government's."

"It's more of an inconvenience than a cross," returned Walking Einstein. "I'm so out of touch with these mainstreamers these days that whatever they say or write about me is like water off a goose's ass. I just plain don't give a damn. Besides, there isn't one of these liberal academic loonies who's seen what I've seen."

"Exactly, Dr. Chase, and that is precisely the reason you're here."

"There's nothing more I can tell you. I have a couple of hunches, but nothing definite."

"Hunches?"

"Theories, if you prefer."

"We're more interested in facts, Dr. Chase."

"Why would the government be so interested in a chunk of rock?"

"We're willing to pay for the information you have."

"I need time to analyze some recent data," returned Chase.

"We'll give you whatever time you need, and a place to work, with only a couple stipulations."

"Let's hear the stipulations."

"We have first refusal on your current research, and all subsequent work when you contract with us."

"I need more on the *we* part. In other words, I need to know precisely who you are."

"Yes, that's certainly legitimate, and it will all be made clear to you once you're aboard."

"That sounds Navy."

"To a point it is," Smith admitted.

"I thought clandestine organizations like yours just took what they wanted without the sweet talk," Chase confided. "Or is all that nothing more than Hollywood?"

"I'm not a Hollywood kind of guy, Dr. Chase. You've been thoroughly vetted, and your work correlates with a classified government project."

"What little I know about governments too often distresses me. It's my opinion that benevolence is not an identifying characteristic. Like many other ordinary people, I just don't trust governments—or politicians. Politicians are pompous snobs invested for the long haul. Their constituents are expected to endure incompetence and meaningless promises. I don't think any differently about organizations like yours, whatever the hell it is."

Seconds later, the door opened again. This time, the big man in uniform entered the room. Dr. Charlie Chase was sitting in front of Lt. General Moro Eugene Elkins. It was immensely evident that this was a man used to throwing his weight around. "So, you're Dr. Charles Chase?"

"Yes, I am, General."

"Some of your current work has gotten our attention."

"I tend to talk a lot, get excited easily, especially when I think I'm onto something important."

"It's what you *haven't* said that we are interested in."

"Now that is interesting," replied Charlie seriously, "but it's not the first time someone has told me that."

"We have plenty of overpaid people working projects that use language and theories I could not begin to comprehend. We need a practical thinker who will take a pragmatic approach to research we consider critical. Smith will brief you, give you the specifics, and we'll proceed from there." The big man, with three shiny stars on his epaulets, turned and walked out the door.

"Can I get my bag now?" Charlie inquired.

"Of course, Dr. Chase. We're very accommodating here."

"Accommodating is definitely not a word I'd use to describe you or your organization."

Ignoring Chase's chiding remarks, Smith told him there was routine paperwork Charlie needed to sign, and that would be followed by a briefing, during which the government's expectations would be detailed.

"We'll set you up with your own laboratory at the University of Vincennes in Indiana. You'll have a secret clearance, and you'll answer to me weekly, and have no connection to the University in any way at all."

Charlie nodded, "I'm impressed."

"You should be, Dr. Chase. We respect the integrity of your work and expect you to have the same regard for what we're trying to accomplish."

"And what exactly are you trying to accomplish?"

"That information will be revealed in detail during your briefing."

That was the end of the discussion. Chase was taken to another room in another building. That room had the same appearance of sterility as the one he had just left. Listening carefully, he was quick to fill in at least some of the blanks. Smith and his people had clearly connected "gateways" with high magnetic fields. Quite possibly they thought Chase knew how to control these portals. An aspect of this initial meeting that had received insufficient discussion was how ley lines fit into the equation. Maybe that information was already known to them. One thing remained decidedly clear, that in the coming days and weeks Dr. Charlie Chase would be required to provide pertinent research, or he would soon have his walking papers in hand.

Chapter 22

GATHERED AROUND THE kitchen table, Ben, Jenna, and Liz watched Adrian White move a plastic ruler over the placemarks, most of which fell on or near two heavy lines running the length of the map. "Together, we can possibly identify several of these places. In fact, I know some of them well, especially the ones around Evansville," admitted White.

"I grew up in Spencer County," Ben said, "and even then, some of these spots held a particular fascination. The cliffs in Rockport, not a real big deal unless you're a kid with the opportunity to play there. And in Grandview, right on the Ohio River, is the Archaic Period Shell Mound, never professionally excavated, but familiar to local relic hunters. Located on a bluff at the edge of a cornfield, they dug out artifacts before the river got them. I remember how disturbing it was to see human bones washed across the cornfield and scattered on the sandy banks of the Ohio River.

"Creepy," Jenna suggested, "like digging in a graveyard."

"Angel Mounds," declared White, using the edge of the ruler to indicate a site near Evansville, "Middle Mississippian mound builders, and one of the best known archeological sites in Southern Indiana."

"I know the Old Newburgh Presbyterian Church," Jenna began, "has a reputation of being haunted. It's even on the Ghost Walk tour every Halloween. And here, Preservation Hall, also on the Ghost Walk."

"Fernwood Pioneer Cemetery, Ewing Young Burial Site, Hoover-

Minton House. There are a lot of places here in Newburgh," Ben declared, "and all near or inside one of these red circles."

It was Liz who identified what the others had apparently overlooked. Pointing, she said, "The William Gilbert Atwood House."

How about that?" smiled Ben. "I don't know whether to be pleased or worried."

Liz kept looking at the map and noticed other red circles without any identification of what was there. One larger circle held her attention, until she finally asked Ben if he knew of any other surrounding landmarks. "This location northwest of Newburgh is very interesting. It falls between the two heavy lines, but what is it?"

Looking at where she was pointing, Ben recalled something he had read not too long ago in the *Booneville Standard*, about excavations a few miles from Atwood House, the Ellerbusch-Martin Site, where several pieces of Middle Woodland pottery and artifacts had been discovered. "The entire area has multiple Native American sites. Most of the smaller ones are still intact and unexcavated. Artifacts are always turning up in plowed fields."

There were other open circles all around Atwood House, and numerous smaller ones running north toward the Ohio state line. Some nearby Indiana sites identified were in Haubstadt, Yankeetown, Bedford, Shoals, Bethel, Jasper, and Ferdinand, as well as several other towns and cities all the way through the northwest corner of Ohio into Michigan's Lower Peninsula. Primary focus was on the extensive number of locations near and around Atwood House. Only one other area was circled almost as heavily—Saint Meinrad, Indiana.

Just past five o'clock that evening, Liz Raymond had a premonition as she sat with Adrian White on the stone patio at the back of Atwood House. "There's something strange out there," she remarked with an air of conviction. Pinching the collar of her jacket tighter to ward off the dampish air, she went to the edge of the patio, where she remained silent nearly a minute before speaking again. "Something doesn't fit, Adrian. I don't know what it is, but there's something unusual in those woods."

Ben came out the back door carrying a bottle of red wine, and

Jenna, behind him, had a large platter of cold cuts, cheese, and crackers. Heavy shadows appeared at the edge of the lawn and deepened visibly as the evening advanced into early night. Darkness was already settling under the trees. The star most visible in the darkening sky, and boldly bright above a few remaining deep purple swirls on the horizon, was Venus.

"What's back there, Ben?" Liz asked, pointing toward the woods.

"Forty acres of trees is all."

"Nothing else?"

"Shanklin's pond. It's nothing more than a fishing hole."

Liz continued with, "This afternoon I saw some small undulations on the east side of the house, and a larger rise just beyond the apple trees, at the edge of the woods."

"I've never noticed them," returned Manning. "I seldom go that far back, and the few times I've been back there, I didn't pay much attention to the topography."

"Except for the one larger mound, the others are subtle rises, easy to miss, but they are there," Liz assured him.

"Most likely nothing more than natural formations indigenous to Southern Indiana landscapes," offered Ben, as a possible explanation.

"That's probably all they are, but I'd like to walk back that way, see what's there."

"Now?" asked Manning seriously.

"Well . . . "

"How about it, Jenna?" interrupted Ben. "You up for an adventure?"

"I suppose," she answered, "if you're sure we won't get lost."

After putting another log in the fire pit, Adrian White poured his second glass of wine. "If you don't mind, I'll stay behind and restudy the map, see if I can connect the dots—make more sense of it all."

Ben remembered a few nights before when he saw lights, then again last night, when he heard an engine in the woods near Shanklin's pond. Though he hadn't thought too much about it, he now dismissed the possibility of coon hunters. "I think someone's been snooping around out there at night. Why, I don't know."

"You've seen them?" Liz asked.

"Just lights. I thought it was Shanklin's sons coon hunting. Now I'm not so sure."

With the lights of the patio behind them, a sizable moon slowly rising on the eastern sky, and a slight breeze in the apple trees, the three of them walked steadily toward the woods, not one, unless it was Liz Raymond, expecting to find anything more than trees. Liz stopped to sit a minute on the same bench where she and Ben had sat earlier in the day. The seat, still warm with sunlight, was only wide enough for two, so Ben stood a little to one side, looking at Jenna, who had her eyes closed and was seated close to Liz. Her hands folded in her lap, Liz regarded the woods as though she saw something the others did not.

Pointing to fireflies that flicked their small fires across the lawn, Liz appeared entirely at ease with the night. "They're such beautiful little things," she said, "their tails flicking on-and-off as they brighten the darkness—one of God's charming little creatures."

"Do you really expect to find something back there?" Jenna asked.

"Maybe we'll find something that will help us answer at least some of the questions about Atwood House."

They went on until they found the dirt road that went in the direction of the pond. With Liz several feet ahead, and the beam of her flashlight casting a bright glow, wide enough to illuminate the roadway on both sides, Ben deliberately slowed his pace. He whispered to Jenna that he was happy they were together in the "deep dark woods." He was sure she was smiling.

Twenty minutes later, the noise stopped them in their tracks. There was no longer any need for flashlights. Thirty yards ahead of them, Shanklin's pond was engulfed in white light. Instinctively, they ducked into the trees.

"They're draining the pond," Liz proclaimed.

The sound of a generator was muffled slightly by trees, most of the larger oak trees still with leaves. Only recently had the beautiful deep colors that came with fall begun to appear. Lights from a pickup truck cast distinct shadows on the water, while two men in overhauls stood at the edge of a wooden pier smoking.

Liz pushed her way deeper into the woods, Jenna and Ben a few steps behind, both more apprehensive than Dr. Raymond. Their footsteps were silent on the hard ground. With each step, they moved closer to the action—until Jenna recognized a third man, just coming into the light.

"Matt Jennings!" Jenna exclaimed out loud.

"Probably a friend of the Shanklin boys," guessed Manning.

"Why are they doing this at night?" Liz asked rhetorically. "This is the kind of work more easily done in daylight."

"My dad and I drained a pond once on our farm in Chrisney, Indiana. Just opened a drain tap behind the dam and walked away while the water drained out into the pasture. I was out there at night, curious about what was in the pond. Nothing but fish and turtles, which we moved to a large lake farther back on the farm."

"I guess there isn't a drain on this pond, Ben. Just got to pump it out," Jenna whispered.

"But they don't have to stand there watching it drain," he returned.

"Not unless they expect to find something at the bottom," hinted Liz.

Before speaking again, Ben caught her eyes in the weak light. "What could be at the bottom of a country pond?"

"Well something's keeping them here," Jenna agreed. "I don't think it's fish or turtles they expect to find."

The deep throaty sounds of the generator bit into the early night like steel teeth. In the white glow of the truck lights, the night took on an ethereal appearance. That piece of sky directly above the pond, blacker now, had filled with stars, and a couple familiar constellations were visible. The Big Dipper caught their attention. While Liz Raymond looked at an earth mound that rose nearly 20 feet into the darkness, Ben and Jenna searched for the Little Dipper. Not far from this large mound, and nearer the pond, was a cluster of smaller mounds each rising more than five feet.

Pointing, she asked Ben, "What do you think those are?"

"Don't know. Kind of strange though, so many of them scattered around that big one."

"Could be Native American, part of an effigy mound," surmised Raymond.

A shout from the end of the pier, "Look at that," yelled one of the men, his voice barely audible over the generator noise.

From their vantage point in the small thicket of trees, no more than 25 yards from the pier, they could distinguish a dark image in the center of the pond. They saw one of the men disappear into the shadows, and soon after, light on the object in the water became more concentrated. Having moved the truck closer to the edge of the pond, the man returned to the others with a large spotlight, which he flipped on even before he was on the pier. Instead of aiming the beam of light at the object, he moved it slowly around the perimeter of the pond. The light was so bright that it illuminated clearly 20 yards into the trees.

"Get down," Ben cautioned, only seconds before the light came around to where they were hiding. "Don't move."

Suddenly, an explosion of white light near them. The night was gone. Trees stood out like a small army of ghost soldiers anxious to march. The oak tree, large enough to hide them, had cast a fat shadow, until consumed by the white light that was stealing way too much of this early autumn night. After what seemed minutes, the light moved away to expose other parts of the woods, leaving Ben and the two women once more in the dark.

"You expect to find someone out there, Kevin?" questioned his brother, Ray.

"It's the Shanklin brothers," Ben whispered.

Suddenly, Jenna's mobile phone began playing the first notes of "*Yankee Doodle Dandy.*" And then Liz sneezed.

"Good Lord," said Ben in a muffled voice.

The light that had passed them by came back around, moving fast through the trees, until it stopped at their oak tree. Crouched low behind the tree on a ground hard enough to be rock, Ben grabbed Jenna's hand, which seemed cold. Liz had her other hand, squeezing lightly, as if to say things would be all right. Jenna quickly shoved the phone into her jeans pocket and hoped, then prayed, it would stay silent.

It was Matt Jennings who put a rational face on things. "Let's finish the job and forget about ghosts in the night."

"I swear I heard music, a mobile phone."

"Just relax, Kevin," advised Ray. "Who in their right mind is going for a stroll in these woods after dark?"

Matt laughed, "Probably a bunch of pixies in frilly dresses."

Kevin kept shining the light on the thing emerging from the water. "It's nothing but a damn rock."

And that is exactly what it was. They could see the top of it from where they were hiding. Tapered slightly at the top, the rock became more imposing as more water drained from the pond.

"Maybe it's a meteor," surmised Ray.

"I don't think so. A meteor that size would have caused a major sensation," returned Jennings.

Ray conceded, "Then it's nothing more than a big funky rock."

"Why is a rock that size in our fishing hole?" Keven asked.

Matt hesitated a few seconds before saying, "The way the landscape is sloped, maybe it rolled down the hill—over there in that opening. Probably broke away from that rock face."

Puffs of smoke off the generator, caught momentarily in the truck lights, hovered like miniature rain clouds above the pier. It was a larger pond than Ben expected, more than 50 yards across, and from their perspective among the trees, the pond appeared to be perfectly round. Ben's first thought was that the pond had not been dug but was instead a natural depression—a sinkhole on the landscape.

"No sense hanging around here," Matt told them. "We'll come back in the morning and transport whatever's alive to the lake."

Ten minutes later the truck drove away, and with a greenish glow coming from the rock, there was more light than any of them expected to find this deep in the woods at night.

"Do you see that?" asked Liz.

"Strange, really peculiar," Ben replied. Almost as soon as he said this, the light began to fade, until seconds later, only darkness remained.

"Well that's it. The show is over for tonight," said Jenna, "no reason to stay any longer." Already, she tried to put the pathway in a narrow beam of light.

Liz dropped in behind her, but not before looking back at the large mound, which was directly under a generous expanse of open sky. "I think there's something else here, something special . . . forgotten over time, and never documented."

"Like what?" asked Ben, as they began their journey back to Atwood House. "You said the area had a considerable Native American history," Liz reminded him. "After all, there are several sites identified on the map, and many of them are at locations not far from Atwood House. I'd even go so far as to say you have undisturbed Native American sites on this property."

"You're probably right, Liz," Ben agreed. "There are several sites in Southern Indiana, which remain unknown, unmapped—virgin sites, which collectors would love to excavate."

When they were back among the apple trees, Jenna slowly stretched an arm in front of her, pointing beyond the trees. "Look."

A green aura enclosed the entire house. It was in the windows, shining on the chimneys and doorway lentils, and illuminating shrubbery, as it washed across the grass all the way to the stone bridge.

"There's dancing on the patio," murmured Liz.

Chapter 23

"I SEE IT BUT I don't believe it," Jenna proclaimed.

Hoping Liz would have an answer, Ben asked, "What's happening?"

"One thing's sure—we all see it," Liz said excitedly. But it was what she said next that held their attention. "Could this have something to do with Shanklin's pond?"

"That rock?" Ben replied. "How is that possible?"

Liz regarded them both before saying, "Again, though I can't explain what it is, I'm absolutely convinced that the strange appearances at Atwood House are in some peculiar way connected to that pond."

Staring with disbelief, they stopped near one of the large oak trees at the back of the house, watching two dancers, dressed in clothes from a century before, move rhythmically across the stone patio. The man, with a well-trimmed mustache and beard, was in his early 40s, and the woman several years younger. Once or twice, the woman dropped her head back, releasing coils of dark curly locks down the back of her purple gown. Incredibly light on their feet, executing each turn with precision, they seemed entirely caught up in the music—in the night, and in each other.

"Are they friends of yours?" asked Jenna pointedly.

Both Ben and Liz looked at her curiously, and it was Ben who said what both were thinking. "I never saw them before."

"Then they must be ghosts." Even as she spoke, Jenna's words sounded macabre and shockingly uncanny.

Liz smiled. "This is without a doubt the most extraordinary thing in my entire career. Call me crazy, but we are witnessing what few others have seen, a real time slip, a fracture in the fabric of time. There can be no other explanation."

"Impossible as it seems, there they are, dancing across the patio of Atwood House," admitted Ben hesitantly.

"Adrian," shouted Liz. "Where is Adrian White?"

The music stopped. The dancers spun each other for the last time. The green illumination began to fade, until only a crease of radiant light appeared near the far edge of the patio. Slowly, as though they regretted that the dance had come to an end, the young man and woman turned toward the light. The man continued into the brightness and was instantly gone. The young woman, however, her arms outstretched, turned back to regard the three of them separately for several seconds, as though she wanted to speak.

Taking several steps closer to the woman, Liz reached out to touch her. Their hands were just inches apart, when the light behind her began to dim. "Please," began Liz, "please don't go," she pleaded.

"It is time," said the woman, drawing back her hand, leaving the three of them staring at a line of low stars in the sky above the Ohio River.

Minutes later, they went into the house, to find Adrian asleep in a rocking chair near the fireplace. With only a weak fire burning, the room was oddly silent. On the desk were both maps.

"Look at him. Poor thing's been working too hard. He doesn't eat, doesn't sleep, always trying to figure out what it all means." Liz took a blanket off the couch and put it over White, who moaned softly. "Never heard a thing," she smiled.

Hoping he could revive the fire, Ben stirred the ashes with the tip of a poker until orange sparks appeared. After putting fresh kindling on the grate, the flames took hold and in 15 minutes the fire would mute the shadows that were so often present in this large room. As he snapped on a couple of lamps, the library began to take on a homey relaxing ambiance.

As the room warmed and night passed into the deeper hours, Liz and Jenna looked at the two maps, and were surprised to see a few new notations White had made while they were in the woods. Liz was especially interested in a circle around the town of Saint Meinrad and a line connecting that town with Newburgh. Had Adrian White found a connection of some kind between these two towns that were only 50 miles apart? The word Abbey was written in and underlined. A longer line was drawn from Saint Meinrad south to the town of Rockport on the Ohio River. The short distance between these two river towns of Newburgh and Rockport was also connected by a line, with all three lines forming a triangle.

"I wonder what it means?" asked Jenna.

"I'm not sure how Rockport fits in," Liz answered, as she traced the three lines with her index finger, tapping the map near the town of Rockport, which White had circled in pencil. "I think he's discovered points of relevance near the three primary locations of this triangle. Anything special about Rockport?" she asked Ben, as he crossed the room to join them.

"It's a small river town. Several old buildings, and a scenic road along the Ohio River, where people used to stop for picnics, or to explore caves high up in the bluffs."

"Caves?" pressed Liz.

"Long limestone overhangs in the cliff face. Disappointing as caves but fun to climb the cliffs if you're looking for a small adventure. I recall great views of Kentucky across the river. Apparently, sometime in the early 1800s, a family spent a winter inside the lower cave. There's quite a bit of history attached to the area, but I don't recall anything really significant, unless it's the excavation done near the caves."

"Do you remember what was excavated?" Liz asked.

"It's been several years ago. But from what I remember, the excavation uncovered remnants of a Native American site. There's still a large boulder only a few yards away from the precipice of the cliff. The land was privately owned, and all the artifacts found there were moved to a reconstructed village at the other end of town."

"The boulder is still there?"

"As far as I know it was never moved."

"If not, then there are three large rocks, one at each place. The Abbey, Rockport, and here in Newburgh in Shanklin's Pond," Liz offered thoughtfully.

"Do you think that means something?" Jenna asked. "Or is it just coincidence?"

"I don't know," Liz replied. "Maybe Adrian has already made that connection."

Later that night, after Liz had turned in and with Adrian still asleep near the fireplace, Jenna sat on the stone railing of the bridge. Ben stood next to her. It was the first time in recent days that they had found time to be alone together. Jenna traced constellations with her fingers.

Oh, silent night . . . not a creature stirring. It was not a night for tender kisses and soft words under starry skies. There was an eerie sky already lingering menacingly above the treetops, and both knew something strange was about to happen.

"Look, a falling star, Ben. Maybe a meteor from the Orionid Meteor shower—the one Lacey's been talking about."

He looked to where she was pointing—a place in the low sky over Shanklin's pond. "Quick, make a wish before it's gone," he encouraged.

The falling star did not vanish as expected. Instead, it was no longer falling at all. It seemed suspended from the handle of the Big Dipper, larger and brighter than all the stars in that part of the sky. Ben decided it had to be Venus.

"I don't think Venus is ever in that part of the sky."

"Then it's probably Jupiter or Mercury. It's got to be a planet."

"Planets don't move like that, Ben."

"Then it's a helicopter or a small aircraft coming this way."

"There's no sound," declared Jenna. After regarding the sky again, "And why is the Big Dipper upside down? I don't recall seeing it upside down before. And how many stars are in the handle? Do you remember?"

"There's an extra star, one that shouldn't be there," declared Ben.

But the extra star was not a star at all. It was not a meteor from the Orionid Meteor shower. Its movement across the expanse of black sky obliterated the icy sparkle of starlight, eclipsed constellations, as they watched. Both knew this was something very unusual, and it was coming closer—until it became an improbable shape.

A chunk of night vanished above their heads. A huge piece of Indiana sky, which had been there seconds before, was now gone, and in its place was something extraordinary, an object much out of place in this unfamiliar sky. It's shape was triangular. Black, slick beveled edges, with tiny lights that were barely discernible, it was a craft like neither had seen before—a UFO that had appeared without warning.

"I never believed in these things," Jenna confessed. "How ridiculously naïve this presumption that anything and everything in the sky has an explanation."

Ben was mesmerized by what was hovering above Shanklin's pond, so bewildered by it that it took almost a minute before he could even speak. "Come on, Jenna."

"What?"

"Under the bridge, we have to get out of sight." Grabbing her hand, he immediately began pulling Jenna toward a narrow pathway that led down a steep incline.

"Ben!"

"We have to hurry."

"If it's not one of ours, hiding won't make any difference," she protested. "If they want us, there's no place to hide, no place to run." She was breathing hard as she spoke. "Slow down before we both end up in the water."

"What would they want with us?" he questioned. "Why is it in the sky above Newburgh, Indiana?"

The rocky terrain under the bridge was hard to negotiate in the dark. Only a few feet from the water, Ben stumbled, almost taking Jenna down with him. The sound of water rushing over rocks was louder than either expected, and both knew the stream was at least three, maybe four feet deep. As their eyes grew more accustomed to darkness, they found themselves standing nervously on a large flat outcrop of limestone that ran six feet in any direction.

Much to Ben's surprise, Jenna turned on the light on her mobile phone and began shining it into the cracks and crevices in the stone foundation. Her intention was to make a cursory inspection of their surroundings.

"Jenna," he grunted in disbelief.

"I want to see where I am. For all I know there are creepy crawlers under here."

"I'd rather deal with creepy crawlers than that thing up there," Ben declared.

"Okay," she muttered, turning off the light.

Suddenly, there was a loud cracking, breaking noise—as if the entire sky had been ripped apart. Peeking around the edge of a stone support column, they could make out a narrow split in the sky—a black seam unzipped, leaving the ruptured sky devoid of starlight. In the space where stars should have sparkled, was muted pink light the color of cherry blossoms. With green light less diffuse in the center of this vertical fissure, it was difficult to look too long without squinting.

Ben knew the same thing had happened that night in the library—just before Anna disappeared. "It's an opening that won't be there much longer," he said with confidence.

Twenty seconds passed before she whispered, "Look."

Instead of disappearing, the UFO dropped even lower in the sky, and above it another appeared, and then a third—each identical in appearance to the first, each with several small white lights, that might have been mistaken for stars in the Aquarius or Pegasus constellations. Several bright lights against the northeastern horizon, and not one of them a star. Abrupt angular movements yet precise and controlled, until the three UFOs formed a triangle above Shanklin's pond. Still no sound in this night of nights. Tapered black edges darker than the night, outlined in lights that were small splinters of ice, tiny sparkles like the shine of distant stars, these UFOs had an inexorable but unknown purpose.

"This is so impossible." As Jenna spoke, she managed a slight smile.

Still trying to rationalize what they were watching, Ben replied, "Maybe they're helicopters from Grissom."

"Helicopters make noise, Ben." Only inches from his face, she looked directly into his eyes. "They aren't helicopters."

A twisting funnel of white light shattered the tranquility of the woods and lasted nearly 30 seconds before vanishing. The unzipped cleft, with the green light inside, began to zip shut. In less than five seconds, the three UFOs were gone. A familiar night sky returned with its immense expanse of sparkling constellations. They had not disappeared into the alien space, as Ben and Jenna expected. Instead, it was like each UFO was hooked to a long zip-line, and the end of that zip-line connected to a place on the northeastern horizon, which was the direction of Saint Meinrad, Indiana.

Still under the bridge, and still perplexed by what had transpired, Ben took Jenna in his arms and kissed her passionately. Holding her face gently in both hands, he saw her trepidation and wanted to kiss it away, but instantly realized that fear was not so easily kissed away. "I wanted to do that before."

"Before what?" she grinned.

"Before the sky exploded," he said calmly.

Her smile was wide and spontaneous. "So, do it again then."

And he did. Afterwards, they climbed the grassy bank to the bridge, where Anna Atwood had once stood in cold autumn rain.

The early morning air was damp. As they walked beneath a sky on fire, in the direction of Atwood House, mist settled on the grass. The moist misty air grew colder, heavier, until the sudden threat of rain began to dim the stars. Darker clouds were already approaching. Soon, they would settle in the sky above Atwood House.

"Looks like more rain," she remarked.

They walked a little faster under this darkening sky, thinking more about UFOs than the coming rain. Each was brought closer to the other by the strange events of this remarkable night.

Chapter 24

As Smith came into the office, Walking Einstein, dressed in a white shirt and tie, sat at a large oak desk working complex computations on his new computer. Looking up, Charlie Chase was surprised to find the man standing in front of him, a newspaper tucked under his left arm. Smith had been serious when he told Charlie that results were not only expected but demanded.

"Did you see this?" asked Smith, holding out the newspaper so Charlie could read the headline.

"I haven't read a newspaper in years. Anything I need to know is right here in front of me, but yes, I've seen it."

"And what do you think?"

"They're here."

"Don't tell me what we already know, Dr. Chase. Overpaid thinkers on government payrolls are already stretching appropriations and internal budgets. I've told you that I want fresh thinking."

Tapping the monitor screen, Chase replied rather casually, "There's a high concentration of sightings near the 37th and 38th parallels. The question is why so many verifiable accounts at these particular latitudes?"

"I suppose you have an answer?"

"Ley lines," offered Chase.

"Ley lines . . . ley lines," Smith repeated.

"There's more. Take these recent Indiana sightings in Newburgh and Saint Meinrad, especially what happened last night at the Abbey."

"Yes . . . we're aware of these. What about them?"

"They also occurred on or near these latitudes."

After a long pause, during which he regarded Walking Einstein carefully, the man known only as Smith said rather sharply, "I don't believe in coincidence, sir."

"It is definitely not coincidence."

"You want me to believe there is a connection between ley lines and these particular latitudes?"

"It's a connection easily made."

"Don't hold back on us," Smith ordered. "If you know something, let's have it."

"Another large rock has recently been uncovered at the bottom of a pond in Newburgh. When a straight line is drawn from there to the site at the Archabbey at Saint Meinrad, both sites fall near the 37th parallel corridor."

"Go on," Smith prompted.

"It's right there in your hand. There were recent sightings in both places."

Smith set the paper on the corner of the desk before speaking again. "Those were nothing more than Sikorsky's from Grissom, on maneuvers in that area, and easily mistaken for UFOs. It's happened several times before."

"If you want straight shooting from me, Mr. Smith, then I should get the same courtesy from you."

"National security is not your concern."

"We both know they're here."

Smith went silent, and Walking Einstein thought the conversation was over. One of the fluorescent lights flickered overhead, and the hum from the transformer was increasingly audible. Both men seemed noticeably uncomfortable with each other. Smith was not the kind of man who was ever too far from a military uniform, and Charlie Chase was sure that that he would do whatever was necessary to protect all information pertinent to national security.

"I'll have to get maintenance to do something about that damn light." Charlie pointed to the defective fluorescent light.

Smith looked up at it. Then he sat down in a chair near Walking Einstein's desk, looked at the man curiously before speaking again, "Tell me how in the hell you got such a pretentious name?"

"Colleagues. It was meant to be a sarcastic condemnation of me personally. I didn't think like those pretentious bastards, would not bend, and they didn't like it. So, they branded me an imposter who too often turned his back on progressive thinking."

Smith smiled as he spoke, "I'm around these people every single day, and believe it or not, I listen carefully to their research. Rarely anything new, nothing but the kind of rhetoric academics use when they apply for government grants. They have ways of making their hypotheses sound compelling, even the ridiculous ones."

"I'm genuinely sorry for you, Smith," returned Charlie.

"Let's get back to these time slips."

"They are shifts in the fabric of time, cracks and fissures—what you refer to as portals," stated Chase frankly.

"There has to be a way to identify or predict with some accuracy their locations," suggested Smith with a directness that caused Chase to immediately think the man expected him to provide that answer.

"This is where it gets complicated."

Smith leaned back in the wooden chair across from Walking Einstein. "We're not unfamiliar with current theories."

"I'm sure you're not, and again, that's what confuses me. What I know, you either know or have already considered."

Pushing on with questions he thought Chase could answer, the man in the dark blue pinstripe suit cleared his throat and said, "Tell me more about these time-shifts. How do they happen? Can they be initiated?"

"I think so."

"That's it? You think so?" Smith was pushing hard, hoping for a glimmer of light in a world where gray eclipsed even the smallest anticipation.

"There's more."

"Let's have it then," Smith demanded. "These mainstream thinkers can't think beyond their data. I don't want more phony conjectures.

I want fresh thinking, possibilities beyond the same damn data that lead to more dead ends."

"There is no key, if that's what you're thinking."

"Look, Charlie, I know you got ideas, maybe definitive ideas, maybe nothing more than speculations. But I need something to hang a hat on, something that explains how these things come and go so damn easily."

"You're keeping me too much in the dark, Smith. If I knew a little more about this project you're working on, maybe then I could offer something more specific . . . more substantial."

"*Project Firefly*," returned Smith abruptly.

"Well, that's a start," said Chase. "And what exactly did the Air Force retrieve in 1947 Newburgh, Indiana?"

"Much of that remains classified, Dr. Chase," Smith confessed.

"I've seen what's been released. The declassified material is so heavily redacted that's it's virtually meaningless."

"You're talking about an event that occurred years before my time."

"But not an event unfamiliar to you," Chase implied.

"That was then, and this is now, as they say." Smith looked closely at Chase before adding. "What happened there in 1947 has been thoroughly documented."

"I don't buy the meteor story, Smith."

"We're not dealing with 1947, Charlie," shot Smith angrily.

"I need a starting point," Chase stated calmly.

"And you think 1947 Newburgh is the place to begin?"

"Whatever information was secured from the Newburgh event has some huge holes in it, or I wouldn't be needed," Charlie declared. "Not unless you're going in another direction—considering other objectives." Charlie looked at Smith and waited for an answer. "Which is it?"

"It's both," admitted Smith.

"Let me see if I can fill in some of the blanks for you." Charlie saw Smith's expression change from irritation to curiosity. "Let's suppose magnetic energy is the fundamental component of *Project Firefly* and that what happened in Newburgh, Indiana and also in Roswell, New Mexico in 1947 provided the military with, well let's say, a few new tools in their toolbox, and that what was discovered was much more than rudimentary information." He kept his eyes on Smith as he continued to speak with subtleties and innuendos he knew Smith would understand. "The hammer was no longer the tool of choice. Moving forward, the laws of physics weren't working. Bring in the cavalry, the cookie-cutters, the talking heads to figure out how the *visitors* had altered the laws of physics. Both science and national security had been compromised."

Smith leaned forward on his elbows, regarded Chase with eyes as serious as any Charlie had seen. "What if I told you that your narrative had omitted one essential component?"

"I'd say you got the abridged version."

"You're saying you know what that component is?"

"I'm saying you're dancing with the devil."

"What the hell does that mean?" asked Smith, whose patience with Chase was beginning to wear thin.

"You're being manipulated by a bunch of sheep . . . thieves of taxpayer dollars who are contracted to the sins of conformity.

"My God but you have a high opinion of yourself," proclaimed Smith.

"Not so much as a low opinion of those working in your echo chambers."

Smith got up and went over to the only window in the office, which looked out on a faculty parking lot. "Which one of those do you drive?"

"None of them," revealed Chase. "I don't live far from campus, so I walk when the weather's nice."

"Do you even own a car?"

"An old Ford Explorer."

"I was beginning to think we weren't paying you enough," smiled Smith.

Dismissing Smith's remark and before speaking again, Charlie came over to where Smith was standing. "Thermal currents," said Chase without looking at Smith.

"What about them?"

"I'm convinced certain weather formations are capable of creating vortexes or vortices," revealed Chase.

"Yes, we know that. They are frequently observed."

"Certain types of weather anomalies can create vortexes in time and space, but too often they occur without warning." Chase had his arms folded as he looked at cars in the parking lot. "A lot of expensive metal out there, some of these people must be knocking down huge bucks."

"Let's stick with weather anomalies," suggested Smith. "We've reviewed Ivan T. Sanderson's work more than once, thinking his *Vile Vortices* might explain why there are so many accounts of disappearances at 12 identified locations."

"No matter what some scientists proclaim, Sanderson's work is not outdated. In fact, his planetary grid research goes back to Plato's geometric patterns, which suggest how earth's energies are organized. Maybe that's where we begin again."

"You do have some ideas, don't you?" Smith smiled. "I think you and I might be close to working on the same page, Charlie."

Chase nodded, "Maybe so. Think simpler. Sometimes less works better than more."

"That is certainly a place to begin," smiled Smith who was trying to sound ingratiating.

For the first time in a long time, Walking Einstein was convinced someone was genuinely interested in his work. It was work not entirely off the scientific grid, but still far enough away from prevailing theories that most of his former colleagues would brand him as too much of a risk-taker. And now, standing next to him was a man who just came out of the night, a man whose intentions were not entirely known to Chase, but a man who was not only willing to listen, but anxious to put Charlie Chase at the head of the line—at least for the moment.

Chapter 25

"X-RAYS . . . TRIANGULATION . . . THE PIEZOELECTRIC EFFECT," said Charlie as he walked across the room to a table strewn with papers and books. Picking up a book, he returned to the desk, but didn't sit down. Instead, he opened the book, removed a paper that was heavily creased with two folds, and put it on the desk in front of Smith who took a pair of glasses from his pocket. "We know they occur in outer space as a form of light. Electromagnetic radiation. Perception of this light, call it the Chandra Effect, can be observed with the use of special telescopes."

"Yes, that's right," agreed Smith.

"What if I told you that certain conditions make it possible to observe this light with the naked eye?"

Smith nodded, "Explain how that's feasible."

"It's been proven that ley lines have certain properties and these properties have electric charges. There are times when unusually heavy charges are produced."

"Batteries," suggested Smith.

"Yes—batteries. At or near these ley lines, especially at latitudes north of the 37th parallel, certain rocks, especially those under pressure, can act as insulators, and then become semi-conductors that produce electric current and create outbursts of light. Granite is an excellent conductor of electricity, and the more pressure exerted, the stronger the electric current passing through the granite. Ionized air begins to glow, much the same way gas is activated in a fluorescent tube."

Smith looked at him closely, "You're speaking about the Piezoelectric Effect."

"To some extent, yes."

"In theory, it makes sense, but . . . "

Cutting Smith off abruptly, "I can assure you it's more than theory."

"You're suggesting deliberate actions are required?"

"That's right," answered Chase. He walked around the desk to open one of the drawers, and took out a canvas bag, which Smith recognized at once. Placing the bag on the desk, he slowly unfastened the straps, looking at Smith the entire time. Removing a rock, the size of a softball, he placed it gently in front of Smith, "You need a trigger."

"Quartz?"

"Or feldspar."

Shaking his head and looking at the rock in front of him, Smith asked, "So let's say you have found a way to manufacture this light and observe it without the use of a telescope, what's the point?"

He picked up the newspaper that Smith had brought with him, unfolded it, then took a few seconds to glance over the article, until he found what he was searching for. "This is the point. Witnesses reported seeing a green shaft of light at both the Newburgh and Saint Meinrad sightings. It's right there in front of you."

"We've had numerous reports of green lights at various sightings, not to be denied. But we decided these were a phenomenon relative to atmospheric conditions, nothing more than that," said Smith.

"This is not about atmospheric conditions. It's not ball lightning or anything like it, if that's what you're suggesting," Charlie stated. "I think you're seeing a split or crack in time . . . a portal."

"What comparative data do you have—if any?"

"Not much," Charlie confessed. "There are reports of strange lights in several places. Those places with higher frequencies of UFO recurrence need to be considered more seriously. Though academics are studying these phenomena, too many questions about their origins remain unanswered. You'll agree that some sightings are reminiscent of *foo fighters* so prevalent during World War II."

"We're aware of all that," admitted Smith. "It's old news."

"To frame this in a more recent context, and primarily out of curiosity, I ran spectrum analyses on the Marfa lights, and the strange lights at Brown Mountain in North Carolina."

"And . . ."

"I'm convinced we're dealing with different phenomena."

"If you're asking us to read between the lines, Charlie, there are still too many pieces missing, important pieces that offer definite resolutions to a complex phenomenon, which some of the best minds have studied for decades. It can't be something as simple as quartz or feldspar."

"Deposits of feldspar are abundant as veins in both igneous and metamorphic rocks, and though this mineral is found in many different types, only the parallel striations of K-feldspar seem to create the right properties necessary to generate a charge. Excessive amounts of electricity create magnetic fields, which in turn create lift."

"I'm listening," Smith assured him.

"That's where we begin." He sat down behind his desk, regarded Smith carefully, as though he wanted to be sure of the man's reaction to what he was about to say. "I tell you again that the answers are in energy grids, and unless you're willing to consider them in a broader context, beyond what you expect to find, those answers will remain light years away. You know as well as I do, or I wouldn't be sitting in front of you now, that the parameters of many hypotheses are too narrowly defined. Confinement leads to presumptuous narrow-minded thinking, which always comes up short. Discovery is too often outside of the box. Nikola Tesla was on the right track with his Wardenclyffe Tower idea, just way too far ahead of his time—or ahead of J. P. Morgan's money."

Smith stared at the carpet, his arms crossed and both feet fixed firmly on the floor, as though he was hesitating to respond to Chase's remarks about Tesla. "You are not the first to express this more radical perspective, and as far as I know nothing definitive has come from such thinking."

"I'm saying there are times when chance has a higher probability rating than the methodical, time-intensive, plodding rigidity of mainstream science. Suppose Tesla was really onto something with his alternating current research, his wireless transmitter concept."

"Go on, Dr. Chase."

"What if equally powerful transmitters could be created by using natural resources? Furthermore, what if there are numerous places where these Tesla-type towers already exist, and have existed for millennia? Consider the possibilities."

"Suppose you're right," began Smith, regarding Walking Einstein carefully. "If you know the matrix, so to speak, then you can create a gateway?"

"No, not yet anyway. The fundamentals are there, but not the solution."

"I don't understand."

"There are too many variables."

"Screw the variables," snapped Smith. "We're not the only ones working on this."

"I think these time slips are natural phenomena," admitted Chase. "But suppose there is a way to control a source of power that is essentially unattainable."

"Controlled, but unattainable. You're playing both ends against the middle here," Smith alleged sharply. "The question is why is this power so damned unattainable?"

"Because it's generated or manufactured power that needs to be manipulated," Charlie answered.

"You want me to believe it's alien intervention?" Smith was trying to get a more precise response and seemed irritated at Chase for proposing what Smith considered, "ambiguous clutter, in the way of clear thinking."

"No."

Smith, still regarding Chase with a hint of skepticism, "Then what are you saying?"

"Not unless we're the aliens. It is often prudent to look behind—at the past. Solutions are not always in the present or discovered by looking ahead."

"There's nothing profound in that thinking."

"It's not meant to be profound. Suppose ancient Egyptians had contacted another civilization in the Orion star system, for example. We know how important the Orion belt was to other cultures like the Hopi of Northeastern Arizona, whose mesas are said to correlate with the three belt stars of Orion. The point is that a transmitter was needed to make the connection. Again, ley lines played a significant role in these early efforts, the same as they do today. So, I'm saying there are key geographic regions, many of them already identified, and these are the places where we begin to establish accelerators. If you continue to underestimate or deny the importance of these sites, you'll move backward—not forward. That much I can assure you."

"You're holding something back, Dr. Chase," stated Smith firmly. "What is it?"

"Only that by synchronizing the vibrations of certain towers, possibly in patterns yet undiscovered, and with enough current passing through them, it might be possible to generate energies strong enough to create a portal, a wormhole in the fabric of space and time."

"What else?" Smith pressed.

"We already know that musical notes create patterns of sound waves. Pushing further, and with the right technologies, these energies or vibrations can be transmitted into space with one specific intention—to communicate."

"We're already doing that, Chase. The Sirius star system has been a target for decades and we're still looking at recent data that suggest a possible response."

"But to manufacture the necessary energy for a time portal these rock transmitters, especially those at sacred sites, need to be utilized. These particular sites are there for specific reasons, and because many of these sites have been rebuilt on over the centuries, there needs to be a thorough chronological examination of them as places where existing energies are still present—places where those energies can be manipulated."

"There must be a logical reason for rebuilding at these same locations, something that's always there—something indigenous and found at each site."

"Sand," said Chase.

After looking closely at Walking Einstein, Smith removed a mobile phone from his suit pocket and punched in one number. "I think we've got something."

Chapter 26

Charlie Chase knew he was walking a tight line. Government people were usually impatient and wanted answers immediately. National security was always an issue. No reason to think this time was different. The whole situation had shadings of the space race. With technology this extreme, the ones who controlled it had the assurance of utilizing its capabilities and powers to accomplish several hegemonic objectives. Although that kind of potential was still not entirely comprehended, Chase was convinced that interdimensional travel, if it could be called that, could eventually alter the landscape so enormously that the world in which he lived would never be the same. He knew also that Smith was not going to let him drag his feet too long. Something continued to cause anxiety. These were thoughts that the military was less altruistic than Smith wanted him to believe, that already being considered were dark sinister motives, which had everything to do with military directives.

Whether signals had been received from the Sirius star system, as Smith had implied, Chase couldn't say with complete assurance. With the enormous technologies available, it was entirely possible that transmissions had been broadcast and received. If sent messages had been returned, then Smith was in search of something else, and every indication pointed to magnetic fields and their influences on theoretical time portals. Chase suspected that Smith already realized the potential for a portal was not to be discovered in the stars, but in terrestrial locations where there were strong confluences of ley lines.

Charlie was not entirely in the dark, but he was reluctant to reveal too much. Maybe he had said too much already. Smith would quickly realize the conductive properties of sand and make the logical connection to energy grids. When Chase caught Smith's expression at the mention of Tesla's name, he was convinced the man was after other information, which had nothing to do with communication towers or time portals. Charlie had a hunch, a seriously troubling hunch that General Moro Eugene Elkins had objectives that were exclusively terrestrial.

Plurality of worlds, or the multiverse, was undeniably prioritized at the highest levels. Whether the military had discovered all the finite elements of a matrix allowing for interdimensional travel, was in Chase's mind, unlikely. Not only that, there remained too many think tank academics whose idea of time travel involved walking from their desks to the nearest bathroom. These disbelievers were not capable of a single original thought. They sailed merrily along, across smooth seas, the ship always steady, always upright. If originality bit them in the ass, their liberalism would numb the pain. Self-aggrandized freeloaders with inflated paychecks, these narcissistic bastards were the mouthy hypocrites spinning their narratives at universities everywhere—bloggers of progressive insanity.

For Walking Einstein, the future might be in the very same space he was living his life, and if he could discover how to push though the invisible wall, that future would be accessible to him. Reports of pilots lost in magnetic fogs were not uncommon. And there were numerous accounts of people disappearing into thin air—while in the presence of others. Were these people destined to leave this universe for another?

As far as Charlie could figure, Smith did want him to determine with certainty those locations where there were extremely high concentrations of regenerative energies. He already knew about Sedona, Dulce, Marfa, as well as other mainstream locations. The man was asking for something bigger. Walking Einstein knew precisely where to begin, or more to the point, where to continue his search for hot zones, where energy grids had both kinetic and elastic properties. One of those places was along the Ohio River. Like the Abbey at Saint Meinrad, places farther south had magnetic fields that were off the charts. If Smith didn't already know this, he would want that information as soon as possible.

Dr. Charlie Chase had always been reclusive, had no close friends, and had very little regard for ostentatious people. Progressive liberals were nightmare creeps, and the farther away from them he could get the better he liked it. The problem was that these sanctimonious phonies were too heavily entrenched in academia. College and university administrations were full of them. In classrooms everywhere, impressionable students sat in front of them, listening to these idiots espouse their bleeding-heart rhetoric, and enduring their leftist political rants when election results were not what they expected or wanted. Their fundamental purpose in life was to dazzle the less endowed with their brilliance—and they always came up short. Their hate was suffocating, their whining insufferable, and what they created, deplorable. Group think was imprinted indelibly on their foreheads, pinned to their chests, and they wore this stamp like a badge of honor, as an endorsement, as a definitive statement of everything they were not.

Chase was entirely immune to their insidious venom, and the world they continued to hammer out would continue to be misrepresented by bigoted news media, which no longer had the vaguest idea what journalistic standards were—if they ever knew at all. It was just a matter of time before these egotistical jerks would destroy the Constitution and push society back to the Dark Ages—and then play the blame game for the chaos that they created.

Then there were the take-your-guns-to-town people, always behind the times, the never-willing-to-take-a-chance people, more like sheep with each passing day, the slow-to-speak people, those cautious, righteous, and safe-inside-the-flock people, the revolutionaries who talked the good fight until their conservative proclamations were chastised by shortsighted liberals. Watch the weak scatter. These were the people who always finished in second place and were entirely okay with that. Cowardice and indecision defined them. As far as Chase was concerned, they came up short on every issue, and their words were too easily, too often silenced by their innate fear of being criticized. They would never find the courage to be independent thinkers.

Chase was not a man dazzled by much of anything. His father had left when Charlie was born. Two years later, his mother remarried an educated man nearly 20 years older. Jim was Charlie's salvation. He was kind and taught Charlie all the things a father should teach a son. The bond between them was infinite. He never knew why his real father had left, knew only that he was not inclined to know the kind of man he was. Jim was the father any boy would love to have, and even when Charlie went away to school, they were always in touch.

After Chase had finished his doctoral work, he had a short tenure as an associate professor in the physics department at Southern Indiana University. His liberal colleagues found him strange. The Department Chair and the Dean considered him too much of a freethinker, whose research projects were always unfinished and pushed to extremes the established dogma of the University. At one faculty meeting at the end of the academic year, Charlie referred to the Department Chair as incompetent, more concerned with his neighbor's wife than he was about endorsing legitimate research grants from faculty. As expected, this didn't go over well.

But that was Charlie Chase. Right or wrong, always his own person, impulsively outspoken, and always quick to defend his work, he accepted a research position at the University of Chicago, which lasted, much to Charlie's surprise, seven years, or until a young hotshot elitist, whose family had donated heavily to the University, was appointed the new Dean. The Dean had referred to Chase's work as fanatical and unprogressive. Late one night, Charlie drove over the state line to a small farm in Valparaiso, Indiana, scooped a few ripe cow patties into a large shopping bag, which he put into the trunk of his Ford, then drove to the Dean's house and placed the bag on the man's front porch, set it on fire, rang the doorbell and left.

Charlie moved on from the University of Chicago to relocate in Jasper, Indiana. Around town he became known as Walking Einstein. He managed to publish a book at a conservative publishing house, which sold better than anticipated, but a book that academia panned, referring to it as "inane rambling and borderline lunacy." Somewhere along the way, Smith became aware of the book. Something in the research had caught his attention, and that was the reason Dr. Charlie Chase found himself signing a security disclosure, which he took quite seriously. At last, he had a voice that was being heard. How long that would continue, he couldn't say.

Visionaries like Chase considered failures as nothing more than temporary obstacles—steppingstones to success. Life was not neat and orderly. It was messy. Failures were necessary clutter, momentary mistakes easily brushed aside and forgotten. He realized from the beginning that working for people like Smith was risky. These were people who demanded to be taken seriously. If they didn't get the information and results they wanted, Charlie knew this door, like others that had closed behind him, also swung outward. Charlie now had another chance to continue research that he was convinced was at the threshold of significant discovery.

One unmentioned objective of his new position had strong intimations of military stratagem. Though confrontation didn't bother him, Charlie despised war. If he had been conscripted to advance a military mission, he'd be forced into a decision Smith might not like. That was still far enough down the road, so he'd continue with what they asked him to do, until he realized his work was too heavily compromised by military manipulation and intrigue. That realization had first occurred the moment Chase was introduced to General Elkins. He knew then it was just a matter of time before the General came knocking again.

With the government, disinformation campaigns were as frequent as lying to Congress. Maybe these campaigns did begin in 1947 Roswell, New Mexico, as many people suspected, and had over the years become increasingly more complex and convincing. Chase knew General Elkins had his hands full, stretching truth as far as he possibly could, while keeping every storyline completely believable. It would be a few days before the General would call on him, and there was always Smith to buffer any military protocol.

If there was one thing Charlie was sure about, it was the importance of quartz in the construction and operation of what he continued to refer to as communication towers. When triangulated, ley line influence and strong magnetic fields had the potential to reveal at least some of the answers Smith wanted. It would take time to work through new calculations, and even now, Charlie realized there might never be any significant developments. Those answers that Smith was pushing so hard to get might still be decades away—if they were to come at all. The possibility of failure was a predicament that Chase considered seriously. Smith was giving Charlie all the freedom he wanted, while at the same time providing sufficient rope to make a noose. People like Smith were movers and shakers, the untouchables who emerged from the shadows with hammers large enough to pound anyone six feet into the ground. That was enough to frighten even Dr. Charlie Chase.

Chapter 27

IT WAS THE week before Thanksgiving. Christmas decorations hung along the streets of Newburgh and Evansville. Many downtown stores had Christmas music playing for eager shoppers. Christmas displays were in all the franchise stores, and probably no place had bigger displays than Walgreens and the Walmart super stores. It was the festive time of year, time for colder weather and shorter days.

Still standing on the southeast lawn of Atwood House was the structure dug from the ground and resurrected into a thing which still had no decisive purpose. Ben had recent thoughts of taking it down and transporting it to the town recycle center. Maybe it was Jenna's influence and persistence that prevented it from being demolished. She'd told him there was something missing, and that in time they would discover what it was. So, reluctantly, Ben gave in, and there hadn't been much discussion about it in several days.

Most days, Ben was busy painting, preparing for a December exhibition at the River City Art Gallery in downtown Evansville. His other exhibitions there had been successful, so, anxious to get some recent work in front of the public, he made himself stay busy painting. Jenna said several times how happy she was to see him take on this renewed interest and commitment.

The unfinished portrait of Anna Atwood was wrapped and placed in a foyer closet, where it was all but forgotten. Late one afternoon, Jenna unwrapped it and studied it closely, as though she was searching for something. Holding a photograph from an old newspaper in one hand and the painting in the other, she noticed a striking similarity in the faces. Enthralling midnight eyes, articulated cheekbones, thin lips accentuating a rather pouty mouth, the face partially revealed behind the veil had unmistakable similarities to the face in the photograph.

Chopping firewood was not one of Manning's favorite chores. However, laying in for the winter as much wood as possible was good exercise, and both he and Jenna enjoyed a warm fireplace on cold evenings. He cut some of the dead oak and hickory trees in the woods south of the stone bridge, split the logs and stacked them in the woodshed a few yards off the back patio.

"Look at this, Ben," she said when he came inside.

"What is it?"

"I found a picture of Anna Atwood in an old newspaper."

"Really?"

"Look at her face." Jenna held up the painting and handed Ben the photograph. "The similarities are unmistakable, don't you think? You can't deny that this is Anna Atwood you're painting."

Ben, looking from the photograph to the painting, smiled and agreed. "I can't deny it, Jenna. There are similarities, but that's about all." After a pause, he added, "She's a pretty thing, not a doubt about that."

"Okay, Ben, that's enough. I just wanted you to see her face, not fall in love with it."

He reached out for her hand and took it in his. "Your face . . . that's the face I want to see."

"She is beautiful, though," agreed Jenna.

"But she isn't real."

"Well somebody that looks a lot like her has been in your house more than once."

"Let's forget about that. You're the real deal, Jenna. Anna Atwood stopped being the real deal a hundred years ago."

"I just thought you'd like to see the photograph."

"What do you want to do this afternoon?" he asked, adroitly changing the subject.

"I think you should finish her portrait, Ben. I like it very much and wish you were more serious about finishing it."

"As soon as I have time, I'll finish it," he promised while putting the painting back in the closet.

"You've had time, so I know you're only talking."

"No, seriously, I'll do it—just for you."

"Not just for me, Ben, for Anna, too."

"Why is that so important?"

"I don't know why, but I want you to finish it."

"I would rather paint your face instead," he admitted.

"If you do, I swear I'll never speak to you again. Besides, I don't dress like that."

"You're making too much of this, Jenna."

"I want her to live in this century."

"What a strange thing to say. Anna Atwood doesn't belong to this century."

"Well, she sure does show up in it frequently."

"What's really bothering you, Jenna?"

"I don't know. It's just that she has such a mysterious face. I'd like to know her better is all."

"That's not what you're thinking."

She looked at him closely, wanting him to know exactly what she was thinking. "That painting has a soul."

"What?"

"I mean it, Ben. It's calling out to you, and I'm sure you've heard it." Still looking at him, more curiously now, "Or, do you expect her to finish painting it?"

"Why don't we take a drive, do some small towns—early Christmas shopping?"

"Sounds fun. Maybe we can eat at Maddy's," she replied excitedly.

"Great idea," he smiled.

It was not the first time they had shopped the small towns north of Newburgh. Both enjoyed searching the antique malls, especially those in Huntingburg and Jasper. With Christmas coming fast, it would be a good opportunity to beat the rush.

As a boy, Ben loved the Christmas holidays, and each Christmas was every bit as exciting as the one before it. He always looked forward to buying "Toys for Tots." Just the thought of giving toys to underprivileged children was one of the highlights of each Christmas. His only sister taught English in Japan, and his parents lived in the Florida Panhandle and no longer traveled at Christmas. He'd told Jenna earlier in the week that he would spend Thanksgiving in Florida and was anxious to visit his mother and father who'd asked him to come for the holiday.

Their plans to shop ended abruptly when they both heard a recurring humming, that sounded very much like the sound of discharges from high–voltage power lines. Coming from somewhere inside the house, it was loud enough to keep their attention for almost a minute before either was inclined to move.

They knew, even with the doors closed, that the strange noise was coming from the library. Jenna stayed a step or two behind Ben as they continued cautiously down the hallway, until, only a few steps from the library doors, they hesitated, realizing someone else was in the house. The noises were louder now, vibrations in the oak floorboards, subtle at first, but stronger near the entrance to the library. The space beneath the large ornate doors was filled with a faint glimmer of fluctuating green light.

With his hand on the doorknob, Ben looked at Jenna, and seemed reluctant to open the door. "It's Anna," he said confidently. "I know she's in there."

Light under the door intensified. Beneath their feet, heat lasted only seconds, before the space around them turned colder. Not a sound of any kind, and it was a heavy foreboding silence. Hesitating no longer, Jenna pushed past Ben, and slowly opened one of the doors wide enough for them to peek inside the room.

The interior of the library was flooded with white light, streaming through windows on the other side of the room. It had to be sunlight, but looked more like manufactured light, and it was strongest in the center of the room.

"I don't see her?" Ben said softly. "Do you?"

Before Jenna could answer, a hand appeared in the space between the doors. Instantly, the crack through which they were peeking was gone. Jenna backed up so suddenly that she nearly took Ben off his feet. Then, both heard the latch snap shut.

"It *is* her, Ben. It's Anna."

"She's locked us out."

Desk drawers squeaked open, squeaked shut. Another opened, then closed. "She's searching for something," whispered Jenna.

Light continued to spill out from under the doors, illuminating the tips of their shoes, and pushed across the floor into the hallway. It seemed there was too much light for the library to contain, and it was stretching the very seams of the room. Again, a drawer slid open, and the rustling of papers was audible. Then, it was the sound of a chair or table being moved that held their attention.

"The brooch!" exclaimed Ben.

Jenna grabbed him by the arm. "You have to give it back."

"Come on." He took her hand, and led her outside, around to windows at the front of the house. Working their way past the hedges and taller shrubbery, until they could look inside the library, they were surprised to see a shape standing with her back to them, bent over the same table on which she had placed the vase of flowers.

"What's she doing?" asked Jenna, thinking Ben would know.

Shrugging his shoulders, "I think she's writing something."

"I want to meet her, Ben."

"What?"

"You heard me. I really want to meet her."

"Why?"

"There's something strange about this whole thing. I don't think she is what she wants us to believe she is."

"If she's not a ghost, then what is she?"

"She's no ghost, and I'd bet she's as much a part of this century as you and I."

After straightening herself, Anna turned toward the window like she knew she was being watched. The white light intensified, causing Ben and Jenna to cover their eyes. Behind them a car drove up the lane. It was a sleek black Ferrari, and Ben knew it belonged to Bob Bergman.

Apparently unaware of Bob's arrival, Jenna continued to peek inside the window. "She's gone." When she looked for Ben, he was already on his way to meet Bergman.

Chapter 28

SLIGHTLY EMBARRASSED AS she emerged from behind the shrubbery in time to see the Ferrari roar to a stop in front of the house, Jenna followed a few yards behind Ben. The sun burned through a bank of heavy clouds that had moved in from the south, leaving a beautiful blue sky and a stunning autumn day ahead. Though their agenda had changed, both Jenna and Ben realized these strange and continuing events at Atwood House needed answers, and they were anxious to pursue recent suspicions, largely those that Jenna had suggested.

Bergman, wearing a broad smile, gave a slight wave as he approached them. Dressed in a navy suit, his hair slicked back, he said warmly, "Looks like a great day and warmer than weather reports predicted."

"Hi, Bob," Ben greeted politely, "how's that Ferrari running?"

"It needs a good workout on one of those back roads off the Interstate."

"I'd love to be with you when you do it."

"Mr. Bergman," smiled Jenna, reaching out to shake his hand.

"How are you, Jenna? And please call me Bob."

Her smile widened. "You're probably wondering why we're creeping out from behind the bushes."

"No, not at all," Bergman assured her. "I was just passing by," and here he looked at Ben, "and thought I'd say hello, and see if you've thought more about selling the brooch."

Looking at Jenna before answering, Ben said, "I really haven't thought much more about it, Bob . . . just been busy with things around here."

"Well, not to worry. I assure you it's in safekeeping."

"I'm sure it is," he smiled. "Give me a little more time to think about it, will you?"

"Sure, take your time. I have a few clients who are always looking to buy something unique . . . something expensive." He walked back toward the Ferrari, but before getting in, turned to regard Atwood House. "This place really is special—and what a location." Glancing out across the front yard he saw the structure near the stone bridge. "Is that yard art?"

"Just something we dug out of the ground . . . might as well be yard art," Ben answered. "We don't know what it is."

"Do you mind if I take look at it?"

"Not at all."

They walked across the lawn until they came to the structure, which was shining with sunlight. "Odd looking thing," admitted Bob. "You say you dug it out of the ground?"

"That's right—over by the bridge."

Bergman glanced toward the bridge, then walked around the structure. "Is it all here?"

"As far as we know; we couldn't find any more pieces," Ben replied.

"I wonder what it was, if anything at all." He ran his fingers along the surface of one of the verticals. Looking at both Ben and Jenna before speaking again, he said in a voice barely audible, "Strange."

"What is it?" asked Ben curiously.

"Put your hand here," directed Bergman. "Maybe it's something I'm imagining."

"We know about the pulse," returned Ben evenly.

Bergman stepped back to where they were standing. "This is much more than a pulse, Ben."

Ben put his hand on the structure in the same place where Bergman had touched it, but drew back instantly, like he'd received a shock. "It's stronger, much stronger than before. It feels like current is passing through it."

"Exactly," agreed Bergman.

"You know what it is?" asked Ben, thinking Bergman might have an answer.

"There has to be a reason why this is passing current," he replied slowly.

The sound of water running over the rocks filled the silences between words. Shadows cast by the structure were surrealistic shapes, asymmetrical twists and turns on the lawn. Leaves the color of molasses, caught on a stiff breeze, floated on the crisp air before falling softly to the ground. In the distance, and beneath the large oak trees on the perimeter of the woods, pools of blue haze lingered like smoke from small fires. Across a deep blue sky, yellow rays of sunlight edged a few white clouds, which were slowly drifting toward the northern horizon. This day was art on canvas, already captured in the paintings of Impressionists like Renoir and Claude Monet.

After circling the structure a few more times, Bob Bergman's increasing interest seemed surprising. He looked closely at an indention in one of the horizontal bars, pushed his index fingers inside and rubbed the edges a few times. Whether he knew what the edifice was, neither Ben nor Jenna could say, but Bergman was certainly giving the thing his complete attention.

"These symbols," he began, "any idea what they mean?"

"We have a few ideas," Manning admitted.

"And something must have been inserted into this space," Bergman added, continuing to run his fingers along the edges.

"Any ideas?" Jenna asked. "We just assumed it was a natural space in the rock."

"I think it's more than that. These are sharp edges, deliberate incisions, probably cut by a laser—incised for an insertion of some kind. When I was a young boy, I carried a quartz crystal around with me. Always had it in my pocket, expecting it to strengthen my inner energies."

"And did it?" Jenna wanted to know.

"Maybe, but it was hard to tell, since it was such a subtle thing if it happened at all. But I always believed there was something to it."

"You think a quartz crystal went into that hole?" Ben guessed.

"Why not? This area is full of quartz veins. If not quartz, maybe some other stone was used."

"Used for what?"

"I don't know, Ben. Stones give off energies. And quartz crystals are capable of wider energy bands, which can amplify the more latent energies of other stones. They can even affect emotions. Remember mood rings?"

Manning nodded.

"Well, it's just a hunch."

"That's interesting," Jenna said, "and if you're right, for what apparent reason was it done?"

"I know stones and a bit about crystalline structures, but I can't answer that one." Shaking his head, he smiled at them. "That's a tough question all right."

While listening carefully to Bergman talking about the properties of stones, and how crystals emit energies, Jenna examined the small depression. "Oh, my goodness," she said, her face taking on the kind of excitement that comes with discovery.

"Did you find something, Jenna?" Ben called from a few feet away.

Even Bergman was startled by the sudden outburst and moved closer to see her drawing her fingers across the sharp edges of the incision. Ben watched Jenna carefully trace the edges with the fingers of her right hand. Both men were beginning to think she had discovered something. But it was Bergman who sensed what she was thinking.

Jenna turned abruptly to regard each of them before speaking. Her face was more relaxed, and the slightest hint of a smile was evident. "The brooch," she said calmly. "Maybe it could be inserted into this space."

Even as she spoke, Bergman pushed past her to have a closer look. "Why use an expensive piece of jewelry? For what possible purpose?"

"You said," she continued, "that stones emit energies. Since this incision is not a natural anomaly, there has to be a reason why it's there."

Bob glanced at Ben who looked surprised to hear the brooch being mentioned in such an extraordinary context. "Strange as it sounds, she might actually have something, Ben. It's a bold presumption, no doubt about that, and I have no idea why such a thought should even be considered with any seriousness." He looked at Jenna. "We can always try it, I guess, see what happens—if anything."

"You're actually serious?" Ben laughed.

"I can't explain it. I'm convinced this," and he pointed to the space, "was cut for a reason, for an insertion of some kind. There's an outside chance that with the right stones in place . . . " He stopped abruptly to consider what he was about to say next, perhaps thinking he'd already pushed this idea too near ridiculous. Yet, he knew he'd not said much at all, only suggested Jenna might have an idea worth considering.

"What is it, Bob?" Manning asked.

"We know some current is passing through this thing, and it's drawing it from somewhere, possibly from a vein of crystal or quartz cache beneath the ground. I have absolutely no idea if it's complete or even reconstructed in the way it was originally built. But I can assure you that what's there in front of us did have a purpose—as ridiculous as that sounds."

"That much we know," agreed Ben," and even after digging it up, there is still confusion about what it is—and I don't think we're any closer to an answer now than we were then."

"It sure does get your attention, doesn't it?" Bergman smiled.

"We did run GPR over a wider radius but got nothing out of the ordinary."

"Could be other pieces scattered farther out," suggested Bob.

Pausing to regard both Jenna and Ben, he said with a hint of confidence, "I don't think the brooch works—but possibly a deliberately incised piece of quartz crystal." Again, a lengthy pause before he continued, "This is going to sound extreme, but crystals, especially galena crystals, can be used to construct a radio. Let's suppose that when the crystal is placed into the depression, these vertical columns represent antennas. It's nothing more than a supposition, but certainly possible. We would need to find a ground, possibly an underground water pipe, or any piece of metal buried near here."

"You think this was a radio transmitter?"

"I don't know, Ben. My mind's working overtime on this one. I do think Jenna has the right idea though—and she might be right. Maybe the stones in the brooch would jump start this thing." After another reflective pause, "I think the larger the stone or stones, the more energy produced, and distance will increase proportionately with a larger transmitter."

"Lacey has taken your mineralogy class and said she learned a lot about gems," Jenna offered as an affirmation of Bergman's expertise with stones and crystals. "She told me it got kind of metaphysical at times. Are we dealing with metaphysics now?"

"To some extent, but first it's the basics we're trying to piece together. If the basics work, who knows where we go from there? If this thing could capture electromagnetic waves, even those that can travel great distances at a speed of 186 miles per second, then we've got a receiver. That could be significant. Again, that's only a theoretical possibility, and critical pieces that should be here, as I've said, could still be buried." After a sheepish smile, he said, "Probably best to keep these ideas to myself . . . leave this thing, whatever it is, to the scientists."

"I suppose we could consider widening the perimeters," Ben replied.

Bob looked in the direction of the creek before speaking again. "If the creek flooded, the water could have moved pieces of this thing to the other side of the bridge." There was another pause during which he looked across the stream to a field that was nearly 20 acres of unused pasture. "Is that where the military dug?" and he nodded toward the field.

"Somewhere over there," replied Manning. "Nearer the woods, I think, but don't know exactly where."

"There was never much information, not public information

anyway, and I've often wondered exactly what they recovered all those years ago," confessed Bergman.

"Maybe nothing," Ben suggested. "Maybe this was a classic example of doing nothing more than moving equipment around—disinformation or diversion possibly. There are also those who think they dug in the wrong place."

"And I'm sure that's a possibility," agreed Bob, "but why the pretense?"

"I don't know," admitted Ben. "It wouldn't be the first time the military has overreacted."

"Well," Bob began, looking at his watch, "didn't mean to take up so much of your time. Got to get on with the day. I'm driving up to Tell City to appraise some jewelry for an elderly couple. They are conscientious about leaving something valuable to their daughter."

Ben shook his hand and said, "I have to say that you're leaving us plenty more to think about."

"You got something here. No doubt about that," Bergman replied. "Even if it's a radio receiver, or even a transmitter, who put it here and why? Get a piece of galena crystal or even a piece of pyrite and fit it into the depression. See if anything happens."

The sun had climbed higher in the sky and any shadows that were on the lawn earlier that morning were long gone. Again, Bergman made a couple of cursory remarks about how nice the house looked. A couple of minutes later, the Ferrari rumbled to life and Bob Bergman was on his way to Tell City, Indiana.

"I sure didn't expect any of that," admitted Jenna as the two of them walked toward the house.

"The man knows stones, not a doubt in the world about it."

"What if he's right, Ben? What if it is some kind of communication tower?"

"I guess the military is not in the habit of digging holes on private property. If something happened out there, somebody outside the military knows what it was. I think I know who that person is."

"Larry Collins?" she asked.

"He's a cautious man, Jenna. I don't think he trusts anyone. He always seems to be holding something back, revealing just enough to keep you interested, but not much more than that."

"He does seem to trust Adrian White," Jenna reminded him.

"Maybe we're too intellectually inferior," Ben laughed.

She shook her head and smiled. "I'm surprised he ever agreed to talk to a couple of corncobs like us."

Chapter 29

A FEW DAYS AFTER Thanksgiving it happened again. Jenna saw them as soon as they came into the library, another vase of flowers on the table, the entire room filled with sweet fragrances. On the table beside the vase was a small yellow envelope addressed in ink to Mr. Ben Manning. Jenna handed it to Ben who hesitated to take it.

"Go ahead, Ben," she urged. "Read it."

Ben slipped a finger into the envelope and opened it easily. Folded inside was a note neatly penned on yellow paper. He read it silently to himself before reading it again out loud.

"'Dear Sir,

Winter jasmine were my husband's favorite and were set each Christmas holiday in this corner of the room.

Yours, Anna'"

"Can you imagine that?" Jenna's tone was slightly contentious.

"What?"

"Seems a little audacious, don't you think?"

"Not at all. She's only being polite."

"Yours, Anna is more than polite. It sounds like she's got a crush on you."

"Come on, Jenna," he smiled. "It's nothing."

"She could have said, Yours Truly or Happy Holidays, something more formal."

He put his arm around her waist and kissed her lightly on the forehead, but drew back suddenly, "Better be careful, we don't want to make her jealous."

"Ben Manning," she shouted. "You *do* think she's flirting with you."

"Maybe a little, but it really doesn't matter, does it?"

"It does matter. She comes and goes whenever she pleases."

"But she doesn't come to see me. She wants the brooch returned."

Jenna went across to the fireplace, got on her hands and knees, and immediately began to search for something.

"What're you doing?"

"I found the brooch here in this niche," and as she spoke, she pushed her fingers into a sunken space on the left side of the fireplace. "There's something here, a small gap . . . an impression, and it looks like it was put there deliberately."

"It's probably a crack in the mortar?"

"She wants that brooch for a specific reason. It's more than a sentimental gift from her husband. I would bet on that." Kneeling at one side of the fireplace, Jenna looked thoughtfully at a space in the buildout just above the cantilevered hearth. There was an indention in a section of the masonry. "Look at this, Ben. Look closely, and you'll see what I mean."

Kneeling beside her to get a better look, he saw it at once. It was stone, not brick as he expected, and cut into it was a space about three inches wide, "It does look like this was intentionally done." He scraped a fingernail across the surface only to see paint flaking off the stone. "This section has been deliberately painted to look like brick, but it isn't really brick."

"That's right, and not easily noticed—deliberately concealed."

"It sure looks that way."

"I think the brooch fell out of this space."

He observed the indention closely before suggesting that there would be no reason at all to keep an expensive piece of jewelry embedded in such an unusual place as a fireplace chase. Shaking his head to show his confusion, "It makes no sense."

"It does if that brooch is more than a piece of jewelry."

"I don't know, Jenna."

"Look at how this is shaped."

"I see that. It could have held missing ornamentation. Maybe even a maker's mark or construction date plate."

"You have to get the brooch from Bergman."

He realized she was serious and knew the only way to silence her curiosity was to do what she said, get the brooch. "It's just plain odd."

"Trust me on this, Ben. I don't know how I know, but I know."

After standing, he helped Jenna to her feet and gave her a hug. "I'll call Bergman and arrange to get the brooch. But I don't feel comfortable with jewelry that valuable in the house."

"I realize that, but this could be important."

Changing the subject, he said, "I have to go to Evansville this afternoon. Do you want to come?"

"I can't. Rikki has two closings, and I need to be in the office. Probably won't get away until after five."

"Okay," he nodded.

"You'll get the brooch then?"

"I'll stop by Bergman's this afternoon."

Around noon, he called Bob Bergman and asked to meet with him. Ben knew that when he saw Jenna later that day she would ask if he had the brooch, so he'd do what he told her he'd do—get the brooch and have it there when she returned. "Jenna has an idea that the brooch is more than a brooch," he told Bob.

"And she could be right," Bob agreed. "I'll be here all afternoon, Ben. Stop by whenever it's convenient."

Glancing at the note Anna had written, he read it again slowly. Jenna was overreacting, and there was something about that he liked. But there was absolutely no reason at all for her to be jealous. With those thoughts still lingering, he was sure he heard someone in the foyer. Deciding Jenna had forgotten something, he went out to meet her. Instead of Jenna, it was Anna Atwood who stood in front of him. His jaw dropped. His eyes widened, and for several seconds, he was frozen to the floor, staring into eyes mysterious enough to momentarily frighten him.

"I did not mean to startle you."

When he realized he was staring at someone who hadn't come in through the front door, he quickly tried to pull himself together and regain his composure long enough to speak. "Hello," was all he could manage.

"Do you like the flowers?"

"Yes, yes, of course, they're quite beautiful actually. Thank you."

"There were always flowers in the house."

"I love flowers."

"Please do not be nervous at my presence, sir."

"It's not an easy thing to relax in the presence of a gho—"

"Ghost?"

"I'm sorry," Ben apologized.

"I can assure you that I am as real as you."

"How do you come and go without using the door?"

"It just happens sometimes. I cannot explain it."

He reached out to shake her hand and saw her draw back. "What is it?"

"Please do not think me coy, so much as vigilant," she said.

He was starting to relax, maybe too easily caught up with Anna's beauty. He reached out again, and this time she slowly extended her hand. He took it in his, shocked at how cold it was. With her hand in his, he looked at her cautiously before saying, "I can't believe this. Can it really be happening?"

Slowly, even reluctantly, she withdrew her hand, but did not lower her eyes from his. "You have a kind touch," she told him, looking deeper into his eyes. "My husband's touch was gentle."

"Excuse me, but I don't know what to say. Even though I want this moment to last, I know it cannot."

"It is possible."

Aware of the mesmerizing effect she was having on him, he could not lower his eyes from hers. Strange as it seemed, he felt compelled to regard Anna with both suspicion and fascination. "You appear so suddenly, out of thin air it seems, and as much as I want to believe and accept it, you must surely realize the improbability of this happening."

"You have touched me. You look in my eyes. You see me standing before you. Is that not enough?"

"I . . . I can't seem to stop my hands from shaking."

Her smile, small, somewhat cautious at first, gradually became bolder, until pale delicate lips parted enough to reveal the tips of her teeth. He'd seen pictures of women dressed this way, thought the long dresses cumbersome and pretentious—until now. But it was his sudden inclination to hold her that occupied his thoughts. Did she know what he was thinking?

"May I ask about your husband?"

"He died in a motor car accident not far from this house."

"I'm sorry. I don't know what else to say to you."

"The young woman is your wife?" she asked.

"Jenna—no, we're not married."

"There are things about this house and its property that you do not know."

Was she asking or telling him? He couldn't be sure. "Yes, I'm sure an old house like this has many mysteries."

"Occurrences," she corrected. "There have been occurrences, and there will be more of them unless . . ."

Her hesitation confused him. It was as though she had second thoughts about saying more. "Unless what?"

"The future has happened beyond these walls on the long field near the bridge."

"Again, I'm sorry to say that I don't understand."

The smell of jasmine became stronger. The sweet scent filled the foyer, and he inhaled it deeply. When he dropped his gaze to look behind him, it happened. Anna Atwood left him standing alone in the foyer, without so much as saying good-bye.

Chapter 30

DURING THE 30-MINUTE drive to Franklin Street on Evansville's West Side, Ben could think of nothing but beautiful Anna Atwood, who minutes before had stood in front of him in a striking blue taffeta gown. He'd been thoroughly enchanted by a woman from another century, a sensational young woman whose age could not have been more than thirty. To deny that it had happened, was no longer possible. He'd touched her, and that was the moment he knew it hadn't been a dream or some crazy hallucination or out-of-body experience. He had seen and spoken with Anna Atwood at length and was admittedly distressed by her sudden disappearance. Unthinkable before, but now very much in his thoughts, was this ardent wish to see her again. He realized only Anna could make that happen.

In orange neon, in a lower window of a two-story brick building that still had intact the original plaster moldings and cornices, the words *Rogers's Rocks & Minerals* was prominently displayed. Ben had driven to Roger's after his meeting with Anna had ended abruptly. About a week earlier, he'd purchased a chunk of galena quartz that Roger had cut to specific dimensions. Though it had set Ben back nearly a hundred dollars, following Bob Bergman's suggestion had seemed a good idea at the time. If it worked, as Bergman expected, then it would certainly be worth the money. Otherwise, it was nothing more than expensive ornamentation for an occasional table or bookshelf in Atwood House.

His brown hair slicked back with gel, dressed in jeans and a tee shirt, Roger was one of those past middle-age men who loved classic rock 'n roll. His voice was deep enough to be heard over Elvis Presley's song, *Jailhouse Rock*, that was playing on a vintage Rock-Ola jukebox located in one corner of the store. He wanted to explain what he referred to as the articulation of the cuts he'd made to the quartz, which Ben thought informative but unnecessary. Still, he listened to Roger's concise explanation.

"It's not the best quartz crystal, but it has good clarity, good cleavage, and the point termination should be good enough. Might be a rough edge or two, but you said that didn't matter much."

"Thanks, it'll be fine."

"I get collectors in here all the time, but they want clusters with great presentation. Don't get much request for galena, though."

"Well, it's just something for a friend," Ben lied.

"Best of the holidays," Roger offered graciously as Ben went out the door with a slight wave over his shoulder, which he hoped Roger saw.

It was cold in Indiana. A super cold front had moved south out of Canada. Weather forecasters were already calling for snow, quite possibly heavy snow. There had been other Christmases not so long ago when snow piled into high drifts along the roads, and covered the roofs of houses in Newburgh and Evansville. Already, several residents from farther north had moved to Florida, just to escape cold weather, and although many were older, there seemed to be a recent exodus of Millennials to warmer climates. With winter a couple weeks away, Ben Manning was eagerly looking forward to the colder weather.

Although Christmas was not just a come-and-go holiday for Manning, it had lost some of its magic. He remembered days when his younger sister and he would sit with their parents in front of an early morning fire. His father had loved the sharp crackling sounds of logs burning in the stone fireplace. Those days were long gone. His mother and father were happy eating Christmas dinner with friends, who like them, had retired to the Florida Panhandle. His sister Beth, who taught English at a high school in Hokkaido, Japan, returned to Florida only briefly during the summer.

He already knew that Jenna would spend Christmas with her family. She had relatives coming from out of town, and said she was "really anxious" to see them again. Already thinking ahead to Christmas Eve, Ben Manning had Mrs. Anna Atwood indelibly on his mind. Never in his life had he met such an enigmatic woman. Her looks were devastating, and the emotion of seeing her so near to him, in a foyer filled with yellow sunlight, had taken hold of him like nothing else in his life.

Ben entered the jewelry store and found Bob Bergman sitting behind a counter of expensive jewels. An ocular in his right eye, he examined a piece of jewelry, which Ben immediately recognized. With no one else in the shop but the two of them, Ben was not sure if the man in the tailored suit even knew he was there. "Hey, Bob, how are you?"

"Ben." When he looked up, the ocular fell to the end of the neck string. "Didn't hear you come in . . . been studying this brooch a little more and found something I can't explain."

"What's that?"

Reaching into a desk drawer, Bob took out another ocular and handed it to Manning. "Ever use one of these?"

"Not that I can remember," Ben smiled.

"It's essentially a magnifying glass with high resolution." He handed the brooch across the counter to Ben. "I want you to look closely at the back of this."

Awkwardly at first, Ben managed to get the ocular fitted in his right eye. "Am I looking for something special?"

"You'll know it when you see it."

Seconds passed before several striations came into focus. They hadn't been incised into the metal but seemed to be raised seams with what looked like several tiny bubbles. "Glue lines?" Ben asked, still not sure what he was seeing through the lens.

"That's right. Why glue, for what possible reason?"

"I have no idea," admitted Manning.

"You said Jenna found this near the fireplace?"

"Yes, that's what she said."

"Well it beats me, but I'd bet that's crystallized glue, and that somewhere around the fireplace you'll find other traces of glue. I can't imagine why though." He shook his head as he spoke.

Ben immediately recalled the space in the fireplace, which Jenna had earlier discovered. Because it seemed such an impractical place to put an expensive brooch, he didn't say anything to Bob about it. Its purpose, if it had one at all, was another of those weird and unexplained things that made Atwood House both unique and mysterious.

"Oh, by the way, Bob, I had a piece of galena quartz cut to size. Just picked it up at Roger's."

"That old boy loves rocks and knows them better than anyone I've ever met."

"He seems anxious to tell you what he knows, doesn't he?" Ben laughed as he reached into his jacket pocket for the quartz, which he handed to Bergman. "I thought you could buff it up, put a shine on it."

"Sure, I'll do it later—don't know if it'll make any difference though. This idea, it's just a hunch, Ben."

"Like you said, it's worth a try. Maybe you could run it out to the house when you get a chance. I'd feel better if you were there."

"I have a couple from Evansville stopping by later this afternoon. They're good clients who usually spend big. They're very particular about what they buy, so I'm sure I'll be tied up with them until late."

"Okay, Bob, whenever you got time. It can certainly wait until after Christmas,"

Ben was in a hurry to get to Atwood House. One thought persisted. Anna was living in his head, a resolute image that could not be shaken loose. Each time he closed his eyes, she was there. He had to see her again and was already praying the brooch held the magic to make that happen.

Removing the brooch from the case, he held it out in front of him. His breathing was sharp and uneven, his entire body tense, and his hands shook as he placed the brooch into the space near the fireplace. To his surprise, it didn't fit. So, Jenna had been wrong. Instantly, another thought struck him. Turning the brooch different ways, attempting to make it fit, he was still unsuccessful and nearly convinced that it had been a crazy thought from the beginning. What if it fit the other way—in reverse? When he turned it around with the gems inside the space, the brooch fit perfectly, and suddenly, Ben Manning was undeniably afraid.

Chapter 31

FIVE MINUTES HE waited, then ten. Standing in one corner of the room, he felt his body begin to relax. Gradually, almost imperceptibly, the room began to dim, everything around him starting to fade. For a minute or longer, nothing seemed real. It was an image seen through a convex lens . . . through a gossamer veil. An image coming to life behind a stage scrim. Atwood House was changing, transforming into another time. Standing motionless, his heart began to beat rapidly. Every muscle in his body tightened as he watched in disbelief the transformation that was slowly occurring.

The heavy mahogany desk was gone. Other furniture seemed to melt into the large oriental rug. The drapes were not the ones he and Jenna had hung. The kind of furniture he'd seen at auctions and in antique shops began to appear, while familiar furniture and everything he remembered about the library was sucked into an invisible vortex. The walls were covered in green wallpaper with a distinct pastoral theme. Afraid he would succumb to the vortex, sink into it and be lost forever, he closed his eyes and held firmly to one of the plaster columns. The world he knew continued to spin insanely out of control.

At last, when he opened his eyes again, he saw at once the fire in the fireplace. The room was hot and smelled of jasmine. It was a room from another century, and still unable to move, he remained as rigid as a black marble statue that stood near the front windows. His entire body continued to shake. No matter how hard he tried, he could not stop the awful shaking. He felt like screaming but managed to put one hand over his mouth.

"Oh, my God," he muttered under his breath. "This is too impossible."

But the impossible soon lost credibility. The impossible was all around him. His memory of the library was quietly vanishing the same way early morning dew evaporates at sunrise. On a table near him was an extraordinary bouquet of flowers, neatly arranged in a beautiful porcelain vase decorated in a motif of pink cherry blossoms. Beside the vase, was a small Japanese dish with coins in it. Hurriedly, he slipped a coin into his pocket, thinking if he made it back the coin would be the proof he needed.

Above the fireplace mantel was a painting of Anna. She was dressed in a black gown with a low neckline. Against her skin was a string of white pearls. Once more their eyes met, and finally he realized that he'd stepped uninvited into Anna Atwood's parlor.

Almost coincidentally, he spotted what he thought was the brooch in the weak light cast by the small fire. He had to recover it. But to his regret, the room began to expand. To retrieve the brooch, he would have to cross this enormous space and walk directly to the fireplace, which seemed dimmer and decidedly farther away from where he stood, hesitating. The first step was nearly impossible. He was even unsure that his legs were still under him—until he felt the edge of a thick rug through the soles of his shoes. Why had walking become so impossibly difficult? He took another step. Floorboards creaked.

Knowing he was being watched every step of the way, he kept his eyes on the fireplace. The eyes in the portrait moved when he moved. After a few more steps, he felt compelled to look at the painting and was shocked when he realized her eyes were missing. The eyes he had admired only moments before were morphing into one enormous eye protruding from her forehead, and where a pupil should have been, was a white light pulsating like a heartbeat. Fear caused him to immediately look for the brooch. The excitement he had felt earlier was gone. He didn't want to be there, no longer wanted to know where there was, even though he knew Anna Atwood might walk in at any moment. He had to get the brooch.

But something was wrong. The brooch was not there, only the indention into which he had placed it, which now resembled a large gaping hole in the side of the fireplace. He was sinking into a hole large enough to swallow the entire room. Knees too unsteady, his legs were going out from under him at any moment. Panic set in, causing him to bump against a chair. Without the brooch, he was trapped there for sure.

A small glint of white light appeared. A reflection coming from a niche below the space where he had inserted the brooch. He decided it must be the same place where Jenna had found it. Dropping to his knees, he recovered the brooch, and after brushing it against his jacket, as if to clean it, he pushed it into the hole. It seemed strange that he had to use both hands to do it. He felt a sharp pulse in his fingertips, like electrical current passing from the brooch to his fingers. At the same instant, the room grew hazy, increasingly indistinct, causing him to draw back, as though he knew what was happening.

Moving as cautiously as possible across the room to the same corner of the library, where he had stood only minutes before . . . he waited. Piano music, someone was playing the piano in an adjoining room. Could it be Anna?

Voices! Soft at first, then louder, as though those speaking were coming nearer. Then, footsteps on creaky floorboards. He knew his discovery was now inevitable and was already searching for words to explain his presence in this early 20th century parlor or drawing room.

Another thought, Anna would recognize him. She was his salvation. She would realize that he had discovered the secret of the brooch. But recognizing him was no guarantee of his safety there. After all, he was an intruder from the future. Then, almost instantly, the thought that Anna Atwood had been several times into his future, the one he had left behind, the future he had sacrificed for a chance to be with a woman who could be two places at once. This thought confused him even more, causing him to realize, despite the impossibility of existing in one place, which was also another place, that Anna had never left Atwood House. It didn't matter if yesterday was today, or even if tomorrow belonged to yesterday. They were somehow connected, and Anna was alive in all three times.

A pulsating shaft of greenish light appeared instantaneously in front of him, causing him to close his eyes. Instinctively, he put up his hands to prevent it from striking him. Then came blackness, deep, silent—sticking to his skin like wet clothes. Easier to get there than it was to get back, and searching for an exit when he'd had enough, was exactly what he was doing now. No exit. This was it—the end to it all. He would never see Jenna again.

But good luck prevailed.

When he finally forced himself to squint through eyes reluctant to open, he expected to see Anna Atwood staring him down. Instead, he was standing in a room filled with vanilla sunlight that hurt his eyes. Unable to focus for almost a minute, he was surprised to see with enough clarity, where he was standing.

Rising out of the floor and barely distinguishable in the haze that was gradually evaporating, familiar furniture gradually took shape. He'd done it. He had traveled in time, despite all those lead-head scientists who said it wasn't possible, that time travel was science fiction, and that anyone who thought it possible was severely uninformed and pathetically disillusioned. These were the great scientific minds, the gatekeepers of all that was sane—the executioners of freethinkers. He'd done what none of them would ever do. Another more disturbing thought quickly took hold of him—a disparaging thought that tempered the euphoria that comes with momentary achievement. Who would believe him, when he said that he'd traveled years . . . decades, more than a century into the past?

As each piece of furniture emerged from the dissipating mist, he continued to think about failure. He was sure Jenna wouldn't believe it. For a few seconds, he drew back, deciding he wouldn't mention it to her, just keep it all to himself, until he could make some real sense of what had happened. Though he was nearly convinced he had traveled to Anna Atwood's parlor, he could not shake loose the possibility of hallucination. Real as it had been, illusion could not be dismissed. The mind was capable of extreme imagination. He recalled how easily he'd found pareidolic images in water stains, and clouds, and how quickly abstraction was converted to specific shapes and forms. Deep inside, he was sure the experience had been real, and now his mind needed time to sort it all out . . . if sorting out the impossible was even possible.

And what about Adrian White and Liz Raymond? Wasn't this the discovery they expected? Wasn't that why they had come to Atwood House, to learn its secrets? What secrets? Ben still wasn't sure what happened, or for that matter, if it had happened at all. Consequences of revealing such an extraordinary event would be devastating. Others would accuse him of lying, think him crazy for telling such a story. There were no gateways or portals. Such thinking was the provenance of science fiction writers. No, he'd stay silent, at least until he had the chance to consider the experience in the light of more practical thinking.

He didn't hear Jenna come in through the front door and was slightly startled when he saw her standing in the doorway to the library. The collar of her long winter coat was turned up, and she unwound a scarf as she looked at him across the room.

"What is it? You look like you've seen a ghost."

He fabricated a small laugh that probably sounded phony. His thoughts still captivated by what had happened to him only minutes before her arrival, Ben became conscious of the darkness that seemed to have come in with Jenna. Sunlight had vanished. In its place were the early shadows of late afternoon. The grandfather clock in the foyer was just striking six o'clock.

"How was your day?" he asked at length.

"Busier than usual. I'm relieved to have it finished."

"You hungry?"

Shaking her head, and still looking at him, she asked, "Did she come back?"

"Who?"

"Come on, Ben . . . Anna. Was she here again?"

"No."

"She'll come again. I'm sure of that."

Trying hard to avoid any further conversation about Anna Atwood, he was finding it too difficult to get the beautiful woman out of his thoughts. As much as he wanted to share with Jenna what he had experienced, he felt such a disclosure would be impossible for her to accept. Another thought prevailed though, and that was that in time, Jenna might be the one person who would believe it all. Nevertheless, he'd wait it out, think it through repeatedly, until he was convinced that what occurred had really occurred. Again, a more sobering thought quickly overtook him—the realization that he'd never traveled to the past at all. That it really had been nothing more than hallucination, or even more drastically, the idea that the past had traveled to him.

"I got the quartz this morning, left it with Bob Bergman to polish."

Jenna came into the room, looked closely at him, and said, "You sure you're okay? You look kind of pale."

"I'm fine, Jenna . . . really."

"Did you get the brooch?"

"Bob was busy with customers," he answered deceitfully. "I'll get it later."

"You'll excuse me for saying this, Ben, but you really seem a little off."

Another manufactured laugh before replying, "Maybe I'm just tired."

"Well I have a surprise."

"What?"

"Liz is in town."

"Oh . . . "

"Have you checked your voice mail lately?" Jenna asked.

He glanced at the message center on the desk. It was blinking red. "Imagine that, I actually got messages."

"Anyway, she's in town for the weekend, staying at the Evansville

Regency. We're going Christmas shopping later—a girl's night out. I hope you don't mind."

"Not at all," he answered warmly. "There's no reason for Liz to stay in Evansville. She knows she's always welcome here."

"Maybe she didn't want to impose, or maybe she just needed some self-time."

"Oh, by the way," continued Ben, "I got in touch with Collins and he agreed to a meeting at his place, kept saying he wasn't sure if he could help much, but seemed willing to tell us what he knows about the time the Young family lived at Atwood House."

"That's good, Ben. I'm sure he knows plenty—probably needs a little prodding is all."

After Jenna had gone to meet Liz Raymond, Ben hurried over to the fireplace. The brooch was in the same niche where Jenna had found it. If there were traces of crystallized glue on the back as Bergman had suggested, the glue had been necessary to keep the brooch in place. Or something else, possibly a photograph had been affixed to the back. Maybe Bergman had been mistaken, and it was not glue but something else entirely. He'd read or heard about women putting perfume or scent trails on jewelry to intensify the effect, possibly the same idea as a pheromone. Quite possibly Anna could have done that with the brooch—maybe a brooch that she had never worn at all.

Chapter 32

OUTSIDE HIS HOME located a mile south of Newburgh, Collins sat near a fire pit, looking at the flames, and blowing smoke rings into a frosty night. Behind him, the yellow glow from the porch light was strengthened by the illumination of a lamp in a large front window.

"Don't know if I can help you much," said Collins, watching them approach before stopping a few feet from the fire.

Logs circling the fire, which had been cut from dead trees on the property, now served as seats. Under a tin-roofed shed, cords of firewood were stacked in several rows. Near the shed, was a log splitter, and several longer logs were nearby in a patch of weeds. The air was crisp and smelled of burning wood.

"We only have a couple of questions, which won't take much of your time," Ben assured him.

"Time and money. Don't have much of either."

Dismissing the man's comment, Manning asked with a directness that surprised Jenna. "Do you know what's buried on the Atwood property?"

"I enjoy the country. Couldn't do this in the city, not legally anyway. But out here, no one bothers you, no one looking over your shoulder shouting out ordinances, got lots of freedom within these tolerable boundaries."

"I think your father knew what it was," pressed Ben. "Maybe he told you about it."

Collins regarded him for several seconds before speaking again. "Maybe it's time to let it go," he whispered, as though about to loosen some heavy weight that had held him down too many years. "There aren't many of us left who know the real story, and anything the government has concluded is nothing but fabrication. Deliberate disinformation—covertly-spread rumors." He looked up at them, and said politely, "Might as well sit down and get comfortable."

Picking up a pointed stick, Collins stirred the fire, which snapped a few times before sparking bright orange. The heat took the raw sting off a cold December night. Sitting on logs close to him, they watched and waited anxiously for Collins to continue speaking.

"The military knows all about the ley lines and the vortexes. What they hauled off the Newland property were pieces of what I think was a communication tower. Though my father saw most of the excavation clearly, he had no clear idea what was loaded onto a flatbed truck. It could have been anything; but whatever it was, I doubt it was a meteor. It's my opinion that the meteor recovery was always the cover story."

"Meteors, ball lightning, and swamp gas tended to be convenient covers frequently used by the military. Even today it's the same storyline." Ben seemed to be speaking more to himself than to the others and was now wishing he had not interrupted Collins so quickly.

"Only when he was hired by the Youngs to conceal a perfectly useable room inside Atwood House, did he begin to take more serious interest in the numerous UFO sightings that were being reported with increasing frequency. He realized something strange had to be going on—something the Air Force had no intention of acknowledging. Since the 1940s, and maybe even several years before that, Newburgh was overwhelmed with UFO reports. The military was routinely aware of these sightings."

Manning seemed confused as he asked, "You're saying the military recovered what might have been a communication tower, which was for some unknown reason in pieces. Then they hauled it away, not as junk, but with the intention of reconstructing it?"

"Possibly," Collins answered. "If it was, think what that would mean."

Ben nodded, "You're right. It would definitely be significant."

"I've seen photographs of what you've dug up near the bridge on the Atwood House property. Dr. White showed them to me. I don't know if it's the same thing the Air Force recovered, but don't think so."

"What do you mean?" Jenna asked.

"My father made drawings of what he saw. Pieces had been laid out on the ground, and there were several of them. I remember him saying each piece cast a pink hue, especially at night. The only way to hide the light was to put the pieces under heavy canvas tarps."

"Do you have those drawings?"

"No, Mr. Manning. They were destroyed by my father when word got out that one of the military officers suspected he had them. From my recollection, what you found does have a few similarities to what the military took away."

"Well, actually there's nothing certain about anything we've considered.," Ben admitted. "But you could be right. If it is a tower, a communication tower, that creates an entirely new scenario. Who put it there, and why?"

"There's talk about the discovery in Shanklin's pond. You're probably aware of it." Collins said.

Hesitating to reveal what they saw that night with Liz Raymond, Ben intentionally kept his response concise and noncommittal. "Heard the Shanklin brothers were draining the pond, digging it deeper to restock it with game fish. I didn't really think much about it."

Collins leveled a look at them, gave a slight nod, and said with an abruptness that neither expected, "Like the two of you, and that psychic, Dr. Raymond, I was there the night they found it. I saw it all, but still don't have any idea why anybody would get excited about a big rock, and even stranger is its reason for being there at all."

Jenna caught Ben's arm. "Yes," she clarified, "we saw the thing in the pond, nothing more than a huge rock like you said," she conceded.

Already in the last minutes of twilight, the night, coming out of the northeast, would soon consume the distinctly jagged tree line that looked like a shaded relief cut into a small expanse of periwinkle blue sky. The lone star Sirius glittered white near the tail of a chalky moon. Shadows around the fire deepened, and the breeze seemed suddenly colder. In the flickering firelight, they could make out the smile on Collins' face.

"What was it we really saw in the pond?" asked Larry Collins, without looking away from the flames. "It must have had a purpose."

Before another word passed among them, there was a huge clap of thunder loud enough to shake the bones of the dead. An explosion of white light as radiant as any Sunday morning sunrise, streamed out of a crease in the night sky. And for almost a minute, they watched in disbelief.

Time for atonement! Time to fall to your knees and pray, or at least drop to your knees and repent a lifetime of sins. Time to ask forgiveness. God have mercy on a world of sinners too stubborn, too proud to kneel. No atonement for those without humility, even if it was Armageddon above their heads. How incredibly soon the End of Days had come, and not even the sanctified meteorologists had predicted such a catastrophic event. Hallelujah! The righteous were ascending. Time to praise the Lord. Although the Golden Gates were opening, there was confusion about who the righteous really were. How perplexing, and yet sublime, to be among ascending angels.

None could deny this miraculous opening of the heavens. Each saw the blue shimmer of water, and not one of them could determine how such a spectacular night could fall apart so suddenly. The three of them huddled together, looking upwards into another time and place. Somewhere, someone had opened a portal. Astonishing as it was, there had to be another, more earthly explanation. What that could be, they could not imagine. Ben thought about holograms cast on a black sky, but knew this had nothing to do with holograms. As strange as it was, what they were witnessing was impossible to dispute and even more impossible to comprehend.

At the edge of a long green field, pushing up against a grove of small leafy trees, was the vacillating image of a church with a modest white steeple. Close by, the indistinct image of a large house. Like melting wax, the image began to dissolve, and in seconds after it appeared, it disappeared. In its place was a starry sky with a crooked moon low on the eastern horizon.

Several seconds passed before Collins spoke in a clear calm voice. "Opening a portal is one thing. Controlling it is another. If they can accomplish that, then the world as we know it will never be the same. I have to admit that I never thought it was possible." After a lengthy pause he added, "I recognized what we saw."

"What?" asked Jenna.

"Yes," Collins replied, "it's a place I've seen before."

Ben was not so quick to believe him. "You can't be serious."

"The church, the stream, and the vague image of a house, all appear in a photograph we discovered among some pictures taken by my grandfather," Collins said. "If I'm not mistaken," he continued after pausing slightly, "we've had a glimpse of the parsonage, which was on Atwood property near where the stream runs into the woods, not far from where a church stood."

"Incredible." Ben stared hard at Collins. "You're serious, aren't you?"

Collins nodded slowly. "Apparently, the parsonage became dilapidated and was left abandoned when the pastor moved to Evansville."

"What about the church?" asked Jenna. "We saw a church."

"Yes," continued Collins, "there was a church farther back, near the Shanklin property. It apparently burned down, but I'm convinced there's more to that story. I'm sure the foundation or part of it is still there, and it shouldn't be too hard to find exactly where the church stood, if you're interested."

"I just can't believe this," admitted Manning. "It's too outrageous."

"Seeing is believing," assured Collins.

"Or, believing it is seeing it," Jenna suggested.

"I can assure you," Collins went on, "that if you look, you'll find the old Baptist Church foundation. It's out there. I remember my grandfather saying how people were afraid that the fire would spread across the dry pastures into the woods, and even into town."

"You say the church was on the other side of the stream, near the woods?" questioned Ben.

"About 200 yards north of the bridge, I think. I'm not sure how the property lines run back there, or for that matter on which side of the stream it was built."

"You've been very gracious, Mr. Collins," Jenna said politely, "and what has happened here tonight, as remarkable as it was, could be an omen, an indication of stranger things to come."

Collins nodded, "But this is not the work of God. On that, I stand firm."

"Amen," whispered Jenna loud enough for both men to hear.

Chapter 33

NOT IN THE past ten years had there been snow as heavy as this in Indiana. Weaker fronts had come and gone, leaving little more than an inch of snow, which was not enough to last through Christmas Day. People who remembered were comparing this storm to the blizzard that had dropped more than six inches of snow on the Evansville area. Twelve years ago, two days before Christmas, the temperature had descended into the teens, and on a bitterly cold Friday evening the fat heavy snowflakes began to fall and didn't stop until New Year's Day. To date, it had been one of this area's heaviest snowfalls.

With temperatures still above freezing, three inches of snow already on the ground and more on the way, it would be a spectacular white Christmas this year, a winter wonderland across the entire state. Many stores in Newburgh and Evansville didn't close their doors until after midnight. Fires burned in the brick and stone fireplaces in the stately homes along the Ohio River, white smoke rising into a blackberry sky, looking like mist, before dissipating into the darkness. It was the kind of day that made the world a lonesome place and Ben Manning felt that loneliness deeply.

The snow was coming out of the north where earlier there had been a trace of orange trying to push through. It had been there only a minute before the heavy gray door slammed shut, before the entire sky went black and sullen. As he watched from the window, a black shape came into view. A thin figure dressed in a long black coat, narrow at the waist, full at the hemline, she was a vivid silhouette cut from the desolate sky behind her. Head bent, a statue chiseled from winter sky, the woman stood motionless on the bridge in a shower of swirling snow. She wore no hat and locks of dark hair hung loose around her collar and down her back. Only once did she look up, before letting her gaze fall across the snow in the direction of the woods surrounding Shanklin's pond. Never had he seen such a lonely and melancholy image as this striking figure standing so dismally still.

Instinctively, he hurried into the library, took a camera from one of the desk drawers and returned to the living room. Pushing the curtains aside, he snapped off several pictures of the woman who was still on the bridge, only now under a black umbrella. It was Anna. It had to be Anna. Without even trying to understand, he pulled on goulashes and took a heavy winter coat from the foyer closet. Hurriedly, he wrapped a woolen scarf around the collar. Removing gloves from his coat pocket as he went out the front door, Ben could hardly wait to be near her again, and gave no thought to the snow falling heavy and silent.

The first blast of cold air stung his bare face and felt like flakes of ice in his lungs. In snow that was becoming increasingly deeper, each footstep was cumbersome. His breath was coming harder with each step, causing him to stop twice to catch his breath and steady himself. Surprisingly, the closer he came to the bridge the easier it became to walk. Even his breathing was more controlled. Stopping behind her at the opposite end of the bridge, his eyes fell on the numerous buttons that ran in a straight centerline from just below her neck to her waist. Her damp hair, partially bound by a red silk ribbon and tied well below her shoulders, was covered with snowflakes.

"Anna." He was shaking again, not so much from the cold as from the fear that at any second, she would disappear and nothing he could do or say would stop that from happening. "Dear, Anna." His voice was louder this time, surer, and he knew she heard him call her name. "It's Ben . . . Ben Manning. I saw you from the window."

When she turned, he felt his body shudder even worse than before. Snow was on her eyelashes and on her collar and shoulders. Her eyes had a distant look and for a moment he was unsure if she saw him standing ten feet away from her. Her lips looked as though they had been drawn with the fine tip of a pencil. Never had he seen lips so delicate. The upper lip was a perfect cupid's bow trailing off in lines so fine that they were barely visible as they reached the corners of her mouth. Surely this woman realized her striking beauty and the effect it had on others. But there was something more to Anna Atwood than her stunning good looks. He'd seen once before in her eyes this strength of character and boldness that could intimidate.

"I hoped you would come," she smiled.

"You must be freezing. How long have you been out here?"

"I do not know how long."

There were no footprints anywhere around where she was standing. Again, how could she so suddenly appear like she did? Somehow, Anna Atwood had a way of traveling through all those years, even if she denied how her transits into the future were accomplished or even possible. Nevertheless, there she was once again, only this time standing calmly, seductively in a flurry of snowflakes.

With snow continuing to fall around them, the sky darkening in every direction, an eerie silence far off in the trees was creeping closer, stilling the wind, which earlier had scattered white mists in the air. Strangely, and much too regrettably, Anna seemed farther away from him than she really was—a shadow so ephemeral that it lacked strength enough to survive at all. Still, even with snow falling between them and the closing darkness leaving ghostly images to inhabit this somber winter landscape, Anna Atwood was as real as the stones that held the bridge together.

"I come with a warning, Mr. Manning." Closing the parasol, and placing it on the bridge, "It is for your safety I speak."

Her voice was flat without the slightest hint of emotion. He'd heard recorded messages with more emotion. A sudden blast of frigid air brought him to his senses. Whether deliberate or not, she was building a wall between them, using blocks of ice cut from the frozen stream beneath the bridge. She had traveled all those years into the future only to put a wall of ice between them.

"Warning! What warning could you possibly bring, especially from so many years ago? Please excuse me for asking so abruptly."

Dismissing his ungracious and chiding tone, she answered resolutely without being disrespectful. "I implore you to return the brooch before it is too late."

"Too late for what?" pressed Ben.

"For both of us, and others like us." Turning slowly and pointing to the thing dug from the ground weeks ago, and covered now in a layer of snow, she said, "That is not what you think, Mr. Manning."

"You know what it is?"

"There are mysteries of many years ago still buried in the dirt. Things you would not believe even if I revealed them. Incredible, even monstrous things that should never have happened."

"If they are monstrous as you say then you must tell me what they are, Anna."

"A monster stands there in the snow, a resurrected monster."

He looked to where she was pointing and realized the thing dug out of the ground concerned her greatly. She seemed to fear it as a sinister presence. But even beyond her fear was a deeper emotion, and that emotion was anger.

"Why does it disturb you, Anna?" he asked deliberately.

Before speaking again, she looked away from it and glanced at Ben. "It is a thing that was forever dead and buried."

Even after a pause that allowed enough time for thoughts, Anna hesitated to explain her remarks, which Ben found frustrating, considering that she knew what the structure had been or had represented. "I'm truly sorry if seeing this thing, whatever it is, distresses you, but it has interest to friends of mine who are scientists."

"In the beginning it offered hope," she finally disclosed. "It soon became a punishment cast upon us by a vindictive God."

"I tell you that it remains a mystery to us."

"A mystery is not always solved so easily in any time."

"Yes, I know that." After taking a step closer, he asked, "The markings, do you know what they mean?"

"I cannot explain them," she answered. "My purpose was only to caution you, and to request that you return the brooch."

He started to tell her that he'd used the brooch and knew of its uncanny powers, but quickly bit his tongue. More important than either the brooch or the villainous thing rising out of the snow, were emotions he could no longer suppress. "Surely you know how often you are in my thoughts." Stepping nearer, until they were no more than inches apart, the impulse to touch her surged through him like volts of electric current. "As extraordinary as such words must seem to you, I profess my thoughts openly."

She laid her hand gently against the sleeve of his coat before speaking. "We are as different as two stars in the heavens, and as far apart."

"The human heart has no boundaries, Anna."

He took both her hands in his and for the first time since that afternoon when they had stood this close in the foyer of Atwood House, he finally saw in her eyes what he had longed to find there. Was she at last beginning to feel that such an extraordinary relationship as theirs was possible, even if her words continued to contradict what she felt? Or, in those deeper, more constrained recesses of her mind, were thoughts there incapable of moving the spirit, existing only as indelible imprints on the brain, leaving impressions that had absolutely nothing to do with love? If only what he saw in her eyes was a glimmer of hope.

"And can the heart alter time's immovable boundaries?"

"You stand here before me now, not a shadow, not a memory, but as beautiful Anna Atwood. Your hands are in mine. I can see myself in your eyes."

"Please, Mr. Manning," she protested, withdrawing her hands from his.

"I've stopped considering the improbability of such a wonderful thing as this and find myself hoping with each day that passes that your presence here will never come to pass."

"So nice those words, which are spoken at a time when I am most vulnerable."

"I say what my heart encourages me to say."

As snow fell silently, he reached out once more for her hands, only to be disappointed when she turned away. "Anna, please believe me when I tell you how very sorry I am for what has happened in your life . . . for what has saddened you so deeply."

"You do not know, sir the severity of such pain."

Ben Manning drew back, wishing now that the coldness would turn every word he'd spoken to her into ice. Turning back into the snow, leaving her words frozen in the cold space between them was all he could do. Once he got back to Atwood House, he'd make a fire, hot enough to melt the heaviness now in his chest. Mrs. Anna Atwood could pack away her sorrows and return them to where they belonged, away from where he lived. His thoughts of such a place were like the icicles hanging from the railings of the stone bridge—long empty years filled with pitiless despair.

A few feet from where she stood was a snowman, wearing a black hat and scarf. It was Anna's husband frozen on the landscape of one of the blackest days Ben could remember. Before lifting his boots out of the snow, he shot a look of absolute disdain in the direction of the snowman. Though he realized it would survive in the bitter cold that had swept across the area, there would come a day when one of God's brightest suns would destroy it.

"Please do not turn away from me, Mr. Manning. What I have said has offended you and for that I am deeply sorry, but . . . "

"You come with this sadness of so many years, and it's a sadness I do not want in my life," Ben said seriously.

Her words came behind small puffs of white air, which stuck much too long to this miserably cold day. His boots were filling with snow, a heavy snow ready to cover first his footprints and then him. If he waited longer, he would become a reluctant winter friend for the snowman Anna had made. Jenna would find him a frozen statue staring into the black icy sky that was suspended low above the Ohio River.

But, like far-off echoes, there were tender words waiting, and they had the strength to slowly melt this offending cold. He could hear ice cracking, breaking into pieces, melting warm in silver puddles that trapped her reflection. He could not turn away from lips so perfect, eyes so deep. But on one of winter's coldest days, Ben Manning was agonizingly conscious of all those summer suns between them.

Anna regarded him closely as she spoke, "I will not deny that I wanted to see you, and there are feelings I cannot disown—feelings I want to confide."

The air was warming again. Where had winter gone? Snowflakes melted before they hit the ground. On the distant horizon, a glimpse of sunlight, which looked artificial. The snowman leaned a little to one side in this space that was no longer winter. Ben wanted it to melt and run off into the creek, wanted it to flow beneath the bridge and into the trees where Shanklin's pond would swallow whatever was left of it. The sunken eyes made from two dried leaves the color of coal and bent at the tops to look like eyebrows, regarded him suspiciously, he thought. The nose, two broken and twisted twigs, was elevated just enough to give the face a haughty countenance. Two crooked arms, branches from a patch of rhododendron growing near the bridge, flailed out in Ben's direction as though they were reaching for him.

"Yet, there is a deep fear that causes me to hesitate," she admitted.

"Then you must listen to your heart, Anna and speak those words you know are there."

"Although the loneliness in my life is harsh, you have been undeniably in my thoughts."

"Every minute of every day I think of you, Anna. There, I've said it. But you and I are too much apart, like you have said, and I know there is nothing I can do to change that."

"It does not have to be that way," replied Anna.

"But it is. You draw back when I reach out to touch you."

"Only because I do not know what is happening to me."

"You are as ephemeral as the snowflakes in your hair. Nothing I can do or say will change that."

"I wish I were not so alone. Surely you understand what it means to lose someone," she told him.

"Yes, I know that sadness. But you are so many years away from where I'm living . . . so very far away, that I cannot comfort you."

"You are a sensitive man, Ben Manning. It is in your eyes, and your words are kind and honest. I am at ease with you and must find a way to show you my feelings."

"How can such a thing as this be possible? As often as you are in my thoughts, there remains a darker foreboding reality I can't ignore," he said.

"Ben."

Someone was calling him, a voice that sounded far away, muffled by the snow, which was once more falling harder across the bleak and dismal landscape.

Turning away from Anna, he saw a figure trudging through deep snow, calling out his name and waving with each step. A red scarf became bolder as the attenuated shape came nearer.

"Ben," she called again, one arm raised above her head to get his attention.

But behind him, someone else called his name—faint, distant, a faltering whisper lost in a piercing wind.

"Anna," he yelled. "For God's sake, speak to me, sweet Anna." But his voice was unheard—empty in so much snow.

"Ben," shouted Jenna again from one edge of the bridge.

With his head down, he turned away from the snowman Anna had made, turned his back on Anna, who was nothing more than a fading shadow against a frozen background of dead words and cold desperate shadows.

Chapter 34

CHRISTMAS EVE, AND Ben Manning sat in front of a roaring fireplace, enjoying music of the season. In the soft light of a tall Christmas tree that he and Jenna had decorated, and as the fire snapped across new logs, Ben felt his body unwind. Atwood House was silent. Nothing stirred in any of the many rooms. With Jenna spending Christmas at home, Ben soon realized that alone at Christmas was too much aloneness.

A couple hours earlier in the evening, he thought about catching a flight to Florida, to spend a few days with his mother and father. But they had their own lives now, so he would just be in the way. His mother wouldn't be cooking a big meal, and his dad wouldn't be basting a turkey, and Christmas Day wouldn't be the kind of day he would remember. It was okay though. They were happy and that's what really mattered. Besides, he hated to fly in bad weather.

But there were ways to minimize aloneness on Christmas Eve. There was always television and if he looked long enough he'd find something he liked. But television didn't feel right on this sacrosanct night. Church did. Newburgh Presbyterian Church was holding candlelight services at seven o'clock. Since he had nothing to do, he'd pull himself away from the cozy fire to spend an hour sitting among people whose faith was more devout than his.

The church, only a ten-minute drive from Atwood House, was the oldest church in Newburgh. As he climbed the stone steps, he was surprised to see Millie Stewart talking with two other ladies in huge hats. She had a large smile and her eyes were sparkling with the magic of Christmas. Under a sky full of stars, a few men stood to one side of the steps talking in whispers. Each time the doors opened, organ music spilled out into the night. Though he was known by many in Newburgh, he knew very few people, and when someone called his name, he hoped it was one of the few he did know.

It was Bob Bergman coming up the steps behind him. Ben turned to see both Bob and his lovely wife, Julia, and waited on the top step long enough to say hello. Bob, wearing a striking camelhair overcoat was holding his wife's hand, and both smiled as they ascended the steps toward him. He'd met Julie Bergman a few times and thought her a bit standoffish.

"Merry Christmas," he said cordially, shaking both their hands.

"Merry Christmas, Ben."

"Season's Greetings, Mr. Manning," smiled Julia Bergman as she passed into the sanctuary.

Though Manning was not a member of Newburgh Presbyterian Church, he did occasionally attend Sunday morning services there. Jenna had managed to convince him that he needed a stronger spiritual self, that he would be right with God if he attended church. Jenna and her family were in the congregation at the United Methodist Church on the other side of town. The Newlands were a close family, and though they would certainly not have objected to having him attend church with Jenna, Ben felt this was one of those nights when families worshiped together.

Ben strongly believed in a Savior who died for the sins of mankind. He also believed it was man's inherent nature to sin. There was no perfection attached to mankind, or to "humankind" as the politically correct preferred. God dealt constantly with the imperfect. Many of the righteous imperfect attended church regularly and prayed fervently for God's forgiveness, even blaming a benevolent God when they realized the tenaciousness of sin. Absolution remained deep in the shadows of human frailty. The imperfect did the best they could, but inevitably offloaded their sins on the doorstep of a God who was their only hope for redemption.

No matter how often Ben attended church, no matter how many times he listened to learned men preach the Word of God, and no matter how often he prayed, usually for the healing of the sick, the protection of children, and for a peaceful existence in a world that was, as Manning saw it, spinning off its axis with hate, no matter how many prayers, Ben Manning remained convinced that he didn't need an ordained minister to intercede for him. As a boy, he was heavily churched at Zion Evangelical, a small white church in the woods filled with small-town people, most of whom were farmers. Sitting in the back of this small church with his friends, he heard repeatedly that there was no forgiveness unless it was through Jesus Christ. Jesus was an intermediary and through Jesus, God lived in each of those who strongly believed that praying to Jesus guaranteed an audience with the King.

The historical figure of Jesus Christ, who died that horrific death on the cross so that the sins of mankind would be forgiven, had long been a source of agitation for Manning. If Jesus had been God's only son and not an ordinary man, a prophet with a fiery temperament, then the miracle of His resurrection did happen as the Gospels proclaimed. But among churchgoers there were doubters, many of them believing that Jesus Christ had been a religious man who accepted and portrayed Himself as the anointed Son of God. Without doubt, Manning so often thought that religions had the power to brainwash, and accepting verbatim religious dictates, too frequently stifled critical thinking.

Jenna had told him several times that faith had no conditions. It was commitment, unbridled love that filled the heart with hope. Christians, filled with the spirit of Jesus Christ, seldom questioned their faith. They prayed to Jesus Christ of Nazareth who took their prayers to God. Manning remained skeptical of Christ's intercession with God, too often thinking that he could find salvation through God without asking Jesus to do it for him. Though he wanted deeply to believe in the Savior, Jesus Christ, he hesitated. Jenna had been right when she said he needed a stronger spiritual self, and he would continue to ask for God's guidance. Ben was a man afraid of what came after these few earth years that for him were a lifetime.

"Merry Christmas, Mr. Manning."

It was Millie Stewart, coming down the aisle with two ladies in big hats. She stopped long enough to shake his hand. In her eyes was the spirit of the Lord, and it showed brighter than the candles burning on the oak chancel table.

Manning's smile was genuine, as he held her hand a few seconds longer than was necessary. "How very nice to see you again, Miss. Millie. Merry Christmas."

"These are my sisters from Tell City."

"Welcome ladies. I hope each of you has a very, very merry Christmas."

The ladies giggled and pushed off toward a pew at the front of the church.

Christmas Eve services were always special. Coming in out of the snow to find a warm sanctuary filled with candlelight engendered memories of better times, and allowed time to reflect, and recall the trials and tribulations of a man who either assumed the role of Savior or was without denial God in human form. The improbability of Jesus Christ's birth on the 25th of December no longer mattered to Manning. This was a night to proclaim that birth, and for an hour on this holy night that was all that mattered.

Another couple of inches of snow had fallen during the service. The Christmas Eve landscape was washed in moonlight. Standing in the cold for a few minutes, he glanced up to see Larry Collins coming down the steps. When their eyes met, Collins gave a slight wave, which Manning returned. He was grateful to Collins for information he and Jenna had discussed several times. If Collins was to be believed, then there was still much to do, still many questions that had to be answered. But with so much snow on the ground, anything buried under the lawns at Atwood House would have to wait, probably until spring. Collins had mentioned a church foundation at the north end of the property, and if remnants of a foundation still existed Ben Manning would locate them.

Chapter 35

AT A FEW minutes before nine o'clock, Manning opened the door to the sweet smell of flowers. Thinking maybe Jenna had slipped in and left the basket of red poinsettias on the foyer table, he went over to see if she had left a note or card. Nothing. But the strange weave of the basket caught his attention. It was undoubtedly old, with traces of red paint visible on one side. Maybe she had found it in one of the antique or thrift stores downtown. The more he looked, however, the more he became convinced that it was not something Jenna had left at all.

After hanging his coat in the foyer closet, he locked the door and went to the kitchen to make coffee. But when he got there, the lights were on and a couple of empty bowls were on the counter. From the kitchen, he could see into the dining room, and saw immediately flickering shadows on the walls. If this was Jenna's doing, he could not have been more surprised.

A candelabra set in the center of the table had long white candles burning. Candlelight was the only light in the room. The table had been set for two, with places fixed at opposite ends. On the credenza, a large bouquet of flowers had been arranged in a pink vase that looked Japanese. If Jenna had put all this together while he was at church, it was a surprise he would never forget.

The scent of jasmine in the room was weakened by another scent, which smelled fresh, like the smell of rain. She had wiped the dust from the furniture. Each piece glistened in the soft candlelight, chairs, the china cabinet and credenza, each shining bright as the Christmas Star.

"I hope you like it," she said from the doorway across the room. "Merry Christmas, Mr. Manning."

"Anna."

"It is such a beautiful night and I was so much alone. I hope you will forgive this impertinence."

"I don't know what to say."

"Please, I hope you are not upset. I wanted to surprise you."

"And you certainly have done that." Looking across the dining room table through glimmering candlelight, he said in words barely audible, "Merry Christmas." The words sounded far away and reminded him of those faint sounds bumping and ricocheting off the stone walls of cliffs he had climbed as a boy in Bristow. But these words were spoken here, in front of a woman who had left her time to spend Christmas with him. Or, was he, instead, in her time?

"You are alone tonight?"

"Jenna? She's with her family."

"I realize how impulsive you must think me."

"No, Anna, it's—"

Before he could finish, she held up a brightly wrapped Christmas present accented with green ribbon gathered into a bow. "This is for you."

She brought the present around the table, stopping so close to him that the alluring scent of jasmine took hold of his senses. With every breath, the fragrance got stronger, until he realized the provocative aroma was having a calming effect. Standing in front of him, offering him a Christmas present, was this striking woman from another time. For several seconds, their eyes met, and the deeper he looked, the more sadness he saw. Once again, the impulse to hold her was strong. If only he could kiss away the awful sadness, tell her he was the solace she was seeking.

He'd been so overwhelmed by her presence that the brooch she had pinned to her dress had gone unnoticed until now. It looked like the one Jenna had found—the one Anna had asked him to return. She must have seen him staring at it. If she did, she said nothing. Why had she stopped asking about it, he wondered? She surely had not forgotten about her request to have it returned.

"Thank you. Thank you very much. How could I ever anticipate such a wonderful thing as this?" Trying hard to put words together while Anna looked at him, he was barely conscious of the present he was holding."

"Please open it," she said tenderly.

Setting the package on the table, he unwound the ribbon and carefully set it aside. The wrapping paper was stiff and had pictures of Santa Clause standing in snow among evergreen trees on a hillside. Santa was dressed in the familiar long red robe with white trim that he'd seen in drawings of Victorian Santa's. Slowly, not wanting to tear the paper, but also looking at the strange way the package was wrapped, he glanced at Anna, who was smiling. After setting the paper aside, he noticed that the plain white box had a small green envelope with his name on it. It was attached with a spot of melted wax. He freed it from the box and opened carefully the lightly sealed envelope. Removing a card bordered in holly leaves and red berries, he was conscious of his hand shaking, conscious of Anna's smile, conscious of the seductive aroma that filled the dining room.

Dear, Mr. Manning,

I would appreciate greatly if you would wear this for me tonight.

Yours, Anna

Folded neatly in the box was a dark tailcoat, beneath which he found a pair of gray trousers with vertical black stripes, a heavily starched white shirt and a black silk tie. Except for the shoes and socks, it was a complete set of gentleman's formal wear from either the late 19th or early 20th century. Though he could not accurately date the clothing, the one thing he knew with certainty was that they were the kind of clothes he'd seen in old photographs. He was astonished . . . speechless—jolted so visibly that he was sure Anna noticed.

"You don't like it."

"No, it's not that at all. It's only that I never expected such a gift."

"My husband was such a particular man about his clothes. I bought this the year it happened, before he had a chance to wear it."

Again, as though it was a burden too heavy to manage, she was remembering her husband's accident while looking at Ben, as though she wanted to talk about it but was unable to do so without being emotionally distraught. During the few moments he looked at her, he was again jealous of her husband. The accident had occurred a lifetime ago, and there had been too many sorrows in Ben's own life for him to anguish over Anna's grief. Even though he felt her pain, he drew back momentarily.

"If it fits, I'll wear it," he smiled.

Fifteen minutes later, standing in the dim light of the foyer, Anna Atwood watched Ben come cautiously down the stairs, and without taking her eyes off him, waited until he was standing on the last step before speaking. "William," she sighed.

Completely shocked by her words, he said nothing.

"Let me straighten your collar. Your tie is crooked," she said, walking over to where Ben stood, still dazed at her obvious confusion.

"Anna, it's me, Ben Manning."

She put the back of one hand across her mouth, and there was a small gasp as she backed away. She managed to get the words out at length. "I am so sorry, Mr. Manning; it is only that you remind me very much of my husband."

Trying to break the despair that had taken hold of Anna, he asked, "How do I look?"

Again, she put a hand across her mouth, but this time to keep from laughing. "Handsome. Quite proper really." Her eyes brightened. "It is a handsome fit, I think."

Standing in his stocking feet, he held one foot out in front of him. "It feels nice to be a proper gentleman, even without shoes."

Anna was wearing a dark purple dress with a low neckline accentuated with tiny pink flowers. A string of pearls against her skin danced like all those sunny reflections he'd seen in the water near the stone bridge. She cut a stunning image, one that left enduring impressions. Turning away from him, she walked toward the library as though these movements were perfectly natural. After all, it was a house in which she was very much at ease. Standing near the fireplace and gazing into the lingering flames of a small fire, which had burned low while he was at church, it seemed to Ben that she was reminiscing again, and he knew immediately there were consequences with that, like that day at the bridge, and he didn't want to experience Anna's sad recollections again.

After replenishing the fire, he said, "Let me get you something to drink, Anna. I'll only be a few minutes."

"Thank you."

It was taking him too long to decide what to bring her, so he took out a gallon of cider and warmed a pot of it on the stove, poured the hot cider into two white mugs and returned to see her standing in the center of the library, as though she was taking in with interest everything around her. Ben placed the tray on the desk and watched as she continued to look curiously around the room.

"You have so many beautiful things." Speaking about the beige couch, she said, "It is large and quite comfortable."

The recessed lights in the ceiling seemed to fascinate her. She looked at them and then at the desk lamp that Ben switched on, only to back away a step or two when the light filled that part of the room. The telephone, the computer, the television, all these caught and held her attention. She was like a child fascinated by things which seemed unfamiliar to her. Slowly coming over to where Ben stood, she looked under the lamp shade, but quickly turned away from the bright light.

"Here you are, Anna, warm cider. Why don't we sit on the couch where you'll be more comfortable?"

The rustle of her dress caught his attention momentarily. For a few seconds, he thought about his own appearance, which to Anna must have seemed quite normal, but to him, extremely confining. Wherever she went, she left behind a trail of perfume, soft aromatic overtones that were very pleasing to Ben.

"Merry Christmas, dear Anna, and thank you again for these fine clothes."

Sitting next to him on the sofa, her hands folded in her lap, she was smiling and seemed much at ease with him sitting so close. "The young lady, you like her?"

"Jenna is a very nice person, and I like her very much."

"You will marry her then?"

"We've never discussed that."

"I envy her."

He took one of her hands in his and held it a few moments before speaking again, "Don't you know how I feel about you, Anna? Can't you see it in my eyes? It's in every word I speak to you."

She put her other hand on his. "The strange frightening occurrences that have taken hold of my life remain most difficult for me. Our time together is little more than moments."

"But you're here now, and there's no danger. There is nothing to frighten you."

Withdrawing her hands from his, she looked at him desperately, as though she was thinking thoughts he should know. "You cannot deny that our time together is regrettably little more than stolen minutes."

He knew instantly she was right. They were living their lives on borrowed time. From the beginning, it was an improbable love affair with too many years between them. No matter how much they wanted to be together, there were so many irresolvable complications. Moments were all they had and moments could never be enough for either of them.

Anna Atwood was a young woman still grieving for her husband, and not even Ben Manning could silence the pain she was forced to endure. Yet, she came through all those years to see him, and each time she did he felt his heart slipping away. She was such a fragile thing, sitting years away from the world she knew. If there was anything at all keeping her from slipping farther into melancholy and despair, it had to be the rooms in Atwood House, and just maybe—Ben Manning.

Chapter 36

SHE LEFT HIM sitting on the couch in front of a dying fire. It was long after midnight when he walked into the foyer and caught a glimpse of himself in the mirror. At first, he was a little shocked to see the reflection of a "proper gentleman" as Anna had called him. He smiled when he wondered if Anna's time could ever be his time. Would he be at ease in her time, comfortable without the modern conveniences of modern society?

It was Christmas morning. In church steeples everywhere, bells heralded the miracle of Christmas. Even heathens and atheists could hear the bells ringing boldly, proclaiming ecstatically the birth of Jesus Christ. No one knew where these anti-Christians lived, maybe in the house next door, or down the street near one of the churches. But they were surely there somewhere, living in the houses of Newburgh, Indiana, and their hands were no doubt covering their ears. But the bells kept ringing—kept right on ringing in their ears and clanging in their heads, and though they seethed with anger they were forced to endure the awful bells. There was no judge to proclaim a violation of church and state. There was no escape from the bells on a day as holy as this. Regardless of political correctness, church bells rang loud, not just in Newburgh, but in cities and towns everywhere.

Still dressed in the clothes Anna had given him, he went into the dining room with a mug of fresh coffee, smiling as the bells continued to clang. His one great hope was that the bells were banging so loud in the heads of the nonbelievers that they were unable to eat breakfast or read the manufactured morning news or watch television news commentators stretch the perimeters of the television screen with phony journalism.

Using a white linen tablecloth and dishes from the rosewood china cabinet, Anna had set a beautiful formal table. The candles had burned into extinction, but the table was so attractively set that he pulled out the heavy chair at one end and sat down to think of her.

It had been a Christmas Eve to remember. Anna was a profound enticement, the kind of woman never forgotten. Although their Christmas Eve supper together hadn't happened, Ben went over the words that had passed between them. He tried hard to imagine what Anna must have felt, sitting not on one of those stiff settees, but on a couch with soft cushions. When she looked around the house, she might have considered herself a piece of old furniture among so many modern things. This thought alone caused anxiety, but it was not a thought to which he gave any real credence. Inside the walls of Atwood House, there was a perplexing strangeness that Anna could not possibly comprehend, and more than likely confusion still reigned in her thoughts, wherever she was on this bright beautiful Christmas morning. At least those were Ben Manning's early thoughts, his presumptions on this snowy Christmas morning. Only once did it occur to him that these presumptions might be inaccurate.

"Good morning, dear Anna," he said softly, looking across the table to the empty chair at the other end. "Merry Christmas, sweet beautiful Anna. How much I wish you were here."

And those church bells kept ringing in steeples everywhere. How loud! How resounding their message. And heathens and atheists must be going crazy as the bells continued to reverberate in their sanctimonious ears. Except for the noisy church bells, there was a great oppressing silence in the dining room. For a few moments, he considered using the brooch. He'd done it once and it had worked. Why not again? What was she doing this Christmas morning? Was she with friends? Was she sitting alone with thoughts of her husband, or maybe even thoughts of him? Was she warm? Was she smiling? Was she wearing the same dress? Did she walk the halls of Atwood

House, hoping to catch a glimpse of him? Maybe she was traveling to a friend's house where she would spend Christmas Day. Wherever she was, would she think of Ben Manning who was so many, many years away from her?

"Anna Atwood, why did you ever come into my life?"

The emptiness in Atwood House remained cruel and painful. The empty chair at the end of the table was nothing more than a piece of furniture. In the doorway behind it, a small ray of sunshine lasted only seconds. Grayness was everywhere. Even the windows in the library had long lines of gray that for some strange reason reminded him of highways he had traveled.

His feet were cold. He laughed out loud. What a sight he must have been when she saw him standing in his stocking feet on the stairs. Remembering her smile, he shook his head as though it hadn't happened at all. But it *had* happened. Her heart had beaten here in the dining room, only hours ago, and he knew she would return. She would come again, and maybe again, and he'd be there waiting.

He heard the front door open and close. but sat there unable to move, unable to think clearly. Who would visit so early on this gray Christmas morning?

"Ben," she called. "I have a present for you."

"In here, Jenna."

She stood in the doorway staring at him in disbelief. "Ben Manning!"

"Merry Christmas," he said softly.

She came up next to where he was sitting. "I don't believe this. It's her. She was here." She saw the note Anna had written on top of the wrapping paper. "Really, Ben."

"It's nothing more than a note, a Christmas card."

Jenna put the Christmas present on the table in front of him. "This is too impossible to accept. I suppose she set the table, too?"

"She's a lost soul, Jenna."

"Can't you see what she's doing? She's making you into her husband, Ben."

"The clothes were nothing more than a Christmas present."

"No, they are much, much more than a Christmas present. The clothes are Anna's way of owning you."

"Come on, Jenna. You're making too much of this."

"Am I?"

"Yes."

"Ben, listen to me. Anna is trying to make you the husband she lost. Why can't you see that?"

"You're confusing me. All I know is that she asked me to wear these clothes, wanted to see how I looked in them, nothing more than that."

"There is more to it than that." Jenna's voice was softer. "Why don't you look at me when I'm talking to you?"

He turned his head and saw the hurt in her eyes. "I'm sorry. I don't even know who I am anymore."

"This whole thing is impossible, and yet, it continues to happen. It's beginning to frighten me, Ben. What if her intentions are not what you think? What if there is something evil motivating her?"

"Jenna, please, I admit it's more than I expected. I don't pretend to understand her motives. But to say she comes with malevolent intent, I just can't believe that."

"Or maybe you don't want to believe it." She took the wrapping paper that he had folded neatly, the green ribbon, and along with the card, which she returned to the green envelope, put them in one of the credenza drawers. "Let's put these away for now. They'll be there for as long as you want them."

He nodded. "It really is beautiful wrapping paper, a lot better than that cheap Christmas paper that always tears when you cut or fold it," he said, managing a slight smile.

Dismissing his comments about the wrapping paper, she asked, "Can you even imagine how lost, how absolutely alien she would feel in a world so different from hers? Even though these are the same walls, it's what's in the house, Ben. Kitchen appliances, a washer and dryer, a vacuum cleaner, photographs of people Anna never knew, the Internet, none of it would make sense to her. Can't you see that?"

"I saw it last night in the library. She was confused, lost in this space that no longer belongs to her."

Outside in the streets of Newburgh, in the streets of cities everywhere, church bells rang even louder. The Holy Spirit was walking on the sidewalks, walking down the streets shouting, "Hallelujah!" And the anti-Christians, those who had no faith, the misinformed, the heartless self-righteous nonbelievers were turning up the volume on their radios and televisions, pulling their blinds and curtains, hoping to stop the confounding bells from ringing across this crisp icy Christmas Day. But the bells kept ringing. And there was nowhere for these angry hypocrites to hide. They kept their ears covered, hoping the walls of their homes would continue to stand against the ringing of the Christmas bells. But like those stone walls of Jericho, these walls, too, were beginning to crack.

"I brought lunch. Why don't you change your clothes and help me in the kitchen? It's not much, but I was hoping you might join us for Christmas dinner later today."

He nodded, "Thank you for the invitation, Jenna," and with indifference he was sure she noticed, he turned away from her. His decision to hang Anna Atwood's Christmas present in the bedroom closet was very much on his mind.

"See you in the kitchen," she yelled as he climbed the stairs.

But someone else was waiting, and she was holding a large butcher knife. On the counter was a platter of roast beef, which Anna was slicing thin as Jenna came into the kitchen. For a moment, Jenna was startled, but regaining control of herself quickly, she stared at Anna contemptuously.

"You have to let him go, Anna."

"No, I cannot."

"Anna, please. Ben is not your husband. You want something that can't happen—something that is not possible."

"There is too much sorrow in my life. You cannot understand the coldness around me each day."

"But the answers you seek, the consolations, they are not here."

Anna lowered the knife, turned toward the doorway, and while church bells rattled the town of Newburgh, Indiana, Anna Atwood vanished into thin air, leaving Jenna Newland a little shaken.

When Ben came into the kitchen, he was wearing black slacks, a white shirt and striped tie and a gray sports coat. “I always liked to dress a little for Christmas.”

She came up to him and gave him a hug. “You look nice.”

“Didn’t expect to see you today. I thought you’d be with your family and friends the entire weekend.”

“I made some time for you. I even left a voicemail on your cell about dinner this evening.”

“Thanks, Jenna, I think I left my mobile in the car.”

“Please don’t get upset with me, Ben, but have you thought maybe this house is no longer what you expected . . . maybe it’s not right for you?”

“Truthfully, I don’t know what to think. There was no way to anticipate any of this strangeness. I won’t deny how strongly this house has hold of me.”

“I never told you what Rikki Whitman said later that day after the closing.”

“What?”

“She said the reputation that went with Atwood House was bigger than the house itself. I didn’t think much about it at the time—but she was right, Ben.”

“I’m sure all old houses have reputations of one kind or another.”

“Rikki really did believe, not only what was said about the house, but also what was written about it.”

“Maybe she knew something,” returned Ben.

“Maybe.”

The God-doubters stood on their sidewalks, some shoveling snow, others looking disdainfully in the direction of Newburgh Presbyterian Church, or Newburgh United Methodist on Old State Road, or toward any of the other churches whose bells took away the serenity of their unholy morning while continuing to ring and clang incessantly inside their pompous heads. Hate festered like sores that wouldn’t heal.

"I appreciate this more than you know, Jenna."

She knew he wouldn't join her and her family for the evening meal. But with some help from Ben, Jenna prepared green beans, mashed potatoes and gravy, cranberry, and hot rolls. They would supplement the few slices of roast beef Anna had left behind. Though hurriedly prepared, Ben realized how thoughtful it was for Jenna to think of him and take time away from her family. Although he hadn't expected it, he found Jenna's company to be just what he needed.

"Excuse me a minute," and with that, she left the kitchen, only to return seconds later with a package wrapped in red and green candy canes. "I hope you like it."

He knew there were presents under the tree for Jenna, one he'd bought a few weeks before, the other more recently. They could wait a few minutes. The package she'd brought was heavier than he expected. After shaking it slightly, he put it back on the table and carefully began to unwrap it, trying not to tear the paper. He glanced at Jenna long enough to catch the anxious expression on her face.

"Don't worry about the paper, Ben."

"Just taking my time," he smiled.

"It was one of those spontaneous ideas," she acknowledged with obvious satisfaction. "Lacey helped me with it."

On the table in front of him was a large book with *Atwood House* embossed in gold leaf on the front cover. At first Ben was puzzled, that is until he opened the book and saw photographs of Atwood House. "A scrapbook."

"You really like it?"

"It's very thoughtful, Jenna."

"We took pictures as the house was cleaned, a before and after portfolio. It's a makeover of Atwood House in pictures."

"What a great idea." He hugged her and kissed her on the cheek. "Thank you very much."

"Glad you like it."

"I have something for you under the tree."

In the library, beneath the Christmas tree, were a couple of packages with her name in bold black letters. He reached for the smaller one, and handed it to her, saying, "It's certainly not as creative as the present you gave me, but maybe you'll like it."

"I'm sure I will." After unwinding the red ribbon and setting it aside, she unwrapped the package and found two tickets for dinner and mystery theater on the Ohio River Queen, which was a renovated paddle wheeler traveling the Ohio and Mississippi Rivers. It was anchored in Evansville during the entire month of January. "What a terrific idea."

"And here's what goes with it."

Excited to see what he meant, she hesitated, trying to think what was in the second present. Then shaking it, she shook her head. "I don't hear anything."

"It's in there," he smiled.

She peeked inside before removing the lid, only to find another smaller box, which she opened at once. "Oh, Ben, they're gorgeous!" She took the pearl necklace out of the box and held it up to the light.

"Bob Bergman recommended them."

"Ben, I never expected anything so nice."

"I want you to know how much I appreciate everything you've done. I'm not talking only about your work here. There's been no one closer to me than you, no one. I could never thank you enough."

"What a spectacular gift, elegant, and yet simple enough to wear with just about anything."

"A special gift for a very special person," he replied tenderly.

"I absolutely love them." She kissed him passionately on the lips. "And you, too, Ben Manning."

Someone else was in the house, waiting for her chance to speak.

Chapter 37

IT WAS A couple of days after Christmas when Ben went into town to get the galena crystal, which Bergman and not delivered as expected. "How was your Christmas, Bob?"

"Expensive. I'm glad it comes only once a year." He came around from behind the counter and shook Ben's hand firmly. "How'd Jenna like the pearls?"

"Great recommendation. They look spectacular on her."

"I got the earrings to go with that strand of pearls."

"Maybe for her birthday."

He went back around the counter and took out a decorative black box, placed it in front of Ben, and lifted the lid. "Perfectly matched, symmetrical, no chalky spots or wrinkles, 95% unblemished, tremendous luster, and they're a perfect match for the necklace. I'll wrap them up if you want."

"That's some pitch."

"I'll tell you what I can do. I'll sell them to you less 40%, and that is a terrific price. I'll guarantee these come from some of the best pearls on the market, Japanese Akoya white 10-millimeter beauties. To tell you the truth, I forgot I had them, or I'd have pitched this set when you bought the necklace. They belong together."

"Okay, Bob, you talked me into it."

"Great buy, Ben. You want them wrapped?"

"Keep it simple, will you?"

"I got something else for you."

"I can't afford anything else."

Turning his back to Manning and opening the door to a large wooden cabinet, he took out the galena crystal, unwrapped a white cotton cloth, and then set the crystal carefully on top of the glass counter next to the earrings. "All polished and ready to go."

"Great."

"I was going to bring it out after I closed the shop, but since you're here . . . "

"I'll definitely wait until you're there before I do anything."

"It might be nothing more than a long shot."

"Let's give it a try and see what happens," said Ben with a hint of enthusiasm.

"Okay."

"It's going to be cold out there tonight."

"I'll wear my boots," Bob laughed. "Should be pretty with a full moon."

After Bob finished wrapping the earrings, he inadvertently glanced out the window to see a young woman in a long black coat looking inside the store. She seemed intent on something, but what it was Bergman couldn't determine.

"Thanks again, Bob," said Ben, ready to leave.

"Do you know her?" Bergman asked.

"Know who?"

"The woman outside the store." Bob nodded toward the window through which the woman was still staring. "I don't know how long she's been there. I thought it might be Jenna."

"Probably a tourist in town for the holidays—maybe just window-shopping."

"She's not looking at any of the displays. She seems to be staring at you, Ben. You sure you don't know her?"

"I haven't seen her before. A bit curious though, isn't it?"

Before the conversation continued, the unknown woman turned away and even when the two men went over to the window they could not see her anywhere. She was there one minute, gone the next.

Even outside the store, there was no one on the sidewalk in either direction, except for Dale Bedford who owned the corner antique store, and he was shoveling snow.

"We'll see you around seven o'clock if that's all right."

Bergman nodded. "See you at seven, Ben."

Later that same day, he took the painting of Anna from the closet and put it on his easel, ready at last to paint Anna's face as he remembered it. Although he still had reservations, his decision to complete the painting was decisive. Since Christmas Eve, her face had been embedded in nearly every thought. He'd watched her expressions, more than once looked deep into her eyes, and when they had sat next to each other on the couch, he saw the way her hair had been pulled back to make the features of her face even more pronounced.

His brush moved easily across the canvas, each stroke and swirl of paint suggesting confidence and determination. The lightness in his fingertips allowed the brush to glide without hesitation, until the face he thought he knew well began to emerge from behind the veil. Every brushstroke was made from memory. Texture, color, both came easier than he expected. But the eyes, he could not finish the eyes, and what he was looking at now were two small whorls of black paint. Yet, they seemed to stare at him, eyes without pupils, vacuous spaces that left him distressed and disappointed. For some unknown reason he could not paint away the blackness that had taken hold of him in a macabre, even sinister way.

Ebbing was the excitement he'd felt earlier. Setting the brush down, he was conscious of a slight trembling in his hands. Why had the steadiness that had guided those same hands earlier left him now? Again, he picked up the brush, but each time he lifted it to the canvas, his hand continued to shake.

The portrait was pulling him in, controlling his thoughts, silencing his voice. It was asking for honesty, integrity, demanding propriety, and the authenticity of each brushstroke, while decisively proclaiming existence—legitimacy. The brush was being guided by an unseen hand. Or was it too soon to paint her eyes? He wasn't escaping from this precarious hold she had on him, so much as he was attempting to understand it. Again, who was Anna Atwood?

The veil! He'd lifted the veil, and she didn't want it lifted—not until he knew with certainty that it was Anna Atwood's face he was painting. That had to be it. She had told him that only when his fingers had lifted the veil would he see the truth, the impossible truth. Anna was beginning to control him like Jenna had said, and he was unable to resist or loosen her hold on him. How was such a thing possible?

The room was empty. Or, was it empty?

"Anna," he called, looking at each corner of the library. "Anna," this time his voice was louder. When the grandfather clock in the foyer began to strike four o'clock, the chimes reverberated throughout the lower floor of Atwood House. But except for the chimes, the house remained ghostly silent.

When Jenna arrived later, at a few minutes after six, Ben was sitting in front of the computer staring hard at a photograph of William and Anna Atwood. On the desk beside him was the newspaper photograph of Anna that Jenna had given him. As she came up behind him, he seemed to be comparing the two photographs.

"She *is* pretty," Jenna acknowledged.

"There's something in her eyes that I can't figure out."

"Like what?"

"I've been looking at her photograph for almost an hour, trying to discover what it is about her eyes that not only confuses me, but also frightens me."

Jenna leaned over his shoulder and looked closely at both photographs before saying, "Look at the backgrounds. They're not the same, yet her expression is identical in both images."

"You're right. But there's no reason for the backgrounds to be the same."

"It's like she was sitting in one of those studios that have changeable backdrops. You know, pick the one you like and slide it into place."

"But these photographs had to be taken at different times in different places."

"The clothes, the expression, the pose, even the tilt of her head . . . all identical," declared Jenna.

"Well, one thing's for sure, Jenna."

"And what's that?"

"The secrets in her eyes are not secrets she's trying to conceal."

"Then, those secrets define Anna Atwood."

"To a large extent, yes," Ben agreed. "The more I look at her expression, the more I'm convinced she knows something we should know. It's as if she's seeing our time clearly, but not her own."

"Well, she has been in our time, Ben, more than once," Jenna reminded.

"No, it's bigger than that. I want you to see something." He took from the center drawer of the desk a manila folder, which he opened so Jenna could see what was inside. "I think you'll find these photographs interesting."

He laid four monochrome photographs out on the desk. "These four men were much ahead of their times. Each to a large extent dealt with the future. Undoubtedly you recognize Nostradamus, Edgar Cayce, and Nikola Tesla, but maybe Srinivasa Ramanujan is a face not so quickly recognized."

"Okay, you got my attention."

"Look closely at their expressions."

"Unsmiling, serious, confident, maybe a little outside themselves," concluded Jenna.

He added the photograph of Anna to the mix. "She fits in nicely, don't you think?"

"You're saying Anna Atwood is a prophet . . . a savant?" she asked.

"I think she has seen the future, knows to some extent a future which you and I have not experienced." He paused long enough to let Jenna look more closely at the photographs. "It's in their eyes. Although each is looking at the lens of the camera, there's something more, something much bigger."

"There are definitely striking similarities," admitted Jenna.

"Each one is looking beyond the camera lens. They are looking into the future, Jenna."

"I suppose it's possible. There are those with reputations, people ahead of their own times."

"It's no longer a secret that our government continues to conduct studies and experiments in the areas of remote viewing, time travel, or interdimensional travel, and much more. Many of Nostradamus' quatrains have in fact been realized. Tesla and Cayce both saw the future long before it happened, and even today, mathematicians continue to be amazed at the accuracy of Ramanujan's equations."

"You really have been busy, haven't you?" she joked.

"I've been painting."

She saw the easel, and the canvas covered with a cloth. "You've finally finished her portrait."

"Not quite."

"Well, may I see it, please?" she asked excitedly.

Removing the cloth slowly, he saw Jenna's expression change from one of anticipation to anguish. He felt her hand clutch his arm, as though she was trying to turn him back toward her. "I haven't decided if I want to finish it, or for that matter, if I can finish it."

"The eyes! What have you done to her eyes?"

"Nothing, I left them unfinished. There's no reason to be upset."

"Look at them, Ben."

When he put the cloth over the painting, it must have smudged paint higher up on the canvas. The fresh paint around the eyes, which caused the unpainted eyes to bulge out of the canvas, inadvertently gave the entire face a distinctly freakish appearance. Realizing immediately the reason for Jenna's distraught reaction, he wanted to explain that he'd not decided how to paint the eyes, but said instead, "It's a rather unnerving portrait."

"If I didn't know better, I'd swear this was deliberately done, just to frighten me."

"It's nothing more than paint smudged in all the wrong places."

Jenna looked hard at him before speaking again. "I can't wait for you to finish painting her portrait, and, furthermore, why should her eyes be more difficult to paint than all the other eyes you've painted?"

"They shouldn't—but they are."

"Why can't you just paint a pair of normal everyday eyes?"

"Sorry, Jenna. I didn't expect that. It's a bizarre coincidence, and not done intentionally. Besides, her eyes are not everyday eyes."

"When she's looking back at me with eyes I understand, I'll feel a lot better about things."

Bob Bergman arrived precisely at seven o'clock. When Ben opened the front door, Jenna beside him, neither recognized him at first. Bundled in a heavy winter coat, gloves, galoshes, and a hat and scarf, he looked like he was ready for a trip to the Arctic.

"Is it really that cold, Bob?" Ben asked.

"It is. Better wear long underwear if you got any." Bob kicked the snow from his boots before entering the foyer. "You have the crystal?"

"It's right here in the closet." He handed a box to Bob while he and Jenna finished putting on their winter gear.

"How are you, Bob?" Jenna asked.

"I guess I'm as anxious as you guys to see what happens," admitted Bergman who smiled and reminded her that the idea remained nothing but a hunch. "Quite frankly, I don't know what to expect—if anything at all."

Ben was just slipping into his boots, when they heard a noise in the kitchen. "It's nothing," he assured them, "all kinds of noises in this old house."

Jenna said, "Sounded like someone opened and shut a drawer."

"Maybe one of the ghosts is in the cutlery drawer," Ben joked.

"Not funny, Ben," she answered, slipping into her coat, then winding a scarf around her neck.

With Ben and Jenna carrying flashlights, the three made their way to the tower, which at night took on extreme surrealistic overtones. Standing out against the sky in a space between the trees and against the low moonlit horizon, the thing looked as if it had legs, arms, and a head leaning to one side. A light snow was falling, and the closer they came to the bridge, the more excited they became. Bob carried the galena crystal in a cardboard box, which he set in the snow when they stood before the edifice that only days before had offended Anna Atwood.

Ben shined his light in the direction of the bridge, until the snowman was trapped in the yellow beam. It was still wearing the hat and scarf Anna had left behind. Cruelly attacked by a few hours of sunlight that had covered the landscape during the past week, the snowman still leaned heavily to one side. The dead eyes looked directly at Ben, leaving him somewhat distressed. To say this was a pilgrimage taking on the appearance of ritual, might have been the case to any clandestine observers. But it was only the three of them in a night full of stars, and standing with their backs to the moon, each wondered if anything unusual was about to occur.

Chapter 38

IT WAS A wonderfully clear evening in Saint Meinrad, Indiana. Walking Einstein and Smith stood in front of a huge rock which had no remarkable features other than its size. Although Smith had no idea what to expect, Walking Einstein hesitated to reveal information that might explain to Smith precisely why they were there.

"This is where it's going to happen then?" asked Smith evenly.

"I don't know."

"Well let's get it over with if you don't mind."

"If the trinity is complete, then we'll see it happen."

"Trinity?"

"The signal must be triangulated. There have to be two other transmitters present if it is to happen."

"You're sure about this?"

"No, not entirely," answered Charlie indifferently, "but it makes sense." After pausing a moment, he added, "There's always the risk of proximity though."

"Quit talking in riddles," shot Smith. "What the hell does that mean . . . the risk of proximity?"

"There can be hallucinatory effects on the brain. Perception can be affected by proximity of light transmissions."

"In other words, what we see might be nothing more than hallucinations—that is if we see anything at all?"

"Possibly."

Another three feet of the larger rock had been uncovered, and the sandy soil dumped at the far end of the ball field. With the new excavation, the large rock had taken on a slightly tapered bottom. In the moonlight, the vein of quartz that circled the base of the rock glistened enough to show a clearly defined circle. Inside this circle, Chase laid down several quartz crystals and then pressed a larger crystal into the fissure.

"What do we do now?" asked Smith.

"Wait."

"That's it?"

"And watch the sky," Charlie said easily.

"Watch for what?"

"You'll know it when you see it—I think."

While Smith and Walking Einstein continued to wait and watch, Ben Manning held in his hands a piece of polished galena crystal. Those doubts that existed before were still present. Standing in snow, a cold wind cutting into them, each was having second thoughts.

"I'll do it," asserted Jenna, and before either Ben or Bergman could protest she attempted to fit the crystal into the space. "It seems to fit perfectly," she smiled, backing away and looking at both men confidently. "So now we wait for something to happen."

And almost immediately, while the three of them looked at each other in disbelief, something did happen. A bolt of green light shot high into the sky. Another, thinner line merged with the heavier line to form an apex. Much to their surprise, a thick green line slowly joined with the other two, until the three intervening lines formed a distinct triangle, the center of which was directly above their heads. Covering the ground all the way to the woods, and pushing deeper into the trees toward Shanklin's pond, a wash of dim greenish light became visible. But that was not the most shocking occurrence, not by any stretch of imagination. It was the thing in the sky above where they were standing that took away any hint of satisfaction or accomplishment, a UFO caught for a few seconds where the three beams of light converged.

On the ball field at the Abbey, Smith gazed into the sky with astonishment. "You've done it, Charlie."

"A trinity is complete. Like I said, X-ray eyes."

Smith had a handheld GPS that marked the coordinates of the area beneath the apex of the triangle. "Got it. You got to remove the quartz—quickly. We have what we need to proceed."

When Charlie took the quartz from the large rock, the three bands of green light faded and then disappeared, leaving the sky just as it was minutes earlier. Methodically, like one who had performed a ceremony he was just now concluding, Charlie Chase took up the several smaller crystals and returned them to the canvas bag, into which the large crystal or "trigger stone" had already been placed. He smiled at Smith who was still looking at coordinates on the GPS.

"You mentioned a trinity."

"Yes . . . it took three transmitters to open a gate."

"That means someone else knows."

"Possibly, or it could be entirely coincidental."

"You already know how I feel about coincidences."

"They do happen," Charlie told Smith.

"Not in my business."

If there was any real euphoria that night it was in Newburgh, Indiana where the three pilgrims regarded each other through the light snowfall, each wondering what had just occurred. For no longer than 30 or 40 seconds, they had seen something spectacular. Not one of them knew what had happened on this frigid December night. But something they did had caused it to happen. They'd figured something out, but didn't know what, only that the polished piece of galena quartz had caused spikes of light to appear in the sky. As confusing as the beams of light were, it was the UFO, that in some strange unexplained way seemed connected to the light, that had caused the most commotion.

Early the next morning, a convoy of military vehicles and equipment passed through town. Ben immediately became suspicious. People were already talking about a possible military presence. The convoy did not stop in Newburgh, however, but continued east on the French

Island Trail. Although it didn't happen often, there were times in recent years when military personnel on maneuvers had used this section of Route 66, traveling either to or from the National Guard Armory in Evansville.

With both Bergman and Jenna working, Ben knew what he had to do. Lifting the cloth from the unfinished portrait of Anna Atwood, he observed it for several seconds, thinking Anna had either tried to guide or deceive him. Looking again at the two photographs, he was convinced that the answers remained in her eyes. There was no deception intended. It was not so much about painting the ethereal, as Ben had imagined, as it was about painting the absolute truth. Ben had wanted Anna Atwood to be the ethereal, and that was why he could not paint the reality she was. It was in the photographs of her. That was the reason her expression was the same in both photographs. She was revealing the truth about who and what she was, just as she tried to do when she had told Ben that the veil she had worn had been a mourning veil—a veil of circumstance. Anna had asked him to lift it and said that he must recognize the impossible before he could paint what she had not tried to hide. The veil was the barrier between them—a barrier of space and time.

At least now, the portrait could be completed with assurance that it was Anna Atwood's face. It took less than an hour to put it right, only 60 minutes of painting to capture the depth of her gaze. She was not staring into her own century, but into his. He knew that now. It was in the two surviving photographs of her, but what she saw, he couldn't even imagine.

Ben recalled what had happened the night before, and previously, on that night at Larry Collins' house when the man had mentioned a church that once stood near the woods north of Atwood House. Both Collins and Anna had spoken of something in the ground, something that shouldn't be there. The sudden thought that Larry Collins knew, or at least suspected the truth, struck him as odd. Ben also recalled Liz Raymond's comments about several undulations she'd noticed. There was still a critical aspect missing. The portrait of Anna Atwood would have to wait just a little longer before it was finished.

Pulling on his boots and slipping into his winter coat and gloves, he grabbed a walking stick out of the foyer closet. Outside under a swollen gray sky, Ben Manning followed the stream northeast. Near the edge of the forest, the stream flowed past a tall cliff face until it disappeared into the deep woods. Although snow still hung heavy on the trees, there were several patches of bare ground, especially in large areas where the weeds grew tall. If there had been a structure somewhere near the woods or stream, there should at least be pieces of a foundation surviving, as Larry Collins had disclosed. After an hour of looking, first in areas where the ground was more exposed, and after poking the walking stick into the snow, he was cold and ready to return to Atwood House.

He thought it was a tombstone sticking out of the weeds. About 30 yards closer to the apple trees, but farther north, he brushed away a light covering of snow, to find several pieces of limestone, which could certainly be part of the church ruins. Without a shovel, uncovering larger sections would be slow going. He was convinced he'd found indications of an old building. Taking ten steps in one direction, then in another, and finally ten more steps in a new direction, he eventually found stone slabs, most pieces flat against the ground. If it was a church foundation, what did it mean? Did it have any real contemporary significance? During the summer and fall, the foundation would have been hidden in the thick broom sage and easily missed. No one really walked out that way, so again the foundation would have remained undiscovered, and even if found, who would have thought much about it?

After uncovering about three feet of what he was sure was foundation, he thought about the parsonage that Collins had mentioned. Maybe this was that foundation, and he hadn't yet found what was left of the church. Walking back to Atwood House, one thing was abundantly clear. If he was going to continue the search, the snow would have to be plowed away. Ben hoped Matt Jennings would be available to do that. He felt sure Collins had a reason for telling him about the church, but he had no immediate idea why it was important to locate where it had stood.

"With all the snow on the ground, there's not much surveying going on around here," Matt said. "But we're staying busy with plowing and removal for now. You say you want to run GPR on a piece of property farther back?"

"Property north of the house near the woods. It's not a large area."

"Are you building back there, or trying to locate something?"

"I've found what looks to be remnants of an old foundation," Ben revealed.

"That's curious. Didn't know there had been anything back there."

"I guess there used to be an old house, and possibly a church on that part of the property."

"I've heard some talk about that from Keith Owen down at Owen's Hardware. According to his father, there was a small church somewhere near the stream, which apparently burned to the ground a long time ago. Anyway, not much we can do with all the snow still on the ground, unless you want me to clear it."

"No, it's not that urgent," replied Ben.

"We can do it when the snow melts, or if you're not in any big hurry, we can wait till spring," suggested Matt.

"Let's at least wait until the weather breaks. I'll call you as soon as we get a couple of good days," assured Manning.

Ben wanted to ask Matt about the thing in Shanklin's pond. He thought it might have some connection to what had happened the night before when three bands of light were visible in the sky. But this didn't seem like the right time to discuss it. The meaning of it all, Ben couldn't determine—not yet anyway.

An Internet search turned up a 1901 article in the *Evansville Courier* that reported a church fire north of Newburgh with causes unknown. Witnesses reported hearing a loud noise after which flames appeared at or near the church. Since it was so late at night, and after fighting a large brush fire the day before, volunteer fire fighters were abruptly awakened from their sleep and equipment was slower than usual to arrive at the scene. The end of the article mentioned a brief military presence after the fire had been extinguished.

Standing in front of the finished painting of Anna Atwood, he stared long into her eyes. The mystery that was Atwood House was in front of him. Of that, he was now certain. Continuing to look in her eyes, there was a sudden and troubling apprehension that something was wrong—still unpainted, a salient aspect, which his mind refused to see. Again, maybe he had painted what he thought should be there, instead of what *was* there. Retrieving the two photographs from the desk, he held them up next to the portrait, studying intently the eyes in the photos and the eyes in the painting. The eyes in the painting did not belong to Anna Atwood.

Nearly 20 minutes passed before he saw it. Anna was not so much looking at the future as Ben suspected when he had painted in the eyes. The longer he looked at those eyes, the more confident he became that his initial presumption was a shocking misperception. The eyes in both photographs communicated a message he hadn't considered—until now. Though he finally saw what was there with undeniable clarity, there was something deeper, something much more profound, and it was frustratingly perplexing. Anna didn't possess those extrasensory capabilities associated with Nostradamus or Edgar Cayce. Anna had already seen the future. There was no doubting it. There it was manifest in the photographs of her, fixed forever in her eyes—and it was unequivocally real. Anna Atwood *was* the future.

Chapter 39

HE HAD TO see her again. A month had passed without a sign of Anna. Even Jenna thought it strange. Still cold, the only snow that remained was in small icy drifts in places where the sun seldom shined. Matt had surveyed the foundations of both the parsonage and what Ben was convinced was the church. Remaining at both sites were several limestone rocks, which distinguished what remained of the foundations. With most stones embedded a few inches below the topsoil, there was no point in exposing them. The GPR readings did, however, show the approximate size of the church, which was small and most likely like those white clapboard churches that still existed, particularly in small towns.

Further research revealed that it had been a Baptist church, and that the pastor lived alone in an adjacent parsonage. Records showed both church and parsonage construction were completed in 1900. The church was destroyed by fire only a year later. The parsonage, though not destroyed, was heavily damaged, and the property eventually abandoned. Ben was glad to have these additional historical data pertaining to Atwood House and its surrounding property, if for no other reason than to get a sense of the bigger picture.

One of Manning's New Year's resolutions was to accept more commissions from those who wanted portraits painted. He would still have plenty of time for landscapes but realized portrait painting generated a rather steady income. It was Jenna who, after seeing the finished portrait of Anna, which now hung in the library, persuaded him to advertise in a couple of local periodicals. "After all," she had told him, "that portrait of Anna Atwood is pure genius." Like an art critic anxious to comment, she was convinced that it was "the eyes" that made the portrait work.

It was early Thursday evening. Ben was napping on the couch in front of a low burning fire, while one of Brahms' Brandenburg Concertos played on the radio. At first, he paid no attention to it, dismissing the voice as the announcer's. But Brandenburg Concerto #3 in G major was still playing. Twice more, a faint whisper near him prompted him to sit up and glance around the room. He expected to see Jenna but was surprised to find the room empty. He called out Jenna's name and waited for her to answer. Maybe she'd just come in and was still in the foyer.

Walking across the room to lower the volume on the radio, he thought he had caught a glimpse of Anna Atwood. With the music muted, there was only the silence of Atwood House pressing in around him. Even an hour of silence in a house as big as this was beginning to wear on his nerves. He never thought that possible. He bought the house, thinking silence a prescription for sanity. Maybe Jenna was right. If there was inspiration inside these ancient walls, it was still hiding in the closets and under the stairs, still waiting to be discovered.

When his mobile phone rang, it startled him momentarily. It was Jenna. She and Lacey were on their way to Atwood House. Though he was surprised that Lacey was coming with her, he was relieved that soon this monotonous silence would loosen its relentless and wretched grip on him. He waited for them on the front porch, waving as the car came to a stop in a gray twilight.

Dressed in winter coats and woolen scarves, they hurried up the steps eager to get inside out of the sharp chill that still held the broader Evansville area in its grip. Lacey wore a tam-o'-shanter appropriately tilted to one side, with a matching pair of red mittens, which gave her a charming schoolgirlish appearance. Lacey was perky and always completely sure of herself, qualities much admired by Matt Jennings who had been dating her.

"How you been, Lacey?" he asked politely once they were all inside.

"Busy, busy, busy," she admitted. "School is kicking me pretty good. But after eight years, mostly night school, I'm graduating this May. Hurray! Hurray!"

"And then what? Are you still doing the drama thing?"

"Not anymore. Too many big heads. Too much ego. Social work seems to be a better fit for me."

"Well, congratulations. I know it'll all work out for you."

The three of them sat around the kitchen table drinking coffee that Jenna had just made. Lacey told them she was "a little uneasy," as though she was being observed by someone she could not see. As she tapped the table top lightly with her fingers, she seemed focused on someone in the dining room. "Who's that?" she asked abruptly.

Ben, sitting with his back to the dining room, looked across the table at Lacey. Jenna, who sat between them at the end of the table, looked at Lacey and then at Ben, as confused by Lacey's sudden reaction as he was. Remembering Lacey's flare for the dramatic, Ben was prepared to ignore it—until he saw her pointing toward the dining room.

"There's a woman standing in the doorway behind you," announced Lacey.

Startled, Jenna drew back and glanced again at Ben, who turned in his chair to see Anna standing exactly where Lacey had said—in the door to the dining room. She reached out as though she wanted Ben to take her hand. "You must destroy it," she said. Before Ben could say a word, she was gone.

Lacey poured herself a fresh cup of coffee and shook her head slowly. "I never know quite what to expect when I'm here."

Dismissing Lacey's remark, Ben asked, "What did she mean by that? Destroy what?"

"I don't know, Ben," Jenna began, "but I don't trust her. For some strange reason, the woman is obsessed with you, and either you can't see that, or you don't want to see it."

Lacey calmly walked into the dining room and immediately disappeared. Both Ben and Jenna saw it happen and looked at each other shocked. But in the next instant Lacey was back, standing in front of them as though nothing unusual had happened.

"What is it? What's wrong?" Lacey asked, seeing the strange expressions on their faces.

"You disappeared," Jenna informed her. "You were there one second and gone the next, and now you're back again."

"You can't be serious."

"She's telling you the truth, Lacey. We saw it happen."

"But I swear I saw both of you standing in the doorway," Lacey replied.

Ben walked over to where Lacey was standing. It was the same place where he'd first encountered Anna on Christmas Eve. Reaching out his arm, he saw it disappear into thin air.

"Ben!" cried Jenna. "Your arm! It's gone!"

"Don't you understand what this means?" He turned away from them, but quickly glanced over his shoulder as though he wanted to be sure they were watching. Then without saying another word, he stepped into what he was sure was another dimension.

"Ben!" shouted Jenna.

Then it was Lacey who stepped across the invisible threshold. Jenna backed away, striking a dining room chair sharply. She watched the space where she had last seen them, only to observe an arm emerging out of thin air. Then it was another arm that appeared. Like the fabled Cheshire Cat, Ben's face appeared, then disappeared, and then appeared again, only this time with Lacey's face a few feet away. Two familiar faces visible and neither had a body.

Again, the faces were gone, and again Jenna waited. Five minutes passed, and still no sign of Ben or Lacey. Ten minutes passed, and she felt panic taking hold. But panic wasn't the only thing to take hold of her. From out of nowhere, a hand shot out and grabbed Jenna by the wrist, pulling her firmly. It was a man's voice, but not Ben's.

"It's finished," said the voice. "There is no longer hope. We are prisoners of another time."

Startled, Jenna managed to pull away.

"Stay away from me." It was Lacey, her voice shrill. Jenna could not decide whether she was angry or frightened.

"It's me, Lacey," Ben said.

"I'm so confused. Where am I?"

"Give me your hand." Again, it was Ben's voice.

The next thing Jenna saw was the two of them reappearing in the dining room. Ben smiled. Lacey looked shocked. Even Jenna was shaken by what had happened. Ben, however, looked at them excitedly.

"We saw you clearly, Jenna," began Ben. "Your movements were hurried, rushed, sort of erratic and jerky, like those movements of characters in silent movies. Even your voice, well it sounded like a recording played at the wrong speed." Then he regarded Lacey, who was noticeably disoriented. "Are you okay, Lacey?"

"Hardly," she answered. "What happened?"

"I think there's an open gateway right here in front of us," replied Ben confidently.

"A gateway to where?" asked Lacey.

"I don't know. I think we stepped into another time, another dimension." Looking at Jenna, he added, "We were gone no longer than a minute. I didn't have time to see where we were."

"You were gone almost fifteen minutes, Ben."

He remembered what Adrian White had told him the day White was driving from Bloomington, Indiana back to Evansville, when he was caught in a time slip and ended up in Nashville, Tennessee. He referred to the event as a "crease" in the space–time continuum. The only explanation Adrian had was that "there are portals that routinely open and close at various geographical locations."

"It was hazy, like being in a dissipating fog," Ben told Jenna.

"I had my eyes closed most of the time," confessed Lacey. "When I opened them, I expected to see something, anything, but there was nothing but fog. It was cold and unsettling. Next time, I'll wear a light jacket or sweater," she smiled, after regaining at least some composure.

"What if there is no next time?" Jenna was attempting to put the incident into a more rational perspective and wanted to minimize the euphoric spin. "This isn't something to fool around with, Ben. It's dangerous. What about the others that exist in this house?" she cautioned, continuing to show agitation with what she considered Ben's cavalier attitude. "How do you know when they open, when they close?" She saw him start across the room toward the door at the other end of the dining room. "What are you doing, Ben?"

Expecting to disappear again through what he was convinced was a portal or time slip, he didn't answer. Much to his surprise, when he crossed what he thought was the threshold, he was still visible.

"It's gone," Lacey declared, brushing the air with both hands. "Just like that, it's gone."

"She's right," Ben confirmed. "It's no longer open."

Jenna shook her head as she spoke. "This is serious, Ben."

"It's exciting," proclaimed Lacey.

"And what if you got stuck there and couldn't get back?"

"Stuck where?" asked Lacey. "I don't even know where I was."

Shaking his head, Ben answered slowly, "I didn't think about that."

"If you can come and go that easily," Jenna went on, "so can people from the other side."

After a moment, he nodded agreement. "You're right."

"There was a man's voice," Jenna told them.

A bit more serious now, Ben said, "It was me. I was the one you heard."

"No," returned Jenna flatly. "It was not you, Ben."

"Who then?"

"I don't know, a strange voice, speaking of being trapped in another time."

"This is getting weird." Lacey smiled as she spoke. "There's always something strange going on in this house. Maybe the entire house is a gateway."

"She might be right, Ben."

"Adrian White needs to see this," thought Manning out loud.

"I'm afraid we're getting in way over our heads with all this," Jenna admitted.

Ben regarded her carefully before saying, "Maybe so, but we need to discover what's going on in this house, because if the government gets wind of this, it'll be too late for all of us."

But the government already had Newburgh in its crosshairs. Even as they spoke, satellite scans were being carefully reviewed by Smith and his colleagues, one of whom was Walking Einstein.

Chapter 40

"NEWBURGH, INDIANA," said Smith to Walking Einstein. "We're talking about an antique river town in Southern Indiana." He laid out a map on the desk before adding, "The Air Force actually dug property there years ago," and he thumped a circled spot on the map with his index finger.

"They missed something. Surely you've considered that."

"Yes, we've considered it, and we're still considering it," snapped Smith.

"These aerial reconnaissance scans show nothing immediately significant, but I'm sure something in Newburgh was responsible for one of the three light beams we saw at the Abbey," Chase stated.

"And we're trying to figure out what that is," declared Smith.

Pointing to Shanklin's pond, "What's this?" Charlie asked.

"Nothing important, just a big hole in the ground."

"But there's something there." As Smith bent down to get a closer look, Charlie took a magnifying glass from a desk drawer and handed it to him. "Here, maybe this will help."

"Construction equipment, looks like a bulldozer."

"No, the thing in the middle of the hole, what is that?" pressed Charlie.

"I don't know."

"Suppose it's a pond or lake that's been drained recently?" Charlie surmised. "Maybe the dam had a leak, or maybe they wanted to dig it deeper. If you look closely, the place near the bulldozer looks like a dam. And right there in the middle might be what we're look for, a power source."

"With the one we discovered in Rockport, this one could be the missing piece of this trinity thing?" asked Smith.

"I think so," Charlie Chase agreed.

"And you think we need to take a closer look at what's there."

"I've seen the declassified briefs from the 1947 dig, and whatever was taken away was either incomplete or nothing more than wreckage of some kind."

"Many details of that excavation are still classified," Smith declared bluntly. "As far as leaving something behind, it's possible, but I doubt it. That site's been surveyed and resurveyed."

"If you look carefully, there's something near this small bridge, and it's near the original dig site."

Smith looked to where Chase was pointing, and again shook his head as if to say it had no significance. He seemed anxious to leave, giving Charlie the impression that what had happened the other night was now prioritized as newly classified information much beyond Walking Einstein's pay grade. Glancing at Charlie, he nodded and left the room.

For several seconds, Charlie stared at the aerial photographs, looking closely at the topography and specifically at some undulations northeast of the bridge. At first, he thought these mounds might be part of a larger prehistoric effigy mound. The Angel Mounds complex was only a few miles away, so it was more than likely that undiscovered Native American sites were still scattered across the local landscape. But there was no distinguishable symmetry, no identifiable pattern. The arrangement was haphazard, and that was sufficient reason to consider another hypothesis.

Scans did indicate those areas where the ground had been disturbed. Though there were several possibilities for these apparent anomalies, the closer he looked the more convinced he was that something had struck the ground near the bridge and had been recovered by the military in its 1947 excavation. Another thought persisted, and, again, that thought brought into focus the distinct probability of something left behind.

Smith, however, went away convinced that the established trinity so important to Walking Einstein had gone beyond expectations. More concerned about the beams of light that converged to form a huge triangle, than about any terrestrial reconnaissance reports, the man known only as Smith poured over celestial maps in his office. General Moro Eugene Elkins stood next to him, waiting impatiently for an explanation. With his index finger on Sirius and nodding to General Elkins, Smith was prepared to make a declaration.

"There's no doubt about it, the light was directly in line with Sirius—just as we suspected."

"You're sure about this?" asked Elkins.

"We have Arecibo verification."

"Are the power sources secured?"

"No, sir, only two. The Saint Meinrad site and the site in Rockport, Indiana," Smith disclosed.

"And the location of the other site is also in Indiana?"

"Yes, sir, and each site is near the 37th parallel as predicted by Dr. Chase. We have data that show the other location on private property near Newburgh, Indiana. We can have a go team in transit tomorrow, if you think it's necessary."

"Newburgh, Indiana," said General Elkins. "The town sounds familiar."

"It was the site of the 1947 excavation and retrieval."

"Is it possible that something was left behind?"

"I don't think so, General. I've been over the files, which indicate a thorough recovery."

"What does Dr. Chase think?"

"Well, sir, let me just say he's considering it."

"What does that mean?" asked Elkins, raising his eyebrows.

"I'm not sure, sir." He looked at General Elkins a few seconds before speaking again. "I'm not sure Dr. Chase can be trusted."

"In what respect?"

"Again, I don't know. He's not one of those mainstreamers who takes military protocol too seriously. He might be a security risk."

"It was his research that opened the portal."

"Yes, sir, and he's perceptive enough to see the bigger picture—if you know what I mean, sir."

"If there's any violation of the disclosure agreement, we'll take action."

Before the conversation continued, an Air Force staff sergeant came in with a look of urgency on his face. "Excuse me, sir."

"What is it, Sergeant?" asked Elkins.

"Arecibo has picked up another transmission, General."

"Proceed as planned," Elkins told Smith before turning abruptly to leave.

"If you'll excuse me, sir, there is one other very real possibility."

"What possibility?"

"This trinity thing Chase keeps referring to does not hold up when we review satellite scans," said Smith.

"You're saying three sites are unnecessary?"

"Yes, sir, the third site was, in my opinion, unrelated to the other two. We already have the information we need and I'm convinced Dr. Chase knows that."

"Possibly, this trinity idea is some type of religious experience or reference," Elkins smiled. "If we have what we need, we leave it at that for now. There's no reason to snoop on private property or create a military presence that will get people talking. In no time at all it would turn into a damn circus, just as it did in Roswell, New Mexico." With that said, General Elkins and the Staff Sergeant left the office.

Smith was considering how to transition Dr. Charlie Chase into a capacity that would keep him available as a consultant, while at the same time minimizing his accessibility to classified information. He wanted to keep Chase close, but not too close. A possible solution was already being considered.

Meanwhile, early that same morning, Dr. Liz Raymond continued to drive south on Interstate 69 in rain so heavy that she decided to stop for coffee in Elnora, a few miles north of Vincennes, Indiana.

As she drove into the small town, where she had stopped several times before at the Main Street Café, she was quick to realize that something was wrong. In such a heavy rain, it was becoming difficult to recognize any of the buildings along Main Street. Or was she even on Main Street? With rain striking sharply against her windshield, and the wipers unable to push enough water away to permit a clear view, she pulled over to the side of what she thought was Main Street, with the intention of waiting out the storm.

She was accustomed to driving in rain, but not in such a heavy rain as this. And hadn't the weather forecast called for a cold but sunny day? She'd heard it only minutes before on WFIU FM? Could the forecast be this ridiculously inaccurate, she wondered? Never had she driven in rain this intense. Rain continued to beat incessantly against the roof and windows. But she was safe and even comfortable in the SUV, so after reclining the seat with the idea of a longer wait than she had anticipated, she took some recent research from her backpack and settled in to reread a few articles she had collected from the library archives at Indiana University.

Claps of thunder were loud enough to disturb her concentration. Lightning flashed violently and illuminated the interior of the SUV. A few times she attempted to look through the curtain of rain to get a sense of where she was parked, but those efforts were futile. Nothing outside the car was visible. She'd read accounts of cars being washed away in heavy rains, and although increasingly nervous, she hoped the large SUV would continue to be safe. Maybe the wind, which had come suddenly, was causing the most anxiety. Her GPS had stopped working. WFIU FM was off the air, or so she thought.

The storm continued to rage for several more minutes, before the rain subsided long enough for her to get a glimpse of her surroundings. Neon signs blinked brightly against a gray landscape. She could not remember seeing neon signs this large in the small town of Elnora. And what had happened to the Main Street Café? Across the street from where she was parked, a row of tall buildings pushed so high into the sky that she could not see the tops of them, no matter how hard she tried.

With her confusion continuing to mount, and a sudden calm settling around her, she began to realize that she had not stopped in Elnora at all. She must have driven farther than she realized during the early minutes of the storm, more than likely all the way to Vincennes. Looking at the time on her mobile phone, she realized she'd been driving for less than half an hour. Another thought struck her. Somewhere along the way she must have made a wrong turn. Reluctantly, she realized this was not Vincennes, and the closest city with buildings this tall was Indianapolis, which was nearly a hundred miles behind her.

Dr. Liz Raymond was not the kind of woman who panicked easily. Sensing that something unusual had happened, she carefully considered her options. Then, the already strange got even stranger. Several years before, she had traveled to Hong Kong for a research symposium. There for a week as a presenter on paranormal occurrences, she experienced a typhoon that had come in off the South China Sea, causing the symposium to be delayed three days. One morning, surprised by the calm that had set in, she went outside to find the eye of the typhoon passing over. With this thought in mind, and the wind and rain subsiding, she cautiously opened the door of the SUV and stepped outside with her cell phone in hand. Quite possibly she was stepping into the eye of what was an incredibly powerful storm, much like she had experienced in Hong Kong.

If this was Elnora, Indiana, it had changed beyond recognition. The distended sky appeared to drop lower, until the tall buildings were lost in a strange and heavy fog. Even the bright neon had dimmed, and cars were not moving at all. Flat, two-dimensional shapes, the buildings resembled stiff outlines cut from painted wood. In front of her was a Coca-Cola truck, and stenciled on the door beneath the yawning driver were the words, Nashville, Tennessee.

No matter how hard she tried, she couldn't explain what continued to happen around her. When she looked south, a modern city was set in relief against the sunken sky, a cluster of silhouetted shapes that grew fainter the longer she looked. To the north, along a narrow street, were clapboard houses, gleaming in sunlight—the same sunlight she'd left behind in Bloomington, Indiana. On both sides of the street, people passed slowly on the sidewalks. A pickup truck coming down the street toward her, never seemed to get closer to where she was standing. Only a few yards down the street, and motionless on a grassy lawn, was a dog with bulging eyes.

Before she realized what was happening, that imagery to the north grew brighter with each passing second. The sunny images were visibly moving toward her, past her, moving south, until rays of sunlight fell into the street where she stood. Ahead, the outline of a building she recognized slowly emerged from the mist. It was the Main Street Café, coming steadily into focus. Two men in coats and hats shook hands on the sidewalk. She heard honking and turned to see a car approaching. She had to step aside to let it pass. Sun beat down on the town of Elnora, Indiana. Whatever it was that had existed in the gloom under a bleak and somber sky had disappeared.

Once inside the SUV, she started the engine and immediately WFIU FM was back on the air, playing a Vivaldi violin concerto. The GPS, however, showed Interstate 40 West with the city of Nashville, Tennessee just 12 miles away. Glancing at her cell phone, she was surprised to see that nearly 31 minutes had passed. What had happened to her was not possible. Yet, she knew the strange phenomenon had occurred. As she attempted to sort out the possibilities, she realized instantly that those possibilities were few. Since she hadn't imagined any of it, that eliminated one of the possibilities. So, if she hadn't imagined it, then it had happened, and there had to be an explanation.

It had gone wrong about a mile north of Elnora. The sky had darkened without warning. Although weather anomalies were not uncommon, she was sure this was much more than just an abrupt change in weather. This was something spectacular, a rare and fascinating rupture in time, an exceptional opportunity to view two completely different places simultaneously. Had the GPS confirmed that she had glimpsed Nashville, Tennessee from Elnora, Indiana, or had she really been on Interstate 40 only minutes from Nashville? Whatever had happened could certainly happen again. That thought alone frightened Liz Raymond. If there was an answer that had veracity, Dr. Adrian White would have it, and she had the pictures on her cell phone to prove this strange phenomenon had happened. This one thought persisted, as she drove the remaining miles to Evansville, while the same Vivaldi violin concerto played another 15 minutes on WFIU FM.

Chapter 41

IT WAS EARLY spring. Lacey Laurens had announced her engagement to Matt Jennings, whose father had recently retired, leaving Matt and Matt's younger brother David to keep the business profitable. With Ben's guidance, and based on what Larry Collins had revealed, what was left of the church was discovered only 40 yards west of the north woods. Remnants of the parsonage, located by Manning a couple months before, had remained the primary point of interest, that is until several other larger stones were found. Although only the tops of the stones were visible, Matt was still able to get reliable dimensions, which revealed the approximate size of the church. Perhaps the most significant find was made by Matt while digging the perimeter with a backhoe. On the south side of the foundation and oriented more to the southwest were stone steps, and it was Matt's opinion that those steps had been at the front of the church.

With what remained of the entire foundation now exposed, they began running interior GPR scans. One afternoon late, with the sun setting behind the trees, they got a strong hit on the east side about five feet from where one of the walls had stood. Digging more than a foot into the ground, they uncovered pieces of untarnished metal, that when fit together, formed a triangle. The two pieces forming the apex of the triangle had opposing beveled edges, only lightly chipped. Though the pieces fit together perfectly, both ends had broken and jagged edges, suggesting other undiscovered pieces were still in the ground.

Light to the touch, and with a glossy patina, all the uncovered pieces looked new, as if they had been recently manufactured. Distinguishable on one piece was an impression, possibly a symbol, lighter in color, not painted or stenciled, but rather incised into the metal—if it was metal at all. Closer observations revealed this same lighter color along one of the jagged edges, leading them to think the piece had broken and the rest of it was still buried.

Not more than five minutes had passed before Matt got a strong hit near where the other pieces had been excavated. After pushing three red flags into the soil, Ben glanced toward the western sky, and quickly realized the remaining light, spread purple across the entire horizon, was what was left of the sunset. Digging into the ground with a spade, he exposed another piece. Although much like the others, it appeared to be longer. Even in the dim light, they saw traces of the same light color along the jagged edge, which when completely exposed, could be one of the missing pieces they expected to find. In the ebbing light, with darkness closing in, they considered placing lights at the site, so they could continue the dig into the night.

"I think it's better to get some rest and continue in the morning," Matt told Ben at length. "I still need to finish the interior scans and want to run GPR scans around the exterior of the foundations."

Ben nodded his agreement. "What I find interesting is that these pieces are turning up inside what was once a church. They certainly don't seem to be what I would call church artifacts."

"Maybe tomorrow we'll have some answers," admitted Matt.

Liz would be in town tomorrow on spring break and told Jenna she was glad to have a place to visit, "far away from academia." Adrian White had been notified but was attending a conference on the West Coast. Jenna was shopping with her mother in Evansville. Meanwhile, Ben was anxious to take a shower, then once again look over the research Dr. Raymond had left behind on her last visit to Atwood House.

What he found fascinated him. Published in a small local

newspaper called *The Herald* was a 1901 account of the church and its fiery destruction. According to the article, a meteor air burst had occurred and was solely responsible for the devastation, although no pieces of meteorite had ever been located. That was the prevailing contention for decades, until in 1947 a local resident by the name of Albert Ruston, now long deceased and buried near a large chestnut tree in Newburgh's Rose Hill Cemetery, had started a rumor that the church had been struck by "a craft of unknown origin." The rumor, which had taken on some apparent credibility, was quickly dismissed by the Air Force that same year, with a subsequent report stating that a meteor had caused the damage, and that a sizable meteorite *had* been recovered and taken away for examination. Most residents at the time never bought the meteorite story, remaining convinced that something "black and sinister" had destroyed the church, "a thing from out of the sky" but certainly not a meteor.

Ben, hoping to get an early start, was up and dressed by six o'clock the next morning. After a cup of black coffee, he headed out to the site. He was surprised to find Matt already working in the early mist of a cool morning, and even more surprised to see several red flags pushed into the ground at various places around the church foundation. Matt had used a metal detector to identify places where he'd gotten solid GPR hits and was now scanning an area near the woods.

"Morning," he waved, when he saw Ben approaching.

"You definitely believe in getting an early start, Matt."

"This is exciting stuff. I've had some good hits this morning," and he gestured toward the flags.

"Looks like we got plenty to keep us busy," Ben returned.

"There's a place over by the stream, about 20 yards this side, where the creek narrows. You can see it if you look closely," and he pointed to the area in reference. "There is a distinct depression. Might be nothing, but often sunken areas like that indicate disturbances in the ground. I'll look at it a little closer later."

They had continued interest in the larger pieces they had discovered the day before. Ben grabbed a shovel and an hour later took a long narrow piece out of the ground. It had the same shiny patina as those pieces already recovered. Different in some respects to those retrieved, this piece resembled more closely those pieces dug up the previous fall near the stone bridge. Extremely light, a six foot piece could be held and balanced easily in one hand.

After closer observation, the surface, which they thought might be polished metal, seemed now more like a skin or sheath stretched tightly over an aluminum framework. In the early morning sun, the patina sparkled even more, causing Ben to look away momentarily. When struck lightly with a hammer, a deep reverberation could be heard against the backdrop of trees.

At this point, neither had any idea what they had dug out of the ground. Manning had certainly not forgotten Anna's reference to something malevolent still buried on Atwood House property. She had spoken fearfully, calling it a huge evil. Larry Collins had told Manning the military had not made a clean sweep of the area. Ben could not be sure if what the military had left behind were those pieces being discovered now by Matt and him. However, one thing remained clear, that these pieces being unearthed shouldn't be there at all. Something unusual, even improbable, had happened here many years ago, and Ben was beginning to think he knew exactly what it was.

Liz was staying at the Tropicana Evansville. She had invited Jenna to spend a couple of nights with her, and both had enjoyed playing the slots at the adjoining casino. Though neither was a gambler, these nights together were enjoyable, and Ben was happy to have this opportunity to work with Matt at the church site.

Not wanting to be left out entirely, Jenna called to say she and Liz were coming later that afternoon, telling him they would bring fried chicken, so he wouldn't have to worry about preparing anything. She knew he was working the church site and regretted they could not get to Atwood House until what was looking like the end of the day. Liz loved coming to Newburgh, and she and Jenna really hit it off. Once, by invitation, Jenna had driven to Bloomington to attend a couple of Dr. Raymond's classes, and told Ben how much she had enjoyed them.

Another 30 minutes passed before he heard Matt calling. "Look at this, Ben. We might have something here."

The width of the creek narrowed to about eight feet at a point where it bent heavily to the east, before straightening out into the woods. It was shallow enough, especially during the summer and fall, to use seven large stones to get to the other side. Since they provided a shortcut to the woods on the east side of the property, there had been evenings when Manning used these rocks as a natural bridge. Deer often grazed at the edge of the woods, and on several occasions Ben had come close enough to hear and see the bucks rutting. Cautious as they were, they didn't seem to fear him.

It was near there where Matt poked with a stick into a clump of tall weeds. Ben thought he might be poking at a snake or dead animal. But when he saw him drop to his knees and reach into the dense growth of weeds with his bare hands, he knew Matt had found something in the dirt.

Concealed in a tangle of bromegrass, morning glory, and chickweed was a large section of flat rock, which Matt had managed to expose, after clearing the weeds around it. Digging down with the sharp edge of a spade to nearly three inches, Ben was unable to loosen or get underneath the stone. While he continued to dig around the edges, trying to move it, Matt got a bucket from the truck and went down to the stream to fill it. Returning with the water, he splashed it on the rock, and began wiping his bare hands across the surface, brushing away cheatgrass and pennywort that had adhered to the porous stone.

Pouring more creek water over the bare surface, Matt said, "Might be something written there."

"If it's a gravestone, it's a huge one," Ben admitted.

"It's not uncommon to find small cemeteries near these old churches." He glanced up at the terrain before speaking again. "The land slopes noticeably from the woods down to the creek, so there's a chance that some downhill creep occurred and moved this stone to where it is now. But then it might not be a gravestone at all."

"It's definitely been here a long time."

Nodding, Matt brushed his fingers over part of the stone, before drying that section with a rag removed from his back pocket. With sunlight illuminating its surface, they were both able to see what looked like numbers or maybe dates. "They're almost gone. I don't think there's enough left to make them out."

"Why don't we try to get the rest of it out of the ground," Ben suggested.

And that's what they did for the next hour, until they had completely edged the large slab of limestone and cleaned the surface as well as possible with water from the creek. As the surface of the stone brightened, they inspected it carefully, both wondering what they had uncovered, and what was beneath it. So, Matt brought in the GPR unit and they soon had the readings both had anticipated.

"The ground has definitely been disturbed, and there's something down there, maybe steps—and what looks like a large void," Matt reported.

"Maybe it's an old well capped–off."

"Could be, but until we lift this slab, it's impossible to determine what's there."

"Then it's a project for another time," Ben smiled.

Looking at eight red flags, each indicating a dig site, Matt nodded his agreement. "We've got plenty to keep us busy. This one can wait."

Chapter 42

IT WAS NEARLY six o'clock before they had a chance to consider what had been recovered. The flags had been pulled and the many pieces lay on the ground where they'd been dug out. Among them, was considerable similarity, particularly in color and surface appearance. Black shiny pieces varying in size from a foot to seven feet were scattered all around the interior of the church foundation. As they regarded them, they knew the work ahead was more than the two of them could do, at least as quickly as they would like it done. Since Adrian White was detained on the West Coast for a few days, Jenna, Lacey, and Liz Raymond were the ones who could provide the much-needed help.

When Jenna and Liz arrived later than expected, both were eager to learn what they could about the large limestone slab Matt had located. With Jenna and Ben looking on, Liz walked around the limestone slab before kneeling to get a closer look at its surface. In the degraded sunlight, she used the light on her mobile phone to take several pictures. Along with cracks and chips were indentions at various places on the surface. It was extremely difficult to decide if these were deliberate markings that had been severely compromised by time and weather.

As she traced a row of indentions with smooth edges, Liz remained focused on what she said felt like numbers, "I just can't make them out. Might not be anything at all, but it seems they're evenly spaced on a line."

Matt was just now coming over to join the group, "Got any ideas, Dr. Raymond?"

"Not yet, Matt." She looked around at the many pieces they had excavated before saying, "It's beginning to look like a debris field."

Ben picked up at once on her comment. "Suppose something came in from the north over the trees, hit the church, and those undulations out there are places where it struck the ground before stopping on the other side of the creek," he suggested.

"If so, what did the military recover?" Jenna wanted to know.

"We know now that they didn't get it all," Ben answered. "If Liz is right, this *is* what's left of a debris field."

Liz, still occupied with what she felt sure were numbers etched into the limestone slab, removed a notebook from her backpack and with the edge of a pencil rubbed the lead across a sheet of paper, then did another lower down on the stone. She slipped them inside the notebook with the intention of looking at them more closely when they returned to Atwood House.

Jenna had gone off to look at the old parsonage foundation, which hadn't yet been entirely cleared. Considerably smaller than the church foundation, she wondered about the man who had lived there, wondered what he was like, who he was, where he had gone. Heavy patches of weeds covered much of the foundation on the north side, which was most likely the main entrance to the house. Walking along the outside of the foundation on the western side, she saw what looked to be another slab of limestone, barely visible in a clump of weeds. Even in the weakening light, it had caught her eye.

A small section of stone was exposed enough to show heavy marks across its surface. After looking closely at them, Jenna had the distinct impression that something heavy and sharp had been repeatedly dragged across this section of stone and had left deep lines, which she felt were not deliberate incisions. Was it possible that the other stone showed the same or similar marks?

Twilight was now across the entire sky, a pale blue wash beneath a deeper blue, and in this distressed light it was difficult for closer examination of the stone surfaces. Coming over to where Liz was still rubbing her hand across the surface of the first slab, Jenna inspected the other end of the stone. With the light on her cell phone brightening the area, she immediately noticed what looked to be faint drag lines and snapped a couple of close-ups.

As Matt prepared to leave for the day, promising to return around ten the next morning, shadows were deepening on the lawns around Atwood House. While Ben regarded one piece that was about five feet long and angling inward about 35 degrees at each end, he noticed the entire outward edge was sharply beveled the same as many other pieces already uncovered. Though several pieces were obviously missing, he was beginning to think they had retrieved exterior parts of a crashed aircraft.

All the pieces remained now in those heavier shadows creeping deliberately across the entire church and parsonage foundations. The three of them walked back to Atwood House in the crisp shades of evening. Ben knew that a very plausible scenario was taking shape. It looked increasingly like there had been at least one event, and possibly a second. Whether they were connected was still impossible to determine.

Behind them, in the trees and deep in the blacker shadows, a light moved up and down the rock face and then across the surface of the water. A thin man in a dark jacket and jeans, wearing brown wingtip shoes, was bending down to pick something out of the stream, a piece of metal with a black glossy skin, beveled along one edge. He wiped the piece, about four inches in length, on his jeans, then slipped it into his jacket pocket, after which he drew the fingers of one hand across the tips of his shoes.

In the beam of his flashlight, and with curiosity still pressing him, Charlie Chase caught a glimpse of something shiny embedded in the soft soil less than a foot from the water's edge. Removing a jackknife from his pocket, he carefully removed a coin from the soft ground. Water from the creek quickly filled the hole, but not before he was able to retrieve a second coin. Washing them in the creek and rubbing his fingers across both, he was surprised by what appeared to be two gold coins, which glinted in the bold rays of the flashlight.

Slipping the coins into his pocket, he immediately widened the hole, thinking there might be more coins buried there—but found none.

Smith had released Dr. Chase from all further "contractual services" or, possibly it was Chase who had asked to be released from any further obligations with Smith's organization and from *Project Firefly*, a top-secret project that reached much deeper into military stealth than Chase imagined. He told Smith he'd received a research offer from Vincennes University to finish out the year for an assistant physics professor who had recently taken sabbatical leave. After signing all appropriate paperwork, they parted ways, and Walking Einstein was relieved that their separation was an amicable one, or so it seemed at the time. Smith had told Chase that if his services were needed again, he'd be notified, saying further, that he'd done "admirable" work and had provided a critical piece that had long been missing.

Although never privy to *Project Firefly*, as Smith had mentioned once or twice, Charlie knew with absolute certainty that Smith and his clandestine organization had the capability to create and control magnetic fields, as well as possessing cutting edge research on Doppler effects and plasma vortexes. It was also conceivable that either a gateway or portal, and not a communication tower had been retrieved and reassembled, or that Smith was searching for a way to power and control outgoing and incoming laser transmissions. The portal idea didn't have enough strength and was quickly dismissed from Chase's hypothesis. Everything seemed to point to the recovery of a communication tower. Without a doubt, something was recovered in 1947, and Charlie Chase was sure he knew what it was not.

Now that they knew the matrix of the transmitter, others could be used to snap the on-off switch. Charlie realized early on that coordinates could be derived by using two transmitters or towers. The trinity which he had mentioned to Smith could possibly provide the triangulation needed to ascertain a wider grid, inside which were deeper mysteries, some that might never be understood or solved. But Smith had already located other large stone transmitters nearby, one in Ferdinand, Indiana at the Monastery Immaculate Conception, the second in the small town of Bristow, Indiana. While Smith and his colleagues continued to look skyward, Charlie considered possible ways to locate a gateway, a portal that had allowed accidental visitors to arrive late one night while the good people of Newburgh were sleeping.

Chapter 43

A NEW ARRANGEMENT OF flowers in the library. Anna had been there—the first time in weeks. With Liz and Jenna at the Tropicana Evansville Hotel and Casino for the night, Ben took the finished portrait of Anna Atwood off the wall and put it in front of him on a desktop easel. Staring into her eyes, he remembered the day when their eyes met in a winter snowfall.

The longer he looked, the more lifelike her face became. He realized he had caught in the painting the fascination and enigma she was. How easily she could apprehend his senses, how undeniably enduring her effect on him. This was reminiscent of another time, years ago, when he'd admired the face of Nefertiti, reproduced in a plaster bust after the original in the Egyptian Museum Berlin. He'd traced her lips with his fingers as though such an intimate gesture would cause her to speak. But as now, it didn't happen. There were no words, and even in the dead plaster eyes, the beauty of Nefertiti lay cold and distant as the moon.

Even though he had lifted the veil, Anna's portrait, as evocative as it was, remained oil on canvas. It would always be that—forever lifeless. Forever silent. A portrait rendered not from imagination but from passion. If she had guided his hand, it was for no other reason than to leave her true image in his life. If she couldn't stay in his time, he would live in her time for as long as possible. Taking another look at the painting before going upstairs, a new thought struck him and this thought had claws already reaching for him.

He dressed in the clothes Anna had given him at Christmas and then went downstairs. Wearing a pair of men's early 20th century shoes he had found in the storeroom behind the great room, Ben was surprised how comfortably they fit. If he was going back in time, he'd have to look like he belonged there. Walking into the dining room, he thought she might be there like she had been on Christmas Eve. But he found only furniture and the shadows it cast on the walls and floor. Stained glass windows at the top of the stairway were flushed in moonlight. He was disappointed when Anna was not there as he expected. Then, as he turned toward the library, he heard music coming from the great room. The dancers were back, and this time he'd join them.

Slowly opening the doors to the great room, he drew back in astonishment. There were no dancers. Except for a solitary shape standing in moonlight that poured in through the windows, the room was empty. Music continued to play softly. With her back to him and coils of dark hair loose against her skin, she was looking at a moon that filled the entire windows. Her skirt, deep purple with a gathered hemline, was high enough to reveal black-laced shoes that stopped above her ankles. The green blouse with puffed sleeves and tight cuffs, and a long closure of back buttons, made her strikingly thin.

"Anna," he whispered.

She turned with her back to the moon, and in front of her a long slender shadow stopped near his feet. Except for her eyes, which had caught and held the moonlight, the features of her face were indistinct. Both arms extended toward him, she whispered his name. She wanted him to hold her. Exhaling slightly, he brushed his fingers across his lips, as if there were no words left to say. This time, words gave way to silences.

For a few moments, he saw near Shanklin's woods someone building a church. As ancient sunlight poured out of the sky on a hot and humid summer day, a small man with a red beard hammered nails into clapboard. On a limestone base, a tower shaped like a pyramid pushed into a blue sky. Moving closer, as the room brightened, the windows filled with morning sunlight. Anna inclined her head to one side and seemed to regard him with both curiosity and fascination. In her quiet eyes were ghosts from another time, looking at him with deep sadness in their eyes. She'd brought them with her, let them live again in her eyes, one face emerging from another, until at last only Anna's eyes called him. But these extraordinary images faded—much too fast. Once again, the beautiful image of Anna Atwood caught fire in the blazing moonlight.

He and Anna danced slowly across the great room. Neither said a word. The fragrant aroma of jasmine was unmistakable and seemed to come, not from Anna, but from the room itself. So close now, never this close to her before, he inhaled her until his senses were completely overwhelmed by the sweet scents of her hair, her skin, the clothes she wore, and her breath, that smelled like apple blossoms. His world spiraled away from him faster than he perceived, and even if he wanted to stop this enchanted insanity he could not.

Moonlight stretched their shadows across the floor as they danced. On the walls two dark shapes moved so slowly in those shadows that lingered that they were nearly imperceptible. His arm was around her waist, his fingers entwined with hers, the gentleness of her touch on his shoulder, and nothing anywhere in his world was as he remembered it. Anna had taken all those memories away. When she laid her head against his shoulder, his feet no longer touched the floor. The music was spiritual, that kind of music that heals the soul, and if ever there was a soul with cracks in its foundation, it belonged to Ben Manning.

Minutes passed, as music continued to play, music he'd never heard before. It was taking hold of his emotions so entirely that he felt like a man pushing desperately through a heavy mist—just to find himself. Stumbling, his efforts futile, he thought he no longer wanted to find who he was now, or who he had been, or would be—not with Anna Atwood in his arms and her head gently against his shoulder. Next to him in this endless haze was hope. Anna would guide him among the stars until the windows in the great room once more caught fire, much like the fire in those diamonds Bob Bergman had in his showcases.

High in the corner of one window was the star Sirius, which for a moment appeared to be the only visible star in the entire sky. Its sparkle was enormous tonight, as though its light was salvation for all the sinners caught in its radiance. It was a moment of realization, a time of reconciliation. In Anna's arms the redeeming light of Sirius poured over him, and when he looked at his fingertips, there were tiny specks of fire like the shine of fireflies on a warm summer night, all this righteous light from a star he had never noticed—until now.

Still, not a word passed between them. Anything that needed to be said was in her touch and deep in her eyes. She looked at him with that soft fire in her eyes, to find his heart melting, and he wanted it to happen on this glorious night in Newburgh, Indiana. He wanted to hollow out, erase everything he was, begin again, fill himself with moonlight and let the white pulsing light of Sirius beat forever in his chest. No longer would he be consumed by sin. Absolution was in the pure honest light burning in her eyes. So quickly, so near his atonement, he saw dark clouds move across the face of the moon, and Sirius climbed higher in the night sky until heavy shadows fell on each window, until once again he felt his heart beating and redemption fading. The anticipation in his eyes became suddenly cold, as if the wind outside had found an open window and extinguished the promise of hope.

Again, the distance between them had overwhelmed the moonlight. The small fires burning in her eyes were the sunsets of a hundred years ago, and yet, they were one more sunrise on a daring new day, not in his life, but in hers. On this night when lights in the houses of Newburgh burned away another day of memories, he found himself wanting this sunrise of another place and time to remain forever in the great room of Atwood House. When the music stopped, he watched her arms slowly drop to her sides. For a few more moments they remained silent. Each knew what the other was thinking.

At length, Anna reached out to take his hands in hers. "I have missed you more than I deserve."

At first, Ben thought these words were meant for her husband.

Once before when he'd worn these same clothes she had mistakenly called him by her husband's name. This time, however, was not at all like before. This time, she held his hands tightly, as if to let him know it was not her husband in her gaze. Relieved, he managed to speak. "Dearest, Anna," he began, "how very much my life changes when you are here."

"And mine also," she admitted.

"The days are long without you."

"You are in my every thought, in every beat of my heart. You are the beautiful flowers of spring, Ben Manning. I could wait no longer to be with you. Can you ever forgive me for coming into your life?"

He held her face with both hands. It was a delicate touch, as fragile as a soft spring breeze against her skin. When he kissed her, she pulled him closer with both hands behind his head. He kissed her again, this time more passionately, and surging through his body were hot impulses dormant much too long. But once again in her eyes was that loneliness of too many years between them, and he could not kiss away those years.

When he drew back, she said sadly, "You are disappointed."

"No, dear, dear Anna I'm forever lost in your eyes. I love you so very much, but as you said once, we live so many years apart. We continue to steal minutes from a clock that ticks us both into eternity."

"You said the heart has no boundaries."

"And that's true. Time lays down those boundaries—not the heart."

"Then time is villainous and cruel," she sighed. "It is a flower that blooms at midnight, only to pass into eternity in the morning sunlight."

"Yes," he nodded, "it remains the enemy of even the purest, most celestial souls. But you're here, not as a dream, but as one not stopped by the cold hands of time. You are in my arms, Anna. I feel your heart beating, and your words are not silenced by time. They are beautiful, honest and tender words that will live unbroken in the long shadows of eternity."

"Minutes taken from time's evil and relentless clutch. I tell you this with a heart that has been pierced by an arrow—a heart that will not heal, and I must continue to endure this awful pain."

A chilling silence suddenly took hold of the great room. The moon, higher in the windows, showed an angrier face, as though it had been frozen too long in an alien sky. Unable to smile longer on two hearts beating furiously, it was the great round face of a clock, ticking minutes off their lives together.

"You do not know how I long to see you, how I want to be held in your arms and hear my name on your lips." With tears welling in eyes that only minutes before were bright with moonlight, she sighed, "I can no longer bear this appalling darkness that comes between us. This fire that rages so violently inside me now must die, as surely as stars fall to their death each night."

The great room, for the most part unused by Ben, did have a few chairs, a large oak refractory table stacked with books, and an early 20th century settee beneath the tall beveled glass windows. Two people whose emotions for each other were no longer concealed sat quietly. Anna's pale hands were nearly concealed in the folds of her skirt, as though she was trying to keep them from being exposed to the cold that had fallen across the large room.

For nearly a minute, Ben wondered if there was something—anything—he could say to acknowledge the strong emotions she was feeling. Anna, unaccustomed to declaring so openly such deep feelings, seemed to draw back, possibly with thoughts of impropriety. He sensed it when she deliberately looked away as though slightly embarrassed. Or, possibly, she realized once again that the years between them were too many. Any declarations of love were decisively vain. But both, despite the futility of such beautiful words, felt compelled to express the deep feelings they had for each other.

"Sweet, Anna, my wish to be near you is spoken without remorse."

"So lovely are the words you speak that I can hardly believe they are meant for me."

"I speak words too long silent. They are meant for no other than you."

"Then you must kiss me again . . . and again, until there has been a kiss for every year between us."

Though passions of the heart were expressed convincingly, and with the conviction of love, not so the thoughts that were unrelenting hammers drumming furiously inside his head. They were noisy saboteurs already drawing their swords to cut away his heart. Anna's beauty was unforgettable and each moment with her was captivating. Such enthralling emotions he refused to dispute.

Such enchantment would have impacted her husband every day of their lives together, just as it affected Ben now. Appearing in front of him that day on the stairs, must have been coincidence, or had she always known how to travel from her time to his? He knew the brooch she'd asked him to return had a kind of sorcery, because he had used it, what seemed now like a lifetime ago. Continuing to push through the sweet moonlight were those provoking doubts at the top of this steep and rapturous mountain. Maybe these were the illusions of a man who had lost his way too many years ago, at a time when he no longer remembered it happening at all.

When he kissed her again, he was sure that there was no turning back. Anna had him. The clutch of her fingers on his heart was tightening. But he would have it no other way. Let the world spin out from under him. He'd survive. With Anna in his arms, nothing else mattered. That thought was in every kiss, every touch, and she must have known, because the grip she had on him tightened even more. Still, there was a tightening in his chest, a suffocating emotion apprehending his senses. Maybe it was the fear of taking a chance, the echo of Jenna's admonishment.

"I can no longer imagine a day when we're apart," he admitted. "You have hung the moon low enough in the sky for me to touch, and I cannot, I will not let it go. I love you and could never stop telling you how completely you've taken my heart from me. Love is not blind as they say, Anna. It's as bold as the full moon, as dazzling as the stars above our heads."

"If propriety has put a shroud across my face, you must remove it, so that you will remember forever the love that is in my eyes. Can you see it shining like starlight? Can you see the great sky full of stars and the two of us riding the wings of Pegasus? Look carefully, Ben, before it is too late." She put her arms around him and pulled him closer. "Kiss me, please kiss away my fears. Show me again what is in your heart. Let me feel the love you tell me is there."

"Oh, dear Anna, how could such a wonderful thing happen to us?"

"Come with me, Ben. Stay in my life forever. I love you so deeply."

He knew instantly it was the beginning of an ultimatum he didn't want to hear. Turning away from her, he took a few steps toward the doors to the great room. "I can't go with you, Anna." He looked at her with tears in his eyes. "You know I cannot."

"I love you so much."

"You're taking my heart from me, and I can't stop you from doing that."

"You said you loved me, Ben."

"I do love you . . . more than you know."

"Yet you hesitate."

"Oh, Anna, how could I not love everything you are? You're the mist, the sunlight in the morning sky, and the moonlight at night, the soft rain breathing life into the flowers. You are everything beautiful, your smile, so bright in this dismal world of mine. How many times I have prayed you'd come in the night and lay beside me?"

She looked at him with stardust in her eyes and when the music began again, they danced, and danced, through the entire night. He held her so close that her breath sometimes came in short gasps. Still she smiled and begged him to hold her tighter, and tighter, until she would become part of him, and if such a thing as that was possible, it was going to happen that night in the great room at Atwood House.

"I love you, Ben Manning. I have not known this kind of love in my life."

Pink early morning skies appeared in the windows, with the slightest trace of orange deepening as each second passed. Ben finally let her go. She looked at him from across the room, in the same place he'd seen the dancers disappear the previous autumn. He knew it was inevitable. She was only seconds from leaving, and nothing he could do would stop it from happening. She continued to reach out to him, her arms motioning him to follow—and this time in the pink glow of morning sunlight, and much to his surprise, he did.

Chapter 44

When it came to research, Dr. Charlie Chase was as skilled as any in the business. Thorough in every respect, his exhaustive search of the literature usually turned up what others missed or weren't looking to discover. He looked through Warrick County, Indiana plat books from 1895 to 1900 until he found it—a two-acre plot of land deeded by Ollie Jessup. This was property on which the church and parsonage were constructed in 1900, and later after the fire, the land was purchased by William Atwood. Chase had found the 1901 *Herald* account of the church fire, which appeared to be the only mention of a Pastor Thomas Arnold.

Further research in Bible records of the same period made no reference to Pastor Thomas Arnold, and even after a careful search in the *National Registry of Ordained Ministers*, there was still no mention of the man. Responsible for rebuilding the church in 1902, and a man of immense mystery, Arnold had supposedly spent less than a year in Newburgh before moving to Evansville. After a thorough Internet search and a review of public records, Charlie found three Thomas Arnolds, but all three had owned businesses in the Evansville area. Presumably, not one of these men had been an ordained minister.

No matter how deeply he searched, there was no record of Pastor Thomas Arnold during the years 1902 to 1930. Either the man was a self-ordained minister or hadn't been a minister at all. If he was an impostor, there had to be a reason why, and Chase was sure he knew what that reason was. There was still a Jessup family living in Newburgh and after further searching, Charlie learned that the Jessup property was adjacent to what was now the Shanklin farm, and northwest of the Atwood property. The deeper he dug, the more Dr. Chase was convinced a strange event had occurred in 1901 Newburgh, Indiana, and he was slowly putting all the pieces together. It all made perfect sense to Chase.

With the extremely heavy confluence of ley lines converging between the 37th and 38th parallels, and the high incidences of UFO reports in the Evansville and Newburgh areas, Chase's explanation reached deep into the paranormal. Though a scientist, whose contentions were derived not exclusively from facts, Walking Einstein was once again thinking beyond the rigid constraints of mainstream science, considering with serious purpose an explanation that fit the circumstances as he knew them. These circumstances were terrestrial in nature and had nothing to do with the Sirius star system, as he was sure Smith and his colleagues still believed.

Using X-Ray fluorescence or XRF spectrometry, as it was often called, he'd analyzed those pieces of metal gathered from the creek near the site of the old church, and found each to be nonferrous, with an oxide layer or skin called a passivation layer, that was nonporous to oxygen. He'd forged the metal alloy, which had high concentrations of the elements, iridium, magnesium, tellurium, germanium, and palladium to several degrees Fahrenheit, with no trace of decomposition. When put to yield strength and tensile strength stress tests, the pieces had an extremely high tensile strength-to-density ratio and were virtually indestructible. Nothing he did altered the shape or composition in any discernible way.

Evidence piled up, all of it supporting, not an extraterrestrial craft but one from earth's own future. Though it was impossible to determine when, Chase remained convinced that what the military recovered in 1947 was something they hadn't anticipated. Consequently, they created a cover story, that upon real examination was preposterous.

A group insisting what was retrieved in Newburgh was from

another planetary system could not determine with any certainty from what system the craft had traveled. Chase was convinced that the Sirius star system remained the most likely contender among this sanctimonious bunch of elitists, whose rhetoric was little more than repetitious thinking, whose members continued to beat the extraterrestrial drum; but their shockwave was nothing more than one disinformation campaign after another—a noisy shudder, easily shrugged off as blatant hypocrisy. It was left to clandestine groups like Smith's to put it all together, by searching out the facts, no matter how improbable or impossible the results.

Chase realized that he had not been called in as a consultant to something as ancient as the 1947 retrieval. But while a member of Smith's team, he'd heard and seen enough to know that extraterrestrial intervention was one of two contentions still on the table. The other, and the one Chase was sure of, was increasingly more than a possibility, and a contention with high probability—that the future had already occurred in 1947, and this was considerably more perplexing than the alien assertion.

General Elkins had weighed in with his usual aggressive demeanor, by adding to the mix a distinct concern for national security. Aliens from destinations unknown would pose manifest threats, and the United States military might be helpless against what he referred to as advanced technologies. "If we're outgunned," he was heard to say, "extraterrestrial incursion would be catastrophic."

Since no bodies were recovered, and if what had crashed in Newburgh in 1947 was an unmanned craft, a possible drone from the future, it would certainly have been taken apart and even replicated. If that was the case, the military would already have those advanced technologies, frequently spotted in the skies, and mistakenly identified as UFOs. As plausible as that was to Chase, there was another very intricate piece that many in the established scientific community refused to consider with any real seriousness. Though Charlie felt his contributions had been minor and not fully understood, Smith considered the simplicity of the transmitters the beginning of something bigger, and further felt his organization had the information needed to flash messages out into space—messages aimed specifically at Sirius.

What if a craft recovered on the Newland property in 1947 had a pilot, or possibly more than one occupant? What if these occupants had been left behind and reconstructed a church on property originally deeded by Ollie Jessup? And what if there were seams, rifts in the space-time continuum that existed at various places across the earth, at sacred places, at places where ley lines created portals? And had parallel universe research been sacrificed to other military dictates, the most prominent of which was national security? Did national security rhetoric fail to consider a multiverse? Or did the government already know that portals opened and closed, and where these portals were, and how they were controlled? Had Chase misread Smith's intentions? Had the man deceived him into thinking the military concern had focused entirely on establishing communication towers?

There were, however, a few reputable physicists much involved in the study of parallel universes and interdimensional travel. Something, maybe weather anomalies, caused these gateways to open and close. Maybe there were no controls. Dr. Charlie Chase, now outside the constraints of the laboratory, was on the hunt for answers.

Newburgh was just a one hour drive from Vincennes, so he'd resume snooping in the area that seemed to have the most answers. After all, the craft had been retrieved from property in Newburgh. Charlie thought himself innocuous enough, and even when he started asking questions, he'd simply say he was doing research on the 1947 retrieval. There was no reason to lie about it. His credentials could certainly be verified, but he didn't think it would come down to that. He'd start with those who would remember what Charlie was calling the "event." Old-timers could be found in any restaurant that served up home cooking. He'd stop at the Knob Hill Tavern, conveniently located on Old Highway 662 at the west edge of Newburgh, serving hot fiddler crabs since 1943.

He got there early one Friday evening a few minutes before the crowd arrived. Securing a corner seat at the bar, he had a good view, especially of those tables in the tavern side of Knob Hill. It was a dim cozy room with a definite small-town atmosphere. Charlie ordered a beer and prepared for a lengthy stay. The bartender's name was Mack. In his 70s, Mack had what was left of his gray hair pulled into a short ponytail tied off with a piece of black ribbon. The few others at the bar were probably regulars whose butts fit perfectly into the black-cushioned barstools. A couple of seats away from where Charlie sat on the corner stool, was an older man dressed in faded overhauls, with bright red suspenders over a green flannel shirt. This was John Deere farmland and the four–legged deer on his hat had been leaping that way since mid-century.

Mack served up a large platter of fiddlers to the man. Charlie wondered how much of the fish would stay in the moustache and beard, both so thick and unruly that they resembled the worn bristles of a paintbrush. But the man found the small hole that was a mouth and chased down each bite with a slug of beer. Since the man had a jovial demeanor, Charlie decided he'd often been a mall or department store Santa Claus.

Eating fried fish at the opposite end of the bar were a well-dressed man and woman in their forties. Behind them on the wall was a large mounted catfish that looked like it had been there several years. It was a big one, probably a trophy fish pulled from the Ohio River that was a couple of hundred yards to the south, where the Big Bend, as it was called locally, turned in the direction of Evansville. There were other fish mounted on all the walls. It was clear to anyone that this was a proud river town floating lazily into a predictable future. It was not a town in a hurry to go anywhere. A scenic town with small businesses on both sides of Main Street, there were no dilapidated or boarded buildings. A Farm Bureau Insurance office had been in the same building for several decades. Newburgh was a survivor. Since everything they needed was as close as Evansville and the Internet, most people living in Newburgh had no reason to travel, unless they wanted to view new scenery or visit family or friends who had moved away.

Chapter 45

AS THE DINING room gradually got busier, crowd noise started spilling into the tavern. A few of the tables near the bar were already occupied, most of them by couples who seemed comfortable in each other's presence. The bar and backbar were turn of the century mahogany, polished by decades of wear. A beveled glass mirror ran the length of the bar, making it easy for the bartender to see everything going on when his back was turned. Nicked and chipped in many places, especially along the top edge, the wainscoting was probably original. The Knob Hill Tavern was what you'd expect in a small town, especially on a Friday night—kind of homey, a suitable place to eat and drink away the week.

Every so often, Mack retrieved a flyswatter from the back counter and took a whack at a few persistent flies. It must have been a routine action, because nobody but Walking Einstein even noticed. The entire place smelled of fried fish. Charlie didn't care much for fish, too boney for his palate. He did like chili so that's what he ordered from a Millennial in a stained apron, whose frown seemed permanently fixed, and who was given to long exhalations at the end of each order she took.

Ten minutes later a bowl of chili was placed in front of him by Mack, who asked if he wanted crackers. Across the room, the girl with the forced smile was busy clearing a window table for customers standing nearby and anxious for her to finish. Her lethargic efforts were beginning to wear thin on the two men and two women, so Mack came around from behind the bar to help.

A few minutes later, "You're not from these parts, are you?" Mack asked.

"Just passing through."

"I know most all these good folks . . . mostly locals."

"Charming town," Charlie told him.

"And it's a good town full of hardworking people."

Chase nodded, "Got quite a history I imagine."

"No more than any other town," Mack replied. "I remember the big paddle wheelers and the excitement they caused each time they came in down at the docks. Now it's barges pushing freight from Cincinnati to St. Louis and back. The only paddle wheeler I've seen in ages is The City of Evansville."

"A city with its own paddle wheeler, I suppose that brings back plenty of memories."

"It's been dry-docked for years anchored in several tons of concrete. The only wheel turning now is the roulette wheel."

"It's a gambling casino?"

"That's right, three or four decks of slots, crap tables, roulette wheels, bars, and restaurants."

"Mack," a man called from the other end of the bar.

After Mack had drawn a couple more drafts, he returned to continue his conversation with Chase. "Many small towns around here have folded, overnight it seems. Kids are moving to bigger cities where the jobs are, and small business can't compete with the big discount chains. It's a shame to watch the old ways disappear."

"They call that progress, I think."

Mack laughed, "Isn't that the truth." Then, after a pause, he asked, "Where you from anyway?"

"Here and there. I've moved around a lot. Living in Vincennes now."

"How about another beer—on the house?"

"Thank you, Mack. Can I get you something?"

"No thanks," he smiled. "I've been riding the wagon these past ten years. Fell off a couple times but managed to climb back on."

"Good for you, sir." After taking a couple bites of chili, with Mack watching, Charlie nodded and smiled.

"You like it?" Mack asked.

"It's excellent—much spicier than the canned chili I usually eat."

"Made right back there in the kitchen by Marge Curtis who has been here longer than I have, maybe longer than any of us."

"Give her my compliments, will you, Mack?"

"You bet," Mack assured.

"There sure are a lot of people coming in the door," observed Charlie.

"And probably just as many waiting outside."

"So, business is good," smiled Chase.

"And has been for as long as I can remember. This is a nuts-and-bolts kind of place. Nothing fancy about folks around here."

Charlie decided he'd better ask the questions that brought him here before Mack got too busy. "I've been in a lot of small towns, and it seems they all have something unique in their histories."

"I'm sure that's true. We got our own oddball stories, but most go back several years."

"Isn't Newburgh where the military dug up something, in 1947 I think it was?"

Mack looked at him somewhat suspiciously, before asking, "You work for the government, sir?"

"No, not anymore, just mentioning one of those stories like that Roswell event."

"It was kind of crazy around here . . . never quite knew what was really taken away. Nobody saw anything as far as I know. You can imagine all the wacky talk that went on for months."

Chase nodded.

The long frown moved slowly toward the bar with drink orders, and Mack saw her coming. "It's time to pop the caps on some long necks. The mixed-drink crowd usually shows up later, around ten o'clock." Mack walked over to meet Long Face.

The man whose mouth was lost in a mound of whiskers had finished his fiddlers and snapped his overall straps a couple of times as though this was his way of complementing the chef. Without so much as a word, Long Face came up and took away his empty plate. The bearded man looked over at Charlie, who sipped the draft beer Mack had set up for him.

"Name's Keith—Keith Owen," he said, reaching out to shake Charlie's hand.

"Charlie Chase," smiled Charlie.

"That was a long time ago. Most people have all but forgotten it."

"It must have been a huge thing for a small town?"

"For a few months, but it was hushed up good. None of us ever knew what really happened out there. In those days, government's word was good enough. Not like today."

"I guess even the military changes over time," Chase suggested.

"Whatever it was they found was loaded on a flatbed truck and taken away expeditiously as the military is prone to say. That's the way the story went by most of those who saw it happen."

Walking Einstein was suddenly thinking back, to a time long before 1947, and was quick to perceive reasons why the military had taken so long to retrieve whatever they had discovered. The United States had been in two world wars, experienced a stock market crash, and was heavily invested in postwar reconstruction and development programs. Though the Space Race was on, there were no eyes in the sky—no surveillance or reconnaissance satellites until 1957, the year The Soviet Union successfully launched Sputnik into a low earth orbit.

With these reasons considered, Chase was amazed that the thing was found as early as it was and thought it could have gone unnoticed for several more years. He'd managed to find only a couple of reports that mentioned the Newburgh event, and they were in local newspapers. Though it was all beginning to acquire a chronology, there was one other possibility that needed to be checked out.

Mack came over and stood by them. "How about another one, Keith?"

"Not tonight, Mack. That's it for me, got some work to finish." He nodded to Charlie and disappeared into the night.

"Keith Owen is one of those stand-up men who would help anybody and never expect a thing in return. He and his boy Tim own the hardware store downtown."

"Mack," called a man toward the far end of the bar. "Set me up here, will you?"

It all seemed to fit, even the 46 years that passed before the craft was recovered, if it had been recovered at all. Even if the ground was uncultivated and overgrown, there would still be indications that something had crashed. He had a hunch, which meant he'd have to do some nosing around at the site.

He brought the subject up with Mack. "I guess that landscape has changed a lot since the military dug into it."

"Not as much as you'd think," Mack answered.

"Any ponds or lakes near there?"

"The old Atwood house is still there, just recently purchased by a local artist. Several years ago, the Newland family built a place on property near the military dig site. There's a large lake south of the house, used by the city as a reserve water reservoir. In fact, you can see the dam if you drive the French Island Trail east, about a mile past the Old Lock and Dam House."

"Thanks, Mack. It's been a real pleasure."

"Stop in again when you're this way."

"I'll be sure and do that."

Instead of returning to Vincennes, Chase spent the night at a motel east of Evansville and about five miles from Newburgh. The craft might not have been dug out of the ground at all. From all the reports he'd found, the recovery had been during daylight hours. Was it possible that the craft had been submerged in the lake, and what was recovered were only pieces broken off when it had struck the ground? After the Great War ended, a strong Nationalism had taken hold. It would have been anti–American to mention the words conspiracy or cover-up. The people of Newburgh could have been deceived and never even suspected it.

Saturday morning at a few minutes before sunrise, Charlie Chase drove the French Island Trail east near the Old Lock and Dam House. He noticed the abrupt rise in the landscape ahead, where several expensive homes had been constructed along the summit. But after another mile, the expensive houses gave way to a heavy stand of trees that rose like the masts of sailing ships high into the morning sky. Refusing to dissipate, a sluggish mist clung tenaciously to hillsides and vegetation, as though it still had hours before sunshine rose high enough in the sky to burn it away.

Like Mack had said, the dam, or what looked to be about 20 yards of dam, was visible at the top of a steep rocky incline. With woods from the road all the way to the top, Charlie could climb without being seen. Parking his car on the river side, in a small open space with a scenic view of the Ohio River, he got his camera and began to climb. It took nearly 30 minutes to get to the top. Pausing to catch his breath, he sat a few minutes on a rocky outcrop, looking back at the road below, and at the Kentucky side of the river that could be easily seen above the trees.

There was a large lake at the crest of the hill with tall trees surrounding it on three sides. Looking at the size of the dam, he realized the water was probably more than 40 feet deep in the center. The only construction at the site was a brick pump house and two filtration tanks, built near a spillway that ran off toward a creek. On the far side, a long open field stretched north more than half a mile, ending at a broad expanse of trees, and near the place in the creek where he had found the strange pieces. The town of Newburgh had posted signs prohibiting swimming and boating. Shore fishing was by permit only. The Newland house, which would not have been there in 1947, was between the lake and the far woods. If something had crashed or even landed in 1947, it could certainly have ended up at the bottom of the lake, or for that matter, even in the Ohio River.

After taking several pictures with his digital camera, he began the descent back down the hillside to his car, convinced that there was another more tenable storyline to the 1901 event, also to the military recovery of a possible craft 46 years later. The Ohio River was not more than 300 yards from where he was standing. Immediately, Chase realized the proximity of the river brought a whole new set of circumstances into play.

Chapter 46

THE FRONT DOOR was unlocked and ajar when Liz and Jenna arrived at Atwood House. Nothing, not a sound came from inside. The first thought was that Ben was upstairs and hadn't closed the door after coming in earlier in the morning. It was Liz who felt that something out of the ordinary had happened, and that it had occurred during the night.

"He's gone, Jenna," she said evenly. "Ben is gone."

"What do you mean he's gone?"

They stood in the doorway to the library and both saw the new bouquet of flowers in the vase. "Anna has been here again, and he's gone with her."

"I don't believe that, Liz."

"You know it's true. Something happened here last night, not a thing to speak of casually, but it did happen, nevertheless. If he's not out there at the church site, or shopping in town, then he's with Anna. I can't explain it, but I do feel it—as sure as I'm standing here, Jenna."

"That woman is too much. Where does she get off doing such a thing? She shows up and works a spell on him and he's too blind to see it happening."

"It might be more than that."

"What do you mean?"

"Maybe he wanted it to happen. You blame Anna for what Ben wanted all along."

"This whole thing is ridiculous," scoffed Jenna.

"Yes, but to deny it would be foolish."

"Maybe so. After all, the man doesn't really have it all together anymore."

"Anna's a tantalizing enticement."

"You might be right, but Ben is no pushover. I just don't think he would be naïve enough to think that such a preposterous thing would be possible," Jenna admitted.

"I don't think there's anything we can do, Jenna. If he is with Anna, I suppose we wait—and hope he finds his way back."

"So that's it? Just wait until he shows up again? You know as well as I do that he might never show up again. Ben Manning might be gone forever."

Liz didn't answer right away. Her eyes closed, both hands over her ears, she rocked back-and-forth on her heels, and was either putting herself into a trance or already in one. When she finally opened her eyes, she stared into the interior of the house, which was just now coming to life with sunlight through the eastern windows. At the end of the hallway were two rooms in the back of the house, one recently converted by Manning into an art studio, and the larger room, now a gallery where several of Ben's paintings were already displayed. He and Jenna had painted the rooms more than a month before, but the only work done since was the addition of track lights, which Matt Jennings had installed. Liz started down the hallway, but stopped abruptly after only a few steps, as though she'd suddenly changed her mind.

"What is it?" Jenna asked.

"The great room—something happened there last night. I'm not sure yet, but something strange happened to Ben in that room."

Opening both doors wide enough to reveal a bright interior, Liz entered cautiously, Jenna following a few steps behind. Stopping in the center of the room, she again closed her eyes and began rocking deliberately. In seconds, shards of sunlight dissolved, leaving the great room in gray tones.

Two images emerged.

The moon was an enormous face peering through the windows, its mouth a twisted gaping hole, in which appeared the silhouettes of two people tightly embraced. For a few moments, these images floated rhythmically across the floor, before spinning absurdly inside the huge mouth that had no tongue, turning, twisting convulsively—two attenuated shapes quickly sucked into oblivion. The moon pushed closer to the windows, until nothing but a huge sardonic smile pressed against the glass.

Lightning flashed. Walls in the great room disintegrated. A wide expanse of white appeared, as flashes of green ripped away the ceiling. With nothing beneath her feet, nothing to steady her, Liz Raymond sensed a tremendous force tugging, pulling her into a churning vortex.

She opened her eyes abruptly, looked at Jenna as though she was seeing her for the first time. If she had put herself into a trance, or if some unseen force in the room had affected her, it was impossible for Jenna to determine what had occurred. She unbuttoned her jacket and drew the back of her hand across her forehead to wipe away light perspiration.

"You okay?" Jenna asked with a note of concern.

Without answering, she closed her eyes again, only to find the malicious smile replaced by a man standing in a mist at the edge of a pond or lake. His sandy hair was disheveled and slung over one shoulder was a canvas bag. Although she was sure she'd seen the man before, she didn't remember where, only that he seemed familiar. When he sat down on a rocky outcrop and brushed the tops of his wingtips, she realized where they had met briefly.

"Sorry, sometimes this thing takes hold of me, and I have to run with it, go wherever it takes me. Can you understand that, Jenna?"

"Not exactly," Jenna answered.

"Somebody is putting the pieces together," she assured Jenna.

"What about Ben?"

"Ben and Anna were in this room last night. She must have convinced him to go with her."

"Go where?"

"I don't know, but possibly through a gateway that opened here in this room."

Jenna quickly remembered the night in the dining room, the same night she had seen Lacey and Ben disappear. She had not revealed this to Liz, who was now suggesting the same thing had happened last night in the great room, and that Ben had gone voluntarily into another dimension. Sure that Anna was responsible for his disappearance, a shudder of disbelief went through her as she looked helplessly at Liz Raymond.

"You must have faith, Jenna. We'll find the answers."

Nodding, Jenna managed a slight smile. "I hope you're right."

"I saw something else . . . a man I met briefly some months ago at the Abbey in Saint Meinrad. I don't know who he is, but I do know he is in Newburgh."

"What?"

"I'm sure this all sounds a bit improbable to you, but you're going to have to trust me, Jenna."

"Where do we find him?"

"He'll find us," Liz answered confidently.

"I swear, if I didn't know you, Liz, I'd think you were crazy."

"It wouldn't be the first time someone thought that." Liz put her arm on Jenna's shoulder as she spoke, "Maybe we better go out to the site. Matt's probably wondering where we are."

When they neared the site, they saw Lacey sitting in the seat of a white Bobcat parked a few yards away from one of the limestone slabs. She gave a slight wave when she saw them. Matt, who was kneeling at one end of the slab, was clearing dirt away, until one corner was entirely exposed. Waving, he got up and came over to meet them. Lacey climbed down from the Bobcat happy to see them.

"I thought we'd look under at least one of these slabs," he said. "Something's down there, just can't make out with the GPR what it is."

"It's surely not a grave?" asked Jenna hesitantly.

"Doesn't look like a grave. Seems more of a void in which there appears to be steps."

"Where's Ben?" Lacey asked.

"Ben's gone," Jenna replied.

"Gone? What do you mean he's gone?"

It was Liz who attempted to put Lacey's curiosity at rest, at least for now. "We're not sure, Lacey. It's nothing to worry about. He'll show up later."

But Lacey wasn't so sure Ben would show up later as Liz suggested. She had her own ideas about what had happened. "What if he went through one of those invisible boundaries, a gateway, or whatever it was we experienced in the dining room? I'll say it again. Strange things happen in that house."

"Ben knows what he's doing, Lacey," Jenna assured her.

Shaking her head, Lacey said, "That woman seems to have a thing for him."

"Lacey told me about the incident in the dining room," Matt revealed. "That house really is a mystery."

"We start by believing everything will be fine," suggested Liz, who was curious about the dining room incident. "Maybe we can talk about what happened in the dining room later."

Jenna looked at Liz, as if to get her approval before speaking again. "Dr. Raymond had a premonition in the great room."

"Really," replied Lacey excitedly.

"Why don't you tell them, Liz?" prompted Jenna.

"As soon as people hear the word premonition, they start shaking their heads. Nevertheless, I can assure you that premonitions can certainly be real." She looked at each before speaking again. "I don't know his name, and I only met him once, but he knows about these strange phenomena, and I'm sure it's only a matter of time before he shows up here."

"A couple nights ago a man at the Knob Hill Tavern was asking questions about the 1947 military recovery," revealed Matt. "Keith Own was there and thought it a little peculiar that a man who was just passing through town would ask so many questions."

"You were there?" Lacey wanted to know.

"Dad ran into Keith Owen in town Friday, said the man looked kind of bookish, one of those eccentric types who knows things. Said his name was Chase—Charlie Chase," Matt announced.

They looked at Liz for her response. But Liz Raymond was looking off in the distance at someone standing near the woods. "I think he found us." She pointed to a man coming closer with each step.

Chapter 47

HE RECOGNIZED LIZ immediately. "I'm sure we've met before."

"Saint Meinrad Archabbey."

"That's right," he nodded.

She looked closely at him as did the others, each wanting to know more about this man now standing among them, looking around curiously. "I never got your name, sir," coaxed Dr. Raymond politely.

"Well, we didn't have much time together, did we? If I remember correctly, you were shocked by what I told you."

"You'll have to admit it was all kind of sudden. I didn't really expect a stone to have a pulse."

He laughed at that, and reached out to shake her hand, "Charlie Chase . . . Dr. Charlie Chase."

"Liz Raymond," returned Liz warmly, surprised to learn Chase was not the itinerant she first suspected.

"Yes, I know who you are, Dr. Raymond. Carl Hewitt told me after you left that day."

Liz introduced the others and when Charlie and Matt went over to look at the limestone slab, Jenna pulled Liz aside and whispered, "Is he the one?"

"He's the one," she nodded.

"Are you sure?"

"Yes, Jenna, I'm quite sure."

The fact that Liz had met Chase at Saint Meinrad seemed good enough for the others. Something about the man made him a bit eccentric, but also engagingly provocative. His sandy-blond hair, parted on one side, was long in the back and touched the collar of his jacket. He had sparkling blue eyes so pale that they looked ethereal. Dressed in jeans, a blue nylon jacket, and shiny wingtips, Chase had a canvas bag over his right shoulder, and Liz knew from the first time they met that just about anything he needed was in that bag.

"Got any ideas?" Matt asked him directly.

"Yes," responded Chase, while running his fingers over what Matt had decided were numbers so heavily weathered that they could no longer be discerned. "What do your scans show?"

"A large void, and there could be steps."

With the rest of them looking on, Charlie moved from one corner to the next, and with a hand trowel, which he took from his canvas bag, they saw him dig until the bottom of the slab was exposed. "If you dig a bit more along the edges, and loosen the stone from the ground, I don't think you'll need the Bobcat."

Matt dug the entire perimeter deeper. When he finished, he looked for Charlie, who was digging the perimeter of the other slab. "Okay, got it," Matt yelled.

Chase was the kind of man who kept his thoughts almost exclusively to himself—unless pushed to reveal them. Even then, he said no more than was necessary. These people were different. They had no obvious ulterior motives, and not one, except possibly Dr. Liz Raymond, knew what had happened here. There was much, much more Chase could reveal, but first things first.

Returning to where the others stood, Dr. Chase acknowledged, "I've seen marks like these before. They're pivot marks."

With Chase once more on his hands and knees, the thin man with the polished wingtip shoes, the man capable of putting it all together, carefully examined the marks on the slab, as if he wanted to be sure before he did anything. Matt also knelt. Chase glanced at him, and what he did next surprised all of them. He tapped the end of the trowel against the south end of the stone. Nothing. Getting up, he went to the opposite end and tapped with the trowel a second time.

Amazingly, the stone began to rise at one end until it was vertical, leaving open spaces on both ends. With some creaking, it rotated on an iron axis that was at the center of the stone. Walking Einstein took a flashlight from his bag, but instead of shining it into the hole as the rest of them expected, he removed the batteries and placed the positive ends against the stone, which immediately began to glow in an almost imperceptible soft white light, which disappeared when he removed the batteries. The mechanism that enabled the large stone to be raised was a series of small vertical wheels connected to a pushrod that, when freed, allowed the stone to rotate on a heavy metal rod approximately five feet long, which was a foot or more longer than the width of the limestone slab.

"This is absolutely unbelievable," Jenna said excitedly.

"What is it?" Lacey wanted to know.

Liz, standing beside Walking Einstein, knew what they had uncovered. Before speaking, she looked at Chase who nodded as though he knew what she was thinking. But instead of Liz speaking, it was Charlie who revealed her thoughts.

"You're right, Dr. Raymond. We saw something similar at the Abbey. And this has been carefully constructed to have the same purpose."

"What is it?" called Jenna from a few feet away.

"A communication tower," Liz replied.

"The underside is not entirely limestone," Walking Einstein informed them. "It has a thin layer embedded with grains of copper," and here he looked at Matt, "much like those pieces you've been digging up. It's a reactor capable of generating a power source."

"Sunlight will activate it?" asked Matt.

"Only slightly. Think of a stove. A burner on low will produce only low heat. Sunlight only warms the surface. It takes another charge to make it function."

"And what's that?" Jenna inquired.

Charlie pointed into the hole, which the sun was beginning to illuminate. "The power source is down there."

The others pushed nearer to see for themselves what Chase referred to as the power source. They saw several rocks, nearly transparent in the noon sun, piled at the bottom of what was nothing more than a pit which looked like it had been dug by hand.

"Rocks," Lacey proclaimed.

"Not just rocks," Charlie acknowledged. "Those are quartz crystals. If you look closely, you can see a protrusion of quartz, probably a large vein running in that direction." Here he pointed to the other limestone slab.

Matt glanced over his shoulder toward the other stone slab before saying, "I guess the other one is the same thing as this?"

Charlie nodded. "A quartz crystal was loaded into that depression." In the overhead sunlight, the depression was obvious to everyone. "At night, the entire stone slab could be rotated, exposing the crystal to the sky."

"You seem to know a lot about this," Lacey alleged.

"I only want to solve this thing before the government shows up, so we can keep them off the hunt, so to speak."

"Pardon me for saying," began Jenna, "but you could be the government."

He nodded. "I certainly could be, but I can assure you that I am no longer contracted in any way with any government program or project. The government has already got what it needed from me. What's going on around here is a much larger event than any of us can fully comprehend, and that would include the government, or more specifically, the military."

It was Liz who came to Chase's defense. "We need to listen—give him a chance to explain what happened here."

"I want to show you something," announced Walking Einstein, reaching into his bag to withdraw a manila folder. "A couple of days ago I was in the woods there," and he nodded toward the woods that concealed Shanklin's pond, "when I found these near the creek." He handed photographs of two coins to Dr. Raymond, who held them out for the others to see. "After cleaning the coins, I shot these photographs and had them enlarged," Chase revealed. "I wanted to be sure that I was absolutely correct about them."

"You say you found these near the creek?" Liz asked.

"That's right."

"What is it, Liz?" Jenna asked, after catching Liz's surprised expression.

"Look at the date."

"I don't understand—2150," Jenna proclaimed. "It says, 'One Hundred United States Dollars'. You can't be serious."

"That's what I thought," returned Charlie, "but I guarantee that these are the real deal." He pulled the two coins from his pocket and held them out on the palm of his hand. "Any jeweler could easily confirm them as gold coins."

"Oh, my God, Liz. Can this be possible?" Jenna looked hard at Chase before asking, "You're absolutely sure about this?"

He nodded, "They are authentic in every respect."

"Dr. Chase," began Liz, "just what is your purpose, your interest in all this?"

"What crashed here in 1901 was not an alien spaceship. All indications point to a craft from our own future. In 1947, that craft was not dug out of the ground by the military as I initially thought. I don't think the government ever suspected a crash site."

"How could you possibly know this?" Jenna asked.

"You do seem very sure," admitted Liz.

"It all fits. This was an attempted controlled landing that went wrong. There are still indications where the craft struck the ground—those rises across the field. After exhausting research, I'm convinced now that the military was searching for something else entirely. This is confirmed by later reconnaissance satellite technology, which never showed anything suspicious—nothing on the Newland or Atwood properties, and nothing in the town lake or Ohio River."

Liz listened carefully to Chase, thinking he presented a plausible scenario. What she suspected was that Walking Einstein knew much more than he offered now. "This is extremely profound, Dr. Chase," she said.

"I think way outside the parameters laid down by lazy, self-aggrandizing academics who never look holistically at anything. They begin with preconceived hypotheses that they spend careers trying to support. I do the research, and I don't care where it takes me," Charlie informed them.

"There had to be a pilot—someone in control of the craft," intimated Liz.

"And maybe a crew, or passengers," suggested Lacey.

"Do you think it's possible they survived?" Jenna asked.

"There's every reason to think they did," Charlie assured them. "I can only tell you what I've decided based on 15 years of research."

"What happened to them?" inquired Jenna.

"I have some ideas, but I don't know for sure. I do think that those answers are still here—on this property."

Matt, descending the eight steps to the bottom, picked up one of the crystals and fit it into the depression. Looking up at Chase, who was watching him, he asked, "Is this how it's done?"

"Yes," Charlie replied. "That's precisely how it's done."

"And then what?"

But before Charlie could answer, the stone slab began to rotate. The mechanism clicked, and the slab went flat against the ground—with Matt Jennings trapped in the hole beneath it. The bottom side of the slab now faced toward the sky. The quartz Matt had fit into the space, cast a soft greenish glow that caused everyone except Charlie Chase to back away. Seconds passed before a thick bolt of green light shot high into a blue sky.

Chapter 48

He felt Anna's hand slipping loose, heard her calling him from far away, calling his name with an urgency that frightened him. Calling, calling, until silence fell on all sides of him, heart-wrenching silence that left only echoes ringing in his head. Ben Manning had no idea where he was.

A gallery of unfamiliar faces appeared, each with a gaping mouth, shouting out warnings that had come too late. The support beneath his feet was gone. Spinning madly, as if he'd been caught inside a swirling wind, sucked into a tenacious vortex, he tried to open his eyes in the vacillating mist that was everywhere. The swirling wind had hold of him. At the mercy of this alien wind, there was nothing to reach for, nothing to steady him, nothing to keep him from blowing into oblivion.

He could not tell in which direction his body was moving. There was nothing to anchor him, nothing to stop the sensation of turning, then floating, then tumbling and spinning again. But he believed that when it finally stopped he would be upright on his feet with beautiful Anna Atwood beside him. It was the terrible silence that disturbed him, especially when he felt this spiraling wind was transporting him back in time. Maybe that was the way it happened, a sweep of wind dragging him away in dead silence, inside a vacuum of shadows and confusion. Why had Anna so quickly slipped away from him? He recalled how easily her fingers had slipped from his. Had she deliberately left him alone, or was she somewhere inside the mist reaching out, trying to find him?

It had happened so quickly. Whether he'd gone with Anna willingly, he couldn't say. What did it matter? Here he was shackled to this ungodly wind that deliberately transported him farther away from the world he knew. But what happened next was so frightening, so disturbing, that he was on the verge of losing consciousness.

Eyes! Hundreds of eyes watching him. Vindictive eyes. Everywhere, the eyes of strangers, watching, staring, unblinking. Eyes without faces. Huge bulging eyes. Were these the eyes of angels, or the eyes of devils—evil, punishing eyes that saw every solitary sin? Eyes that saw into the dark places unhidden from God? It was not a time for nakedness in front of eyes that knew every dirty secret. But there he was, scrutinized by hundreds of cold intrusive eyes that watched him attempt again to steady himself in a greenish mist that was now beginning to evaporate. Finally, his hands rubbed against something with rough edges.

Even with his feet touching what he was sure was a wooden floor, and still leaning to one side, Ben attempted to regain his balance. Knees wobbly, his thoughts hazy, leaving him slightly disoriented after what had happened, and still unsure where he was, he reached out to steady himself and touched what felt like bricks. In darkness this deep, he could not see anything. Holding his hand in front of his face, he could barely make out his fingers. This was what the grave was like, and for a few moments, that's exactly where he thought he was—deep in his own grave.

With one hand trailing behind him, he walked ten feet one way, before coming to a corner. Fifteen steps to his left was another corner. If he was in a room, where was the door? Where were the windows—the furniture? Where were the lights? What was wrong with him? The light was in his pocket.

He took out his mobile phone and pushed on the flashlight. Instantly, shadows relented enough to reveal a large empty room without windows, a room without doors, a room with a plaster ceiling, ten feet above his head. He was entombed inside four brick walls.

What appeared to be the only doorway was bricked shut. Alone in a room without any visible way out was a daunting situation. And with the only light in the room coming from his cell phone, the situation was even more demoralizing.

This was how it ended. God, what a way to go! He could be anywhere in time. When he looked at the time and date on his mobile phone, he was somewhat relieved. It was nearly noon. The date verified the next day after a long night of dancing with Anna. What if the date was wrong? What if the phone didn't work? He knew he had one chance, and only one chance.

His hands and fingers trembled as he held the phone. No signal. Even moving to different places in the room, there was still no signal. He'd have to endure the dark, save the battery. Knowing his chance to survive was slight, he sat down and leaned against the bricked doorway. Without tools, he could not break through the bricks. He remembered seeing karate people break bricks with their bare hands. Maybe he could kick the bricks loose. Then again, if he broke his foot or leg, he'd be worse off than he was now.

The air was thin and rancid, stale air that had been there since the room was walled shut. Shining his flashlight up to the ceiling, he did see a pipe, which probably vented outside. At least he wouldn't suffocate. Then the thought occurred to him that hypoxia might be the quickest way out. Ben had never found himself in a life-and-death situation, so remaining as calm as possible was essential. It was too soon for panic.

Moving to the back of the room, he tried Jenna's mobile again—nothing. If her phone had at least picked up a signal, maybe they could trace it. He'd heard accounts of this being done when hikers were lost in heavy timber. People missing in woods or mountains were sometimes found because they had cell phones. But this enclosure was like a tomb, and in the end, it might *be* a tomb.

Then it hit him. Was this the room the Youngs had walled shut? According to Larry Collins, it was a gateway they had closed. If this was that room, the portal should still be here. Or was that just too illogical to consider? Switching on the light again, he walked carefully around the room, searching every crease and crevice for a possible exit. He even walked every inch of the room, brushing the air with his hands, attempting to find a portal. Absolutely nothing, except a slight crack in the bricks along the back wall.

Putting his fingers up to the space, he felt a pulse of cool air. If only he had something to use as a tool, anything, even a pocketknife. But he had nothing—except his fingers. It was a ridiculous thought to expect his fingers to loosen the mortar between the bricks. If it worked at all, it would take weeks. By then, it would be too late. Ben Manning was a man who needed a miracle—and he knew it.

Shining the light across the floor revealed nothing more than a few pieces of brick and loose mortar. Maybe he could use a piece of broken brick as a knife. Would it be substantial enough to widen the crack? He pushed a few pieces of broken mortar into the small opening, and heard them drop on the other side. So, there was a space behind the bricks. But how much of a space? With the light aimed into the hole, that was a three-inch vertical crease where both brick and mortar had fallen away, he thought he could make out a void in the narrow beam of light. It seemed to go on for several feet. Maybe there was another room behind this one.

Trying to pull himself together before real panic set in, he looked more closely at the area around the opening and noticed several other areas where the mortar was either loose or had cracks. Concentrating on one specific vertical seam in the wall, he realized the bricks were aligned in a straight line, unlike the pattern repeated on the rest of that wall. Six feet from the floor was a horizontal line running about four feet, before stopping at another vertical line. With a sharp piece of brick, he was able to chip away the mortar, which had many age cracks, and to his surprise, pieces of masonry fell to the floor. He kept chipping until he had a two-foot section where most of the mortar had been removed. After several more minutes, other sections loosened, and Manning was ready to try something else.

Leaning his shoulder against one of the vertical seams, he was sure he felt movement. More pieces of mortar fell to the floor, and when he put the light on the other vertical seam he saw cracks at various points along that seam. He could get a running start and strike the wall harder with his shoulder, but this was too risky. What if the bricks didn't budge?

He'd kick it lightly and see what happened. When he heard the breaking sound, he was sure one of the bones in his lower leg had snapped. Instead, a brick fell to the floor, then another, and mortar shook loose along the line where he had snapped a forceful kick. When he looked again, there was separation along the seam, so he kicked again, this time harder. Other bricks gave way.

A door on a vertical axis creaked open to reveal two stone walls and a tunnel stretching several feet into darkness. Six feet in height, the ceiling, though reinforced with timbers, had several cracks, and debris lay scattered on a dirt floor. Someone had gone to a lot of trouble to construct this tunnel. What was it though, and where did it lead? Dust particles floated in the light from his mobile phone. Gradually, he made his way into the tunnel. He shined the light into the darkness ahead, turned it off, and then took several steps before turning it on again to reconnoiter the next few yards.

After he'd walked at least 40 yards, the tunnel split off into two others, one running west, the other northeast. Continuing in the same tunnel, which he thought went northwest, and walking less than 20 more yards, he soon came to a wall, or what he hoped was a door. Why would this tunnel end here? He could see no reason for it ending so abruptly, so he pushed hard against one side. Nothing moved. Trying the other side, he expected something to give way, but again, nothing moved. It was only after he kicked hard against one side that a door began to move. He kicked until there was space enough for him to enter what he realized was another room. He'd have to use the light to see what was inside, and after turning it on, he saw three strange people looking back at him.

"I give up!" he yelled.

But there was no response.

Chapter 49

LOOKING MORE CAREFULLY at the three people, he realized that if they were people at all, they were certainly not alive. They wore black helmets with visors over the eyes and slotted opaque covers over their mouths. What seemed to be lights and other technology were identical on all three helmets. They were dressed in identical uniforms, unlike anything he'd ever seen—white porous material, with black and red vertical piping at various points on the legs, thick circular piping around the arms near the shoulders, and the wrists were banded with more black piping, only larger and heavier. Thin black breastplates were impressed with UAC in red lettering. He poked at one as though he expected it to move, then poked again sharply into the side, and was amazed at how light the material was to the touch.

Already assuming there might be a corpse inside each, he looked away to see what else was in the room. This entire ordeal was getting more bizarre with each passing minute. He snapped three pictures with the mobile camera. The flash was weak, but strong enough to capture much of what was in this unusual room, which, the more he looked, could have been constructed inside a natural cavern. Because his light was weakening, he could not be sure of the enormity of what he had discovered.

To Ben's amazement, the room was substantial in size, and looked as if it had been lived in many years ago. Near several wooden crates and what he was sure was electrical equipment arranged on metal tables, a rising stairway stopped under a large piece of black rock, resembling closely what they had found in the ground near the church foundation. His body was on the edge of convulsing, and he knew if he didn't escape from this tomb soon, he was going to lose his mind.

At the top of the steps, the stone slab wouldn't budge. No matter how hard he pushed, it wouldn't move. He had two options left, to take the tunnel west, or return to the one that led northeast from Atwood House. After backtracking, he headed down the northeast tunnel, walking in darkness as much as possible, or at least until he could no longer endure darkness. After ten minutes of stumbling, he arrived at another wall, or doorway, or dead-end.

To come this far and find no opening, no way out, was frustrating. Panic gripped him. In a few minutes the battery would be dead. Turning off the light and sinking to the floor dejectedly, he prepared to accept his fate. His back against the wall, he felt something sharp poking his ribs. He jumped to his feet quickly and backed away. Shining the light on the wall near where he'd been sitting, he saw a large protrusion of rock glinting in the weakened light. It looked like a large vein of quartz crystal, and these tunnels were probably old mining tunnels sealed decades ago. In several places, gaping holes indicated removal of large chunks of quartz.

One peculiar aspect of his hurried observation deserved more deliberation. The quartz vein passed through the obstruction in front of him, and that was enough to suggest something on the other side. Leaning heavily against what he thought was another door, he was sure his weight had dislodged it slightly. Pushing harder against it, he heard chunks of mortar and brick falling to the floor. Undoubtedly, like the other doors, this one had been sealed for many years and Ben was sure the builders had intended to keep the tunnels, the doors, the stairs, and all that was down here, sealed forever.

Turning the light on the floor, he noticed what looked like a gap between the door and floor. Kneeling to get a better look and thinking that these bricks remained enough of a barrier to make escape impossible, he pushed his fingers into the space beneath the door. Nothing. No breeze, nothing but more brick. His anxiety mounting, the mobile phone battery continuing to weaken, the darkness increasingly frightening, his determination to survive abating, Manning turned off his phone and sat down in what had to be everlasting darkness—and much too soon, the formidable blackness of his own grave.

Surprisingly, there was a distinguishable creaking—and movement. Something was here in this dark labyrinth with him. He thought about running, but to where, back the way he came? No, he already knew what was behind him. Going back was not going to work. Maybe the wall was coming closer. It was a trap, the kind ancient Egyptians built into their pyramids. But this was Indiana. At least, that's what he thought. Something was on the other side of the door—a door slowly opening.

The sounds of stones crushed under the weight of movement. More creaking, as the door rotated on a center axis, exactly the way the other doors had opened. Only this time, Ben wasn't opening it. A slender wrinkle of dirty light crawled along the wall and caught the quartz, which slowly brightened enough to reveal movement in the narrow opening. Ben saw a shape, dark, sinister, barely discernible, but moving deliberately, menacingly around the door, which was clearly opening wider.

Something gnawed at his shoe. He looked down and saw a rat the shape of Pennsylvania. If there was one, there had to be more behind the door that continued to squeak open. With no weapon to defend himself, he shook the rat loose and started kicking furiously, until he heard it scurry away down the dark tunnel.

He raised the mobile phone and started snapping pictures, hoping the flash would frighten any other rats. The door swung shut immediately, leaving him more confused, and wondering about his fate in a darkness deeper than before. Again, he thought about going back to the other tunnel, find a weapon among the things in the room he had discovered. Before he could move, he caught sight of a white light spilling under the doorway. The light brightened, dimmed, brightened again. Then, after a couple of seconds, it was gone.

A mutant rat with a flashlight! That was not possible. He had to know what was on the other side of the door.

Pushing the right side of the rock inward about six inches, he heard deep exhalations, as though the thing had difficulty breathing, or was trying to catch its breath, as it prepared for an attack. Another blast of light, and then another. Something shot through the light and fastened itself to his wrist. He could not tell if it was pulling or pushing him back into the tunnel. He was sure he caught a glimpse of two large eyes. In each flash of light, the eyes grew bigger and more appalling.

Then, without warning, the Pennsylvania rat was gnawing at his other shoe. The unholy beast was starving, and right now Ben's shoe, and possibly his foot, were dinner. He felt the teeth cutting like knives through the leather. If only he had a weapon. But something stronger was fastened to his arm and kept yanking at it as though it wanted to pull him into the space behind the door. Trying to pull away, he felt the grip tighten.

If it was another mutant rat, Ben Manning was finished. He still had battery power and thought if he pushed on the light suddenly it might scare at least one beast away. He'd better do it fast before he lost his arm. Illuminated by the weak light, he could at least get a look at what he would have to fight, and what was most likely going to kill him.

Before he could switch on the light, the grip on his arm loosened. Again, the rat darted off down the dark tunnel. The rank air smelled strangely fresh. A small stream of light plunged into the room. Whatever had grabbed his arm suddenly relented, allowing Ben to draw back his arm. At least he'd have two arms to defend himself. More fresh air came from the other side of the door that was not quite wide enough for him to push through. Thrusting his face into the crack, trying to see what was behind the door, he caught sight of an ascending stairway.

Just as he was about to push his head deeper into the crack, something shot through the opening, nearly striking him in the face. The thing had shot out at him like a snake striking. Shocked, he fell against the wall and was instantly conscious of a sharp pain in his back. He knew a jagged edge of quartz had pierced his clothes into his flesh. He was bleeding but couldn't tell how badly. Putting his hand where the crystal had struck him, he felt a small dampness in the jacket. He thought it strange that he should worry about what Anna would think when she saw the damage to the coat that she had bought him at Christmas.

Anna might never see him again. He'd be dead, down here with the Pennsylvania rat stripping away his cold flesh. Since he would never be found, Jenna would assume he was living happily with Anna, more than a hundred years in the past. If he could only see where the light was coming from, there might still be a way out. What about the jumbo rat though, and what waited for him behind this door that would no longer budge?

"There's something down here."

He heard the voice clearly and thought he recognized it but stayed silent at least until he could be sure. Footsteps crushing stones. The sounds of metal scraping against the bricks. Was someone attempting to beat down the door? He tried to clear his thoughts. If there were people, then they would get him out of this tomb. He would get a second lease on life.

It no longer mattered whose voice he heard. There was hope on the other side of these bricks, while on this side, certain death. Just as he was about to yell out, a hand poked through the space, and to his surprise, the door squeaked slowly on its axis. Manning would soon be face-to-face with someone, and that was much preferred to the darker option of retreating into the tunnel.

Chapter 50

THE SHAPE ON the other side had a hat pulled low on his forehead. In front of him was a shovel that he was prepared to swing at Ben, who drew back against the opposite wall, this time striking his head sharply against the bricks. Dazed, he felt his knees begin to buckle. As he fell, he saw clouds, wispy clouds in a blue sky, and four faces staring down at him.

"It's one of them—one of the aliens!" yelled Lacey, backing into Jenna.

"Get a grip, Lacey. There aren't any aliens," said Jenna.

"Well, it's something awful. You heard it, grunting like some wild beast."

The man with the shovel was helping the counterfeit alien to his feet. "I don't believe it."

"Nice to see you again, Matt."

Once he was out of the hole, Ben stood silently, looking first at the sky, then across the long lawn at Atwood house. "Hello," he smiled.

"Dr. Chase," said Jenna, "let me introduce Ben Manning. He's the owner of Atwood House."

"Mr. Manning," Charlie nodded.

Lacey noticed blood on Ben's fingers. "Something bit him down there."

Smiling at her, he shook his head, saying, "I fell is all."

As Jenna helped him out of his jacket, she saw the cut through the rip in his shirt. "I think you'll survive," she said warmly, "but we need to clean this before it gets infected."

Everyone except Liz, looked at him curiously. He realized they had questions, especially Jenna, who must have been upset, seeing him in the suit that Anna had given him. He was happy to be alive and back home. Still a bit dazed and unsettled, he could not say for sure how long he'd been in the dark. He squinted. His eyes still hadn't adjusted to the bright sunlight.

"How are you, Liz?"

"Fine, Ben. I'm sure you have plenty to tell us."

"I'm not sure what happened, or how I ended up down there."

"Dr. Chase has some information we think you'll be interested in hearing," informed Liz.

"What is this thing, other than a big hole in the ground?" Ben asked.

"A communication tower," Charlie answered.

Almost as soon as he said it, a terrible thought went through Charlie like a shot of electricity. What if he'd been wrong about Smith's intentions? What if Smith's entire purpose had been so well concealed, that Chase had been deliberately deceived and hadn't even considered, until now, something that had maniacal potential? How could he have been so naive? If it was true, Chase realized he had sold out, never suspecting that Smith and his colleagues had wanted to develop a particle beam accelerator—Nikola Tesla's Death Ray Machine. It was now a frightening possibility to be considered seriously, and Charlie Chase was shaken by the thought that he had not considered this possibility before now.

If Chase had provided critical pieces, innocently enough, he'd still have to accept ownership for what Smith had been so anxious to discover. The thought that Smith's organization was already in possession of Tesla's papers was much more than presumption. These important papers had been immediately confiscated at the time of Nikola Tesla's death, and among them were the constructional and operational plans for a particle beam accelerator, or Teleforce, as Tesla had called it—the Death Ray Machine. If successfully constructed, its capabilities would be enormously consequential, especially to a government wanting the ultimate super weapon. Chase didn't like where these thoughts were taking him.

Liz had a way of keeping things in focus. She suggested they go to the house to continue any further conversation. "Why don't we get that cut taken care of, Ben? Then we can talk."

"Lacey and I have a house to look at in an hour, so maybe we'll see you afterwards," Matt informed them. "It's a nice place on Second Street, and a house inside our budget."

After Matt and Lacey had gone, the others walked across the lawn to Atwood House. Charlie and Liz were several steps behind Ben and Jenna. Although their conversation was pleasant and sustained, neither Jenna nor Ben paid much attention to what was being said. Jenna recounted her surprise at seeing Ben climbing out of a hole in the ground, while he talked of blue skies and apple trees that were blossoming.

At length, "Who is Dr. Chase?" Ben asked.

"Liz met him in Saint Meinrad, at the Abbey. That's all I know about him, other than he seems to know quite a lot about the 1901 event." Jenna looked at him closely, moving her hand up and down to let him know the clothes he was wearing revealed what she was thinking. "You actually went with her last night."

"When I attempted to enter the portal in the great room, something extraordinary happened."

"What do you mean when you say something happened?"

"The portal must have closed suddenly. I didn't make it. I didn't get to the other side."

"You must love her very much."

"I'm sorry, Jenna."

"You're not the kind of man to let something go—not even when you realize you should walk away. I'd have been surprised if you hadn't attempted to follow Anna, despite the obvious dangers."

Shaking his head, he said, "I don't know what's happened to me."

Jenna smiled. "If you want to talk about it, I'm available."

Taking her hand in his, Ben was glad it was Jenna Newland walking beside him. "Thanks."

Jenna cleaned and bandaged the wound on Ben's back. Everyone was soon settled in the library, a pot of fresh coffee on Ben's desk. When Chase spoke, his comments were usually extremely concise, but inclusive of his reasons for coming to Newburgh, Indiana. With so much to discuss, it was necessary to establish a chronology of events, so Dr. Raymond recommended that Charlie provide sufficient information to get the others up to speed. Agreeable to her request, and anxious to explain his interest in the 1901 event, Charlie volunteered to offer pertinent data, especially those recently compiled.

The others, particularly Liz Raymond, were excited to have such a dedicated and competent scholar among them. Liz was convinced that he was the one person knowledgeable enough to reveal the missing pieces. Furthermore, Chase was a man without pretense, direct, extremely confident, and perceptive to the point of being psychic. Liz was increasingly fascinated by a scientist whose divergent thinking frequently collided with mainstream ideas. To some extent, Charlie was a romantic, a stargazer, a man who marched to the beat of no drummer. No one was ever going to change that, unless Smith had already done it—circuitously, deceptively.

"One of two things happened out there, and neither has anything to do with aliens." Charlie spoke with enough assurance to be convincing. Even though his ideas were largely conjecture, they were logically conceived possibilities that he felt would eventually be supported by facts. "Suppose a craft successfully traveled through a time-shift, and its passengers found themselves isolated more than two centuries from their own time. They constructed these communication towers to transmit their location. Here's where the narrative diverges. Either another craft from that time managed to arrive at the same time and place as the first craft, or there was no second craft. Either way, those who came were marooned, and left to make the best of it."

Liz looked at Charlie and smiled. "That's interesting, Dr. Chase."

"Stop and consider that for a moment—people from our own future unable to return to their time," said Chase. "Suppose these travelers were caught in a time-warp that inadvertently sent them into the late 19th, early 20th centuries. The knowledge these people possessed would be extraordinary, but they were trapped in an almost primitive past. It was later, maybe by coincidence, that they located or manufactured the time portals connected to Atwood House. But returning to their own time remained impossible—for whatever reasons."

"But they never stopped trying," suggested Liz.

Chase added, "The communication towers they constructed failed, so they eventually gave up—resigned to live out their lives in a time that must have been extremely backward and undeveloped to them."

"And gradually acculturation occurred," added Liz.

Chase nodded. "That would make sense."

"Coincidence would explain it. They probably had no intention of traveling beyond their own time, and at first, had no idea what was happening to them. The time slip took them into the past by accident," suggested Liz.

"Then, they soon realized it was a one-way ticket?" asked Ben.

"Not exactly," added Chase. "Certain conditions had to exist for the time slip to occur in the first place. That's the reason I lean more toward the first idea, that only one craft arrived. I'm convinced there was never a second craft. What you've located by the bridge was one of their communication towers. Communication remained the only alternative they had. After the towers failed them, they were intentionally destroyed and buried. You have unearthed not only their hopes, but also their frustrations and failures."

"What about the pieces we've recovered out by the church foundation?" asked Ben.

"Parts of the space craft that brought them here. A debris field that the military never suspected," answered Chase confidently.

"What evidence do you have to support this idea that the craft was from our future?" Ben inquired, a hint of doubt evident in his tone.

"Not much," he confessed. "Why don't I begin with these?"

He handed the two coins to Ben who recognized them immediately. They were like the one he had taken from Anna Atwood's sitting room. Much surprised by what Chase showed him, he had no idea what to say. Dr. Charlie Chase had certainly caught Manning entirely off guard

"I dug them up near where the creek goes into the woods, north of the house," Chase confessed.

Catching Manning's surprised expression, Liz asked, "What is it, Ben?"

"Nothing, I was only considering what Dr. Chase said." Looking at the three of them looking at him and knowing he had more to say, Ben exhaled nervously. "I found something down there," he began, his voice strained and showing signs of anxiety.

"It's okay, Ben," Jenna assured. "Take your time and tell us what's bothering you."

"There's a room. The light on my cell was dim so I didn't see the interior clearly for very long, though I did see what I'm sure were three spacesuits hanging on one of the walls."

There was a sudden gasp in the room.

Chapter 51

NO ONE HAD expected such a remarkable comment. Each sat silently for what seemed like minutes, considering the implications of Ben's remarks. Here was further proof to support Dr. Chase's contention. Though Ben was not a man given to exaggeration, he could certainly have been mistaken. Not one of them thought this, however. He said he had seen three spacesuits and they believed him.

Several seconds passed before Chase said, "What we already know is certainly fundamental to what we don't know, and that missing information is most likely in the tunnels beneath our feet."

"There's much more. It was so dark, and my cell battery was so weak." Ben faltered, as though he didn't really want to remember.

"How did you get where we found you?" Chase asked, his curiosity apparent to the others.

It was Jenna who answered. "There are things about this house, strange things, very strange things."

"I guessed as much," Charlie admitted. "Dr. Raymond briefed me on some of what's been happening. I assure you it's not the first time I've been involved with the paranormal."

"I have told Dr. Chase about the portals in this house, the gateways to other dimensions," stated Liz. "If we're going to solve this, then he should know what we know."

Charlie looked from one to the other before speaking again. "I'm sure you've discovered that this entire area has a high concentration of ley lines, and that any sustained convergence of these lines produces strong magnetic fields."

Liz nodded to confirm with Chase that they were familiar with the ley lines and the anomalies created by them. Before she could speak, she was conscious of a shadow passing by the entrance to the library. She was sure what that meant. If Anna Atwood was back, she had come again for Ben.

Liz's change of expression was instantly apparent, particularly to Jenna, who glanced toward the doorway. "It's Anna, isn't it?" shot Jenna.

Liz nodded.

Chase, quick to pick up on what was happening, hurriedly withdrew from his bag what looked like a small digital recorder and put it on the corner of the desk facing the door. They all looked at the doorway as though each expected someone to appear. They didn't have to wait long before a black fluttery shape came into full view. A silhouetted shadow, much like a hologram, loomed faintly in the doorway. Although the shape of a woman was apparent, her face had no distinguishable features. The only thing vivid enough to be seen clearly was the vase of cut flowers that was placed methodically on the table beside the door. The shape became gradually insubstantial, disappearing into thin air.

"I assume this has happened before," Charlie said calmly. He turned the camera off as he spoke and set it in his lap momentarily.

Liz looked at Chase before telling him, "Yes, but not entirely like this."

"How do you mean?"

"That was Anna Atwood," said Liz. "This house was built in 1903 by her husband."

"You might as well know, Dr. Chase," Jenna begin, "Anna Atwood is a frequent visitor here, and she most assuredly has form and substance, right Ben?"

Ben nodded.

"We have a distinct trail camera image of her and Ben during a snowstorm—taken this past winter out by the bridge," revealed Liz, "and yet another image, not quite so distinct, captured near the thing on the lawn. We were never quite sure what it was we had discovered," conceded Liz.

Charlie nodded. "That's a whole new dynamic, isn't it?" he returned. "Have there been others?"

"Occasionally," Liz admitted. "We've done a sustained and detailed investigation, Dr. Chase."

"I'm sure you have," Chase said. "You can feel the magnetic fields here. I'm certain there are portals that come and go throughout this house. You probably know their locations. Question is, how are these portals controlled?"

"If we knew that we'd shut them down," said Jenna abruptly.

Charlie looked at Ben. "I wonder if you would walk me through the house later, show me these hot zones?"

After Ben nodded his agreement, Liz began with, "The stairway, the foyer, the great room, and here in the library, those are the primary locations. There were other incidents outside the house, one on the back patio, and the one I mentioned near the stone bridge."

Chase looked at Ben, hoping for some response that would at least reveal why he was dressed the way he was, and perhaps provide further information regarding what he had recently experienced. But Ben remained silent. He looked at the bouquet of cut flowers, as though he had nothing more to say.

Jenna, whose love for Ben had deepened considerably these past few weeks, was going to do everything she could to end the unnatural hold Anna had on him. How she would do that, she couldn't say. She thought Dr. Charlie Chase was asking all the right questions. With what he already knew, information he seemed willing to divulge, Jenna might get the kind of help she desperately needed.

Slowly, Ben got up and walked across the room to the desk, opened a drawer, and took something out. "I found this in Anna Atwood's sitting room," he said as he placed the coin on the desk.

"You what?" shouted Jenna, his comment taking not only her, but also the others by complete surprise.

"Ben," started Liz, "How, how can that be possible?"

Chase looked carefully at the coin before saying, "It's the same coin . . . the same date and denomination. You say you took it from Anna Atwood's sitting room?"

"It's true."

"You were there?" he asked in disbelief.

"Yes."

"How did you do that?" pressed Charlie gently.

Ben withdrew something from a bottom desk drawer. It was a small box, which he opened so they could see the brooch inside. He had no idea what to say. Jenna would recognize it at once, so he stayed silent, waiting for her response.

"So, it *does* work," Jenna said bluntly.

"Yes, I wanted to tell you, Jenna, but I couldn't. I wasn't even sure it had happened at all."

She took the brooch from the box and walked across the room to the fireplace. "Why don't we try it?"

"No, Jenna," Ben cautioned. "You have to believe me."

But already she was kneeling and attempting to fit the brooch into the hole.

It was Liz who stopped her. "No, that's not the answer, Jenna, not yet anyway."

Jenna gave the brooch to Liz and walked away. Still not convinced that it had happened, that Ben only wished it had happened, she shot a look across the room at him before exclaiming, "So why don't you tell us about your trip? Tell us what you did back there with the beautiful Anna Atwood."

He didn't like the cutting accusatory edge to her voice. In fact, he was beginning to regret showing them the coin, and regretted even more his comments about traveling back in time. "Maybe I imagined it all. It happened months ago, and it was all so confusing."

Dr. Chase looked closely at the brooch, rubbing his fingers over the raised edges. "Well, there is one way to find out."

"You're not serious," declared Liz.

"I'd be willing to take that chance. Think what it would mean if it *does* work."

"The risks are too great, Charlie," said Liz.

"Nobody's going to miss Charlie Chase."

"I will," she admitted.

It was Jenna who tried to put an end to what she considered unabashed nonsense. "Suppose it does work, what happens if you can't get back?"

"Ben did it," Charlie stated.

"He was lucky," Jenna said.

"You know I have to try," Charlie replied. "I have to know."

Liz looked at Charlie. "Then you'll need a witness."

Chase reached out his hand to her. "Are you sure?"

"Why not take a chance? That's what it is, isn't it?" Liz was showing some excitement.

"There are no guarantees," Ben said. "It worked once for me, but when I tried to enter a portal a second time, something went wrong."

"A second time?" questioned Jenna.

"Last night in the great room," he reminded her—"when I found myself trapped in those awful tunnels."

"What a shame," she chided. "Did you wonder why she didn't save you?"

Charlie jumped into the middle of their conversation "So how does this work?" he asked, holding up the brooch.

"You're sure about this?" questioned Ben.

Chase nodded. "It's an opportunity not to be missed."

Chapter 52

BUT SECOND THOUGHTS prevailed. After minutes of deliberation, Liz recommended taking time to consider what Dr. Chase seemed almost too anxious to attempt. "Let's give it some additional thought, instead of rushing into something that we don't really understand."

"I agree with Liz," Jenna said. "This is not a thing decided so quickly. I'm not so sure it should be considered at all."

Again, Dr. Raymond attempted to put a practical face on what she considered an impractical and dangerous idea. "Something this extreme requires more planning."

Charlie nodded. "Opportunities like this are impossibly rare. They're beyond cutting edge, and if I sound too anxious, I'm sure you'll understand why. I'll walk the razor's edge for knowledge this extraordinary."

"Ben," began Liz, "can you tell us what happened here last night?"

Manning poured out a fresh cup of coffee. Shaking his head, he explained, "I was trapped in the same room the Youngs bricked shut. I don't know how it happened. For what seemed like minutes, I was in a dense fog that slowly began to dissipate. It seemed my body was being transported by this heavy fog, which felt like it was attached to me. And then the awful wind took hold of me. There was nothing to hold onto, only this horrible gray nothingness pulling me deeper and deeper into a sea of eyes that started at me vindictively. They were everywhere—eyes without faces looking at me, watching me, never blinking as they bulged out of their sockets. If it had not been for the door on the back wall of that room, well, I don't want to think about what could have happened."

"It's okay, Ben." Knowing he was still troubled by the experience, and imagining the fear which had apprehended him in so much darkness, Jenna tried to comfort him. She put her arm around his shoulder and gave him a look that said he was safe.

After sipping his coffee, he went on, his eyes closed, as he tried to remember details that might be important. "A long tunnel, which intersected with two others. Rats, big ones, gnawing at my shoes. At the end of the tunnel, I managed to move what I'm sure was a door. That's when I saw these," and here he passed his mobile phone to Jenna.

With the others gathering to see three pictures, it was Charlie who was the most animated. "If you look past the uniforms or spacesuits, there's something else."

Ben nodded, "Yes."

"I think we're looking at something not seen since 1901, deliberately hidden there," added Chase.

"Hidden where?" inquired Jenna.

"We know where one of the tunnels exits. Ben said another one ran west, which could put it on the other side near the smaller foundation, most likely under the other stone slab." Charlie attempted to generate enough interest among the others to persuade them to return to the site. "Did Matt run GPR scans on the ground from the house to the south edge of these foundations?"

"No," Ben admitted. "We had so many hits near the foundations that we didn't really have a chance. Didn't think much about it actually."

Jenna's phone rang. "Hi, Lacey." The call lasted less than a minute. Jenna told the others, "Matt and Lacey made an offer on the house."

"I'm sure it'll work out for them," Liz smiled.

Jenna added, "They're on their way here in a few minutes."

"If we're going down there, we'll have to have lights, maybe some rope." Though Ben was not necessarily excited about returning to a place where he'd almost met his demise, he knew that the answers to many of their questions could be 25 feet under the ground. "Jenna can you give me a hand?"

"Yeah, when you get out of those clothes, and change back into the 21st century."

Nodding, he smiled at her, and went upstairs to change.

After Ben and Jenna had secured the necessary gear and put it on the back patio, they saw Matt and Lacey approaching. Lacey had her arm around Matt's waist, and in her eyes was the look of a woman in love.

They gathered in the warm afternoon sunlight. What they had seen in Ben's photos warranted investigation. Not one of the intrepid six doubted that. What else the darkness concealed, they could only imagine. Although Charlie was used to taking risks, the others, except for Lacey, avoided risks whenever possible.

Excitement was in the spring air, and thoughts of discovery were rampant among them. In a way, this was the beginning of an expedition about to happen on Atwood House property, an expedition that Ben Manning was getting more nervous about with each minute that passed. After the gear had been loaded into the back of Matt's pickup, it was go time. Lacey and Liz sat in the truck with Matt, the others riding in the back as Matt drove the short distance to the site.

They unloaded the gear near the stone slab that hadn't been opened. Then they looked at each other for a few seconds before Charlie went over and kneeled beside the large limestone slab. Rubbing his fingers across the surface, he found what he hoped to find—impressions, just like the balance marks on the other one.

Ben and Matt shoveled the edges of the large rectangular slab to loosen it so it would open more easily. Once they had freed the stone, Charlie put his fingers on the balance marks. Nothing happened. He tapped one end with the palm of his hand—still nothing. He slapped the other end with his hand, and again nothing. It was clear to the others that Chase was just as surprised as they were—surprised but not at all perturbed.

Charlie Chase was not a man easily beaten. With Ben and Matt's help they retrieved a few flat rocks from the creek and returned with them to where the three women waited and watched. Placing two of the rocks on the north end of the slab, Charlie gently pushed on them, but only slight movement occurred. With two more rocks set on the same end as the others, he pushed again.

This time a definite noise from below caught their attention. It sounded mechanical, like steel wheels turning, grinding noises as the south end lifted slowly before rising to a height of eight feet. There, it locked into a perpendicular position, much the same as the other one had done. As the large limestone slab rose, the four flat rocks used as counterweights dropped noisily to the bottom of a deep pit. About 15 feet below, at the bottom of 12 steps, was a brick wall, which looked like it had been recently constructed.

The space was larger than the similar space at the other site, and spacious enough to be a room, although now it contained nothing more than chunks of quartz. The wall below them, that Ben was convinced was a door, held their attention for several seconds. They knew even before descending the steps, that if there was a room behind that door, what happened in 1901 Newburgh might be explained by artifacts concealed in darkness for several decades. Following their persistent efforts, the door began to move, eventually revealing, not a room as Ben expected, but five steps descending into a passageway that ran east.

"I guess this is it," Ben sighed. "We go in together and come out together."

"That's a great plan," Lacey admitted. "It's the coming out together part I like best."

Descending the steps, until each was standing another five feet deeper below ground, they hesitated again, before proceeding slowly. As their flashlights created tunnels of soft white light, their eyes gradually adjusted to the heavy shadows around them. The ceiling was high enough so that none of them had to crouch or stoop to negotiate the tunnel. They took their initial steps into the eerie darkness, that very slowly began to melt in the beams of their lights. Ben and Charlie led the way, with Liz next, followed by Jenna, Lacey, and Matt trailing the small group. They saw in the bright beams of their lights, quartz crystals protruding from sections of both walls, and there were clear indications that mining had taken place. The entire tunnel had the appearance of a mine shaft. The quartz was probably mined and stored in the room beneath the limestone slab, where it was easy to obtain when needed.

"Is it possible that there was a market for quartz crystal?" Ben asked.

"Crystal was used extensively and still is," Charlie answered.

"Then it was a reliable source of income," Ben surmised.

"Yes," nodded Chase, "and it was a primary source used to power their towers."

They stopped occasionally to regard both the construction of the shaft and the areas where crystal had been mined. After almost ten minutes of walking, they found that the tunnel converged with two others. According to Ben, the one running south went toward Atwood House, and the center tunnel, which ran north then northwest, would lead to the room where he had discovered the three spacesuits.

"If we take the far one," and Ben pointed to the tunnel bending northeast, "it should take us to where you found me, to the other limestone slab. At least that's what I think. It's easy to get turned around down here."

After less than five minutes, they saw an open doorway ahead. Even from 20 yards away they could distinguish what looked like three people standing motionless inside a room. They looked at Ben, who stared straight ahead. He seemed to be in no hurry to proceed, and the longer they looked at him the more convinced they were that he was not looking inside the room at all. Something else, something in the tunnel held his attention.

"What is it, Ben?" asked Jenna, coming up beside him and taking his hand.

"Look." He pointed to a large hole in the tunnel wall, a few feet from the doorway. "There's something in there."

Matt picked up a sizable chunk of quartz, then said, "Let's find out what it is." He walked toward what looked to be another tunnel, but one unsupported by timber, and was most likely an area where a large deposit of quartz had been extracted.

The others followed slowly behind Matt. Suddenly, a large rat shot out of the space and scurried wildly toward the group. It ran across Charlie's wingtips before disappearing into the shadows behind them. There was an audible sigh of relief from everyone. Before they could pull themselves together, however, a massive rat, bigger than a house cat, appeared so fast it startled Matt. The beast seemed confused in the glaring light, and squealing wildly, it jumped into the air, nearly hitting Matt, who dropped the rock on his foot.

"Ouch!" he yelled.

"The appalling thing is on my foot," screamed Lacey.

When they looked, there was no sign of the monster rat, but there were faint scratchy sounds behind them. Then, except for heavy breathing, there was only silence. Lacey continued to shine her light on her legs, until she was convinced the fat rat was really gone.

"I cannot deal with rats," she told the others.

"They're gone, Lacey," said Liz, trying to help her regain enough composure and courage to proceed.

When they found Charlie, he was standing near the doorway to the room. With his light shining deep into the interior, he seemed reluctant to enter. Coming up to join him, they stood several seconds without speaking, letting their eyes adjust to a gritty darkness, which their lights eventually consumed. None expected the room to be so large. It was what was in the room that caused them to draw back in disbelief.

Chapter 53

WHAT HELD THEIR attention were several objects stacked on heavy metal tables. Four tables along the west wall were completely covered with parts of one kind or another. Some of the larger parts had iconography carved on them like the markings on the piece dug out of the ground near the stone bridge. Another table had small piles of quartz crystals. Some pieces were sliced, while others were cut to various sizes.

Matt looked at gold coins in the bottom of two large iron pots. "These look like smelting pots," he told them.

"That might explain some of the financial loose ends," Chase suggested.

Scattered around the room were other miscellaneous pieces, many looking like new old stock. What they were could not be determined with any assurance. Chase picked up a piece from a pile on the floor, and spent a minute attempting to comprehend its function, but said nothing. Other pieces looked familiar, but after examining them, they remained as alien as everything else in the room.

Stacked in neat rows on two other tables were, after examination, not empty boxes as Jenna initially thought, but containers filled with what looked to be several smaller parts, none larger than an inch in length. Among them, were what appeared to be electrical components. Again, after brushing away layers of dust, many parts seemed new, as if manufactured only recently.

Chase looked at the ceiling, more than 15 feet above them. Heavy wood beams ran parallel to each other, 12 of them. Their ends rested on vertical wooden posts placed at corresponding places in the room. Other posts, scattered intermittently, provided additional support for the ceiling, which appeared to be a natural formation of limestone. Each post, and several sections of the ceiling, were coated in black with what Matt thought was a polymer skin, soft and pliable to the touch.

"What is it?" Liz inquired.

"The church," started Charlie, "I'm convinced it's directly above us."

"That would mean . . . " began Liz.

"After it was rebuilt in 1902, it was not used as a church. It had another purpose," Chase said. "It was a front to conceal construction down here. I think they utilized this cavern as a laboratory. There's probably an entrance hidden somewhere in that large escarpment of rock just inside the north woods."

"This is the right place," Ben acknowledged, pointing to three uniforms hanging a few feet from where they were standing. They hung like flat people whose heads were on a shelf a foot above them. "Seeing them a second time is even more shocking than when I discovered them."

The others poked deeper into the room, while Jenna focused the beam of her flashlight on one of the uniforms. She grabbed Ben's arm, pulling him closer. "Does she look familiar?"

"What?" Ben asked, his face pale, his eyes focused on Jenna.

"Look closely at her eyes, Ben." It was obviously an identification tag with the photograph of a woman easily visible.

"It's Anna." And following a pause, "but that's not possible."

"Take a good look," Jenna told him.

The name beneath the photograph was not Anna Atwood. Instead, the tag read, Kii La Rey. His hands began to tremble, as cold shivers shot up his spine. The flashlight clicked off, and he turned away as though he wanted to leave. He could not believe this startling revelation.

Jenna knew the mystery was not yet solved. Loose pieces to a complex mystery were scattered everywhere, particularly around this room. There remained a slight chance that Kii La Rey was just someone who resembled Anna.

"This would explain some things, wouldn't it?" Ben's voice was barely audible.

"Maybe," she replied, looking at the names and faces on the other identification tags. The last two were photographs of men, one older than the other.

"Jay La Rey," she read aloud, then, "San Lando."

Both Liz and Charlie continued putting together what they presumed were the missing pieces to the 1901 crash. There were not many options to consider. The time travelers probably salvaged what they could of their craft, including what most likely was a communication system that was scattered in pieces on and beneath some of the tables.

"Maybe plans to repair the craft had been unsuccessful. Or they stripped as much of the craft as possible, hoping to build a new ship to escape." One prominent consideration Chase had was that the military had never found the craft, had known nothing about it. "Instead, I think a tower was excavated on the Newland property, maybe nothing more than a large rock, like the one uncovered at the Abbey in Saint Meinrad, or, possibly something like what was excavated last fall near the stone bridge." Charlie Chase was convinced that he had it all figured out. The missing pieces were no longer missing. The craft had been retrieved and probably stripped.

Liz pulled Charlie to one side. "Suppose the craft is still out there, in the lake or the river?"

"It would have been discovered by now. A satellite scan would have revealed it."

"You really think they retrieved it?" She pointed toward the three flat people hanging on the wall.

"Yes."

"Something that large would be extremely hard to hide."

"It's possible that these people possessed levitation capabilities—or technology we couldn't begin to comprehend," said Charlie.

"Remember, military retrieval occurred in 1947—and I don't think the military investigated invasion or violation of air space. Though the documents could have been manipulated over the years, those declassified documents and the literature I found did not disconfirm a communication tower, so much as play up the meteor story. Although the government's capable of spinning any narrative, we're still talking about an event that happened a long time ago."

"Those unfortunate people," lamented Liz, "trying desperately to communicate their location and coordinates into their future."

"Coordinates never received," Chase added.

Liz shook her head slowly. "Eventually they gave up any hope of returning to their time. Anger and despair took hold."

"And yet they managed to survive, adapted successfully," Charlie stated. "That itself is huge."

Jenna thought Kii La Rey was probably Jay La Rey's young wife, and they had lived under the assumed names of Anna and William Atwood. She wondered who San Lando might be in this unfortunate trio. Could he be the counterfeit pastor—Thomas Arnold?

At the back of the room, a set of steps rose and abruptly stopped a foot or so beneath the ceiling. "Where do you think these go," Lacey asked, "these steps to nowhere?"

"Probably an access to the church interior," Chase decided.

"That would sure make it convenient, wouldn't it?" Lacey replied, as she continued to rummage through boxes under one of the tables. After moving aside some boxes located at the bottom of the steps, she noticed what looked like the outline of a doorway cut into the floor. "What's this?" she asked excitedly.

It resembled a rectangle about four feet wide and six feet long. On one side was a metal handle, which Matt yanked. Much to his surprise, he heard the raspy sounds of a steel door opening.

"Come into my parlor said the spider to the fly," whispered Lacey.

Another tunnel, descending deeper and running east, opened into a room large enough to hold what was undoubtedly the wreckage of a craft. For several seconds, they stood in semidarkness, shining their lights on a crumpled black mass. The ceiling and walls were covered in a black skin, like the coating or skin on the pieces dug out of the ground inside and around the church. Chase was sure this was stealth protection, making the chamber impervious to any kind of laser beams, radio waves, energy pulse technologies, geometric or radiometric imaging. It was never meant to be found. Yet, here they were, standing in front of what was left of a craft from the future, that crashed in 1901 Newburgh, Indiana. **UNITED AIR COMMAND** was distinctly visible on a part pushed up against a wall. Each saw it, and not one of them knew what to do or say.

Chapter 54

LATER THAT AFTERNOON, when Ben came into the library Chase was talking to Liz, while Matt, Lacey, and Jenna talked among themselves. Overhearing parts of their conversations, he knew they were very much concerned about what they had discovered, and even more concerned about what to do with these discoveries. Although they had unraveled a mystery, Ben was starting to regret it. He considered the new information much too dangerous for any of them.

"You okay?" Jenna asked, coming across the room to meet him.

"I guess so. No point in pretending any longer."

"I think she wanted you to know, Ben."

"So that's what she meant about seeing the impossible."

"Think what she's been through. She probably had family, a life not so unlike people today, and because of some screwy twist of nature, she found herself living so far in the past, that I'm surprised she survived at all."

"She tried to warn me several times, kept referring to something evil in the ground."

"She was in love with you, Ben. Wasn't that enough?"

Ben nodded slowly, "More than I deserved."

"So where do we go from here?"

"You know I tried to go with her, don't you?"

"Yes, I know."

"Something went wrong. Maybe in the end, that was a good thing."

Jenna looked curiously at him, knowing what he was thinking. "I suppose you'll try again?"

"No, I don't belong there."

"She can be persuasive, Ben."

"I'm going to sell the brooch to Bob Bergman, Jenna," Ben announced abruptly.

Smiling, she replied, "That's a new beginning then, isn't it?"

"I hope it is."

"And what about the tower out by the bridge? Maybe it's time for that to come down?"

"Yes," Ben agreed.

"You realize we are really in over our heads," Dr. Liz was saying when Jenna and Ben came into the conversation. "We have seen and touched the future. So, what do we do about that?"

Charlie, quick to put what had happened into sharper focus, wanted to reestablish a chronology, one the others might have forgotten. "Again, let me lay this out for you. Everything, except what was hauled away in 1947, was recovered and concealed by three people who had somehow entered an accidental breach in the fabric of space and time. Three people were able to reconstruct a church, which their craft had destroyed, and used this church and what was left of the adjacent parsonage as a cover so they could construct in existing caverns sufficient space in which to conceal who they were. As amazing and improbably as this sounds, these events did happen, and their secrets remained undisclosed, undiscovered—until now."

"Then there never was a Pastor Arnold or a congregation," Ben stated confidently.

"That's right," Charlie assured, "unless San Lando was a counterfeit preacher."

"Preaching to a phantom congregation," proclaimed Lacey. "I wonder what happened to him?"

"The rumor was that after the fire, the pastor took up residence in another church in Evansville," Chase told them. "Except for a story in a 1901 issue of a local paper, I was unable to locate any other information on Pastor Thomas Arnold in the literature I researched."

Shaking her head slowly, Lacey said, "Maybe from the start they realized the impossibility of being rescued and broadcasting their location was nothing more than desperation."

"Knowing what we know, what do we do with this information?" asked Jenna.

"If they never meant for any of it to be found," Ben began, "we seal it and walk away."

"I think Ben's right," agreed Jenna.

"Or we destroy it all." Matt spoke with enough seriousness to get and hold their attention.

"Good idea, honey," Lacey said, before giving him a kiss on the cheek.

Chase continued to construct what he considered a plausible narrative. "If the military had any additional interest, or thought they had left something important behind, they would have returned. But I don't think that's going to happen." He paused to emphasize what he was about to say next. "If any of this got out, it would be disastrous. Even though I realize how much there is to learn, I can't help but think it would be morally wrong to reveal what we've discovered. Please realize I'm speaking to you, not as a scientist, but as a man greatly concerned with our own future. And who's to say that the government hasn't already recovered this advanced technology from other crash sites?"

"Like Roswell," suggested Lacey.

"Quite possibly," Charlie nodded.

"What about the portals?" asked Liz.

"Yes, I know what you've told me and I'm afraid I can't give you an honest answer," admitted Chase. "Ben said he experienced a time-shift that was triggered at least once by the brooch."

"It *did* happen. As crazy as it sounds, there's no denying that I was transported back in time, to her sitting room."

"There's a very good chance that any portals have to be closed from the other side," Charlie told them seriously. "The idea that they can be deliberately directed or managed is too implausible, that is unless you take into consideration that aliens from other planetary systems have visited earth during its prehistory by bending quantum mechanics and applications to create stable portals."

"That's pretty heady stuff," Ben stated bluntly.

Charlie smiled at them. "It's just something that's out there. I only mention it to suggest that though these earth portals do exist, that any control or reliable governance, even manipulation of them is still theory. If the brooch worked, then it was conceived by someone from the other side, using knowledge decades, even a century or more beyond what we know today."

They all looked at Ben, who was convinced they expected him to make the journey back in time. "I wouldn't know what to do," he protested. "And besides, it might not work again."

Jenna looked at Ben before speaking. "You said Anna has asked you several times to return the brooch. Maybe it's the brooch that would finally put an end to all this."

Charlie nodded his agreement. "It is a sensible consideration, Ben."

"Before we do or say something we might regret," Liz started, "only we know what's out there. No one else has seen what we've seen. I think it's imperative that we promise to keep this to ourselves. I know temptations will be strong, but we must at all costs protect this knowledge. As Dr. Chase has suggested, if this information gets out, I know you can imagine the consequences. Life will never be the same for any of us."

Everyone nodded.

"What about Adrian White?" asked Ben. "After all, he's been as involved with this as any of us."

Liz said, "Adrian is a man who can be trusted implicitly."

"Does that mean we tell him?" questioned Ben.

"He has his own suspicions about Atwood House," Liz acknowledged. "His research on the multiverse will keep him busy. So maybe we just leave it with the six of us, at least for now."

There was more nodding among them, which meant each agreed with what Liz had said. If a time came when they were forced to tell

White about their conclusions, the topic would be revisited. And that was the decision made among the six who had glimpsed the future.

Although Chase stayed silent in the conversation regarding Dr. White, he accepted what had been said and went on with what he was thinking. "There will be no fame, no glory, nothing that would benefit any of us financially. If we disclose what we know, the military will immediately clamp a lid on this place, and the truth will be twisted into another disinformation narrative. It's imperative that we remain silent."

"You mentioned shutting down the portals from the other side," Jenna reminded Chase.

"Yes," Charlie began," but that would require getting to the other side. Even if the brooch has the power to do that, these portals could be unstable and decay sooner than we realize. As I've said, there's been some study regarding time portals, but nothing definitive that I'm aware of, so stabilizing them might not be possible. This has been referred to as the zipper effect for many years. Time was an entity that could be controlled to a point, much like a zipper opening and closing. We do know density shifts have been reported by those who have experienced what's known as magnetic fogs. Why these magnetic fogs occur is still not clear. I do believe there's a good chance that portals move frequently, and those that don't are somehow controlled, but, again, not from this side. This might have happened to Ben when he tried a second time. The portal collapsed."

"Then we must return the brooch to Anna?" Jenna suggested once again. "What if she is giving us that chance?"

"What chance is that, Jenna?" asked Lacey.

"If the portal can't be controlled from this side, she must surely know that," continued Jenna. "I think that's what she's been trying to tell Ben."

"Why don't we talk about that later," Ben said. "I'd like to get that tower down and buried."

"We can do that very quickly," Matt assured them.

Ben looked at them and said, "I sure don't see any reason to leave it there any longer. It causes way too much attention, and not only that, it's lousy yard art."

The sun, low in the sky, barely broke the horizon. They had spent the afternoon talking. As evening began to descend, they stood near the bridge, ready to dismantle the tower. It took less than an hour to strike it, load it into Matt's pickup, and bury it, along with the several other pieces they had recovered, beneath one of the limestone slabs.

"We've all got some serious thinking to do," Jenna told them, with a note of authority to which she was not accustomed. "I'd like to take a shower, get cleaned up and maybe we could meet somewhere for dinner."

"How about the Knob Hill Tavern?" Lacey recommended.

The others were agreeable and arranged to meet at Knob Hill Tavern around seven o'clock. There would be no talk of anything but good food and friendship. Anything else was considered too risky. Even though both Charlie and Ben showed little enthusiasm, they did accept Lacey's suggestion graciously. Apparent to the others, before they left Atwood House, was the distant look in Manning's eyes. Jenna saw it and didn't like it. She told them she'd stay behind and come later with Ben.

When they were alone together, she asked, "What is it, Ben?"

"Jenna please understand that I have to see her again, if for no other reason than to say good-bye."

"It's that easy?" Jenna admonished. I mean that's how it's done? It's too bad you can't call her on your cell phone and tell her. Or, if by some outside chance you got her mailing address, do it that way, and be sure to include a picture of yourself. That will surely ease her pain."

"You're embarrassing me."

"That woman would cut out her heart for you, Ben Manning. That's how much she loves you, and you want to say good-bye as casually as you would brush off a bad day?"

"What else can I do?"

"Your heart has to tell you that. I can't. Let's get you cleaned up. You can't see her like this."

"I don't know what to say."

"Maybe you could say, Jenna I'm sorry it wasn't you. No that sounds much too, ah . . . pitiful."

"What?"

"You heard me, and I don't have the courage to say it a second time."

"I never realized you felt that way."

"With someone else that much in your eyes, it's not possible to see what's in front of you."

He took her in his arms and kissed her.

"Really, Ben?"

"I've been such a fool."

"No, you fell in love with a beautiful and evocative woman. With the exception that she lives in one century and you live in another, there's nothing foolish about what you feel for her."

"You're a special person, Jenna."

"I think somewhere along the way, I've heard that."

Her smile was genuine, but in her blue eyes was melancholy Ben had not seen before. "What is it?"

"Everyone at some time or other goes to sleep at night, wishing, hoping, even praying for the kind of experience you've had. Dream lovers inhabit the world of sleep, but you're one of the lucky ones, Ben. You truly are one of the lucky ones." She had tears in her eyes.

Ben held her tighter in his arms and realized that Jenna Newland would always be there if he needed her. In those moments before they left to join the others, he wiped away her tears, and saw Anna Atwood in her eyes. Later that night, when they returned to Atwood House, a consensual decision had been made. They wouldn't attempt to create the portal that Ben had revealed. For the time being, they would leave things as they were. With the future that had arrived in 1901 Newburgh, Indiana concealed beneath the church and parsonage foundations, Ben, Jenna, and the others realized life went on, not in 1901, but now, in this century, where each had several years ahead of them.

Chapter 55

JUNE ARRIVED BREEZY and damp. All along the streets and avenues of Newburgh, Indiana trees were in full bloom. The sweet scents of fruit trees were thick in the air. A new restaurant had recently opened on the banks of the Ohio River, not far from Atwood House. With the heavy rains of the previous week, the river at Newburgh Lock and Dam House was cresting near 30 feet, which was still a few feet below flood stage. But with a sunny warmer forecast for the coming weeks, no one even talked about the possibility of the Ohio River rising above 33 feet.

Matt and Lacey had a simple wedding on the lawn at Atwood House and moved into the three-bedroom bungalow on Second Street. Matt had the necessary skills to repair just about anything, and with Jenna and Ben helping, the house was quickly transformed into a home. Lacey's excitement was infectious. Everyone saw it, and they were astonished at how it affected the rest of them.

The brooch was not sold to Bob Bergman for $30,000. Instead, Ben left it on the table where Anna was sure to find it.

Recently determined was the disposition of Atwood House. After conversations, especially with Jenna, it was mutually decided that Ben would not sell it. The thought that new owners might find on the property what Ben and the others worked so hard to conceal had heavily influenced his decision.

Even Liz and Charlie were spending considerable time together. Liz had published her second book on paranormal realities, which detailed specific accounts of a fictitious house in Bloomington, Indiana, and the book was selling much better than anticipated. Walking Einstein had some recent success with his research on parallel universes, which was receiving favorable reviews in scientific journals. Smith had called to congratulate him and asked if Charlie would provide some additional information on what Smith was now referring to as the effects of anomalous weather on electromagnetic vortices. Charlie reluctantly agreed.

To keep a secret among six people was no small task. New beginnings were coming for each, leaving them to consider the future with hope and excitement. Maybe that was enough to ensure that what they knew would remain undisclosed.

One late evening when Ben returned to Atwood House without Jenna, who was there virtually every spare hour she had, the sweet aroma of flowers was very strong. He went directly into the library to find a large arrangement of yellow roses in a stunning hand-painted porcelain vase, decorated with purple blossoms and white buds. The brooch was gone. His hand shook and his heart beat rapidly as he reached down for the note that was folded in half and tipped against the vase. With his eyes teary and every muscle tense, each breath pushing hard against his chest, he opened the note and read the few lines written in Anna's hand.

My Dearest, Ben,

The ivy is blooming, and the songbirds are back, and yet I sit alone with memories of you, holding onto them each day. I long to see again your face each night in the emptiness of this house, where we live alone together. In the shade of the evening, you will find the crimson water lilies blooming in the stream near the bridge. They are for you. I am forever in your shadow, dear Ben . . . always remembering that the heart has no boundaries.

Always Yours,

Anna

He read the note twice more before slipping it into his coat pocket. If ever a person longed for a miracle under a sky on fire with starlight, it was Ben Manning. Though he was excited about his upcoming July marriage to Jenna Newland, never in his entire life had he felt this alone.

Under this sky of shimmering stars, he inhaled the crisp night air deeply, hoping it would clear his head. A gigantic and spectacular rose-colored moon had taken hold of the eastern sky. Rising just above the trees, its bewildered face with one unblinking eye, stared down on a world of small people, who were as ephemeral as those rare and delicate flowers that bloom only in moonlight.

After walking down to the bridge, he found them, several large magenta flowers, floating on the water in this stunning strawberry moonlight. In the blackness between stars, a pulsating redeeming light, brighter than moonlight, a chaste, jubilant, and exonerating light, fell across the warm enchanting landscape. All around him shadows came to life. The sweet scent of jasmine filled the air as one haunting unforgettable shadow paused near him on the lawn, where it remained for several seconds—before vanishing into this remarkably uncommon and extraordinary night.

CPSIA information can be obtained
at www.ICGtesting.com
Printed in the USA
BVHW03*0439230818
525399BV00010B/6/P